By Salman Rushdie

FICTION

Grimus
Midnight's Children
Shame
The Satanic Verses
Haroun and the Sea of Stories
East, West
The Moor's Last Sigh
The Ground Beneath Her Feet
Fury
Shalimar the Clown
The Enchantress of Florence
Luka and the Fire of Life
Two Years Eight Months and Twenty-Eight Nights
The Golden House
Quichotte

NONFICTION

Joseph Anton: A Memoir
The Jaguar Smile: A Nicaraguan Journey
Imaginary Homelands: Essays and Criticism 1981–1991
Step Across This Line: Collected Nonfiction 1992–2002

PLAYS

Haroun and the Sea of Stories (with Tim Supple and David Tushingham)
Midnight's Children (with Tim Supple and Simon Reade)

SCREENPLAY

Midnight's Children

ANTHOLOGIES

Mirrorwork: 50 Years of Indian Writing, 1947–1997 (co-editor)
Best American Short Stories 2008 (co-editor)

QUICHOTTE

QUICHOTTE

A Novel

SALMAN RUSHDIE

RANDOM HOUSE

NEW YORK

Published in the United States by Random House,
an imprint and division of Penguin Random House LLC, New York.

RANDOM HOUSE and the HOUSE colophon are
registered trademarks of Penguin Random House LLC.

LIBRARY OF CONGRESS CATALOGING-IN-PUBLICATION DATA
NAMES: Rushdie, Salman, author.
TITLE: Quichotte: a novel / Salman Rushdie.
DESCRIPTION: First edition. | New York: Random House, 2019.
IDENTIFIERS: LCCN 2019016494 | ISBN 9780593132982 (hardback: acid-free paper) |
ISBN 9780593132999 (ebook) | ISBN 9780593133262 (international)
SUBJECTS: | BISAC: FICTION / Literary. | FICTION / Sagas.
CLASSIFICATION: LCC PR6068.U757 Q53 2019 | DDC 823/.914—dc23
LC record available at lccn.loc.gov/2019016494

Printed in the United States of America on acid-free paper

randomhousebooks.com

2 4 6 8 9 7 5 3 1

First Edition

Book design by Barbara M. Bachman

For Eliza

CONTENTS

———

A QUIXOTIC NOTE
ON PRONUNCIATION

―――

Quichotte, pronounced "key-SHOT" in French and
"key-SHOT-uh" in German, and *Chisciotte,* pronounced
"key-SHO-tay" in Italian, are alternative spellings/pronuncia-
tions of the Spanish *Quixote* or *Quijote,* pronounced
"key-HO-tay." Portuguese also uses a "sh" sound rather than a
"h" sound for the *x* or *j* in the middle of Don Quixote/Quijote's
illustrious name. Cervantes himself would probably have
said "key-SHO-tay" in the Spanish of his time. For the purposes
of this text, the recommended pronunciation is the elegant
French "key-SHOT," for reasons which the text itself will
make clear; but, gentle reader, suit yourself. To each
his/her/their own articulation of the universal Don.

PART ONE

PATHOSE

Quichotte, an old Man, falls in Love, embarks on a Quest, & becomes a Father

*T*HERE ONCE LIVED, AT A SERIES OF TEMPORARY ADDRESSES across the United States of America, a traveling man of Indian origin, advancing years, and retreating mental powers, who, on account of his love for mindless television, had spent far too much of his life in the yellow light of tawdry motel rooms watching an excess of it, and had suffered a peculiar form of brain damage as a result. He devoured morning shows, daytime shows, late-night talk shows, soaps, situation comedies, Lifetime movies, hospital dramas, police series, vampire and zombie serials, the dramas of housewives from Atlanta, New Jersey, Beverly Hills, and New York, the romances and quarrels of hotel-fortune princesses and self-styled shahs, the cavortings of individuals made famous by happy nudities, the fifteen minutes of fame accorded to young persons with large social media followings on account of their plastic-surgery acquisition of a third breast or their post-rib-removal figures that mimicked the impossible shape of the Mattel company's Barbie doll, or even, more simply, their ability to catch giant carp in picturesque settings while wearing only the tiniest of string bikinis; as well as singing competitions, cooking competitions, competitions for business propositions, competitions for business apprenticeships, competitions between remote-controlled monster vehicles, fashion competitions, competitions for the affections of both bachelors and bachelorettes, baseball games, basketball games, football games, wrestling bouts, kickboxing bouts, extreme sports programming, and, of course, beauty contests. (He did not watch "hockey." For people of his ethnic persuasion and tropical youth, hockey, which in the USA was renamed "field hockey," was a game played on grass. To play field hockey on ice was, in his opinion, the absurd equivalent of ice-skating on a lawn.)

As a consequence of his near-total preoccupation with the material offered up to him through, in the old days, the cathode-ray tube, and, in the new age of flat screens, through liquid-crystal, plasma, and organic light-emitting diode displays, he fell victim to that increasingly prevalent psychological disorder in which the boundary between truth and lies became smudged and indistinct, so that at times he found himself incapable of distinguishing one from the other, reality from "reality," and began to think of himself as a natural citizen (and potential inhabitant) of that imaginary world beyond the screen to which he was so devoted, and which, he believed, provided him, and therefore everyone, with the moral, social, and practical guidelines by which all men and women should live. As time passed and he sank ever deeper into the quicksand of what might be termed the unreal real, he felt himself becoming emotionally involved with many of the inhabitants of that other, brighter world, membership in which he thought of as his to claim by right, like a latter-day Dorothy contemplating a permanent move to Oz; and at an unknown point he developed an unwholesome, because entirely one-sided, passion for a certain television personality, the beautiful, witty, and adored Miss Salma R, an infatuation which he characterized, quite inaccurately, as love. In the name of this so-called love he resolved zealously to pursue his "beloved" right through the television screen into whatever exalted high-definition reality she and her kind inhabited, and, by deeds as well as grace, to win her heart.

He spoke slowly and moved slowly too, dragging his right leg a little when he walked—the lasting consequence of a dramatic Interior Event many years earlier, which had also damaged his memory, so that while happenings in the distant past remained vivid, his remembrances of the middle period of his life had become hit-and-miss, with large hiatuses and other gaps which had been filled up, as if by a careless builder in a hurry, with false memories created by things he might have seen on TV. Other than that, he seemed in good enough shape for a man of his years. He was a tall, one might even say an elongated, man, of the sort one encounters in the gaunt paintings of El Greco and the narrow sculptures of Alberto Giacometti, and although such men are (for the most part) of a melancholy disposition, he was blessed with a cheerful smile and the charming manner of a gentleman of the old school, both valuable assets for a commercial traveler, which, in these his golden years, he became for a lengthy time. In addition, his name itself was cheerful: It was Smile. *Mr Ismail Smile, Sales Executive, Smile Pharmaceuticals Inc., Atlanta, GA,* it said on his business card. As a salesman he had always been proud that his name was the same as the name of the corporation whose representative he was. The family name. It lent him a certain gravitas, or so he believed. This was not, however, the name by which he chose to be known during his last, most foolish adventure.

(The unusual surname *Smile,* by the by, was the Americanized version of *Ismail,* so the old traveling salesman was really Mr. Ismail Ismail, or, alternatively, Mr. Smile Smile. He was a brown man in America longing for a brown woman, but he did not see his story in racial terms. He had become, one might say, detached from his skin. This was one of the many things his quest would put in question, and change.)

The more he thought about the woman he professed to love, the clearer it became to him that so magnificent a personage would not simply keel over with joy at the first declaration of *amour fou* from a total stranger. (He wasn't as crazy as *that*.) Therefore it would be necessary for him to prove himself worthy of her, and the provision of such proofs would henceforth be his only concern. Yes! He would amply demonstrate his worth! It would be necessary, as he began his quest, to keep the object of his affections fully informed of his doings, and so he proposed to begin a correspondence with her, a sequence of letters which would reveal his sincerity, the depth of his affections, and the lengths to which he was ready to go to gain her hand. It was at this point in his reflections that a kind of shyness overtook him. Were he to reveal to her how humble his station in life truly was, she might toss his letter in the trash with a pretty laugh and be done with him forever. Were he to disclose his age or give her details of his appearance, she might recoil from the information with a mixture of amusement and horror. Were he to offer her his name, the admittedly august name of Smile, a name with big money attached to it, she might, in the grip of a bad mood, alert the authorities, and to be hunted down like a dog at the behest of the object of his adorations would break his heart, and he would surely die. Therefore he would for the moment keep his true identity a secret, and would reveal it only when his letters, and the deeds they described, had softened her attitude toward him and made her receptive to his advances. How would he know when that moment arrived? That was a question to be answered later. Right now the important thing was to begin. And one day the proper name to use, the best of all identities to assume, came to him in that moment between waking and sleeping when the imagined world behind our eyelids can drip its magic into the world we see when we open our eyes.

That morning he seemed to see himself in a dream addressing himself awake. "Look at yourself," his half-sleeping self murmured to his half-waking self. "So tall, so skinny, so ancient, and yet you can't grow anything better than the straggliest of beards, as if you were a teenager with spots. And yes, admit it, maybe a little cracked in the head, one of those head-in-the-clouds fellows who mistakes cumulus, or cumulonimbus, or even cirrostratus formations for solid ground. Just think back to your favorite piece of music when you were a boy! I know, these days you prefer the warblings you hear on *American Idol* or *The Voice*. But back in the day, you liked what your artistic father liked, you adopted his musical taste as your own. Do you remember his favorite record?" Whereupon the half-dream-Smile produced, with a flourish, a vinyl LP which half-awake-Smile recognized at once. It was a recording of the opera *Don Quichotte* by Jules Massenet. "Only loosely based on the great masterpiece of Cervantes, isn't it," mused the phantom. "And as for you, it seems you're a little loosely based yourself."

It was settled. He climbed out of bed in his striped pajamas—more quickly than was his wont—and actually clapped his hands. Yes! This would be the pseudonym he would use in his love letters. He would be her ingenious gentleman, Quichotte. He would be Lancelot to her Guinevere, and carry her away to Joyous Gard. He would be—to quote Chaucer's *Canterbury Tales*—her verray, parfit, gentil knyght.

It was the Age of Anything-Can-Happen, he reminded himself. He had heard many people say that on TV and on the outré video clips floating in cyberspace, which added a further, new-technology depth to his addiction. There were no rules anymore. And in the Age of Anything-Can-Happen, well, anything could happen. Old friends could become new enemies and traditional enemies could be your new besties or even lovers. It was no longer possible to predict the weather, or the likelihood of war, or the outcome of elections. A woman might fall in love with a piglet, or a man start living with an owl. A beauty might fall asleep and, when kissed, wake up speaking a different language and in that new language reveal a completely altered character. A flood might drown your city. A tornado might carry your house to a faraway land where, upon landing, it would squash a witch. Criminals could become kings and kings be unmasked as criminals. A man might discover that the woman he lived with was his father's illegitimate child. A whole nation might jump off a cliff like swarming lemmings. Men who played presidents on TV could become presidents. The water might run out. A woman might bear a baby who was found to be a revenant god. Words could lose their meanings and acquire new ones. The world might end, as at least one prominent scientist-entrepreneur had begun repeatedly to predict. An evil scent would hang over the ending. And a TV star might miraculously return the love of a foolish old coot, giving him an unlikely romantic triumph which would redeem a long, small life, bestowing upon it, at the last, the radiance of majesty.

Quichotte's great decision was made at the Red Roof Inn in Gallup, New Mexico (pop. 21,678). The traveling salesman looked with desire and envy upon Gallup's historic El Rancho Hotel, which in the heyday of the Western had hosted many of the movie stars filming in the area, from John Wayne and Humphrey Bogart to Katharine Hepburn and Mae West. The El Rancho was out of his price range, and so he drove by it to the humbler Red Roof, which suited him just fine. He was a man who had learned to accept his lot in life without complaint. That morning, the TV was on when he awoke with his bright new identity—he had fallen asleep without remembering to turn it off—and the KOB-4 weatherman Steve Stucker was on the air with his Parade of Pets, featuring the celebrity weather dogs Radar, Rez, Squeaky, and Tuffy. That meant it was Friday, and the newly named Mr. Quichotte (he did not feel that he had earned or merited the honorific *Don*), energized by his new resolve, by the opening up before him of the flower-strewn pathway that led to love, was full of excitement, even though he was at the end of a tiring week visiting the area's medical practices in Albuquerque and elsewhere. He had spent the previous day at the locations of the Rehoboth McKinley Christian Health Care Services, the Western New Mexico Medical Group, and the Gallup Indian Medical Center (which cared for the town's substantial Native population, drawn from the Hopi, Navajo, and Zuni tribes). Sales had been good, he thought, although puzzled frowns and embarrassed little laughs had greeted his jovial hints that he would soon be taking a vacation in New York City itself (pop. 8,623,000) with a new girlfriend, a Very Famous Lady, the queen of Must See TV. And his little quip at the Indian Medical Center—"I'm actually Indian too! Dot, not feather! So I'm happy to be here in Indian country"—hadn't gone down well at all.

He no longer had a fixed abode. The road was his home, the car was his living room, its trunk was his wardrobe, and a sequence of Red Roof Inns, Motel 6's, Days Inns, and other hostelries provided him with beds and TVs. He preferred places with at least some premium cable channels, but if none were available he was happy with the ordinary network fare. But on this particular morning he had no time for the local weatherman and his rescue pets. He wanted to talk to his friends about love, and the lover's quest on which he was about to embark.

The truth was that he had almost no friends anymore. There was his wealthy cousin, employer, and patron, Dr. R. K. Smile, and there was Dr. Smile's wife, Happy, neither of whom he spent any time with, and there were front-desk clerks at some of the motels he regularly frequented. There were a few individuals scattered across the country and the globe who might still harbor feelings similar to friendship toward him. There was, above all, one woman in New York City (she called herself the Human Trampoline) who might once again smile upon him, if he was lucky, and if she accepted his apologies. (He knew, or thought he knew, that apologies were due, but he could only partly remember why, and at times he thought that perhaps his damaged memory had got things upside down and it was she who needed to apologize to him.) But he had no social group, no cohort, no posse, no real pals, having long ago abandoned the social whirl. On his Facebook page he had "friended" or "been friended by" a small and dwindling group of commercial travelers like himself, as well as an assortment of lonelyhearts, braggarts, exhibitionists, and salacious ladies behaving as erotically as the social medium's somewhat puritanical rules allowed. Every single one of these quote-unquote "friends" saw his plan, when he had enthusiastically posted it, for what it was—a harebrained scheme, verging on lunacy—and attempted to dissuade him, for his own good, from stalking or harassing Miss Salma R. In response to his post there were frown emojis and Bitmojis wagging fingers at him reprovingly and there were GIFs of Salma R herself, crossing her eyes, sticking out her tongue, and rotating a finger by her right temple, all of which added up to the universally recognized set of gestures meaning "cray cray." However, he would not be deterred.

Such stories do not, on the whole, end well.

IN HIS YOUTH—WHICH WAS long enough ago for his recollection of it to have remained clear—he had been a wanderer of a purer kind than the salesman he eventually became, had adventured far and wide simply to see what he could see, from Cape Horn and Tierra del Fuego, the ends of the earth where all the color drained out of the world so that things and people existed only in black-and-white, to the eastern wastes of Iran, from the cockroach-ridden town of Bam to the wild border city of Zahedan in the vanished time of the Shah, from Shark Bay in Australia, where he swam amidst the sentimentality of dolphins, to the great wildebeest migration across the incomprehensible Serengeti plain. He played Holi with the Bhojpuri-speaking descendants of Indian indentured laborers in Mauritius and celebrated Bakr Eid with shawl weavers in the high mountain village of Aru near the Kolahoi glacier in Kashmir. However, at a certain point in early middle age the Interior Event changed everything. When he came to his senses after the Event he had lost all personal ambition and curiosity, found big cities oppressive, and craved only anonymity and solitude.

In addition, he had developed an acute fear of flying. He remembered a dream of first falling and then drowning, and was convinced after that that air travel was the most ridiculous of all the fantasies and falsehoods that the comptrollers of the earth tried to inflict on innocent men and women like himself. If an airplane flew, and its passengers reached their destination safely, that was just a question of good luck. It proved nothing. He did not want to die by falling from the sky into water (his dream) or onto land (which would be even less comfortable), and therefore he resolved that if the gods of good health granted him some sort of recovery he would never again board one of those monstrously heavy containers which promised to lift him thirty thousand feet or more above the ground. And he did recover, albeit with a dragging leg, and since then had traveled only by road. He thought sometimes of making a sea journey down the American coast to Brazil or Argentina, or across the Atlantic Ocean to Europe, but he had never made the necessary arrangements, and nowadays his unreliable health and fragile bank account would probably not be able to take the strain of such a voyage. So, a creature of the road he had become, and would remain.

In an old knapsack, carefully wrapped in tissue paper and bubble wrap, he carried with him a selection of modestly sized objects gathered on his travels: a polished "found art" Chinese stone whose patterning resembled a landscape of wooded hills in the mist, a Buddha-like Gandharan head, an upraised wooden Cambodian hand with a symbol of peace in the center of its palm, two starlike crystals, one large, the other small, a Victorian locket inside which he had placed photographs of his parents, three other photographs depicting a childhood in a distant tropical city, a brass Edwardian English cigar cutter made to look like a sharp-toothed dragon, an Indian "Cheeta Brand" matchbox bearing the image of a prowling cheetah, a miniature marble hoopoe bird, and a Chinese fan. These thirteen things were numinous for him. When he arrived at his room for the night he spent perhaps twenty minutes arranging them carefully around his quarters. They had to be placed just so, in the right relationship to one another, and once he was happy with the arrangement, the room immediately acquired the feeling of home. He knew that without these sacred objects placed in their proper places his life would lack equilibrium and he might surrender to panic, inertia, and finally death. These objects were life itself. As long as they were with him, the road held no terrors. It was his special place.

He was lucky that the Interior Event had not reduced him to complete idiocy, like a stumbling, damaged fellow he had once seen who was incapable of anything more demanding than gathering fallen leaves in a park. He had worked as a commercial traveler in pharmaceuticals for many years, and continued to do so in spite of his postretirement age and his incipiently unstable, unpredictably capricious, increasingly erratic, and mulishly obsessional cast of mind, because of the kindliness of the aforementioned wealthy cousin, R. K. Smile, M.D., a successful entrepreneur, who, after seeing a production of Arthur Miller's *Death of a Salesman* on TV, had refused to fire his relative, fearing that to do so would hasten the old fellow's demise.*

Dr. Smile's pharmaceutical business, always prosperous, had recently catapulted him to billionaire status because of his Georgia laboratories' perfection of a sublingual spray application of the pain medication fentanyl. Spraying the powerful opioid under the tongue brought faster relief to terminal cancer patients suffering from what the medical community euphemistically called breakthrough pain. Breakthrough pain was unbearable pain. The new spray made it bearable, at least for an hour. The instant success of this spray, patented and brand-named as InSmile™, allowed Dr. R. K. Smile the luxury of carrying his elderly poor relation without worrying unduly about his productivity. Strangely, as it happened, Quichotte's descent toward lunacy—of which one definition is the inability to separate *what-is-so* from *what-is-not-so*—for a time did not materi-

---

* But Dr. Smile was by no means kindly in all matters. As we shall see. As we shall presently see.

ally affect his ability to perform his professional duties. In fact, his condition proved to be a positive boon, helping him to present, with absolute sincerity, the shaky case for many of his company's offerings, believing wholeheartedly in their advertised efficacy and superiority over all their rivals, even though the advertising campaigns were decidedly slanted, and in many cases the products were no better than many similar brands, and in some cases decidedly inferior to the market in general. Because of his blurry uncertainty about the location of the truth-lie frontier, and his personal charm and pleasant manner, he inspired confidence and came across as the perfect promoter of his cousin's wares.

The day inevitably came, however, as the full extent of his cousin's delusions became known to him, when Dr. Smile finally put him out to pasture. He gave Quichotte the news in the kindest possible way, flying out personally from General Aviation at Hartsfield-Jackson Airport in his new G650ER to meet Quichotte in Flagstaff, Arizona (pop. 70,320), after receiving a worried call from the director of West Flagstaff Family Medicine, D. F. Winona, D.O., M.B.A., F.A.C.O.F.P., to whom Quichotte had improbably confided during their appointment that he was thinking of escorting the delectable Miss Salma R to the next *Vanity Fair* Oscars party, after which their clandestine romance would finally become public knowledge. Quichotte and Dr. Smile met at the Relax Inn on Historic Route 66, just four miles from Pulliam Airport. They were an odd couple, Quichotte tall, slow, leg-dragging, and Dr. Smile small, bristling with dynamism, and clearly the boss. "What were you thinking?" he asked, sorrowfully but with a note of finality in his voice, *this time I can't save you,* and Quichotte, confronted with his nonsensical statement, replied, "It's true, I got a little ahead of myself, and I apologize for getting carried away, but you know how lovers are, we can't help talking about love." He was using the remote in his room to flick back and forth between a basketball game on ESPN and a true crime show on Oxygen, and his manner struck Dr. Smile as affable but distracted.

"You understand," Dr. Smile said as gently as he could manage, "that I'm going to have to let you go."

"Oh, not a problem," Quichotte replied. "Because, as it happens, I have to embark immediately on my quest."

"I see," Dr. Smile said slowly. "Well, I want to add that I am prepared to offer you a lump sum in severance pay—not a fortune, but not a negligible amount—and I have that check here with me to give you. Also, you'll find that Smile Pharmaceuticals' pension arrangements are not ungenerous. It is my hope and belief that you'll be able to manage. Also, any time you find yourself in Buckhead, or, in the summer months, on the Golden Isles, the doors of my homes will always be open. Come and have a biryani with my wife and myself." Mrs. Happy Smile was a zaftig brunette with a flicked-up hairdo. She was, by all accounts, something of a whiz in the kitchen. It was a tempting offer.

"Thank you," Quichotte said, pocketing the check. "May I ask, will it be all right to bring my Salma with me when I visit? Once we get together, you see, we will be inseparable. And I am sure she will be happy to eat your wife's fine biryani."

"Of course," Dr. Smile assured him, and rose to leave. "Bring her by all means! There's one other thing," he added. "Now that you are retired, and no longer in my employ, it may be useful to me, from time to time, to ask you to perform some small private services for me personally. As my close and trusted family member, I know I will be able to rely on you."

"I will gladly do whatever you ask of me," Quichotte said, bowing his head. "You have been the finest of cousins."

"It will be nothing onerous, I assure you," Dr. Smile said. "Just some discreet deliveries. And all your expenses will be covered, that goes without saying. In cash."

He paused in the doorway of the room. Quichotte was watching the basketball game intently.

"What will you do now?" Dr. Smile asked him.

"Don't worry about me," Quichotte said, flashing that happy smile. "I've got plenty to do. I'll just drive."

DOWN THE LONG ITINERANT YEARS, when he was on the road in his old gunmetal gray Chevy Cruze, Quichotte often wished he had married and become a father. How sweet it would be to have a son sitting beside him, a son who could take the wheel for hours while his father slept, a son with whom he could discuss matters of topical worldly import and the eternal truths as well while the unfurling road beneath them brought them close, the journey uniting them as the stillness of a home never could. Deep bonding is a gift the road alone gives to those who honor it and travel down it with respect. The stations along their road would be pit stops on their souls' journey toward a final, mystical union followed by eternal bliss.

But he had no wife. No woman had wanted him for long and so there was no child. That was the short version. In the longer version, which he had buried so deep that even he had trouble locating it nowadays, there had been women for whom he had had feelings, whom he had adored almost as much as he now revered Miss Salma R, and these had been women he had known personally. He knew himself to be a man with a true capacity for adoration, an area in which most of his fellow men, being uncivilized ignorant brutes, were sorely deficient. It had therefore been painful to him that almost all the women he pursued had, quite quickly after his pursuit began, done their best to run away.

And he had quarreled with the Human Trampoline. Whoever had done what to whom, they had not parted on friendly terms. But maybe he could make amends, if he could remember his sins. This he would try to do.

But the "romantic" associations—those ladies were gone for good, and were they even real? Now, as he dedicated himself to the quest for the hand of Miss Salma R, it seemed to him that a small corner of the veil obscuring the past lifted up and reminded him of the consequences of lost love. He saw them pass before his inward eye, the horticulturist, the advertising executive, the public relations dazzler, the antipodean adventuress, the American liar, the English rose, the ruthless Asian beauty. No, it was impossible even to think about them again. They were gone and he was well rid of them and he could not have his heart broken by them anymore. What had happened had happened—or, he was almost sure it had happened—and it was right to bury them deeper than the deepest memory, to place their stories on the funeral pyres of his hopes, to seal them up in the pyramid of his regret; to forget, to forget, to forget. Yes, he had forgotten them, placing them in a lead-lined casket of forgetting far beneath the bed of the remembering ocean within him, an unmarked sarcophagus impenetrable even by the X-ray vision of a Superman, and along with them he had buried the man he had been then, and the things he had done, the failures, the failures, the failures. He had eschewed all thoughts of love for what seemed like an eternity, until Miss Salma R reawakened feelings and desires in his breast which he had thought he had suppressed or even destroyed along with his destroyed liaisons—if indeed they were real, from the real world, and not echoes of the greater reality of women on the screen?—whereupon he recognized a grand passion as it was born in him one last time, and he ceased being an ordinary nobody and became, at long last, the great man he had it within him to be, which was to say, Quichotte.

He was childless, and his line would end with him, unless he asked for and received a miracle. Maybe he could find a wishing well. He clung to this idea: that if he acted according to the occult principles of the Wish, then miracles were possible. Such was his tenuous grasp on sanity that he had become a student of the arts of wishing; as well as wishing wells, he pursued wishing trees, wishing stones, and, with more and more seriousness, wishing stars. After he completed his investigations, both in dusty library books specializing in astro-arcana and on a number of admittedly dubious websites, several of which triggered an ominous dialog box reading *Warning: this site may damage your computer,* he grew convinced that meteor showers were the best things to wish upon, and 11:11 P.M. the best time, and that he would need a quantity of wishbones.

There were seven meteor showers a year, in January, April, May, August, October, November, and December: the Quadrantids, Lyrids, Eta Aquarids, Perseids, Orionids, Leonids, and Geminids. Over the years he had hunted them down one by one, to catch a falling star with a good timepiece on his wrist and a generous supply of chicken bones in his pocket. He could be determined when he wanted to be. He had already, in years past, chased down the Quadrantids near Muncie, Indiana (pop. 68,625), the Lyrids in Monument Valley, and the Eta Aquarids in the Rincon Mountain District of the Sonoran Desert in Arizona. So far these expeditions had failed to bear fruit. Never mind! he told himself. One day soon, Salma R would bear him three, no! five, or why not? seven magnificent sons and daughters. He was sure of it. But, having the impatience of his gray hairs, he decided to continue his pursuits of meteor showers, for which he had more time now that his cousin had relieved him of his duties. The heavenly bodies must have been impressed by his persistence, because that August, on a hot night in the desert beyond Santa Fe, the Perseids granted his wish at the Devils Tower near Moorcroft, Wyoming (pop. 1,063). At 11:11 P.M. precisely he snapped seven wishbones while fire rained down from the skies from the direction of the constellation Perseus—Perseus the warrior, Zeus and Danaë's son, the Gorgonslayer!—and the miracle occurred. The longed-for son, who looked to be about fifteen years old, materialized in the Cruze's passenger seat.

The Age of Anything-Can-Happen! How overjoyed he was, Quichotte exclaimed inwardly, how grateful he was to live in such a time!

The magic child manifested himself in black-and-white, his natural colors desaturated in the manner that has become fashionable in much modern cinema. Perhaps, Quichotte surmised, the boy was astrologically related to the monochrome inhabitants of Tierra del Fuego. Or perhaps he had been seized long ago and now returned by the aliens in the mothership hiding in the sky above the meteors illuminating the Devils Tower, after many years during which he had been studied, drained of color by their experiments, and somehow failed to age. Certainly, as Quichotte came to know the boy, he seemed much older than his years. He strongly resembled the boy in the photographs Quichotte had saved of his own childhood far away across the world. In one of those pictures, Quichotte aged nine or ten was seen in a white kurta-pajama wearing his father's sunglasses. In another an older Quichotte, about the same age as the apparition, had a faint mustache on his upper lip and was standing in a garden with his promiscuous Alsatian bitch. Quichotte when young had been a little short, a little chubby compared to other boys his age. Then, in late adolescence, as if an invisible divine hand had grabbed him and squeezed him in the middle like a tube of toothpaste, he shot up to his present height and became as skinny as a shadow. This monochrome boy was evidently at the post-toothpaste-tube-squeezing phase, as long and narrow a fellow as his father, and he was wearing the sunglasses Quichotte had worn all those years ago. He was not wearing a kurta-pajama, however, but was dressed like a good all-American boy, in a checked lumberjack shirt and denim jeans with turn-ups. After a moment he began singing an old advertising jingle. His voice was cracking. A new Adam's apple bobbed in his throat.

> We love baseball, hot dogs, apple pie and Chevrolet,
> baseball, hot dogs, apple pie and Chevrolet . . .

A broad smile broke out across Quichotte's long face. It was as if his miraculous son, born out of his father's dream like Athena bursting fully formed from the head of Zeus, was singing a song of arrival, a love song to his father. The traveler joyously raised his own voice and sang along with his boy.

Baseball, hot dogs, apple pie and Chevrolet,
baseball, hot dogs, apple pie and Chevrolet!

"Sancho," Quichotte cried, full of a happiness he didn't know how to express. "My silly little Sancho, my big tall Sancho, my son, my sidekick, my squire! Hutch to my Starsky, Spock to my Kirk, Scully to my Mulder, BJ to my Hawkeye, Robin to my Batman! Peele to my Key, Stimpy to my Ren, Niles to my Frazier, Arya to my Hound! Peggy to my Don, Jesse to my Walter, Tubbs to my Crockett, I love you! O my warrior Sancho sent by Perseus to help me slay my Medusas and win my Salma's heart, here you are at last."

"Cut it out, 'Dad,'" the imaginary young man rejoined. "What's in all this for me?"

AFTER THE NIGHT of the Perseid miracle Quichotte spent days lost in a haze of joy because of the arrival of the mysterious black-and-white youngster he had named Sancho. He sent a text message to R. K. Smile, M.D., telling him the good news. Dr. Smile did not reply.

Sancho was darker skinned than his father, that was plain even in black-and-white, and in the end it was this that enabled Quichotte to solve—at least to his own satisfaction—the mystery of the boy's arrival. It seemed that Sancho was of approximately the same hue as the Beloved, Miss Salma R. So perhaps he was a visitor from the future, the child of Quichotte's forthcoming marriage to the great lady, and had traveled back through time and space to answer his father's need for a son's companionship, and end his long solitude. To a person who had gained a deep understanding of time travel from television, this was entirely possible. He remembered the Doctor, the British Time Lord, and guessed that Sancho might have arrived in some sort of TARDIS-like vehicle hidden in the dark sky behind the brilliance of the meteors. And perhaps this color drainage, this black-and-white effect, was nothing but a temporary side effect of time travel. "Welcome, my future son!" he enthused. "Welcome to the present. We will woo your mother together. How can she resist being wooed not only by the future father of her children, but by one of those children too? Our success is certain. . . . What's in it for you? Young man, if we fail, then you will cease to exist. If she does not consent to becoming your mother, then you will never be born, and so it follows that you wouldn't be here now. Does that focus your mind?"

"I'm hungry," Sancho muttered mutinously. "Can we stop talking and eat?"

Quichotte noted his son's untamed, rebellious, outlawlike character. It pleased him. Heroes, superheroes, and antiheroes, too, were not made of complaisant stock. They were out-of-step, against-the-grain, different-drummer types. He thought of Sherlock Holmes, of Green Arrow, of Negan. He understood, too, that he had missed the boy's childhood, had not been there for him, wherever *there* might have been. The lad would very likely be full of resentments and even delinquencies. It would take time to persuade him to open up, to stop scowling, to accept parental love and give filial love in return. The road was the place for that. Men on the road together have three choices. They separate, they kill one another, or they work things out.

"Yes," Quichotte replied to his son, with his heart full of hope. "By all means, let's eat."

—

CHAPTER TWO

An Author, Sam DuChamp, reflects upon his Past, & enters new Territory

*T*HE AUTHOR OF THE PRECEDING NARRATIVE—WE WILL call him Brother*—was a New York–based writer of Indian origin who had previously written eight modestly (un)successful spy fictions under the pen name of Sam DuChamp. Then in a surprising change of direction he conceived the idea of telling the story of the lunatic Quichotte and his doomed pursuit of the gorgeous Miss Salma R, in a book radically unlike any other he had ever attempted. No sooner had he conceived this idea than he became afraid of it. He could not at first fathom how such an eccentric notion had lodged in his brain, and why it insisted so vehemently on being written that he had no choice but to start work. Then as he thought about it further, he began to understand that in some fashion that he did not as yet fully grasp, Quichotte—the loner in search of love, the loser-nobody who believed himself capable of winning the

---

* This is partly because his relationship with his estranged sibling, Sister, will be central to his story; but also for another reason, which will be given on page 31.

heart of a queen—had been with him all his life, a shadow-self he had glimpsed from time to time in the corner of his eye, but had not had the courage to confront. Instead he had written his common-place fictions of the secret world, disguised as someone else. He now saw that this had been a way of avoiding the story that revealed it-self to him in the mirror every day, even if only in the corner of his eye.

His next thought was even more alarming: To make sense of the life of the strange man whose latter days he was setting out to chron-icle, he would have to reveal himself alongside his subject, for the tale and the teller were yoked together by race, place, generation, and circumstance. Perhaps this bizarre story was a metamorphosed version of his own. Quichotte himself might say, if he were aware of Brother (which was impossible, naturally), that in fact the writ-er's tale was the altered version of *his* history, rather than the other way around, and might have argued that his "imaginary" life added up to the more authentic narrative of the two.

So, in brief: They were both Indian-American men, one real, one fictional, both born long ago in what was then Bombay, in neighboring apartment blocks, both real. Their parents would have known each other (except that one set of parents was imaginary), and would perhaps have played golf and badminton together at the Willingdon Club and sipped sunset cocktails at the Bombay Gym (both real-world locations). They were about the same age, at which almost everyone is an orphan, and their generation, having made a royal mess of the planet, was on its way out. They both suffered from physical complaints: Brother's aching back, Quichotte's drag-ging leg. They met friends (real, fictional) and acquaintances (fic-tional, real) in the obituary columns with increasing frequency. There would not be less of all this in the days to come. And there were deeper echoes. If Quichotte had been driven mad by his desire for the people behind the TV screen, then he, Brother, had perhaps also been deranged by proximity to another veiled reality, in which nothing was reliable, treachery was everywhere, identities were slippery and mutable, democracy was corruptible, the two-faced double agent and the three-faced triple agent were everyday monsters, love placed the loved one in danger, allies could not be trusted, information was as often fool's gold as golden, and patriotism was a virtue for which there would never be any recognition or reward.

Brother was agitated about many things. Like Quichotte, he was alone and childless, except that he had once had a son. This child had vanished long ago like a ghost, and must be a young man by now, and Brother thought about him every day and was dismayed by his absence. His wife was also long gone, and his financial situation bordered on the precarious. And—beyond these private matters— he had begun to have a sense of something coming after him, of dark-windowed cars parked on the corner of his block with their motors running, footsteps that stopped when he stopped, then started up again when he walked on, clicking noises on the phone, strange problems with his laptop, telemarketing messages with, he thought, a menace behind the banal words, threats on his Twitter feed, murmurs from his publishing company that mid-list Authors like himself might have difficulty being published in the future. There were issues with his credit cards, and his social media had been hacked too often for it to be a random thing. On one occasion he came home at night and was sure his apartment had been entered even though nothing had been disturbed. If the two guiding principles of the universe were paranoia (the belief that the world had meaning, but that meaning was located at a concealed level, which was very possibly hostile to the overt, absurd level, which meant, in brief, you) and entropy (the belief that life was meaningless, that things fell apart and the heat-death of the universe was inevitable), then he was definitely in the paranoid camp.

If Quichotte's craziness was leading him to run toward his doom, then Brother's anxieties were close to triggering a flight response. He wanted to run but didn't know where or how, which made him more fearful still, because he knew that in his spy fiction he had already told himself the answer. You can run but you can't hide.

Maybe writing about Quichotte was a way of running away from that truth.

It was difficult for him to speak of personal things because he had never been the confessional type. From his boyhood days he had been drawn toward secrecy. As a small child he wore his father's sunglasses to conceal his eyes, which revealed too much. He hid things and watched with glee as his parents searched for them— their wallets, their toothbrushes, their car keys. His friends would confide in him, understanding that his was a serious silence, the silence of a pharaoh in his pyramid; sometimes an innocent confidence, sometimes a not so innocent. Innocent: that they had a crush on such and such a boy slash girl; that their parents drank too much and fought constantly; that they had discovered the joys of masturbation. Not so innocent: how they poisoned the neighbor's cat; how they stole comic books from the Reader's Paradise bookstore; the things they did with the see-above crushed-on girls slash boys. His silence was like a vacuum that sucked the secrets out of their mouths and right into his ears. He made no use of his secret knowledge. It was enough simply to know, to be the one who knew.

He kept his own secrets too. His parents looked upon him with a mixture of puzzlement and concern. "Who are you?" his mother once asked him in annoyed tones. "Are you even my child? Sometimes it's like you're an alien from another planet, sent to watch us and gather information, and one day a spaceship will scoop you up and your little green relatives will know all our secrets." This was how she was: capable of emotional brutality and unable, once a clever conceit came into her head, to stop herself from saying it, no matter how deep the wound it might inflict. His father expressed himself more gently, but made the same point. "Look at your little sister," he would tell his son. "Try to be like her. She never stops talking. She's an open book."

In spite of his parents' urgings, he went on as he was, reticent about himself and gathering other people's whispers whenever he could. As for open books, the books he opened in his youth were usually mysteries. As a boy he much preferred the Secret Seven to the Famous Five, the Secret Garden to Wonderland. And then as he grew, it was Ellery and Erle Stanley and Agatha, it was Sam Spade and Marlowe, mean-streeted and tight-lipped! His secret worlds multiplied with the passing years. *The Secret Agent, The Man Who Was Thursday,* tales of espionage and secret societies, these were his guides. In his teens he studied books about black magic and the tarot—the arcana of hidden knowledge, major or minor, drew him irresistibly toward them—and he learned how to hypnotize his friends, though the target of his new skill, an attractive girl whom he desired, resisted his advances even when under his spell. He grew up wanting to know the secret ingredient in Coca-Cola, he remembered the secret identities of all superheroes, and what was Victoria's secret, anyway? That ladies in her era wore badly made underwear? SIS, ISI, OSS, CIA, these were his initials of choice.

This was how he came to be a writer of pseudonymous spy novels. He wasn't widely known, a situation that was unlikely to be altered by the Quichotte book, if he ever managed to get it written and published. Sam DuChamp, Author of the Five Eyes series, unacclaimed, un-famous, un-rich: when people did ask for a title of his in a store, they pronounced the pen name wrongly, calling him Sam the Sham, like the "Wooly Bully" guy, who drove to his gigs in a Packard hearse. This was a little insulting.

Yes, the name on the books veiled his ethnic identity, just as *Freddie Mercury* veiled the Parsi Indian singer Farrokh Bulsara. This was not because the Queen front man was ashamed of his race but because he did not want to be prejudged, did not want to be ghettoed inside an ethnic-music pigeonhole surrounded by the bars of white attitudes. Brother felt the same way. And after all it was the age of the invented name. Social media had made sure of that. Everyone was someone else now.

Pseudonyms have never been uncommon in the world of books. Women had often deemed them necessary. Brother believed (without daring to compare his poor talent to their genius) that Currer,

Ellis, and Acton Bell, George Eliot, and even J. K. Rowling (who preferred the gender-neutrality of *J.K.* to *Jo*) would have understood.

Brown people of South Asian ethnicity had a confusing history in America. In the early part of the twentieth century Quichotte and Dr. R. K. Smile's alleged common ancestor (not fictional), supposedly the first of their clan to live and work in the USA, had been denied American citizenship on the basis of the nation's first immigration act, that of 1790, which decreed that only a "free white person" was eligible for citizenship. And when the Immigration Act of 1917 was signed into law, South Asians, known as *hindoos,* were officially barred altogether from immigrating to the United States. In *United States v. Bhagat Singh Thind* (1923) the Supreme Court argued that the racial difference between Indians and whites was so great that the "great body of our people" would reject assimilation with Indians. Twenty-three years later the Luce-Celler Act permitted just one hundred Indians a year to come to America and gain citizenship (thanks a lot). Then in 1965 a new Immigration and Nationality Act opened the doors. After which, an unexpectedness. It turned out that *hindoos* were not to be a major target of American racism after all. That honor continued to be reserved for the African-American community, and Indian immigrants—many of them familiar with white British racism in South Africa and East Africa, as well as India and Britain themselves—were almost embarrassed to find themselves excused, in many parts of the USA, from racial abuse and attacks, and embarked on the path of becoming model citizens.

Not excused entirely, however. In 1987 the Dotbuster gang terrorized Indian-American families in Jersey City. A letter from the gang published in *The Jersey Journal* threatened violence. "We will go to any extreme to get Indians to move out of Jersey City. If I'm walking down the street and I see a Hindu and the setting is right, I will hit him or her. We plan some of our most extreme attacks such as breaking windows, breaking car windows, and crashing family parties." The threats were carried out. One Indian man was attacked and died four days later. Another was put into a coma. There were further nighttime attacks, and burglaries too.

Then came September 11, 2001, and young Indian men started wearing T-shirts reading DON'T BLAME ME, I'M HINDU, and Sikh men were attacked because their turbans made them look Islamic, and cab drivers put flag decals on their windshields and stickers on the glass partitions between themselves and their passengers reading GOD BLESS AMERICA, and suddenly it seemed to Brother that maybe the mask of a pen name was worth continuing to wear. There were too many hostile eyes looking at people like him now. Better to be Sam the Sham. The spy guy.

THE FIVE EYES, OR FVEY, were the intelligence services of Australia, Canada, New Zealand, the United Kingdom, and the United States who, in the period after World War II, began sharing the results of the immense ECHELON surveillance system and its successors and now also shared information gained from monitoring the Internet. In the books written by Sam DuChamp the mutual distrust of the five principals was a central theme. Nobody trusted the Americans because they couldn't keep secrets, and that endangered the Five Eyes' most important assets, the undercover agents in the field. Nobody trusted the British, even though they were the best at running moles—in Russia, in Iran, in the Arab world—because of the frequent penetrations of SIS itself by moles from elsewhere. Nobody trusted the Canadians because they acted so goddamn holier-than-thou, nobody trusted the Australians because they were Australian, and nobody trusted the New Zealanders because they had never come up with a single useful surveillance program. (The major post-ECHELON programs, PRISM, XKeyscore, Tempora, MUSCULAR, and STATEROOM, were run mostly by the British Government Communications Headquarters, or GCHQ, and the American National Security Agency, the NSA, with contributions from the Australians and the Canadians.) This network of hostile allies was presently being tested further by British little-Englander separatism and American populist bullying, both of which assisted the enemy in general and Russia in particular. Brother had always been proud of the authenticity of the secret world he had created, but now he was becoming afraid of it. Maybe he had come too close to certain uncomfortable truths. Maybe the people who read the Five Eyes books most carefully were the Five Eyes themselves. Maybe they thought it was time to close the "sixth eye," which was watching them a little too well.

To attract such unwelcome attention from the Phantoms just as he was averting his gaze from Spookworld was an irony he could do without. He was old, and truth had become far stranger than his fictions, and he no longer had the energy to try to outstrip the news. Hence Quichotte, picaresque and crazy and dangerous, a knight's move out of a deteriorating position on the board. Hence, also, his newly inward gaze, his returned yearning for his lost home in the East. He had stepped away from the past long ago and later it stepped away from him. For a long time he pretended, even to himself, that he had accepted his fate. He was a man of the West now, he was Sam DuChamp, and that was fine. This is what he said when he was questioned: that he was not rootless, not uprooted but transplanted. Or, even better, multiply rooted, like an old banyan tree putting down "prop roots" as it spread, which thickened and in time became indistinguishable from the original trunk. Too many roots! It meant his stories had a broader canopy beneath which to shelter from the scorching, hostile sun. It meant they could be planted in many different locations, in different kinds of soil. This is a gift, he said, but he knew that such optimism was a lie. Now, well past the Psalmist's *days of our years,* trying *by reason of strength* to move past threescore and ten toward fourscore, his was often the sad heart of Keats's Ruth, when, sick for home, she stood in tears amid the alien corn.

He was coming to the end of the line, and had moved into the general vicinity of the cowled reaper. The borough, the neighborhood, maybe even the zip code. He wasn't quite foot-in-the-ground yet. But it was sobering that the road ahead was so much shorter than the road already traveled. Before Quichotte drove up in his Chevy Cruze with his imaginary son by his side, Brother had almost come to believe that the work had left him, even if life, for the moment, went on. Here was this thing, however mediocre, to which he had given his life, his best self, his optimism; but even the richest seam in the end runs out of gold. When you were your own quarry, when the material you were dredging up lay buried in the caverns of the self, a time came when there was only an emptiness left.

So, then, quit! said the wicked angel on his left shoulder. *Nobody cares but you.*

The wicked angel on his left shoulder was the shadow. But on his right shoulder sat the cherub of the light, cheering him, urging him on, refusing self-pity. The sun still rose every day. He still had determination, energy, and the habit of work. He took heart from the great Muhammad Ali regaining his crown after the long wilderness years, defeating George Foreman in Zaire. He, too, could hope for a rumble in some welcoming jungle. Sam DuChamp, *bomaye*. Kill him, Sam the Sham.

And so to Quichotte's birthplace, which was also his own, to examine certain intimate matters which were at once extremely close and impossibly distant. The technical term for such matters was *family*. A good enough starting point for a tale about obsessional love.

MANY, MANY YEARS AGO, when the sea was clean and the night was safe, there was a road called Warden Road (not called that anymore) in a neighborhood called Breach Candy (still called that, more or less) in a city called Bombay (not called that now). Everything started there and even though his story and Quichotte's were both travelers' tales, journeying through many places and arriving in this strange and fantastic land, America, all their roads led back to Bombay if you ran the movie backwards. The origin point of Brother's whole world was a little group of maybe a dozen houses on a low hill served by a nameless dead-end lane (nameless no longer; Shakari Bhandari Lane, the maps now called it, even though nobody knew where that was), dwarfed by the megacity that now surrounded them. He closed his eyes and walked backwards across continents and years, twirling his cane like Raj Kapoor's imitation-Chaplin tramp, only in reverse. Backwards up the nameless-but-now-named lane he went, past the (real) apartment building where the (fictional) Smile family once lived, called Dil Pazir, which is to say, acceptable to the heart . . . and arrived at a similar building (also real) named Noor Ville, the city of light, and inside it on an upper floor a long-balconied apartment filled with soft cushions, sharp cactus plants, and the unmistakable yodelings of the famous golden-voiced sisters Lata and Asha singing the latest hit songs from the movies on the *Binaca Geetmala*, the weekend chart show sponsored by a toothpaste brand, emanating every Sunday from the walnut-marquetry Art Deco Telefunken radiogram in the living room. And in the middle of the living room's large Persian rug, martini glasses in their hands, here were his Ma and Pa, in backwards slow motion, dancing.

(That Breach Candy was a tiny, lost world, long gone, preserved in the amber of memory like a prehistoric insect. Or: a miniature universe, the past captured under a glass dome, like a tropical snow globe without snow, and in it the tiny people of the past leading their microscopic lives. If the glass broke and they escaped into the great world beyond their boundary, how terrified they would be of the giants all around them, as terrified as he had been when he en-countered the titans of his adult world! Yet, minute as they were, the whole future flowed from them. The little tropical snow globe without snow was the birthplace of everything Brother had been and done.)

His parents' favorite LP was Sinatra's *Songs for Swingin' Lovers!* Ma, always more up-to-the-minute than her husband, liked some of the quiffed Americans. Ricky Nelson. Bobby Darin. But not only the white boys. Also Clyde McPhatter and the Drifters singing "Money Honey." Not Elvis! She was scornful about the truck driver from Tupelo. Who cared about his pelvis or his curling upper lip? Who wanted to step on his blue suede shoes, which were Carl Perkins's footwear first, anyway?

He let the film behind his closed eyes run forward now. His father owned and ran a celebrated jewelry store called Zayvar Brother on Warden Road, at the foot of the hill where they lived. Brother's grandfather, his father's father, had opened it long ago, and Pa had proved to be an even finer designer and maker of beautiful things than his dad. *Zévar* meant "ornamentation" in Urdu and *Zayvar* was the Anglophile patriarch's Englishing of the word. He had been an only child, the old man, but he thought *Brothers* was a businesslike name, and if he couldn't use the plural, the singular would do just as well. Thus, *Zayvar Brother,* a brother without a brother. People had started calling the whiskered old gentleman Brother Sahib, Mr. Brother, and the name stuck. After grandfather had taken his leave, Pa became Mr. Brother Junior, and so, in time, Brother would be Mr. Brother too. Mr. Brother the Third.

A few doors down from the jewelers was Ma's own little enterprise, the idiosyncratic Cakes & Antiques, a front room boasting the best patisserie in the city and a back room in which treasures from all over South Asia could be found: Chola bronzes in perfect condition, lively Company School paintings, enigmatic seals from Mohenjo-daro, nineteenth-century embroidered shawls from Kashmir. When she was asked, as she often was, why she sold this improbable combination of products, she would answer simply, "Because these are the things I love."

The quality and originality of the two establishments, combined with Pa's and Ma's inescapable charisma, turned both Zayvar Brother and Cakes & Antiques into Places Where Everybody Went. Amitabh Bachchan bought emerald necklaces for his wife, Jaya, at Zayvar, Mario Miranda and R. K. Laxman offered Ma their original cartoons in return for her chocolate cakes, and "Busybee," Behram

Contractor, the chronicler of everyday life for *le tout* Bombay, loitered around both stores watching the cream of the city come and go, listening for the latest gossip.

Ma and Pa's home, too, was full of the artistic and famous. Creative people of all sorts passed through their storied drawing room. The great playback singers Lata Mangeshkar and Asha Bhosle were there in person (though never at the same time!). Also cricketers—Vinoo Mankad and Pankaj Roy, the heroes who in January 1956 shared a world-record opening partnership of 413 runs against New Zealand in Madras! The poet Nissim Ezekiel came to call—the bard of Bombay, the island city he deemed "unsuitable for song as well as sense." Even the great painter Aurora Zogoiby herself came over, along with that no-talent buffoon hanger-on of hers, Vasco Miranda, but that's another story. And, it being Bombay, also movie people, inevitably. Talent, talent everywhere, lubricated by whisky-sodas and lust. There were political arguments, aesthetic disputes, sexual hijinks, and martinis. And towering over it all like the still-mostly-in-the-future skyscrapers that would arrive soon enough to change the city forever, were tall Ma and even taller Pa, twirling together slowly, sipping their drinks, she so graceful, he so handsome, and both of them deeply in love.

And because of such intensive and prolonged childhood overexposure to creative genius of all types, Brother too, like his incipiently crazy Quichotte, fell victim to a rare form of mental disorder—his first, paranoia being the second—in the grip of which the boundary between art and life became blurred and permeable, so that at times he was incapable of distinguishing where one ended and the other began, and, even worse, was possessed of the fool's conviction that the imaginings of creative people could spill over beyond the boundaries of the works themselves, that they possessed the power to enter and transform and even improve the real world. Most of his fellow humans, past and present, treated this proposition with scorn and continued down their personal paths in the pragmatic, ideological, religious, self-serving, venal spheres in which, for the most part, the real life of the world was lived. Brother, however—thanks to his parents' circle—was incurable. Even though he afterwards grew up to earn a living in the lowbrow world of genre fiction, his respect for those with higher foreheads remained undimmed. Many years later, the writing of *Quichotte* would be his belated, end-of-life attempt to cross the frontier separating low culture from high.

He stopped the film. That wasn't true. That was a fairy tale. That culture- and love-blessed boho infancy. Parents like his were mysteries to their children in those days. They didn't spend much time with their offspring, they employed domestic staff to do that, and they didn't tell the little creatures much about their lives or answer any *how* or *why* questions, and only a few inquiries that began *what, when,* or *where.* The *how* and *why* questions were the big ones, and on those matters their lips were sealed. They married young and had two children: Brother and Sister, whom Pa nicknamed Tweety Pie because she was the canary of the family, the only one who could sing. Then—this was where the fairy tale broke down—when Brother was ten years old and Sister was five, Ma and Pa separated. Ma was the one to move out, and after that there was a second apartment in the children's lives, in Soona Mahal (real name), on the corner of Marine Drive and Churchgate (now officially Netaji Subhash Chandra Bose Road and Veer Nariman Road, or VN Road). It was rumored that both Ma and Pa had been multiply unfaithful to each other—oh, the lives of the bohemians, those wild, crazy folks!—but the children never saw any Other Woman in Pa's bedroom, nor, at Ma's new place, where Brother and Sister mostly lived during the Separation, did they meet any Other Man. If the parents had committed or were committing the bruited indiscretions, they did so in the most discreet fashion. Pa continued to do his work at Zayvar Brother, and Ma was a few steps away at Cake & Antiques, and life went on as normal, in spite of the crackle of things unsaid, audible to all who visited either location, in spite of the hum of the little wall-hung electric fans. And then, almost ten years later, just like that!, they reunited, and the Soona Mahal apartment went poof! even though it had come to feel like home to both children, and then they were back in Noor Ville, and the parents resumed their martini-hour dancing, as if the long years of the Separation were the fantasy, and not this reinvented idyll.

Further corrections: By the time of his parents' reunion Brother was twenty and at university in Cambridge, so he wasn't around to watch them begin to dance again. And neither Soona Mahal nor Noor Ville felt like home anymore to a young man intoxicated by the sixties in the West. Meanwhile Sister, at fifteen, stayed in Bombay. At first, the siblings tried to preserve some sort of relationship by playing long-distance chess with each other like good smart Indian children, sending postcards with their moves written in the old descriptive notation, P-K4, P-K4, P-Q4, PxP. But eventually a rift cracked open between the two of them. He was older but she was better than him, and he, a bad loser, stopped wanting to play. Meanwhile Sister, stuck at home watching the nightly parental twirling, grew resentful, understanding that in spite of her academic brilliance Ma and Pa were not inclined to lavish a foreign education on *her*. Feeling (quite rightly) like the less-loved child, she saw Brother (quite rightly) as the unjustly favored son, and her rage at her parents expanded like an exploding star to engulf her sibling as well. The rift deepened and by now had lasted a lifetime. They had fought, stopped speaking, lived in different cities—he in New York, she in London (after she fought her way out of the cage of her family)—and no longer met. Decades passed. They were trapped in the drama from which their parents had escaped. Pa and Ma performed The Grand Reconciliation until the end of their lives. That was their happy-ending script. Sister and Brother, silently, and far apart, enacted The Death of Love.

Seventeen years ago, their mother had died peacefully in her sleep after a last day in which she drove her car, visited friends, and dined out. She came home from her perfect day, lay down, and flew away. Sister had caught a plane home immediately, but by the time her flight landed Pa was dead as well, unable to live without Ma. There was an empty bottle of sleeping pills on his nightstand by the bed in which he had been slain by her unbearable absence. Sister called Brother in New York to tell him about the double tragedy. After that there was only one further telephone conversation, a conversation which killed whatever sibling affection remained.

Then, nothing. An empty cloud filled the space where family should have been. Brother hadn't met Sister's fashionista daughter, Daughter; she hadn't met his dropout son, Son. Son was his lost child. His only child, who had broken up with him, too, who had broken up with both his parents, and disappeared. (And now here was Quichotte, his invention, inventing a child for himself and bringing him to life. There wasn't much doubt about where that idea had originated.) There were times when Brother thought of himself as an only child as well. No doubt Sister often felt the same way. But only children don't have, in the shadows of their souls, a deep wound where once there had been a younger sister's kiss, an older brother's safe embrace. Only children don't, in their old age, have to listen to their inner voice asking accusatory questions, *how can you treat your sister like this, your own sister, don't you want to fix things, don't you see that you should.* So he had been thinking about her, about everyone he had lost but mainly about her, weighing the benefits of putting down the burden of their quarrel and making peace before it was too late against the risk of triggering one of her nuclear rages, and unsure if he possessed the courage to make some sort of approach. If he was honest with himself he knew it was up to him to make the first move, because she had a deeper grievance than he did. In a quarrel that had lasted for decades neither party could claim to be innocent. But the simple truth was that, in plain language, he had done her wrong.

———

CHAPTER THREE

Quichotte's Beloved, a Star from a Dynasty of Stars, moves to a different Galaxy

MISS SALMA R, THE EXCEPTIONAL WOMAN (AND TOTAL stranger) to whom Quichotte had declared his undying devotion, came from a dynasty of adored ladies. Think of her family this way: Granny R was Greta Garbo, a great actress who for unexplained reasons abruptly retreated from the world, declaring that she disliked people and open spaces and wanted to be alone. Mummy R was Marilyn Monroe, very sexy and very fragile, and she stole the sportsman prince (a real honest-to-goodness prince) whom Grace Kelly wanted to marry and that became Daddy, who left Mummy for an English photographer smack in the middle of her last movie shoot, and after that Mummy entered a long decline and was eventually found dead in her bedroom, fatally echoing Marilyn's destiny with bottles of pills lying open and empty on her nightstand. And Miss Salma R? She did not inherit Granny's acting genius or Mummy's super sexiness, everyone agreed on that, but her genes did grant her considerable beauty, ease in front of the cameras, as well as violent mood swings and a fondness for recreational and mind-soothing painkillers. As a result, unsurprisingly, she ended up in Hollywood.

That was her Bombay history briefly translated into American. The official version could be summarized in the following few words: "She had led a charmed life. She came from fame and money and made even more money and achieved even greater fame on her own, becoming the first Indian actress to make it big (very big) in America, to cross what might be called the -wood bridge from Bolly- to Holly-, and then transcended even Hollywood to become a brand, a television talk-show superstar and titanic cultural influencer, in America and India too." The truth was more complex. So then, a longer version: Yes, she was Indian movie royalty, a third-generation member of a family of female legends. Her grandmother, Miss Dina R, had starred in half a dozen of the grand classic neorealist films made in the decade after independence. However, the great star mysteriously fell prey to a whole wolf pack of phobias and dark mental troubles, succumbing to long, silent bouts of the deep blues (which Winston Churchill called the black dog and Miss Holly Golightly would later rename the mean reds) and alternating spells of loud babbling hysteria. She retreated into her beachfront Juhu mansion, remaining behind a veil of secrecy for the rest of her life, never responding to the salacious speculation about her madness that bounced harmlessly off her property's high walls, and until her dying day kept the lights on in her bedroom at night because she was afraid of cockroaches and lizards in the dark. She also broke off all contact with her husband, a well-known Bombay physician whom everyone called Babajan—*Baba* being an honorific title of respect and *jan* meaning "darling"—but they never divorced. They lived in separate suites of the Juhu mansion and went about their separate lives. When she ran into him in a corridor by chance, she recoiled as if he were a dangerous intruder, and often actually ran away. After her death by suicide (an overdose of sleeping pills) Babajan told his few remaining friends mournfully that the balance of her mind had been long disturbed and the end was "inevitable."

Her daughter, Miss Salma R's mother, the renowned sexpot star

Miss Anisa R, remained close to her father for a while, but even before her mother's death Anisa and her father, too, were estranged. Not long after she stopped talking to Babajan she seduced the national cricket captain away from her best friend, Nargis Kumari, also an iconic movie actress. The cricketer was the dashing young raja of Bakwas Senior, popularly known as "the Raj," the prince of a tiny central Indian state (on no account to be confused with the distinctly tinier and obviously much less important state of Bakwas Junior), whose ancestor had once considered employing as private secretary a homosexual Englishman named Forster who was thinking of writing a novel about a passage to India, and looking for a job. (He didn't hire him. Another trivial princeling did.) Yes! A blueblood! But the Raj's true aristocracy was to be seen not in his family tree but in the grace and power of his shot-making on the cricket field, his imperious square cuts, his graceful leg glances, his powerful cover drives and autocratic hook shots. He married Miss Salma R's mother in a glamorous three-day wedding at the Taj Palace Hotel in Bombay (a daring, avant-garde affair, because Hindu-Muslim marriages were rare, then as now, even among the elite). Soon afterwards, in an accident described by his jilted ex-fiancée Nargis Kumari as "God's will," he lost the lower half of his right leg in a car crash on Marine Drive. However, defying divine judgment, he regained his place in the team, wooden leg and all, and became one of the sport's true immortals. They had one daughter, whom he professed to love more than life, but that was before he was overwhelmed by the difficulty of dealing with his wife's Technicolor depressions, the blues, blacks, and reds, and the intervening manias which came in different colors, most often green because during these upswings she went on insane spending sprees, acquiring precious antiquities on the black market at absurdly inflated prices. In the end he retired from cricket and abandoned Miss Anisa R, their daughter Miss Salma R, and his royal inheritance, and ran off to the UK—once again, the peg leg did not prove to be a hindrance—to set up house in a suite at Claridge's hotel which he shared with the previously mentioned English photographer, Margaret Ellen Arnold, who had been sent to do a location story about the film-star wife and left with the husband instead.

It occurred to nobody to attach any blame to the prince, who had deserted two women and who, in time, would desert the photographer as well and return to his deeply cushioned and intricately brocaded princely seat to pass the remainder of his days in a happy opium haze. The closest he came to being criticized was when *Filmfare* magazine ran a photo-story about him titled "Someday My Prince Will Run." But even in this story the (female) writer took the attitude that boys would be boys, and what man would not follow in the Raj's wood-leg-real-leg footsteps if he only could? However, Miss Anisa R was devastated by her very public humiliation. In the words of Nargis Kumari, who was happy to gloat publicly over her former friend's distress, Anisa had "been shown the power of Muslim *kismet* and of Hindu *karma,* both of which exact bitter poetic justice upon traitors and wrongdoers." The words hit their mark. Miss Anisa R gave up her acting career and focused on doing charity work with impoverished widows and deserted women as an act of atonement for the crime of stealing a man from a woman who loved him and for the even more shameful error of being incapable of holding on to her husband. She let herself go physically: That has to be said. She became—there is not a polite way of putting this—blowsy. She sagged; for all her good works, her body became the emblem and manifestation of her grief.

She wasn't a good mother—too self-absorbed for that—but Miss Salma R grew up perfectly anyway. She was a studious, upright, composed, idealistic, blameless young girl, and as her mother entered her last decline toward second childhood, it was the daughter who played the adult. More than one person reported seeing Salma following her drunk mother around at glitzy fundraising events for her women's charities, literally taking glasses of Scotch whisky out of Anisa's hands and pouring the contents into plant pots. "Without the daughter's care," people noted, "the mother would never have lasted as long as she did." Even that daughterly protectiveness proved not to be enough. They had moved into the Juhu mansion after Dina's death and maybe that was a bad move. Babajan still haunted the house, and now it was Anisa who ignored him as her mother had done before her. Miss Salma R had been fond of her grandfather as a child, and at first she tried to mend fences between her mother and Babajan, but it was too late. The darkness that had swallowed Dina R came for Anisa as well. She saved countless women from the gutter but the lower depths claimed her in the end. Miss Salma R was the one who found her mother in what had formerly been Dina's bedroom, cold and overdosed with the lights on in the same bed in which her mother had died, similarly illuminated. There was a cockroach crawling up her dangling arm.

Miss Salma R, by this time a nineteen-year-old who had just starred in her first film, did not cry out. She turned and left the room, leaving the lights on, carefully made the phone calls that needed to be made, went to her own room and packed a bag, drove away, and never set foot in that house of death again, leaving to others the task of cataloguing and selling the furniture, the furnishings, the movie memorabilia, and the personal effects—the gowns, the love letters, the photograph albums in which her mother's life lay embalmed. She wanted none of it, and listened to nobody who told her that she was in the grip of traumatic grief and would regret her decisions later. She turned away from the past with all the steely resolve which would take her to the very top of her profession in two continents. Among the elements of the past which she rejected was her aging grandfather. "He's a ghost," she told people. "I won't let any ghosts haunt me now. He needs to find himself alternative accommodation. The house must be sold at once."

In one of those extraordinary coincidences that enliven real life but are considered suspect in fiction, she moved into a smart apartment on the very same low hill in Breach Candy where Quichotte had previously been a child, though she was around thirty years younger than her future admirer.

Westfield Estate, as this little group of villas and apartment blocks was known—this microscopic urban speck from which the entire universe was born!—was the creation of an Anglophile developer called Suleman Oomer, also the builder of the somewhat similar Oomer Park properties down the road. He gave many of the buildings majestic-sounding English names: Windsor Villa, Glamis Villa, Sandringham Villa, Bal Moral, Devonshire House, and even Christmas Eve. It was in Christmas Eve, the place where Christmas was eternally promised for the next day but never arrived, that Miss Salma R came to roost. And it was there, three days after her mother's death, that she agreed to receive an unexpected guest, her mother's friend-turned-enemy, Nargis Kumari, whose presence allowed Salma finally to grieve for her mother. The veteran actress entered the apartment howling with pain and her voluble sadness overwhelmed the daughter's grim-faced stoicism. "What a fool I have been," Nargis Kumari cried, in full tragic actress mode, "to allow a mere man to destroy my closest friendship. What is a man compared to the love between soul sisters? He is a passing shadow. He is a random sneeze. He is a short rain shower on a sunny day. I should have been beside her every minute, sunshine or rain. Now I am as empty as a bottle from which all the wine has been poured. I am a word in a dictionary whose meaning has been erased. I am as hollow as a rotten tree." Miss Salma R's tears began to flow. "I will do everything for you," Nargis Kumari vowed. "You just sit on here and mourn. All requisite duties and disposals will be handled by myself." A few days later word reached Miss Salma R that Nargis Kumari had been at the Juhu house trying on the dead woman's most expensive garments and taking many of them away with her, plus matching jewelry. Miss Salma R called her to discuss this. "You didn't want anything, isn't it," Nargis Kumari replied without any shame. "So these few souvenirs of my darling I can keep close to my heart?" Miss Salma R hung up without replying.

After she wept for her dead mother the mood swings began, as if they had been transferred by the magic of grieving from that dead mind to this living one. From that moment onward she found herself on the emotional roller coaster on which her mother and grandmother had spent their lives. There was no escape from dynastic biochemistry. In Miss Salma R's family the darkness was always there, sitting like a panther in the corner of the room, waiting for its time.

SOME TIME LATER THE AMERICAN TV producer came to call, to tempt her with a California dream. She did not, at first, fall under his spell. "In the industry in this town," she told the American as they sipped cocktails on her balcony at Christmas Eve, "there are six boys and four girls, and for a picture to be big it must have at least one and one, preferably two and one. The whole annual box office depends on what we choose. So it is a burden, and we must be responsible. The livelihoods of thousands of people are affected by our decisions. This is why it is not easy for me to accept your TV series." The American had come a long way to do what all the Bollywood ultrastars required: to "narrate" the series idea to them personally. Miss Salma R offered him samosas, *gulab jamun,* and dirty martinis (up, with olives) and listened with great, wide-eyed seriousness, using the great, wide-eyed, serious look that had served her so well in so many close-ups. This look was as good as the best card player's poker face. The American could not tell if she was extremely interested, slightly interested, or not at all interested in his pitch. He tried again. "I know you are anxious to expand your range as an actress," he said. She nodded fervently but her eyes very, very slightly glazed over. "Both creatively and in terms of your reach and penetration."

Here her mask slipped slightly. *Penetration, reach:* These were fascinating words. He had her attention now. "I know that your films are huge in the Arab world and the Far East as well as here," the American said, "and your stage performances command top dollar." *Huge, top, dollar,* she thought. *These words are so precise, so true. This is a smart man.* "Our show will be streamed to every country in the world," the American said. "You will be the beloved, the obsession, of gauchos on the Argentinian pampa, of cowpokes in Wyoming, of

Puerto Rican reggaeton singers, of boxing champions in Las Vegas. Teenage boys in colleges will desire you, grandfathers will wish you were their granddaughter in big cities and small country towns from Johannesburg to Vancouver. There will be hundreds of millions of ordinary men, humble men with blue collars, men of low net worth, maybe unemployed men, for whom you will be their greatest treasure, and whose paltry, empty-pocketed lives you will enrich as they binge-watch you in the dark."

"Girls too," she murmured.

"Of course girls too," the American agreed. "To girls everywhere you will be their role model and powerful representative. You will kick ass, if I may say that, on their behalf."

She wanted to kick ass on their behalf. "So there are some things that worry me, and I should say so now, isn't it, because when we are on set we should be totally on the same page."

The American sat up very straight. "Yes, of course," he said.

"On page thirty, here"—she pointed—"my character is in the bathroom and it seems she is, excuse me, masturbating."

"That can be fixed," the American said.

"My character does not masturbate," said Miss Salma R. "My character kicks ass."

"Totally," the American said.

MISS SALMA R CHOSE NEVER to explain the forces that drove her to leave home in her mid-twenties and at the height of her popularity in the Indian cinema (and she was popular, though not as deeply loved as her mother and grandmother), and to seek a new fortune halfway across the world. She loved her hometown and her life in it. And yet she left. There were those who said that her relationship with home had soured after her mother's death. There were voices that blamed her "unfettered ambition and greed" and even more spiteful voices that called her "a deracinated, self-hating, Westoxicated no-talent" and called for her Indian films to be banned. These voices suggested that if she had a husband he could have knocked some sense into her. The generation of Netflix-and-chill was less judgmental and looked forward to seeing her on their laptops. In their opinion her real migration had been from silver screen to computer screen, not from Bombay/Mumbai to L.A., a migration that made her even more fashionable than before in their eyes. She herself was unclear about her motives. She had begun her meeting with the American determined to refuse his advances, but by the end of it she had accepted his offer. Maybe the unending Hindu-Muslim tension in the city had activated a Muslim-Hindu tension within her own mixed self and she needed to get away from that old quarrel, change that narrative, not be in that story anymore. Maybe it wasn't about religion. Maybe her spirit was more adventurous than she knew. Maybe there was something in her that wanted to test itself against the challenges of a wider world. Maybe she doubted her own worth and would not be able to think of herself as valuable if she did not pick up this gauntlet. Maybe she really was a gambler at heart and this was her spinning wheel.

There was one character, one story, missing from all the explanations. That was the man whom three generations of women had first loved and then rejected. He never told his story. Neither he nor Miss Salma R ever addressed the question of why he was ejected from the Juhu mansion as soon as Anisa died and never had any more contact with his granddaughter as long as he lived. He gave up his medical practice, went on the pilgrimage to Mecca, and returned to live out his days in silence, an ascetic in a much humbler home than the film star's residence he had occupied most of his life.

AT FIRST SHE COMMUTED between the two -woods, from Bolly- to Holly-, but as her star rose in the West her trips East became fewer and then stopped altogether. The American showrunner had kept his promise. Her spy drama *Five Eyes* turned out to be the biggest thing since the last biggest thing, even bigger than that, in fact, and bigger also than the big thing that followed it. Her character's name was deliberately written to echo her own, deliberately chosen to blur the distinction between the actress and her screen persona. In the show she was Salma C. The *C* was a private joke, an homage to the initial by which the head of British intelligence was known. The joke was left unexplained because in *Five Eyes* her character worked for American intelligence and any association with MI6 would have misled the audience, whom the show wanted to perplex and confuse, but not in that way.

Spies were becoming news again. At the end of the Cold War, without the Soviet Union as an enemy, they felt for a time like old hat, and after 9/11 they looked foolish and unprepared. The expansion of the Five Eyes system of cooperation between the English-speaking nations was Western intelligence's bid to remain relevant, and in *Five Eyes* "Salma C," with her expertise in cyber-warfare, rose rapidly through the veiled echelons of the hidden world. In the first season she played the invisible woman, the U.S. chief of counter-terrorism, holding the rank of ambassador. Her work was so secret that her existence could not be publicly confirmed, nor could her name be printed or her movements made public. She wore power suits and trademark aviator shades and spoke Arabic and Farsi as well as the new vocabularies of the cyberworld and had a dreadful relationship with the old white man at the head of the CIA who lusted after her in the most unpleasantly old-fashioned way and simultaneously pooh-poohed her professional concern that cyber-terrorists could be the most significant new foes that America had to face, and when he was murdered in the season finale she stepped over his fallen body and took his job. In the seasons that followed she managed to create a screen persona that was simultaneously patriotic, ruthless, and adorably nerdy, so that half the country fell in love with her and the other half delighted in her scariness.

The intelligence world, inside *Five Eyes* and outside it, returned to the front pages when it found itself in conflict not only with its usual enemies but with a willful American president as well. In response to real events the series introduced a wholly imaginary chief executive who was obsessed by cable news, who pandered to a white supremacist base, and who had played golf with Salma C's predecessor and talked locker-room shit to him about girls. This entirely fabulist president was dismayed at Salma C's accession to the Langley throne. His fictional dislike of immigrants led him to think of his brown, female CIA chief as untrustworthy and probably un-American, and his fictitious inability to focus on complex details meant he was bewildered by her fluency in the new argots of cyberspeak, hacking, and AI, and translated that bewilderment into anger, so that her job was perpetually at risk. In one episode she told the TV president that the new cyber-invasive processes that threatened the Internet's security procedures, as well as American voting systems, and therefore democracy, could be compared to certain cephalopods like the mimic octopus which could disguise itself so effectively as coral that human beings could not tell the difference. The imaginary president boomed at her in the voice he habitually used to disguise his incomprehension: "Octopuses? I have to talk about octopuses now? We have hostile fucking octopuses infiltrating our systems?"

"Octopi," said "Salma C," quietly, and the actor playing the president turned so red that it seemed possible to viewers that he might actually explode. After this episode images of Salma C's face with a speech bubble saying "Octopi" went viral on the Internet and OCTOPI T-shirts sold very well. Women across and beyond America began saying "octopi" to one another as shorthand for men's stupidity, and liberals of both genders and all the genders in between used the word to stand for the stupidity of the right. A cartoon of Miss Salma C astride a giant octopus which was crushing the White House in its tentacles became the most popular *New Yorker* cover image of the year. She was depicted in *Time* as a multi-limbed Indian goddess with tentacles for arms, the Octopus Woman whose kiss was irresistible even though it killed the men upon whom it was bestowed.

The show ran for five seasons and at the end of it Miss Salma R shed the skin of her alter ego Salma C and emerged as a fully fledged superstar. It was at this moment that she chose, against all advice, to set aside her career as an actor, abandon Los Angeles and the movie industry and move to New York City, and host a daytime talk show on network television, four days a week: a show she would personally own, so that she would never work for anyone else again. It was also at this moment that she revealed her absolute independence and personal power to the people who believed themselves to be responsible for her success, who were convinced that she owed them everything and that therefore *they* owned *her,* the men who knew they would never fuck her and therefore sought to possess her in other ways, the agents, managers, lawyers, showrunners, and production executives, the personal publicists, the show publicists, the publicists for the streaming network, as well as the exalted individuals who were never named but were at the foundation of everything, who gnawed like the Nidhogg at the roots of the World-Tree—that is to say, the rich people, the super-rich and the ultra-rich, who owned the people who owned the people who owned the network that owned the show that had made her what she was. Ignoring all these people, she launched her show, and within three years was the most influential woman in America, with the exception, of course, of Oprah, who quickly anointed Miss Salma R as her only possible inheritor, and by doing so kept her firmly in second place.

Everything about her new incarnation was exactly as Miss Salma R ordained, except for one thing. She had wanted to call the show *Changing the American Story,* or maybe, more concisely, *Changing America.* But the one American she trusted, the one who came to see her in Mumbai/Bombay and persuaded her to move halfway across the world, to step off the edge of the cliff into the unknown, and who was now her company's president, told her that those were dreadful, smart-ass, liberal-elite, forgettable titles. She deferred to the American on this one point, and so the show was named more simply: after her. *Salma.*

———

THE HIT SHOW'S OFFICES, in a converted warehouse space in lower Manhattan, were bulging at the seams, because the number of persons needed to open, read, categorize, and evaluate the mail that poured in every day had risen to over three hundred and sixty-five, their attention divided between the messages arriving on the website and through social media and the hard-copy correspondence, which still made up the largest part of the incoming material, and which required a fleet of forklift vehicles to carry them from the delivery vans to the mail readers' floor, three hundred and sixty-five mail sacks a day, one year of mail sacks arriving on each and every morning of the year. It became plain that no single human being could maintain control over such an uproar of correspondence, and Miss Salma R was told by her executives that they would sift and select a manageable quantity of letters for her personal scrutiny, because for her to sit with each one of the three hundred and sixty-five first readers to judge which letters, emails, texts, and tweets warranted a response, an invitation, or even a special show built around them would require more hours than the clocks allowed for, it would be necessary to bend the laws of time itself, to which she replied, "Then that's what's going to happen, because that's what I need to do." Monday was the only weekday on which the show did not air and so, on account of the force of Miss Salma R's will, the laws of the universe were indeed suspended at the *Salma* offices building each Monday, so that in addition to all the week's pre-production work, she had plenty of time to visit all three hundred and sixty-five mail desks and to make decisions about every single letter that came in. Unnerved by Miss Salma R's temporal absolutism, the clocks gave up arguing and stopped trying to run the hours in the normal fashion, so that when people looked in their direction to see what the time was, the clocks showed them whatever time they wanted it to be, and in spite of the chronometric havoc that was created by this abdication they still permitted everyone to get home on time.

Miss Salma R loved the letters of America. In most of the letters women confessed their secrets to her, their worries about their weight, their husbands, their lecherous bosses, their illnesses, their children, and their loss of faith in a future in which things would be better than they were; and men, too, whispered to her in their emotionally uneducated manner about their inadequacies, both sexual and professional, their fears for themselves and their families, their hostility toward other Americans who did not share their views, and their dreams of glamorous women and new cars. It fell to her to comfort America's anguish, to calm its rages, to celebrate its loves. She had a special soft spot for the stories of recent immigrants and showcased them, from time to time, in a special feature called "Immigreat!"

Her audiences were the letters made flesh. She caressed their pets, ate their cuisine, congratulated them on their successful gender reassignments and exam results, praised their gods with them, and introduced them to the celebrities who came smiling and telling funny stories through all her studio days. The letters showed her that the material success of America had impoverished the spiritual lives of Americans, but she also saw that that success was by no means evenly distributed across the broad populous nation, and the absence of material well-being was spiritually impoverishing also. She was a hugger and a kisser and in spite of her youth she quickly came to be thought of as wise, and the America of the letters was a place in constant search of a wise woman to listen to, always looking for the new voice that would make its lives feel rich once again. Times were hard all over, and she was the bringer of joy. The avalanche of the letters gave her a belief in her own bounty. There was enough love and care in her to encompass them all. Her arms would reach out to soothe the totality of America's pain. Her bosom would be America's pillow. The letters allowed her to become the most that she had it in her to be. (She had her own demons to deal with, of course, but when she was preoccupied with the demons of America, her own seemed to recede, at least for a while. About her demons there will be more to say presently.)

The two categories of letters which were unlike all the others were the love letters and the letters of hate. Of these, the poison-pen letters were more straightforward and bothered her less. Crazy people, religious nuts, envious people, people who made her the incarnation of their discontents, racists, misogynists, the usual crew. She passed them on to her security team and put them out of her mind. Her distant lovers were more upsetting. Many of them were actually in love with themselves and gave her to understand that they were doing her a kindness by bestowing their love upon her. Others simply assumed their approach would be met with a favorable response. And then there were those who begged. When photographs were included, it was usually an unwise move. When the pictures were pornographic, it was especially unwise. The cascades of boasts, assumptions, and hopeless pleas depressed her because of the image of herself she saw reflected in these obsessive gazes. Was she so shallow that these nonswimmers thought they could paddle their feet in her waters? Was she so two-dimensional that they thought they could fold her up and put her in their pockets? She wanted to know how she was seen by others, but this aspect of the knowledge she acquired gave her a heavy heart.

Some of the love letters were still addressed to her *Five Eyes* character, Salma C. These were the letters whose authors seemed to have sunk most deeply into fantasy, identifying themselves as secret, double, or triple agents, or would-be members of the secret world, offering, as their qualifications, details of their patriotism, their skills with guns, and their ability to pass unnoticed in a crowd. She should love them, the *Five Eyes* guys (and women) said, because who could understand her the way they could? "We are the same," these lovers declared. "I am just like you."

The messages arriving via her Twitter feed were mostly pseudonymous, the work of pimply fifteen- or forty-five-year-old male virgins living with their parents in Woop Woop, Arkansas, or Podunk, Illinois. All of them were on or over the edge of illiteracy. America no longer taught its lovers how to spell. Nor did it teach joined-up writing. Cursive script was becoming obsolete, like type-writers and carbon paper. These lovers who wrote in block capitals would not be able to read the love letters of earlier generations. Cursive might as well be Martian, or Greek. For such correspondents Miss Salma R, whose stock-in-trade was empathy, was guilty of feeling just a scintilla of contempt.

Very, very occasionally, a letter arrived which was not like the others, like an odd-one-out category on *Sesame Street*. When this happened, Miss Salma R (perhaps only for a moment) gave the thing her full attention. The first letter from the person signing himself "Quichotte" was one such missive. The thing that leapt out at Miss Salma R immediately was the beautiful penmanship. The pen that wrote these words was a thick-nibbed instrument, a pen to respect, which allowed the author to create perfect copperplate lettering, as if he were making a wedding announcement or inviting her to a debutante ball. The text, too, was unusual. It was one of the rare love letters that were neither bombastic nor wheedling, and it made no assumptions about her.

My dear Miss Salma R,

With this note I introduce myself to you. With this hand I declare my love. In time to come as I move ever closer you will come to see that I am true and that you must be mine. You are my Grail and this is my quest. I bow my head before your beauty. I am and will ever remain your knight.

Sent by a smile,
Quichotte

The paper on which this message was written in such a fine hand was the vulgar antithesis of the writing, a cheap motel-room scrap with the address torn off. From these few clues Miss Salma R deduced that this was an older man, a man from the age of handwriting, the owner of a good fountain pen, who had fallen upon hard times and, being lonely, watched too much TV. From his choice of alias she further deduced an education, which in all probability, judging by the phrasing, had not been an American schooling. She even went so far as to surmise that the writer had this in common with herself: that English had not been his mother tongue, not something heard in the cradle but something learned afterwards. This was suggested by both the syntax (American English was far more informal in its construction) and the spelling (which was improbably perfect). The only puzzlement was the sign-off, *sent by a smile,* with its imperfect command of English grammar. It would have both gratified and shocked our fool of a protagonist to know that these seventy-two words, seventy-three including his pseudonymous signature, which he believed preserved around him the cloak of invisibility within which, for the moment, he preferred to remain concealed, had revealed so much about him. She had noticed him and was focused on his letter: that was good. But it was as if she saw him standing naked and scrawny before her: not so good. At any rate, he had no knowledge of any of this, and so we may leave him for now in his state of innocence, hoping for favor and believing himself unknown. We can also protect him from the knowledge of what Miss Salma R said next.

"Keep this where we can get at it," she said to the intern on whose desk the Quichotte letter had landed. "I've got a bad feeling about it. Let me know if he writes again."

Then Monday was over, and she walked out of the building into the waiting Maybach, sank down into the back seat, raised to her lips the dirty martini (up, with olives) waiting for her on the armrest, and forgot Quichotte completely.

"Evenin', Miss Daisy," her driver greeted her.

"Stop saying that, Hoke," she replied. "You're making me mad."

CHAPTER FOUR

Brother's Sister recalls
their Quarrel, & is involved in
a different Altercation

*E*NGLAND IS ANOTHER COUNTRY. THEY DO THINGS DIF-
ferently there.

Yes: we must sojourn for a time among the English, for so long
thought to be the most pragmatic and commonsensical of peoples,
but presently torn asunder by a wild, nostalgic decision about their
future; and in particular, in London, once the most pleasing of cities, now much disfigured by the empty apartment blocks of the international rich, the Chinese, Russians, and Arabs who stationed
their money in such buildings as if they were parking lots and
money an armada of invisible automobiles; and in London, on a
street in the west of the city, in a neighborhood once known for its
longhair bohemians, West Indians, and quirky local stores, but rapidly becoming too expensive except for the comfortably short-
haired, its quirkiness replaced by the bland façades of frock shops
and chic eateries, and as for the West Indians, they were pushed to
the margins long ago and now, because of that wild, nostalgic decision about the country's future, faced uncertainty and renewed hos-

tility. Once a year in this neighborhood a carnival filled the streets, modeled on the customs of faraway Jamaica and Trinidad, but the intermingled culture the carnival celebrated had changed now, and felt, to some saddened people at least, like a painful reminder of the time before the country broke in half. And yes, let us admit it, our story's other two countries were badly broken, too, and equally disputatious, and more violent. Black citizens were regularly killed by white policemen in one of these other countries, or arrested in hotel lobbies for the crime of making a phone call to their mothers, and children were murdered in schools because of a constitutional amendment that made it easy to murder children in schools; and in the other country, a man was lynched by sacred-cow fanatics for the crime of having what they thought was beef in his kitchen, and an eight-year-old girl from a Muslim family was raped and killed in a Hindu temple to teach the Muslim population a lesson. So perhaps this England was not the worst place, after all, and perhaps this London was not the worst city in spite of its rising knife crime, and perhaps this West London neighborhood was still a nice neighborhood to live in, and perhaps things would get better in time.

An interjection, kind reader, if you'll allow one: It may be argued that stories should not sprawl in this way, that they should be grounded in one place or the other, put down roots in the other or the one and flower in that singular soil; yet so many of today's stories are and must be of this plural, sprawling kind, because a kind of nuclear fission has taken place in human lives and relations, families have been divided, millions upon millions of us have traveled to the four corners of the (admittedly spherical, and therefore cornerless) globe, whether by necessity or choice. Such broken families may be our best available lenses through which to view this broken world. And inside the broken families are broken people, broken by loss, poverty, maltreatment, failure, age, sickness, pain, and hatred, yet trying in spite of it all to cling to hope and love, and these broken people—we, the broken people!—may be the best mirrors of our times, shining shards that reflect the truth, wherever we travel, wherever we land, wherever we remain. For we migrants have become like seed-spores, carried through the air, and lo, the breeze blows us where it will, until we lodge in alien soil, where very often—as for example now in this England with its wild nostalgia for an imaginary golden age when all attitudes were Anglo-Saxon and all English skins were white—we are made to feel unwelcome, no matter how beautiful the fruit hanging from the branches of the orchards of fruit trees that we grow into and become.

To resume: Here in this West London neighborhood we may intrude upon a spacious apartment above a restaurant—the very restaurant space, as it happens, from which, for many years, the carnival was organized! The apartment boasts two floors and a large roof terrace, a lateral conversion across the width of two row houses. The lower floor has been opened out to form a single, light-filled, high-ceilinged room, and in the open-plan kitchen and bar in the large room's northeast corner, mixing herself a dirty martini (up, with olives), we may now see Sister—yes, the Author's sibling, Brother's Sister—an immigrant, plainly, South Asian, obviously, and also a successful lawyer with a strong interest in civil and human rights issues, a stalwart fighter on behalf of minorities and the urban poor, who has devoted a good proportion of her time to pro bono work; and it would not be stretching things to say that she might be thinking, as she has often thought, such thoughts as the ones we have outlined above. Of her appearance perhaps the only thing that needs to be said is that her decision to stop coloring her hair was made quite recently, and she has had to get used to the white-haired stranger in the mirror—to her mother, we might say, looking back at her across time and through the looking glass. And now that we have introduced her and set her in some sort of context, let us leave her to sip her evening drink and await her dinner guests, while we retreat into the privacy of these pages to tell her tale.

———

SISTER DID SOMETIMES THINK about her Brother, but usually
with a kind of dismissive exasperation. She had boxed him away in
the attic of her memories, along with the rest of her early years:
their Bombay world, the radiogram, the dancing. The feeling of
coming second to her brother, who received privileges not offered
to her. She had clawed her way out of that trap, making choices her
parents didn't want her to make (more will be said about these
choices in due course), winning major scholarships to pay for the
British law school education they didn't want her to have. Now,
after a long and distinguished career, her roots were here, in this
apartment, on this street, in this neighborhood, in this city, in this
country, for all its faults. That old world had vanished, and her parents and Brother along with it. Childhood was just a story she could
tell at dinner parties: a story about the hypocrisies and double stan-
dards of the supposedly free-thinking Indian intelligentsia. She had
decisively moved on and made her own life. Or so, most of the time,
she told herself. But the truth was that she still felt the past moving
like a thrombosis in the blood. It might reach her heart and kill her
one of these days.

    After their parents' death it had fallen to her, as the "efficient"
sibling, to deal with everything that had to be dealt with—a second-
rate spy novelist was clearly too much of an Artist to be involved—
and when she had done it all, when she had buried her mother and
burned her father, disposed of the family property, found suitable
new owners for Zayvar Brother and Cake & Antiques, and organized a memorial event at which the city's best and brightest had
turned out to tell funny stories about Pa and Ma and mourn them as
they would have wished, with dances; and after that, when all was
done, when she had arranged for what Brother in his crass way
called the "division of the spoils," her sibling had called her for that
last phone call and said the unforgivable thing.

    "So what's this?"

"What's what?"

"This wire transfer that just landed in my bank account."

"It's your share."

"My share of what?"

"You know of what. Of everything."

"My share of the cloakroom tips? My share of the piggy bank? My share of the loose change in their pockets? My half of the value of the radiogram? My—"

"Your fifty percent of the estate."

"And what's your share? Nine hundred and fifty percent?"

"I see. You're accusing me."

"Damn right I am. You offer me peanuts and tell me they're diamonds. You give me a cheap forgery and say it's the *Mona Lisa*. You send me a drizzle and say it's a monsoon. You hand me a sack of garbage and tell me it's half of a fortune. You're a swindler. You're such a greedy swindler that you don't even bother to make your swindle look convincing. Maybe I'll call a press conference and tell the world how the eminent Sister, the prominent human rights warrior, the champion of the underdog, the British BAME communities' fucking female knight in fucking shining armor, the fucking brown-skin Lancelotta, the Pakis' best friend, the honorary West Indian Indian, the go-to woman when African countries need a constitution written, the free speech heroine, the evenhanded opponent of religious fanaticism and white racism, the postcolonial Boadicea, is a two-bit crook gobbling up the family inheritance. Give me the rest of my fucking money or I'll see you on the front page."

Anger was her weakness. She knew it. She buried it deep, down at the roots of her being, because if she turned it loose she turned green, burst out of her shirt, and became the Incredible Hulk. It didn't often escape. This time it did. Brother's anger was amateur night compared to hers. He had brought a pocketknife to a gunfight. When she began to talk, when the Hulk roared out of her throat, he fell silent. She did not hold back. The threat he had made was a serious one. For her own flesh and blood to go public with such an accusation would be immensely damaging. The mud would stick and her political opponents, of which there were many, given the high-profile public cases she fought, would relish the chance to attack her. This was the age of the kangaroo court of instant opinions, in which an accusation was frequently the same thing as a guilty verdict. She couldn't afford to go easy on him. She needed to destroy his will to go forward, to install a real ineradicable terror in his heart, strong enough to make him back down and keep his money-grubbing mouth shut forever. She spoke for eleven minutes without stopping. She could feel his fear oozing all the way down the phone connection, digital fear, Wi-Fi fear, twenty-first-century fear. Finally she told him, "Be in no doubt that I will do whatever it takes to defend my good name. *Whatever it bloody well takes.*" Then she hung up.

There was no press conference. There was no further communication. And seventeen years went by, and here she was, drinking her dirty martini (up, with olives), waiting for her eminent guests, and lost, all of a sudden, in the past.

TO BE A LAWYER in a lawless time was like being a clown among the humorless: which was to say, either completely redundant or absolutely essential. It wasn't clear to her, these days, which of the alternatives best described her. Sister was an idealist. She believed in the rule of law as one of the two foundations of a free society, along with free expression. (This was the kind of remark you didn't make too often in white society in London for fear of sounding self-righteous, "preachy." It was also a remark which, if made in brown or black circles, might elicit a loud series of disbelieving horse-laughs.) As a result the direction the world had taken in her lifetime was upsetting. Both the law and liberty were everywhere under attack. The thuggish deterioration of Indian society both allowed her to believe ever more fervently that she no longer wanted anything to do with that increasingly horrible country, and hurt more deeply than she cared to admit. The continuing American convulsion disgusted her, and the vulnerability of immigrants to abuse and worse was a growing part of her daily agenda here at home. On a bad (three-martini) day she came close to despair, telling herself that after all these years she was obliged to admit that she had misunderstood the country of which she was now a citizen and which she thought of as her country. She had deeply believed it to be a reasonable place, broad-minded, easygoing, and good to live in, and now she discovered that it was also—or not *also,* but *in fact*—narrow-minded, delusional, and, for people lacking the great virtue of acceptable skin color, not comfortable to live in at all. When she entered this kind of mood her husband the judge—the High Court judge Godfrey Simons—was a pillar of strength. Here he was now, coming down the stairs from the upper floor, where he had been getting ready to greet their guests. He was wearing the floor-length Vivienne Westwood gown, the pearls, and the new high heels tonight. It was a big night for his wife and he wanted to look his best for her. She applauded him softly as he descended.

"You look resplendent, Jack," she told him. "Dignified, glamorous. And the shoes!"

"Thank you, Jack," said the judge. "Glamor and dignity is what we strive for."

They called each other "Jack" instead of "dear" or "darling" or "honey." It was their little private thing. They had so much in common. They had the same favorite drink, they always chose the same dishes in restaurants, and when they were asked about their preferred books they answered identically, without conferring. *The Magic Mountain, Madame Bovary, Don Quixote.* No English books? Oh, if you want an English writer, then there's only one, they might reply, and then they might cry out, in unison, "Trollope!" They had the same taste in dresses too. Calling each other by the same name made perfect sense.

Outside their home the judge wore pin-striped Savile Row suits and bespoke shoes and with his full head of silver hair he looked splendidly judicial. Even at home, most of the time, he dressed conventionally—a short-sleeved polo shirt and slacks. The dresses and jewelry only came out when they entertained. He never wore a wig. He wasn't trying to be a woman. He was simply a man who liked wearing women's designer clothing from time to time. Everyone knew this and nobody drew attention to it. After all, it was widely rumored that Prince Charles, a great admirer of the Islamic world, received guests at Highgrove dressed like an Arab sheik. This wasn't so different, and much more English.

The doorbell rang. "Ready, Jack?" he asked Sister.

"Ready, Jack," she replied.

The great hall at Middle Temple—"her" Inn of Court—was the place where, in 1601, perhaps even on January 6, the Lord Chamberlain's Men, Shakespeare's "playing company," staged the first ever night of *Twelfth Night* before Queen Elizabeth I, Gloriana herself, and a company of VIP guests, some of whose names were echoed in the names of the play's characters. And Shakespeare himself might have played Malvolio. Four hundred years later Sister had been present in the great hall when a prominent theater company restaged scenes from that original production as the centerpiece of a fundraising gala. She had been seated at a table with various luminaries of the West End stage and, on her right, a loud, fleshy Ukrainian sub-oligarch who claimed to love Shakespeare ("Have you seen Innokenti Smoktunovsky in Russian film *Gamlet*? No? Disappointing!"), did not understand the play ("But there are not twelve nights in this story! Disappointing!"), disapproved of all the cross-dressing, making a series of transphobic remarks ("Men instead of women! Disappointing!"), and thoroughly ruined her evening. The next day she called her host, the theater company's financial director, to thank him, a little coolly, for the invitation. "No, thank *you*," he said. "Why thank me?" "Because this morning the disappointing person you talked to all evening wrote us a check for nine hundred thousand pounds." She had been younger then and people told her she was beautiful, though she had never been convinced of that. Anyway, this had become a favorite anecdote of hers, and here she was telling it to the gathering of grandees who had assembled to offer her a seat on the crossbenches of the House of Lords and, shortly thereafter, the job of speaker in the British upper house. She would be only the second woman to be so chosen. It was if she had ascended Everest alone and without oxygen. And at the very instant that she stood upon this pinnacle, she found herself thinking about Brother, because it suddenly occurred to her that *Twelfth Night* was about a brother and sister who were separated, each believing the other to be dead. And after many tangled tales they were joyfully and lovingly reunited. There was a lump in her throat as she considered her own very different situation. Her asshole brother who had never apologized for his slanderous words, never come close to apologizing. Her loser brother struggling to make a living from his fifth-rate books and fearing, no doubt, that as publishing belts were tightened in these hard times his mediocre career might grind to a halt. Her brother who treated her as if she were dead. (Most of the time, she conceded, she returned the compliment.) What did he think he was doing intruding on her big night? He was a ghost, worse than a ghost, a living phantom. Why had he chosen this of all evenings to haunt her and rain on her parade?

As she emerged from this brief reverie a quarrel broke out among the assembled Lords. The youngest peer, the British-Nigerian baroness Aretta Alagoa, was calling to mind one of the early defining moments of Sister's career. In the early 1980s a fire had broken out in cheap public housing in North London and seven families had died. After that two hundred or so people had stormed and occupied their local town hall to demand safe, habitable housing for themselves and their children immediately. Sister had gone in there to offer her legal services and had immediately become the spokesperson for the group, whose media appearances were highly effective, and had forced the borough council to act. "You became a star for us youngsters then," Aretta Alagoa told her, "so for you to become the first POC to be speaker in the Lords would be a big, big thing."

The assembled peers were a cross-party group, intended to show Sister that her prospective appointment had support all the way across the political spectrum. It was an uneasy coalition, however, and now the oldest member of the group, the septuagenarian Lord Fitch, a former Conservative deputy prime minister, broke ranks.

"It doesn't matter a toss if she's a person of color or not," he declared. "Ridiculous phrase, anyway. Isn't everyone a person of color? What am I? Colorless?"

"Who could ever say such a thing about you, Hugo?" Baroness Alagoa did not go easy on the sarcasm. "However, the fact is that people of color presently, and with much reason, feel threatened by your party and its followers."

"I'm not going along with this if it's some sort of bloody tokenism," old Hugo Fitch cried. "I'm not lending my support to some sort of reverse discrimination."

"Affirmative action."

"Reverse discrimination," he repeated. "All I care about is getting the best bloody person for the job, brown, yellow, pink, green, black, or blue."

"And you're sitting at her dinner table," the baroness pointed out. "So I'd suggest you'd have done well to have thought this through before you arrived."

"I'm not here to solve the bloody immigrant problem," Fitch said too loudly, making a fist by his glass of red wine, which had possibly been refilled too many times. "If you bang on about a person of color getting preferment you'll play right into the enemy's hands."

"And who might that enemy be, would you say?" Aretta Alagoa asked very quietly. "Might it perhaps be you?"

Listening to this petty, bitter spat, beneath which there bubbled the poisonous, xenophobic bitches' brew of the new England, Sister caught her husband's amused eye and had to resist a powerful, a positively Ukrainian urge to cry out, "Disappointing!"

A kind of older, don't-rock-the-boat England reasserted itself then, and her guests smoothed things out and made peace and the evening ended as the celebration it was supposed to be, and then they were gone. But she was still haunted, distracted, her thoughts siphoning away from her imminent political elevation as she fell down a rabbit hole into the past. How angry was she with Brother still? Was the unforgivable thing in fact forgivable, or at least forgettable? Her daughter scolded her for doing nothing to heal the breach. Daughter had read and amazingly liked several of her uncle's pedestrian spy novels and was regrettably proud of her literary relative. "Whatever happened is like a hundred years ago," she told her mother. "You're always pontificating about the Culture of Offendedness, *nobody has a right not to be offended* blah blah, but here you are hugging your own offendedness like a pet dog. Come on. If he dies or something you'll be sorry you never put things right."

Maybe that was true. Or maybe she was more afraid of herself, of his ability to trigger her worst responses. They would meet, they would fall into each other's arms, they would cry and laugh and say how stupid they had both been, they would mourn the lost and vanished years, they would tell each other the stories of their lives, their children, their loves, their work, they would fall back into the easy big-brother-kid-sister love of childhood, and that would last for what? Maybe twenty-four hours? Maybe forty-eight? And then he would say something that would open the locked door to the dark cellar and the monster would come roaring out and after that happened there wouldn't be much left of either of them. She was scared of what he could turn her into. That was the truth.

And there was more than one grievance. There was the memory of a slap.

———

MORE THAN FORTY YEARS AGO, Sad-Faced Older Painter, the grand old man of a generation of Indian artists much influenced by European modernism and abstraction, had been hounded out of the country by religious fanatics whose faces, illuminated by the exhilaration of their bigotry, were bright-eyed and blazing with light. He abandoned his home and caught a night flight to London—and he took Sister along with him in his baggage. It was only then that Pa and Ma found out that Sad-Faced Older Painter had fallen absurdly but irrevocably in love with their daughter several years earlier when she was still illegal, and that she had encouraged him in spite of the sixty-year difference in their ages, because she saw him as her ticket to ride, her way out of the cage of her parents' limited ambitions for her, her freedom from a *desi* Jane Austen future of husband hunting and babies. He seemed to her the noble gatekeeper to a greater world of wide horizons and big skies, in which she could allow herself to expand and her wings to unfurl, and then she would be able to fly. She saw him secretly until she was of age and remained a virgin after that until he told her he might have to go abroad to get away from the madmen, whereupon she took the initiative and told him she didn't want to go halfway around the world with an older man if the sex was going to be no good. So she auditioned Sad-Faced Older Painter and declared that he had passed, not *cum laude,* but well enough, all things considered, and so, fine, she would go with him and the devil take everything else. After that there was a secret marriage, and a passport, and the night flight that broke her parents' heart. At the time, full of the excitement of the big adventure, and full of youthful resentment, she was pleased to have hit back and hurt them, seeing it as payback for their unwillingness to invest in her dreams.

The only person who got to know about her love affair was Brother. Home from college for the long summer vacation, he worked out what was going on and confronted her, wide-eyed with

stupid, conservative horror, and she took him on, didn't give him a
chance, released the Hulk within, and terrified him into silence. "If
you say one word," she hissed, "make no mistake, I will kill you.
You'll be sleeping in your bed and I'll come in with a kitchen knife
and you'll wake up dead. Make no mistake." Just as years later after
another accusation she told him, *Be in no doubt that I will do whatever it
takes.* He did not doubt her on either occasion. He kept his mouth
shut, both times. And no doubt hated her for it.

Two months later, on the night she left her parents' home for the
last time, they were out at a party as usual, and she hoped to depart
without a big scene. As she reached the front door of the apartment,
however, Brother came in. He had guessed what might be happening and stood in the doorway, blocking her exit, bloated with righ-
teousness.

"Move out of my way," she said.

"You're a traitor," he said. "You're betraying us all. You're a dis-
gusting person and a traitor."

"Move out of the way," she said.

Then he did something that took her by surprise, something that
must have taken all his courage. He stepped toward her, very
quickly, before she could get out of the way, and hit her once, very
hard, with an open hand, on the right side of her head. The blow
almost knocked her out and she felt a thin trickle of blood seeping
out of her ringing ear.

"You can go now," he said, and let her pass.

SHE LAY IN BED at the end of her big night, looking up at the ceiling light fixture with its gilded cherubs and frosted-glass flowers.
He had hit her, yes. She had a blood clot removed from her ear two
weeks later and there was some permanent damage to her hearing.
But it had not been her finest hour either, even though it had given
her the life she wanted. She hadn't treated Sad-Faced Older Painter
particularly well once she had her scholarship and entered Middle

Temple. She was immersed in new things and he felt like an old used thing, a thing to discard. He understood, asked her for nothing, and didn't last long. He died in his sleep four years later and left her enough in his will to look after her for the rest of her life. And she became a lawyer and created the character she wanted to inhabit and inhabited it, and met the judge and married for a second time and had a child. And Brother's raising of his hand against her was unforgivable. Or was it? As she slipped toward sleep she found herself thinking, in the old voice of childhood, *Maybe I deserved to be hit.*

And immediately her adult voice replied. *No, you didn't.*

SHE AND THE JUDGE had this in common: that they saw the law as an instance of the sublime, inspiring love and awe but also dread, and being, in the end, akin to that *mood* (Wordsworth) *In which the heavy and the weary weight / Of all this unintelligible world / Is lightened.* The law guided her in most things, but it was unable to help her in this.

If he dies or something you'll be sorry, Daughter had said. But there were things Daughter didn't yet know because she hadn't been told.

It might not be Brother who died first.

"Good night, Jack," the judge called from his bedroom. They had separate bedrooms now.

"I love you," she called back. But that wasn't what he was expecting her to say, and so, being a creature of habit, he didn't reply. That was all right. She did not doubt his love.

CHAPTER FIVE

Quichotte's Cousin, the "good" Dr. Smile, is a Man of many Secrets

N THE LARGE AND PROSPEROUS INDIAN COMMUNITY of Atlanta (pop. 472,522), Dr. R. K. Smile was known as "the Little King." A few of the oldsters remembered Otto Soglow's fun-loving cartoon character by that name, a small hemispherical monarch dressed in a fur-collared red garment with a pointy golden crown and a flamboyant black handlebar mustache. He liked innocent pleasures and pretty women. If you took off the yellow crown, that was a good description of the Smile Pharma billionaire too. He loved to play the games of Indian childhoods, was a whiz on the carrom board at his Colonial Revival home on Peachtree Battle Avenue, sponsored a team in the "hard tennis ball" Atlanta Cricket League ("We play casual cricket but we wear professional outfit!"), and from time to time organized informal *kabaddi* competitions in Centennial Park. He was happily married to his wife, Happy, the biryani expert, but could not resist flirting with every attractive woman who crossed his path, so his other nickname, used only behind his back and primarily by the younger women of the community, was Little Big Hands.

In spite of these grabby tendencies, he was highly regarded, a benefactor of the best Atlanta Indian newspaper and website, named *Rajdhani,* "Capital," as if to assert that Atlanta was the capital of Indian America, and a donor to most of the proliferating community associations in the city, groupings of people by their state of origin back home, but also by language (Bengali, Gujarati, Hindi, Tamil, Telugu), caste, subcaste, religion, and preferred house deities (Devi, Mahadeo, Narayan, and even small groups dedicated to Lohasur the iron god, Khodiyal the horse god, and Hardul the god of cholera). He gave as generously to Hindu groups as to Muslim ones, even though he disapproved of the widespread local admiration for the Indian leader Narendra Modi, his Bharatiya Janata Party, or BJP, and its ideological parent body, the Rashtriya Swayamsevak Sangh, or RSS. The only community gatherings in which he politely declined to participate were those at which money was raised to send back to India to support those organizations. In spite of this he was popular across the whole spectrum of Atlanta Indians, and even spoke of himself as a unifying force, able to bring the seventy-five thousand South Asian Muslims in the area closer to their one hundred thousand Hindu brothers and sisters. He was not a deeply religious man himself, and had never set foot in any of the three dozen mosques in the city, not even the large Al-Farooq Masjid on Fourteenth Street. "To tell the truth," he confided to his closest friends, "I (a) am not the praying type and I (b) in fact like the look of the Swaminarayan temple better." This was the large Krishna temple in the suburb of Lilburn. "But don't tangle me up in any of that, *yaar,*" he added. "I'm a pharmacist. I make pills."

On the subject of prescription medication he was outspoken, severe, and, as events would reveal, utterly dishonest. "Back home in the old days," he said when he spoke at one of the community's many gala evenings, "there was always a street corner dispensary that would hand out drugs without a doctor's chit. Cross-legged in his raised booth, the vendor would wave a forgiving hand. 'Come back and give me later,' he might say, but when you came back for more he never asked where the last chit was. And if you asked for twenty painkillers he would say, 'Why so few? Take the box only. Save yourself trouble. Why come back every week?' It was bad for his customers' health, but good for health of business." There was nostalgic laughter when he said this, but he wagged a finger at the assembled worthies and went *tsk-tsk-tsk*. "Ladies and gents, it is not a laughing matter."

Afterwards, when his house came tumbling down, people would say, "It's like he was confessing to us openly. Standing there in front of us and challenging us. Putting on a straight face even while he was telling us he was crooked, and where he got the idea."

"Many of us have done well in America," he went on. "I, also, by the grace of God. Our life here today is a good life. But so many of us still believe our roots are in the past. This is not true. Our old places are gone, our old customs are not the American ways, our old languages are not spoken. Only we carry these things within us. Our roots are in ourselves and in each other. In our bodies and minds we preserve our identity. Because of this we can move, we can go out and conquer the world."

Afterwards, when his enterprises lay in ruins, people would say, "He was too greedy. He wanted to conquer the world. He told us this also, standing right in front of us, he confessed everything. But we were too stupid to see."

BEFORE WE GO ANY further we must take issue with the good—or, as it turned out, not so good—Dr. Smile, and insist on the significance of his historical roots, or at least, the roots he claimed on those occasions when he wanted to claim roots. We have previously mentioned (see page 26) his supposed ancestor who was denied American citizenship at the dawn of the twentieth century on the grounds that he was not a free white man. We now whisk the veil of anonymity off this individual, as if removing the cover from a gilded birdcage, and the caged bird begins to sing. His name, as far as we can establish, was Duleep Smile, and he first bubbled up into history as a chef in London, first at the Savoy, then at the Cecil, which back in 1896 was the largest hotel in Europe. The owner of Sherry's, then one of the best restaurants in New York, brought this proto-Smile and his English wife to Forty-Fourth Street and Fifth Avenue to introduce the American palate to Indian flavors. (An English wife, by the by! An unforeseen element to hurl into the racial mix! But we proceed.) It's a strange name, Duleep Smile, for if, as Dr. Smile insisted, the "Smile" derived from *Ismail,* then "Duleep" might per-haps be an abbreviation of *Duleepsinhji* (like the great cricketer), and that was a Hindu Rajput name; whereas this Original Smile came, in all probability, from Karachi. When asked about the curious con-tradictions of his putative ancestor's name, Dr. R. K. Smile would shrug. "Go back a few generations in any Indian Muslim family," he would say, "and you'll find a convert." Beyond that he did not care to explain or discuss.

What was important to him was that Duleep Smile became a star, a celebrity chef *avant la lettre,* beloved by women in particular, especially as he stated publicly that his food improved the looks and attractiveness of the women who ate it, even suggesting that curries had aphrodisiac qualities. The opinion of the English wife regarding his womanizing ways is not recorded. However, at an unspecified date, she decamped, which may serve as the clearest expression of her feelings; whereupon Chef Smile married and left a succession of ever more youthful American ladies. He also began to call himself a prince. Prince Duleep Smile, the Emir of Balochistan's fourth son. (He wasn't.) He claimed to have a degree from Cambridge Univer-sity (he didn't), and said he was a friend of King Edward VII. (Amaz-ingly, this part of his fantasy of himself had some truth to it; the king agreed to be his patron for a brief time, at least until he discov-ered that Duleep Smile's other claims were phony.) But the chef's golden era—only a few years long—was ending. His troubles with the law were just getting started.

After his citizenship application was rejected he returned to England and then came back to America accompanied by a mysteriously large entourage. There was a law in America making it a crime carrying a thousand-dollar penalty to give anyone a pretext for immigrating by offering them a job. Duleep Smile had made such offers to twenty-six people. He claimed he hadn't. His large entourage was composed of mere tourists, he said; tourists and friends. The authorities didn't buy it. Sherry's restaurant, facing a fine of twenty-six thousand dollars (seven hundred thousand dollars in today's money), ended its association with Chef Smile, who entered a long decline and eventually left for India with his last American wife and disappeared from history. If he left children behind in America, their names are not recorded.

This story was not known to the Indians of Atlanta for a long time. The version they were given by Dr. Smile, and which everyone accepted unquestioningly, was heavily doctored. The culinary triumphs were described; the lies, deceptions, and hustles were left undescribed. Only after everything that happened had happened did an enterprising researcher exhume the true story of Duleep Smile, and establish that no line of descent from the famous chef to the pharma billionaire could satisfactorily be established. Once again, his fellow Atlantan Indians were left to shake their heads at their own willingness to be deceived. "Not only did he choose to claim descent from a con man, but that claim itself was a con," the Indian newspaper wrote. "This was the level of the man's audacity: he showed himself to us openly, but blinded us with his charm. So he rose high high. But he has fallen now."

IN RECENT TIMES HIS WIFE had raised his profile higher than ever. His sons had left home and gone to college to study useful things, money and machines, but their mother, Mrs. Happy Smile, was a lover of the arts, and now that she had an empty nest she insisted to her husband that they should become involved in that world, even though he thought of the arts as useless and the people involved in the arts as useless people. At first he rebuffed her desire to set up a family arts sponsorship foundation, but she persisted, and when she found out about the extensive involvement of the Oxy-Contin family in this kind of work she saw her opening, correctly guessing that her husband's competitive spirit would be aroused. In the garden of the Peachtree Battle Avenue house, by the rhododendron bush, and over a mint julep at the end of the working day, she confronted him. "We must give back, isn't it," she began. "That is the right thing to do." He frowned, which showed her this was not going to be easy. But she set her jaw firmly and frowned back.

"Give back what?" he asked. "What have we taken that we must return?"

"Not that way," she said, in her most cajoling voice. "I mean only, give back out of our generosity to society in thanks for the so so many blessings we have received."

"Society gave me no blessings," he said. "What I have received, I have earned by the sweat of my brow."

"OxyContin *khandaan,* they give back plenty," she said, playing her ace. "Their family name is so so respected. You don't want your name to be so so respected also?"

"What are you talking about?" he said, sounding interested now.

"So so many wings they have," she said. "Metropolitan Museum wing named after them, Louvre wing also, London Royal Academy wing also. A bird with so so many wings can fly so so high."

"But we are not birds. We have no need of wings."

"At the Tate Modern they have an escalator with their name. At the Jewish Museum in Berlin they have a staircase. They have a rose also, pink, bearing their name. They have a star in the sky. So so many things they have."

"Why must I care about asteroids and escalators?"

She knew what to say. "Branding," she cried. "You buy naming rights, your name becomes loved. It will be so so loved. And love is good for business, no? So so good."

"Yes," he said. "Love is good for business."

"So then. We must give back, isn't it."

"You've been looking into this," he guessed, correctly. She blushed and beamed.

"Opera, art gallery, university, hospital," she said, clapping her hands. "All will be so so happy and your name will be so so big. Collecting art also is good. Indian art is hot just now, like Chinese, but we must support our own people, isn't it. Prices are rocketing, so investment potential is good. We have so much wall space. Also we can put pictures on permanent loan in best museums, and your name will be so so loved. Let me do this for you. Also," she said, clinching the argument, "art world ladies are so so beautiful. This is all I'm saying."

He loved his wife. "Okay," he said. "Smile wing, Smile extension, Smile gallery, Smile balcony, Smile ward, Smile elevator, Smile toilet, Smile star in the sky."

She broke into song. "When you're smiling," she sang. It was their song. "When you're smiling."

"The whole world smiles with you," he said.

VERY WELL. IT IS TIME to reveal certain secrets closely guarded by Dr. R. K. Smile and the upper-echelon executives of Smile Pharmaceuticals Inc. (SPI, everyone pronounced it "Spy"). These secrets have to do primarily with the hidden life of the enterprise's premier product, InSmile™, the sublingual fentanyl spray that made the company's fortune; although they also involve the rest of the opioid products manufactured at the main SPI facility in Alpharetta, Georgia (pop. 63,038). It will not be a pretty story. After all, here was a man at the very peak of his career, a generous man, widely respected and even beginning to be loved. It is never pleasant to tear down such a personage, to reveal the feet of clay. Such exposés tarnish the whole community, and are regarded by many as washing the community's dirty linen in public. But when a façade begins to crumble, it is only a matter of time before the unwashed linens tumble into public view anyway. By the time Dr. R. K. Smile visited his relative Quichotte to terminate their official relationship, SPI had already begun to attract the curiosity of the authorities, even though Dr. Smile was dismissive of their suspicions. Meanwhile, Mrs. Happy Smile had entered the arts donor sphere with high energy, and her donation offers had initiated positive discussions regarding naming rights to a potential new Smile Wing of the High Museum and a much-anticipated second-stage Smile Extension of the Cobb Energy Performing Arts Center; and it even, for a time, seemed possible that the city might agree to the renaming of Pemberton Place, the urban hub where the World of Coca-Cola and the Georgia Aquarium were located. "Give me five years," she told her husband, "and I'll make our name bigger in Atlanta than Coke." And yet, and yet. Lightning can strike out of a clear sky. Dr. R. K. Smile would not have five years to give.

But to begin at the beginning: a long time ago, when he was just starting out in the pharma business, he had gone to India to visit family and friends and in a Bombay street an urchin was distributing business cards. He took one. "Are you alcoholic?" it read. "We can help. Call this number for liquor home delivery."

Excellent business model, he thought.

He had kept that card with him ever since. SPI had followed the excellent business model with great success, sending its products in impressively large quantities even to very small towns. When the indictments were handed down, some startling facts would emerge. For example, in the years 2013–18, SPI shipped five million highly addictive opioid doses every twelve months to a pharmacy in Kermit, West Virginia (pop. 400). Six million opioid doses were sent to a pharmacy in Mount Gay, West Virginia (pop. 1,800.) *Call this number for liquor home delivery,* indeed. A great many doctors and pharmacists made the call.

It was a unique characteristic of SPI's sales force—a characteristic that set it apart from the rest of the pharmaceutical industry—that you could join it even if you didn't have a background in pharma sales or even a college diploma or degree in science. Only two qualities were required. You had to be the driven and aggressive type, and you had to be extremely beautiful.

SPI boasted the most supremely attractive sales force in America. (One of their major competitors, Merck, went down a similar route, but SPI did so with much greater commitment and enthusiasm.) As was later revealed, SPI's Eastern Region sales chief, based in Atlanta itself, was a certain Dawn Ho, previously a dancer at Jennifer's, a strip club in West Palm Beach, Florida (pop. 108,161). At SPI she was in charge of selling InSmile™ to the whole highly populous Eastern Seaboard, a drug so dangerous that it required its own special prescription protocol. Dr. R. K. Smile's national sales chief expressed one hundred percent confidence in her abilities. The national sales chief was called Ivan Jewel and had a background in aquarium sales, sleep apnea testing devices, and an online ticket-resale agency in New Jersey, whose company registration was revoked after it failed to file an annual report for two consecutive years. He was also quite a looker himself, the Clint Eastwood type, as he liked to say. "Anything for a few dollars more." He agreed with Dr. Smile that a Florida strip club was not the kind of place where Big Pharma traditionally recruited staff, but insisted that Dawn Ho was a major asset. "She's the warm, sympathetic, good-listener type," he said. "You gots to picture these pain management physicians. All day, all night, they live around extreme agony and cancer. Then comes this beautiful woman, it's a pleasant distraction, one, and then she wants to listen to all your sadness, she wants you to let out all your stress, maybe a little shoulder rub, whatever, that's more than pleasant, two, and so she wants to sell you something, you buy it, boom,

three, deal closed. To me she's a closer. I use her (a) after a first contact by another salesperson and (b) when there's a client who's unde-
cided, who says yes yesterday, no today, we need him to say yes
tomorrow. A beautiful lady who cares for you is the best thing in
such cases. She's like a super gorgeous no-commitment version of
their wives."

The Little King, a.k.a. Little Big Hands, liked this explanation.
"If there are more like her out there," he told his sales chief, "just
get them all."

But the beauty of the sales force—gorgeous women sent to visit
male pain management physicians, Clint Eastwood hunks of men
sent to visit the female ones—wasn't enough, by itself, to explain
the huge numbers of the sales. Beauty allied to drive and aggression:
still not enough. When you wanted to pitch a restricted drug to
board-certified oncologists, you needed to add a raft of additional
techniques. *Incentives:* that was a better word than *techniques*. A
group of additional incentives.

It was Dr. R. K. Smile himself who thought up the speakers'
bureau. Actually, one part of the idea wasn't original. The idea of
recruiting big-name doctors to recommend a particular medication
to other doctors was an old one. Word of mouth was always recognized as the most effective marketing device. But if you wanted to
go off-label, hmm. That was borderline. Maybe across-the-borderline,
because going off-label meant getting doctors to prescribe a drug
for conditions other than the ones stated on the label, for which the
drug was intended. Or, of course, for no conditions at all, turning a
blind eye to recreational use, or, more seriously, to addiction. Another, more colloquial term for going off-label might be *becoming a
drug dealer.* Or even *becoming a narco lord.*

"I've spent my life crossing borders," said Dr. R. K. Smile, at the
opening of the first session of SPEIK (Smile Pharmaceuticals Ex-
panding Information and Knowledge) in Eureka, Montana (pop.
1,037), a smallish gathering which took place in the historic Community Hall, a single-story log building in the rustic style. "I read it

in a book once: if you fly above the Earth and look down, you see no frontiers. That's my attitude. I'm a no-frontier guy in favor of flying high." That was the secret ethos of SPI. They were all high-flying no-frontier guys.

After the Eureka meeting Dr. Smile allocated a budget of three million dollars toward the speakers' bureau project. Over time the project became even more sophisticated in its methods. Doctors were identified and booked, fees were paid, and then, more often than not, the events unfortunately could not take place owing to unforeseeable circumstances, but the terms of the agreements with the doctors stated that the speaking fees were nonreturnable. A budget of three million dollars a year, handed out in substantial dollops of, for example, $56,000 p.a., or $45,000 p.a., or $33,000 p.a., or $43,000 p.a., or even $67,000 p.a., in return for performing speaking engagements which did not actually have to be performed! Such a budget offered opportunities that were attractive to a lot of doctors. Such a budget bought—or to use a more polite term, booked—some very senior doctors. And these were tough doctors, ready to receive these substantial sums in return for prescribing InSmile™ off-label, willing to recommend doing so to other doctors, and able to take any heat that followed.

Yes, unfortunately, some of them got investigated by their state medical boards, but they just handled it! They paid the fines and carried on. Yes, unfortunately, in the worst cases there was disciplinary action when, unfortunately, some of the tough doctors went too far! When unfortunately they allegedly handed out multiple pre-signed prescriptions to patients and some of said patients died of drug overdoses from the drugs so prescribed! When unfortunately they allegedly prescribed InSmile™ to persons with zero cancer pain! When unfortunately they allegedly defrauded Medicare of multiple millions of dollars! When unfortunately they allegedly billed insurance companies for procedures they never performed! A pain management specialist from Rhode Island who was also a SPEIK speaker was reprimanded! A neurologist who was a SPEIK speaker was arrested! These matters were shocking to Dr. Smile and all the SPI team. They moved swiftly to rectify or terminate their relationships with such medical practitioners. They were a reputable company. They were running a speakers' bureau on the side, that was all. They were not and could not be held responsible for what their speakers might be doing on their own time. SPEIK was a reputable and highly regarded program and if its speakers believed in InSmile™, that was because of the inherent quality of the product. It was ridiculous and even slanderous to impugn the ethics of SPI staff. Yes, it was true, some of the adult children of SPEIK speakers were employed by SPI as part of the sales force, but that was on account of their high levels of beauty, not their parentage. These were grown independent men and women and it would be insulting both to their level of beauty and to SPI to allege that their employment was a ruse to give SPI leverage over their parents. SPI had no need to twist people's arms. The profession liked buying what SPI had to sell.

One of Dr. R. K. Smile's favorite doctors, Dr. Arthur Steiger, an experienced pain specialist from Bisbee, Arizona (pop. 5,200), was ordered to stop prescribing painkillers completely while serious allegations against him were investigated. At that time he had received more speakers' fees from SPEIK than any other medical practitioner, even though unfortunately all the much-anticipated events at which he had been billed to speak had had to be canceled owing to unforeseeable factors. Dr. Steiger fought back when he was indicted. "There is a vendetta against doctors who prescribe opioids regularly," he said. "But me, I'm the aggressive type. I aggressively help my patients. I'm the caring type also. I care aggressively. That's just who I am."

"I couldn't have said it better myself," Dr. R. K. Smile said to Happy when he read this statement.

She nodded lovingly. "You also are a fighter like this Dr. Arizona," she said. "Look how you have fought for your family. So so many achievements, so so much success. And when I have done my work and your name is everywhere, museums, concert halls, fish tanks, parks, then you will be too too respected by so so many people and all this noise will go. It is the Age of Anything-Can-Happen," she explained. "This I heard on TV. And I will make Everything happen for you." Her support warmed his heart. He loved his wife. He wondered if it would upset her if he asked her to lose a little weight.

THE FLICKED-UP WINGTIPS OF the G650ER reminded Dr. R. K. Smile of his wife's hairdo. If Happy Smile's hair were an executive jet, he thought, it would fly him nonstop to Dubai. The aircraft was his favorite toy. Sometimes on a still and sunny day he took it up from Hartsfield-Jackson just to potter about in the sky for a few hours, over Stone Mountain and Athens (pop. 115,452), Eatonton (pop. 6,555), and Milledgeville (pop. 18,933), the Chattahoochee and Talladega forests, or the route of Sherman's march. Stonewall Jackson, Robert E. Lee, Brer Rabbit, the Tree That Owns Itself, and the War between the States were all down there and he was above them, feeling at such moments like a true son of the South, which of course he was not. He had tried to read *Gone with the Wind* and to learn the words of "Zip-a-Dee-Doo-Dah" and "Old Folks at Home," but fiction and music weren't his thing. Also, like all cultural artifacts, they reminded him of his wife; and when he went up in the sky he didn't bring Happy along. Instead he invited a half dozen of the most attractive SPI sales reps, former colleagues of Dawn Ho's at Jennifer's strip club in West Palm Beach, and what happened up in the air stayed up in the air. Dr. R. K. Smile was not a perfect husband, he conceded that in his rare moments of inwardness and reflection, but in his opinion these episodes (a) did not take place on earth and so didn't count on earth and (b) in fact made him a better husband by satisfying his secret recreational urges, his off-label desires.

Flying home from Flagstaff after his encounter with old

Quichotte, he was sad, and not even the ministrations of all six salesladies simultaneously could blow away his blues. His poor relation Ismail Smile had always been an anomaly in the ranks of SPI employees, old among the young, emaciated among the luscious, a lonely figure, permanently out of step, everyone's crazy grandpa. And yet he carried himself with a certain dignity, kept himself immaculately dressed and groomed, was well mannered, well spoken, and possessed an enviably large vocabulary, was almost always cheerful, and could unleash, at any moment, his one weapon of beauty, which was his smile. Dr. R. K. Smile feared the worst now that he had let Quichotte go. The old fellow would deteriorate into some sort of dharma bum, moving aimlessly from nowhere to nowhere, dreaming his impossible dream of love. And one of these days Dr. R. K. Smile would receive a call from a motel in the middle of nowhere and then he would have to climb into the G650ER and bring the old man's body back with him to Atlanta and lay him to rest in Cobb County or Lovejoy. That day would probably not be far away.

In his final exchanges with Quichotte he had hinted at asking him to *perform some small private services,* some *discreet deliveries,* but he hadn't meant it. It had been a way of getting out of the room while leaving Quichotte with a scrap of self-respect and the sense of still being needed. The private services, or VIP, division of Smile Pharmaceuticals did not officially exist, and its unofficial existence was known only to a very small group, which did not include Dr. R. K. Smile's loyal wife. The discreet servicing of the desires of the very famous was a subsection of the American economy which it was important not to ignore, but the key word there was *discreet.* Dr. Smile was discreet, and was willing to make house calls to the right people. Lately the demand for InSmile™ among these special, house-call-worthy customers had increased significantly, owing to a change in the OxyContin formula that decreased its appeal to recreational users, and to the special customers' growing awareness that the sublingual spray offered instant gratification in a way that the other popular products did not. More and more gated properties from Minneapolis to Beverly Hills opened themselves to his unpretentious rental cars. He himself, small, physically unimpressive, was the forgettable type, and being forgettable was an asset in this kind of work, it assisted discretion. Like everyone in America, Dr. Smile was in thrall to celebrity, and when he entered the boudoirs and man caves of magazine-cover faces and bodies, he experienced a profoundly American joy, deepened by his secret knowledge that his net worth was probably greater than that of most of the owners of those immensely celebrated, those erotically well-known eyes, mouths, breasts, and legs, those prime manifestations of what Dr. Smile—a doctor, after all—thought of as professionally assisted perfection. He, too, was a professional. In his own way he, too, could assist.

When, some time later, a whisper reached him, the faintest murmur from one of his top, inner-circle speakers' bureau doctors, that a certain Indian movie actress turned American daytime TV superstar might appreciate a house call, Dr. R. K. Smile actually laughed out loud and clapped his hands. *"Arré, kya baat!"* he cried out in the privacy of his home office. "Whoa, what a thing!" Because now, if it all worked out as he hoped, he just might be able to make possible his poor relation's impossible dream, at least once before the tragic inevitable occurred. He might find it in his power, and in his heart, to bring fantasy-besotted old Quichotte face-to-face with his lady love.

But we are getting ahead of ourselves. The secret approach from Miss Salma R still lay a little way ahead, in the shrinking future of the world.

CHAPTER SIX

Sancho, Quichotte's imaginary Child, seeks to understand his Nature

ANCHO SMILE. THAT'S MY NAME. GOT THAT. BUT THERE'S a whole lot else I'm kind of blank about. I don't know if I'm even really here, to tell the truth. For one thing I'm black-and-white in a full-color universe. I look at my face in a mirror and it looks like not a face but a photograph of a face. How do I feel about that? Second class. Minor league. That's how. Also, I don't seem to be visible right now to anyone except *him*. My "father." Only he sees me. I know I'm not perceived, because when we go into the Subway in Moorcroft, Wyoming, where I was born, and he asks me if I want something, a soda, a sandwich, people look at him. That look people use on crazy people. Like he's talking to himself, and I want to yell out, *See me. I'm standing right here.* But to other people I'm apparently impossible to sense. I'm what's the word. Imperceptible.

I'm a teenager imagined by a seventy-year-old man. I guess I have to call him *Dad*. But here's the thing. How am I supposed to feel properly what's the word. Filial. When we just met. I didn't grow up with him, we didn't play ball in any park or whatever dads and sons do in real life. I'm just here, boom, one minute I wasn't and the next minute I was, and what am I supposed to feel? Love at first sight? I don't think so.

This is a problem.

I'm bounded by the limits of him. Tied to him. I'm guessing this is a thing other kids don't feel about their *dads*. That when I move away from the person who made me, when I get some distance away, I feel, how to say this. Out of range. Like, the signal drops, or it threatens to drop. If I try to walk away from him, if I need my own space for a moment?, without him always breathing down my neck?, if I get too far, I start—I don't know how to put it—breaking up. Parts of me become just static. I look like a bad TV picture. Like, wobbly. It's scary. I have to go back to wherever he is to regain full definition. I have to move back in and stay close, or otherwise maybe I'd stop being here at all. This is something I don't like to feel. To be chained to another human being, like a possession. For this I know what's the word.

Slavery.

Also, not to sound sorry for myself, but I'm a motherless child. I think a lot about mother-love, how that would be, a *mother, mom,* stroking my hair, her bosom for my pillow.

I KNOW THINGS. EDUCATED THINGS. But how do I know so much, being the teenage son of a seventy-year-old, and born just the other day? I guess the answer is, I know what he knows. If I listen inside myself I hear his book learning and all his favorite TV shows also—I know them all as if I watched them myself. And if I look I can see his memories as if they were mine, memories of falling out of a tree as a little boy and needing stitches in his head, memories of kissing an Australian girl when he was nine years old and cutting his tongue on the braces on her teeth, memories of bicycle accidents and school detentions and his mother's cooking. All his memories planted in my head.

There's something else. It's the strangest thing. Sometimes, when I'm in here, rummaging around in my own head, using the words he gave me and the knowledge he passed down, uncovering my memories which are his memories, his life story which I could claim as my own if I wasn't smart enough to know better . . . just sometimes, not every time . . . I get the weirdest sense that *there's someone else in here*. Crazy, right? I'm as crazy as he is, the old guy. But who or what is this third person? I'm just going to say this the way it comes to me to say it, even though it makes no sense and makes me sound . . . *unreliable*. It feels to me, at those moments when I have this sense of a stranger, as if there's somebody under slash behind slash above the old man. Somebody—yes—making him the way he made me. Somebody putting his life, his thoughts, his feelings, his memories into the old man the way the old man put that stuff inside me. In which case whose life am I remembering here? The old man's or the phantom's?

This is driving me nuts. Who is that under there slash over there slash in there? Who are you? If you're his Creator, are you mine as well?

There's a name for this. For the person *behind the story*. The old guy, *Dad,* he has a lot of material on this. He doesn't seem to believe in such an entity, doesn't seem to sense his presence the way I'm doing, but his head is full of thoughts about the entity all the same. His head and therefore my head too. I have to think about this now. I'll just come right out and say it: God. Maybe he and I, God and I, could understand each other, maybe we could have a good discussion, because, you know, both imaginary.

If you get imagined into being, does that mean that after that you can just be? If I knew how to reach him, God, I'd ask him that. And also, does he really feel seen? I understand that plenty of people say they talk to him every day, they walk with him, etc., but does he really truly do that? I mean step out beside them on the sidewalk, looking out for oncoming pedestrian traffic. I doubt it. I'm the one out here trying not to let people bump into me, because I'm imperceptible. See above.

Even God had a mother. That's a difference between us. I'll put that in the plural. Even gods had moms. Holy Mary mother of etc. Also Aditi mother of Indra. Also Rhea mother of Zeus. If I knew how to reach them, I'd ask them about the benefits of mother-love. Were they close? Was it wonderful? Did they talk? Was maternal guidance given and gratefully received? Did they use those bosoms for their pillows?

Also, a question regarding beginnings: Did the mothers have mothers? I'm confused. Is there nothing before the mother, no space or time for there to be anything in, until the Birth and after that, everything? I ask because I have only him, *Dad,* but before him presumably another father and another, begat begat begat. But me, he made me all by himself using what's the word. Parthenogenesis. Water fleas, scorpions, parasitic wasps, and me. Gods could do this also. Dionysus born from the thigh of Zeus. But he, *Dad,* he's not godlike. I say this not to be rude but because it's obvious. This is no Olympian being.

TIME TO BE STRICT with myself. Get real, Sancho. There's probably nothing slash nobody *behind the story.* It's just some kind of illusion. Double vision. Echo chamber. Déjà vu. I don't know what to call it. It's just him, *Dad,* becoming an echo of himself. That's it. I'm going with that. Beyond that, there's only madness, a.k.a. getting religion. I have no intention of going crazy or getting religion. One nutty old coot is more than enough in this car.

However: I'm reserving the right to think about this some more.

SOMETHING MUST HAVE HAPPENED to him sometime. Something went wrong with him somewhere along the line. It's buried deep but I'm looking. I'm looking under Roseanne and Ellen and Whoopi and Carpool Karaoke and all the rest. He's got so much book learning in his head under the TV stuff, it even comes out of my mouth, and I never looked at a book that didn't have a gorgeous lady on the cover, preferably deficient in the wardrobe department. *Maxim, Sports Illustrated* swimwear edition, these are my idea of books. This is what I check to keep in touch with what's going on. Even those I haven't checked so many of, my period on the planet being so far of brief duration. But he has the whole big-word library in his head—and what does he do with it? Watches reruns of old sci-fi movies about close encounters and the end of the world. And *Special Victims Unit,* he would be in love with Mariska Hargitay a.k.a. Olivia Benson if he wasn't already crazy smitten with Miss Salma R, America's Oprah 2.0, specially tooled for the younger demographic.

Regarding Mariska, I see here a gateway to the dark material. On that Pinterest page of his memory there's a comment pinned. His mother passed when he was three years old, just like Mariska when her mom Jayne Mansfield died. But not in a horrible car accident. Cancer is all. I can say things like that, *it was only cancer,* because being a figment such as I am I assume I'm immune to sickness. Therefore I snap my fingers at cancer. I bite my thumb at it. Still, tough for Mariska age three and Jayne age thirty-four. On U.S. Highway 90 just west of the Rigolets Bridge, and future-Olivia was even in the fucking car. That's tough. I see that. And for him too. He was in the hospital room just like future-Olivia in the back seat of the car. Or not just like. But similar. When his mother died he was holding her hand. Three years old and the moment she passed he dropped that hand and ran out of the room crying, *That's not her.*

I see him. He's a boy on a hill in Bombay. What do I know about this city? Less than nothing except what he sees. His mother's death, his father the painter weeping, himself stunned into dry-eyed silence. And then he loses his home as well as his mother, there's no more Bombay, the painter father can't bear to be home anymore, he goes west, so now there's Paris. The boy is homesick. He's literally sick. He has heart palpitations, arrhythmia. He doesn't want Paris. He wants his mother. He wants, what's the word. *Kulfi*. From a stall near where is it. Chowpatty. He wants to play in the Old Woman's Shoe in, what's its name, Kamala Nehru Park. Those places are gone. He's what now, French? In an apartment near the Luxembourg Gardens listening to *Don Quichotte* on his father's record player? He doesn't feel French. His father can't handle the sadness— can't handle his son's sadness or his own—and sends him to boarding school in England. I see him. He's a boy from the tropics trapped in the cold Midlands. He's looking at racist words scrawled on the wall of his little study room, *wogs go home*. He's looking at the perpetrator who's standing there with the crayon in his hand, caught in the act. Then an act of violence. He grabs the little perp, grabs him by the collar of his shirt and the waistband of his pants, swings him off his feet, and battering-rams him headfirst into his racist words. K.O. He thinks he's killed the little shit but he hasn't, no such luck. He wakes up and skulks off, he won't do that again in a hurry. But there are others to take the little perp's place.

So: he's capable of sudden violence. Or he was, once.

I see him. He's looking at his carefully written history essay. Somebody came in when he wasn't here and ripped it into tiny pieces and left them neatly piled up on his prep board. I see him writing letters to his father, letters filled with fictions. *I scored thirty-seven runs today and took three catches in the slips*. He can't play cricket but in his letters he's a star. Here's what he never tells his father: There are three crimes you can commit at an English boarding school. If you're foreign, that's one. Being clever is two. And being bad at sports, that's three strikes, you're out. You can get away with two of the three but not all three. If you're foreign and clever but you're a fine cricketer, if you can score thirty-seven runs and take three catches in the slips, you're okay. If you're bad at sports and clever but you're not foreign, you're forgiven. If you're foreign and bad at sports but you're not that smart, you're excused, you'll do. But he had the full trifecta. I see him listening through the paper-thin walls of his study at white boys maligning him in the room next door. At this school there's no TV for the boys to watch. TV came later for him. At school he went alone to the library and afterwards sat alone in his room and plunged into the yellow-jacketed Gollancz editions and flew away into fantasy worlds and alternative universes, away, away across the galaxies, into interstellar space.

I see him. He's the first and last man. He's an explorer standing on a mountaintop glacier in Iceland, Snæfellsjökull, watching the shadow of the peak move until it points to the hole which leads to the center of the Earth. He's in a submarine called *Nautilus* traveling twenty thousand leagues under the sea with a captain whose name means Nobody. He's a warlord on a mountain on Mars, watching a hostile army advance across a red desert. He's a rebel in a forest memorizing *Crime and Punishment* because all the great texts have to be memorized to survive because all the actual books have been burned; the temperature at which paper catches fire is two hundred and thirty-two point seven eight degrees Celsius, better known as Fahrenheit 451. He's a man with a disc embedded in his forehead that glows brightly when he's sexually attracted to a woman, which is okay because everyone has one, so everyone knows who turns them on, and they can cut right to the chase without wasting time on flirtation and seduction. He's a man with a dog stepping by accident into a freak phenomenon called a chrono-synclastic infundibulum and being stretched out forever across space and time. He's a NASA controller in a state of high excitement because an alien flying saucer is in touch and contains people who look just like earthlings, he's guiding it in to land but he's puzzled because he can't see them and then they land and they are drowning in a puddle on the landing field because they are tiny, their spacecraft is tiny, and as they drown the controller runs out onto the landing field and his foot splashes in a puddle and crushes them. He's a computer engineer flying away from a Tibetan monastery after installing the supercomputer that will count the nine billion names of God, after which, they say, the universe will have fulfilled its purpose and will cease to exist. He's looking out of the window of the plane, knowing that the supercomputer has finished counting, and he sees that one by one, very quietly, the stars are going out.

He mentions these two stories a lot, the tiny drowning aliens and the nine billion names. And when he mentions the second one he also mentions the following, he mentions it every time: that the purpose of the universe might not be the nine billion names. It might be the creation of a single perfect love, or, in plain language, the forthcoming happy union between himself and Miss Salma R.

So what will happen in the unlikely event of his quest ending in success? I asked him this straight out. Does he think the world will come to an end?

Obviously, he says. One by one, very quietly, the stars will start going out.

I see him. Above all he's Bilbo/Frodo, eleventy-one today, no wonder he's crazy for journeying. The Road goes ever on and on. I see him invisible, slipping the Ring on his finger. *Ash nazg durbatulûk, ash nazg gimbatul, / Ash nazg thrakatulûk agh burzum-ishi krimpatul.* Invisibility is a thing he dearly wishes for. He wants to disappear. Here too is the origin of his desire to follow a wandering star. I will diminish and go into the West and remain Galadriel. This is what he longs for. To diminish and go into the West. To be a person not seen, of no import, going where he will, remaining himself, taking what life gives him, maybe a mendicant, like a monk, or a *sannyasi*. Maybe even a thief. What has it got in its pocketses? Thief, thief. Baggins . . . we hates it for ever.

In those days there were T-shirts, FRODO LIVES, GO GO GANDALF, he wore them all. Even then he wanted a quest. There are people who need to impose a shape upon the shapelessness of life. For such people the quest narrative is always attractive. It prevents them from suffering the agony of feeling what's the word. Incoherent.

This old Chevy is driving through the Ute Mountain reservation. North on 491, Ya-ta-hey (pop. 580) > Tohatchi (pop. 1,037) >

Canyon of the Ancients. How did we get here? Who knows? Don't ask me, I wasn't paying attention. I was diving into my head which is also his. Here's what he says to me. He wants to perform a ceremony of personal purification before embarking on this cockeyed pursuit. Indian country, he keeps saying, even though I tell him to stop making that joke, it just doesn't work. He wants to sit cross-legged in the heart of the heart of the country and call upon the forefathers of the quest. I don't know who he's talking about. Yes I do. Here it is. He's thinking about Jason in the *Argo* heading for Colchis to find the Golden Fleece, and Sir Galahad, the only one of the knights of the round table pure enough of spirit to be shown the Grail. His head is full of this nonsense. The journey of the Thirty Birds to find Simurgh, the bird-god. The progress of pilgrim Christian to the Celestial City. And searches for women naturally. Rama searching for his kidnapped Sita, Mario the plumber ascending all those levels to rescue Princess Toadstool from the evil Bowser, and the Italian poet, D. Alighieri, traveling through the Inferno and Purgatorio to find his beatific Beatrice in Paradiso.

Oh, one more thing. I hope he doesn't plan to purify me. I'm okay with staying impure. Can you understand that? I'm no angel, don't want to be one. You know what I want to be. Human. I don't really care about good.

Let him drive. I'm digging deeper, below all the stories. Something must have happened to him sometime.

I SEE HIM. He worked hard at school, took refuge in studies as well as fictions, got his scholarship to the dreaming spires, and then, out there in Flatland/Waterland, while feather-footed through the plashy fen passed the questing vole, came a crisis. Here's the scene as it presents itself. His father the painter blew into town. Invite half a dozen of your friends, he said. I'm buying lunch. And at lunch, the studious son and his friends duly assembled, the two prettiest girls (the future eminent oncologist and the future professor of fine arts) were seated on either side of the parent, who proceeded, under the table, shamelessly, to fondle them, knee and thigh. At first they bore it in silence, not wishing to humiliate their friend by calling out his father. But in the end his hands traveled too far and too freely and they rose to their feet and admonished him, Proto-Cancer-Doc and Proto-Art-Prof, gorgeous, reddening, angry, formidable, sad. And he, the humiliated son, jumped up a moment later and began to shout. He remembers every word he said, I can hear them echoing in my ears now, deafening me, breaking forever what remained of the tie between father and son. I see him. As a son he broke the relationship with his father and so now as a father he wants to build a relationship with his son. Thus, I turn out to be the after-effect of that long-gone day, the consequence of his father's lechery. After which his father never spoke to him again, nor did he, Daddy Q, try to mend fences. He graduated with a fine degree but his father did not attend his graduation. And at some point after that he put his feet on the road and went a-wandering and so began his long decline and in the end there was the job with Smile Pharmaceuticals and then the loss of that job and the arrival of myself and bingo, we're up to date.

Almost, but not quite. There's a whole area of his memory I can't access. I feel pain there, both received and inflicted. There's a lot in there, maybe everything that matters, maybe the whole point of him is locked away in that space. It makes him, what's the word. An enigma. In here is where the darkness has been cornered, where the codes that break the code are located. I want to get inside there. No I don't. Yes I do.

At some point the painter father had died. There was no death-bed reconciliation. Sad story. Lost his mother, his home, his dignity, his father, his sense of having a goal in life. But now he has goals once more, insane as they are. Myself and Miss Salma R. One of us nonexistent and the other beyond his reach. This will be his final act.

I see him. He's still hiding in fantasy and science fiction. *F&SF* . . .

great old magazine. Found that memory in here, as well as the other old magazines, *Astounding,* that was one, and *Amazing,* that was the other one. And the writers of the Golden Age. Frederik Pohl and C. M. Kornbluth. James Blish. Clifford D. Simak. L. Sprague de Camp. But now also the movies slash TV. Therefore that nonsense about the Doctor and the TARDIS. He sees himself in the footage. While he drives he's Lemmy Caution in his Ford Galaxie entering *les environs d'Alphaville.* Or: he's on a spaceship doing battle with a rogue computer. Or: OMG he's like thirty years old, walking into the alien mother ship at OMG OMG Moorcroft, Wyoming, Devils Tower . . . exactly where the Perseid meteor shower granted the old guy's wish and I faded in, in black-and-white, on the passenger seat of his car.

Even my birth, my personal origin story, had its roots in fantasy. Is that who I am? A close encounter of the what is it kind? Yeah. I know. Third.

Where's my mother ship?

HIS MANY GRIEFS, his few joys, his few highs, his many lows, are second nature to me now. And now we're riding in his car and he wants this to be a father-son bonding experience. But really I'm something like his clone, his younger clone, and if he wants to bond with me it's a kind of narcissism, right? It's like a sound wanting to bond with its echo. It's like wanting to get closer to your fucking reflection, which is what the whole Narcissus story was about in the first place. You see how I knew that? I know everything he knows.

So: Geppetto. I'm thinking Geppetto slash Pinocchio. The puppet maker wanted a son, so he carved one out of a block of wood. The old guy—"Dad" is still difficult to say—wanted a son, so he went one better than the puppet maker and carved me out of meteors and thin air. And guess what? Like little long-nose Pinoke, I'm going to turn myself into a real live boy. I don't even need a blue fairy, but if I find one, I'll use her, sure. I'll use whatever is available, whatever comes to hand. This whole only-he-can-see-me shit is going to have to stop. I have big plans. I'm going to, really soon, what's the word. Materialize. Visible to one and all, pinch me and I bruise, if you prick me do I not bleed. I will liberate myself by the force of my own will. A pull-myself-up-by-my-own-bootstraps kinda operation. A sling-my-airhook-into-the-sky-and-yank sorta job. There are no strings on me.

There's this story in his head I like. A man's shadow comes loose from the man somewhere, maybe in Africa?, and goes off by itself, traveling the world. Yeah, another traveler, right, another road movie. When the shadow comes back the man is about to marry his princess but the shadow, who is exactly like him, his spitting image, his shadow, right?, has seen the world and become super sophisticated and cosmopolitan and looks like a man now, and persuades the stupid princess that he, the shadow, is in fact the real man and the real man is the shadow. The real man has lost his mind, the shadow tells her, and thinks he's a human being. And the princess and the shadow have the original man thrown in jail and executed and the princess marries the shadow instead. That may not be exactly the way the story goes but it's the memory-version I have. Wow. Some story. And so here we are: I'm the dark shadow and the old guy's chasing his princess. And maybe that's my fate, to become a man and steal his girl. Maybe that's his fate, to be discarded and die.

I like that. It's a possibility. I'm going to store that away and think about it and if I get a chance, guess what? We all have to grab our chances when they come our way.

I know what you're thinking. Maybe I'm not so nice. But you know? I didn't ask to be here. I was imported. I got put on a ship and sailed away and crossed the mighty ocean into Charleston Bay. But slavery's over, right? I once had strings but now I'm free.

You know when his birthday is? Juneteenth. The nineteenth of June. Freedom Day in the Confederacy. It's a sign. This shadow's going to break free. And if I get a shot at a princess, watch me. That's all I'm saying right now. Just watch me go.

CHAPTER SEVEN

Quichotte & Sancho enter the
first Valley of the Quest,
& Sancho meets an Italian Insect

"WHEN CONSIDERING THE MATTER OF WOOING A great lady," Quichotte said, "I ponder, naturally, the classics. And by the classics I mean, first of all, the show that broke the ground and pointed the way, *The Dating Game,* ABC-TV, 1965, 'from Hollywood, the dating capital of the world.' We must ask ourselves when we summon up the memory of a masterpiece: what is the wisdom it offers us?"

"That we shouldn't go on dumb dating shows?" proposed Sancho, unhelpfully.

"Incorrect," Quichotte admonished him, not unkindly, for Sancho was only recently arrived in the world, and so it was understandable that he would get things wrong when he sought to judge its ways. "Listen and learn, my boy. Prolonged viewing of this seminal program, which originally ran on daytime television in black-and-white but soon burst into full color on prime time, drives home some hard truths to the attentive viewer. Firstly, that when a woman possessed of a high degree of desirability is the goal, you will have competitors. The field will not be open to you; you will have to chop down your adversaries ruthlessly in order to achieve your end."

"That sounds good," Sancho said. "Chopping people down. Who are our targets, and how and when do we waste them?"

"Secondly," continued Quichotte, ignoring his miracle child's pseudo-adolescent arousal by the suggestion of violence, "she will question you, and you had better have the noblest answers to her questions, for she will question others as well. Love is an audition, Sancho. He who knows best how to present himself to the beloved gets the part."

"How do you think you're going to do that," the youth disrespectfully rejoined, "a broken-down old nag like you?"

"Be a little less obnoxious to your only parent," Quichotte reproved him. "I brought you into existence by the power of my wishing and the kindness of the stars, and if I grow weary of you, I can make you vanish as well."

"Too late for that," said Sancho. "Once you're born, you're born, that's all there is to it; by whatever means you arrive, you've arrived. After that you're the boss of yourself, and responsible only to yourself. Responsibility for your own actions: that's the basis of all morality, isn't it? The do-gooder gets the credit for the good deed? The murderer is guilty of the crime?"

"We aren't discussing morality," said Quichotte. "We are discussing love."

Sancho, who had been slumped down in the passenger seat of the car, filled with the indifference of his apparent years, abruptly sat up and clapped his hands. "Okay then," he cried, "let's play. I'll be the girl hidden on one side of the wall, and you'll be the contestant on the other side, Contestant One. Let's see how you do with my questions."

"What about the other contestants?" Quichotte asked.

"Don't worry," Sancho replied. "I'll be them as well."

———

LET US IMAGINE THEM leaving the Canyon of the Ancients, after Quichotte has satisfactorily invoked his mighty questing forerunners and also, to Sancho's intense embarrassment, demonstrated his personal version of the Sun Dance, a slow-motion, lurching, gimpy, unstable thing, with arms outstretched and awkwardly tapping feet, oddly innocent and childlike, as if Laurel without Hardy had gone way out west. This terpsichorean act, Quichotte explains, was also a kind of questing, in this case for spiritual power. "Did you get it, then? The power?" Sancho asked when the dance was over, leaving Quichotte panting and wheezing with sweat staining his shirt, and refusing to reply.

And now they are in the vehicle, heading east from Cortez (pop. 8,482) on 160, aiming at Chimney Rock. If we want we could imagine a Penske truck heading the other way, the driver looking down at the Chevy Cruze, seeing the gent in there, formally dressed, suit and tie and hat, what's an old coot like that doing out here looking that way, talking to himself. Maybe he's lost and on speakerphone trying to find his way. Probably the Penske driver doesn't even think about it that much, just passes by and whoosh, he's gone. But on the other hand maybe he thinks, For a minute there I thought I saw someone else in the car, but then no, there was only the dressed-up gent driving alone. Must've been some kind of reflection. A trick of the light. Forget it.

"QUESTION ONE," SANCHO SAID. "And I'm the lady, remember. I can't see you, you can't see me. There's a wall."

"Pyramus and Thisbe," Quichotte said.

"What?"

"It doesn't matter."

"Please don't interrupt anymore," Sancho said with a shrug, and then raised his voice to sound feminine. "Here's question one. I'm a woman who likes my men tall, dark, and handsome, with strong jaws and a dominant attitude. How do I know you're my kind of guy? Contestant Three?"

Now he deepened his voice and answered himself, "Just wait until I get you in my arms, baby. You won't be disappointed."

And then again as the lady: "How about you, Contestant One?"

"By the height of my emotion toward you will you know me," Quichotte cried out in high rhetorical fashion, "and by the darkness in which I dream of you, and by the handsomeness of the deeds by which I will prove myself, for handsome is as handsome does. And by the determined set of my jaw as I bend the arc of my life toward you, and by the dominant idea which possesses me, which is, that you must be mine."

Sancho let out a low whistle. "Wow, Dad," he said. "I guess I underestimated you." It was the first time he had used the word "dad" and meant it.

Quichotte nodded gravely. "A good knowledge of the classics," he advised his son, "is the sign of an educated man."

THEY LIVE ECONOMICALLY. Quichotte's small pension pays for gas and food and cheap accommodation but not much else. It is, of course, inexpensive to feed and house Sancho, as he is, at least at this point, still non-corporeal, mono-chrome, and visible only to Quichotte. Let us imagine them in Colorado, sitting together outside a tent at the Lake Capote Recreation Area, near Chimney Rock. (There has always been a tent in the trunk of Quichotte's car. Maybe we should have mentioned that. It has been there all the time. Sorry.) Here's what's happening: Sancho, not a patient lad, is fraying a little at the edges.

"WE'RE OUT HERE IN the middle of nowhere," Sancho said. "There's nothing to do and no reason to be doing it. This woman you never stop talking about, she's over a thousand miles away and we're out here looking at a rock. There isn't even a TV to watch her show. What exactly are we here for, 'Dad'?" *Dad* again. This time he definitely didn't mean it.

"We're waiting for a sign," Quichotte replied.

"There's signs all over." Sancho was not a stranger to sarcasm. "That one says *Showers* and that one says *Slow*. And there's one back there saying *Bait Shop*. Also *Self-Permitting Station,* that's a good one. It's right over there. You can just permit yourself to do whatever you want. Problem solved. Can we go now?"

"I danced the Sun Dance," Quichotte said. "So the sign will surely come."

PAUSE.

"AS I PLAN MY QUEST," Quichotte said, drinking from a can of ginger ale, "I ponder the contemporary period as well as the classical. And by the contemporary I mean, of course, *The Bachelorette*. Twenty-five contestants! Twenty-six in season twelve! Thirty in season five, thirty-one in season thirteen! The searcher for love must understand immediately, at the outset of his search, that the quantity of love available is far too small to satisfy the number of searchers. We may further intuit, following on from this first proposition, a second; namely, a quantity theory of love. If the amount of love in the universe is finite and unchanging, then it follows that as one searcher finds the love he seeks, another must lose his love; and that when one love dies *here*—and only when a love dies!—it becomes possible for another love to be born *there*. We may regard this as a variant form of the butterfly effect. A butterfly flaps its wings in Japan, and we feel the breeze on our cheek here at Lake Capote."

"Or," said Sancho, "maybe the wisdom to be gained from a show like that is that you can't trust anybody to be true, not even the woman you're after."

"Already so cynical," Quichotte said mournfully. "No great quest, my boy, was ever achieved except by those with faith."

"But if faith is all you've got," the other answered, "you're going to lose out to the guy with the moves and the looks."

"The stories of the suitors and bachelorettes teach us this," Quichotte said, ignoring Sancho's remark, "that an apparent victory may in reality be a defeat, and that the defeated may yet, long after their apparent failure, triumph. At the end of season two, Meredith Phillips agreed to marry Ian McKee; but they separated a year later, and six years after that, her lovelorn high school sweetheart won her hand. At the end of season four, DeAnna Pappas was engaged to Jesse Csincsak, but they called it off six months before their wedding date, and, if we leap into the future, we see that Jesse actually married Ann Lueders, who was a contestant in season thirteen of the parallel show, *The Bachelor*. Jillian Harris and Ed Swiderski (season five), Ali Fedotowsky and Roberto Martinez (season six), Emily Maynard and Jef Holm (season eight), are all exemplars of the proposition that a ring on a ring finger guarantees nothing; whereas Ashley Hebert and J. P. Rosenbaum (season seven) and Desiree Hartsock and Chris Siegfried (season nine) reassure us that victory can lead to happily-ever-after. The record warns us of the frailty of even the greatest endeavors, and the consequent need to be resolute in the pursuit of love, as strong as a lion in his prime, and as unbreakable as a holy vow; and never to give up hope."

"You know your stuff," Sancho conceded in a grumbling voice. "I guess I'll grant you that."

A little later Sancho spoke up again. "I have one more question for you," he said, and this time he spoke with some caution. "If, in the unlikely event that, in spite of everything, and not questioning your worthiness, and all you're doing and will do, but, just suppose, by some freak of bad luck, some wild, off-the-wall, million-to-one chance, the lady doesn't love you back? If you end up not being the bachelor chosen by this pretty frigging hot and desirable and also super famous bachelorette?"

"What kind of question is that?" Quichotte said, coloring, and he was suddenly shouting. "It's the question of an ignoramus. It's the inquiry of a baboon trying to speak English. It's the splutter of a fish out of water. It's the twitch of an amoeba that thinks it's a human being. It's an insult to the greatness of my quest, and to your father also, by the way. Withdraw the question. I, your parent, demand it."

"It's a totally reasonable thing to ask," his son answered. "You yourself just talked about, what did you say, the frailty of even the greatest whatevers. And every guy knows that rejection is a normal thing. Many men are rejected by many women for many reasons and we just have to learn to accept it and feel grateful when a woman assents. And how would I know this, by the way, if not for your thoughts inside me?"

"What do you mean?" Quichotte shouted, really angry, enraged to such a shocking degree that Sancho was disconcerted, more than disconcerted, actually afraid. "Where have you been sticking your nose? Don't you dare go where you are forbidden to enter. You are a child. You are not me. There are things about me that are not for you to know."

"Okay," Sancho said, and it took some courage for him to say it. "I see that under your old-goof act, beneath your sweet nutty disguise, you're maybe someone else entirely, and that part of you is locked away right now. It's like you've caged the beast."

BY THE BANKS OF LAKE CAPOTE, in the aftermath of this confrontation, Sancho realized that his dream might have begun to come true. At first the nights had been difficult for him, because as Quichotte slipped toward sleep he, Sancho, lost consciousness too. The approach of this involuntary dreamless nonexistence terrified him, felt like a nightly execution. He struggled against it but it overpowered him. Until, suddenly, it didn't. Quichotte slept, and Sancho remained awake. A great firework of joy burst in him, erasing the memory of the quarrel. He was on his way to being alive.

That night after the argument, Quichotte had limped off into his tent and had immediately fallen asleep. Now he was snoring his vroom-vroom NASCAR racetrack snores while Sancho lay up on the roof of the Chevy, listening to the crickets and looking up at the humbling wheel of the galaxy. There was a sign if you wanted one, he thought, a gigantic starlight finger flipping the bird at the Earth, pointing out that all human aspiration was meaningless and all human achievement absurd when measured against the everything of everything. Up there was the immensity of the immensity, the endless distance of the distance, the impossible scale, the thunderous silence of all that light, the million million million blazing suns out there where nobody could hear you scream. And down here the human race, dirty ants crawling across a small rock circling a minor star in the outlying provinces of a lesser galaxy in the inconsequential boondocks of the universe, narcissistic ants mad with egotism, insisting in the face of the fiery night-sky evidence to the contrary that their puny anthills stood at the heart of it all. He might still be half a ghost, Sancho thought, but he was a ghost who saw clearly, without illusions, and had his head screwed on the right way around.

And yet he wanted to be one of those ants, that was the paradox of it. He wanted flesh and blood and bones, and a bisonburger from Ted's Montana Grill that he could touch and taste and swallow. He wanted life.

"He wants it for you too," a voice said.

Sancho, startled, sat up fast. There was nobody to be seen. "Who's there?" he cried.

"Down here," said the voice.

He looked down. There was a cricket sitting on the car roof beside him, unafraid, not making its cricket noise, speaking English with an Italian accent.

"Grillo Parlante at your service," said the cricket. "It's true, I'm Italian originally. But you can call me Jiminy if you want."

"This isn't really happening," he said.

"That is correct," said the cricket. "È proprio vero. I'm a projection of your brain, just in the way that you started out as a projection of his. It seems you may be getting an insula."

"A what?"

"As I was saying," said the cricket, "he wants you to be fully human as badly as you do. He imagines it all the time. And to get you there, he will need to give you an insula."

"I'm talking to an Italian cricket," Sancho said to the stars, "whose vocabulary is bigger than mine, and who apparently wants to discuss insulation."

"Insul-*ah,* not insul-*ate,*" the cricket corrected him. "This is the Latin of science. It means an island in the mind."

"He's giving me an island?" Sancho was confused.

"A part of the brain," the cricket clarified. "In *Gray's Anatomy* it is called the Island of Reil after the German scientist who first de- scribed it. But you can call it, if you wish, the Island of the Real. It is the part of the corteccia cerebrale that gets involved in most of what it is to be a human person. Essere umano, si. It is folded within the solco laterale. This is a fissure that separates the lobo temporale and the lobo frontale of the brain. From the insula comes conscious- ness, emotion, perception, self-awareness, and being able to connect to other people. È molto multi-funzionale, this insula, yes. It is where empathy comes from, it controls your blood pressure, and when you get hit, it tells you how badly it hurts. You want to feel hungry? Taste that Ted's bisonburger? The insula gives you feeling and tasting. It is sex you're after? It processes your orgasms. It helps your concentration. It has to do with ecstasy. Oh yes, it's a hard worker all right! It gives you happiness, sadness, anger, fear, disgust, disbelief, trust, faith, beauty, and love. Also, hallucinations, which is where I come in. Eccomi qua!"

"He really wants me to have this insula?" Sancho asked, dubi- ously. "I thought he just liked having me as a black-and-white ac- cessory for his pleasure alone, tied to him, like a prisoner. I'm not sure he can handle an independent child."

"You are wrong. He is like every parent," the cricket said, so- berly confining itself to English. "He wants you in full color, with full powers, able to lead a successful life. He promises you an insula. Already it is growing in you. Soon you will burst out in Technicolor and spread your tail like the winter peacock of Fellini in *Amarcord* and everyone will see you and then there you are! Life. The sweet life. Look at you: growing up fast! Almost the young Mastroianni."

"And you?" Sancho wanted to know. "Are you going to stick around? Because I don't think I want anyone to be my guide."

"The insula," replied the cricket, "unfortunately has nothing to do with conscience."

"Nor do I," said Sancho. "I'm like the sky at night. The universe has no interest in right and wrong. It doesn't care who lives or dies and who behaved well or badly. The universe is an explosion. It rushes outwards, pushing, growing, making room for itself. It's a never-ending conquest. You know what the motto of the universe is? *Give me more. I want it all.* That's my motto also. That's how I see things too."

"That, I already perceive in you," the cricket said, beginning to disappear. "That's already completely clear. Ciao! Baci!" And it was gone.

When Quichotte awoke the next morning he heard the improbable sound of breakfast sizzling in a pan outside his tent. A dark-haired young man—tall, skinny, his build remarkably similar to Quichotte's own—was frying eggs and bacon. The young man had his back to Quichotte and wore a red-white-and-blue-check lumberjack shirt over blue jeans with turn-ups and held the pan in his right hand over the flame. With his left hand he was waving at the campers in the neighboring tent, and they were waving back at him. Quichotte called out and when the young man turned to face him the old fellow's heart pounded so hard that he feared his time had come. Then, still alive, he understood that a second miracle had occurred, because this was his Sancho in high definition, full color, and wide-screen aspect ratio. Farewell, monochrome phantom! Here was a visible, tall, handsome (if a little bony-faced), strapping teenage lad with a grin on his face and a hearty appetite for food. The disagreement of the night before fled from Quichotte's thoughts. He found tears standing in his eyes.

"A real, live boy," he said. "Truly, anything can happen today. Even such a thing as this."

"Is this the sign you were waiting for?" Sancho asked him, but Quichotte had a lump in his throat and couldn't reply.

"Seeing that this happened," Sancho then said, "there are things I'm going to need."

Quichotte was still in a daze, and shook his head in puzzlement.

"Don't pretend there aren't," the lad cried. "You'll have to get me everything. I can't wear the same thing every day, can I. So, shirts, pants, underpants, socks, sneakers, boots, hoodie, coat, hat. Plus, I'll need to eat regularly from now on, so we'll need to get extra food. Also, when we get away from here I'll need a room of my own, to get away from that steam hammer in your nose. And, as this plays out, it's clear I can't live with you forever. I'll need a job, a place to stay, all of that. Which we're not going to find me any of it out here, so we have to leave asap. You've had it pretty easy with me so far. But going forward, I have needs."

"You will want for nothing," Quichotte finally spoke up. "I have some money saved that will take care of it. There is also my severance-pay lump sum."

"Oh, that's right, money," the young fellow said, snapping his fingers. "Can I get a bank account? That's important. A debit card is important. An overdraft is important. If you're not buying stuff, if you're not making repayments, the system doesn't recognize that you exist."

"You must be patient," Quichotte said to his son. "All in good time. At present I am a man on a great quest and that has priority, as I am certain you can understand."

"In your dreams," the youth said, impolitely. "What quest? As far as I can see, you haven't even made a start."

"On the contrary," Quichotte answered him. "I am in the first valley, through which any seeker must pass."

After breakfast, on a trestle table in the picnic area, Quichotte rolled out a large map of the continental United States. Birds wheeled in the sky overhead: a pair of ospreys with six-foot wing-spans, from the osprey nest on a pole in the heart of the Lake Capote campsite. "The hawk is a great hunter," Quichotte said. "Fish quail before its shadow. It is good to have them here. They grace our pur-suit. Their presence is a blessing."

"What are you looking for?" Sancho asked, jerking a thumb in the direction of the map. "Outlet stores?"

"According to one of the great classic descriptions of the quest," Quichotte said, "the seeker must pass through seven valleys."

"What TV show are you talking about now?"

"This is not a TV show," Quichotte said. "This is old. From be-fore there was TV."

"Awesome," Sancho said. The concept of a time before televi-sion impressed even his sarcastic self. That had to be a really long time ago. "Where are these valleys located, anyway?" he wanted to know. "San Fernando Valley where the Valley girls live? And the vampires, moving west down Ventura Boulevard? Or maybe Sun Valley? Death Valley? Happy Valley? Valley Forge? That's all the valleys I've got."

"It doesn't have to be an actual valley," Quichotte explained. "The valley is a metaphor. The seven valleys can be anyplace, any-where."

"Then why," the youth asked, not unreasonably, "are we look-ing for them on a map?"

"Every quest," Quichotte answered, "takes place both in the sphere of the actual, which is what maps reveal to us, and in the sphere of the symbolic, for which the only maps are the unseen ones in our heads. Still, the actual is also the road to the Grail. We may be after a celestial goal, but we still have to travel along the interstate."

"You lost me there," Sancho shook his head. "But that's okay."

"The first valley is the valley of the quest itself," Quichotte said. "Here the searcher has to cast aside every kind of dogma, including both belief and unbelief. Old age itself is such a valley. In old age one becomes detached from the dominant ideas of one's time. The present, with its arguments, its quarreling ideas, is revealed as fleeting and unreal. The past is long gone and the future, one recognizes, is not a place in which one will find a foothold. To be separated from the present, past, and future is to entertain the eternal, to allow the eternal to enter one's being."

"But if you cast aside unbelief as well as belief"—Sancho scratched his head—"then there's nothing left. Right? All you've got is an empty head. That can't be good? Can it?"

"Systems of thought will not help us on our journey," Quichotte answered. "Systems of thought, and their antitheses as well, are merely codifications of what we think we know. When we begin by abandoning them, we open ourselves to the immensity of the universe, and therefore also to immense possibilities, including the possibility of the impossible, in which category I place my quest for love."

"Sounds like one of those shows where you get marooned on an island and your city-slicker knowledge can't help you. *Wrecked, Marooned, Man vs. Wild, Dude You're Screwed*. Or is it more like *The Quest* or *Galaxy Quest*?"

"We will see," Quichotte told him.

"Anyhow, that's right about the universe, I get that part," Sancho said. "The universe doesn't have positions or theories or rebuttals or any of that. The universe is just up there, out there, all around, and it doesn't give a fuck."

"And now we too must seek to be *just there,*" Quichotte replied.

"And not give a fuck?"

"There is no need to give a fuck," Quichotte answered gravely, "about anything except the goal of our journey."

"Namely the lady."

"Exactly. All else is vanity and must fall away."

"Cool," Sancho said. "I can focus on the lady too. That's no problem at all."

"I will write to her," Quichotte declared. "I will say, I am in the first valley of the quest, and am casting aside all dogma, no longer believing anything nor disbelieving. Consequently I am becoming open to the possibility of the impossible, in which category . . ."

"Yes, yes," Sancho said. "There's no need to say everything twice."

"I will say, I am a sleepwalker, walking as if through a dream, until I awake into the reality of our love. It will be a magnificent letter," Quichotte said, "and will do much good work on my behalf."

"I guess," Sancho replied. "Sounds kind of off-putting to me."

"You know nothing," Quichotte reproved him. "Until an hour ago you were just a figment of my fancy. I don't think your opinion carries much weight at present."

"Whatever you say," Sancho shrugged. "Right now, in my life, you're the one holding all the important cards."

At that exact moment, an osprey flying directly overhead sent them a communication. The communication landed *splat* on the map of the United States and obscured the city of New York; after which the osprey, having nothing further to communicate, had completed its role in our story and flew away.

"Ugh," expostulated Sancho. "Fucking bird."

But Quichotte was clapping his hands. "This is it!" he cried.

"This is what?"

"The sign. The hunter has guided us, and the hunt is on! We must go immediately where we have been told to go."

"*This* is the sign?" Sancho demanded with some indignation. "My transformation from a figment into a flesh-and-blood person, that's *not* the sign? *Birdshit* is the sign?"

"On the road to New York we will find the second valley, and, I now believe, all the others as well," Quichotte told him. "In the concrete canyons, where the Beloved awaits me."

"I could have told you that without the help of some crappy bird," Sancho said. "And what's the second valley, anyway?"

"The second valley," Quichotte solemnly pronounced, "is the Valley of Love."

CHAPTER EIGHT

Wherein, turning away from the Brightness of the Beloved, we examine her Darkness

THE SECOND LETTER FROM QUICHOTTE UNEXPECTEDLY touched the heart of Salma R—or even Salma—we have gotten to know her well enough by now to drop the formality of "Miss." *I am a sleepwalker, walking as if through a dream, until I awake into the reality of our love,* it began, and continued through several pages of increasingly purple expressions of adoration. And again, at the end, the oddly ungrammatical sign-off, a peculiarity at the end of a linguistically competent, if overly baroque, piece of writing. *Sent by a smile, Quichotte.* "I'm still worried about him," she told her security chief, "because it goes without saying that stalkers, like groupies, are one hundred percent always and absolutely out of their minds. But the man has a turn of phrase." And the metaphysical aspect of the letter, the surrender of all vestiges of belief, but also of the processes of un- or disbelief, so that one might simply face reality with an open heart and receive its messages, was not without interest.

She made a copy of the letter and read it in the Maybach on the way home, too many times. Her driver asked, just to have some fun with her, "Miss Daisy, is that the light of love in your eyes?"

She snorted at him. "Hoke, just drive the car. There are driverless limos now, don't forget."

"Yes, Miss Daisy," the driver said, and hummed under his breath, "But will you still love him tomorrow?"

It may be that one reason why Salma responded as emotionally as she did to the second letter from Quichotte is that she was herself all too familiar with the battle against mental illness, being a third-generation sufferer herself. For a long time after the family plague manifested itself in her, it was strong medication that kept her going, so much so that she made up a rhyme about it, and even recited the rhyme on her show, where she was open about the ecstatic disorder of her brain. "It's lithium and Haldol and Haldol and lithium," she chanted in front of her laughing studio audience, and then got them all to sing along. "Can't do without those pals, doll, and so I just live withium." She had had to get used to the word *bipolarity,* because both her mother and grandmother had called it *manic depression* and so *manic depression* felt like the right term for what she had inherited from them, the dangerous darkness sitting every day and every night in the corner of one eye and the blinding brightness in the corner of the other one. The meds had controlled the monster within, just about, but there were bad moments, such as when, during a trip to San Francisco, the elevated mood, the hypomania, seized hold of her and she started running around town buying a slew of expensive artworks—an ancient wooden mask from Cameroon, a set of rare pornographic ukiyo-e drawings from Japan, and a small late Cézanne—which her young assistant, also occasionally her lover, had to return to the galleries later that evening, after explaining her condition to them delicately when she wasn't listening. After this episode her attending health professionals had expressed concern that her condition might be becoming treatment-resistant, and suggested the possibility of electroconvulsive therapy: ECT.

"Shock treatment? You want me to have therapy by voltage?" she demanded. "But my dears, don't you know by now that I'm unshockable?"

Nevertheless, she acquiesced. She had to come off the lithium, the health professionals said, because it could be toxic in combination with the juice. ("Well, that ruins a good song," she told them.) When she awoke from the first treatment her first words were, "So, that felt exceptionally good. And I suppose I should have asked this before, but are there any side effects I should worry about?"

"You may experience some temporary confusion," her senior health professional replied.

"Darling," she said, "how will anyone be able to tell the difference?"

"And there may be some temporary, or in some cases permanent, memory loss."

"Ah," she said. "So I suppose I should have asked this before, but are there any side effects I should worry about?"

SHE HAD TO BE "on" from the moment she walked into the studio until the moment she sank into the car with her dirty martini (up, with olives), and she got through it perfectly every day. Well, most days. There was a Latina woman, a rival who wanted her job, who "sat in" for her on the few occasions when her condition did not allow her to appear. She did not care to recall this woman's name. She had also forgotten the driver's real name. She called him Hoke after the character Hoke Colburn because he might as well have been Morgan Freeman in that movie, he looked and sounded so damn much like him. He saw the moments of collapse and said nothing, not so much because of admiration or loyalty as because to say something would have meant he'd be out on his ear and never get a dime from Miss Daisy again. The most daring thing he had ever said to her was this: "There's sure a lot of different folks in there inside your skin, Miss Daisy. I reckon I've seen twenty or thirty of them and I'm not positive I've seen them all." She hadn't liked that. After that he kept most of his opinions to himself.

On the roof of the old chocolate factory on Lafayette Street there was a high-ceilinged modern penthouse, which could have housed a substantial family, in which Miss Salma R lived alone. The word *alone,* in this context, should be understood to mean "plus hair and makeup, plus personal assistants (three, including the aforementioned casual lover, a white boy named Anderson Thayer who claimed descent from a *Mayflower* pilgrim and who was at least a dozen years younger than Salma, a smallish man with long red hair and a Zapata mustache who reminded her at times of Rumpelstiltskin from the Brothers Grimm and at other times of Yosemite Sam from Looney Tunes), personal publicists (three, two for the U.S., one for India), and security (two, one outside the penthouse door and one inside it, plus one more in the lobby downstairs)." At night this number dropped to two: one assistant in a spare bedroom on call to help with nightmares or other forms of nocturnal anguish (this was a female assistant—definitely not Anderson Thayer, with whom Salma's occasional liaisons were carried out discreetly, away from the eyes of other members of her staff), one security guard (also female) to cope with all other issues. To Salma herself, however, the word *alone* meant "without a serious man in her life." She was grateful (mostly grateful) for Anderson Thayer, who was attentive to her when she was down and managed situations well when she was in the grip of her over-bright upswings, but she thought she might have to fire him soon, because he was getting to be a little too bossy, a little too controlling, for her liking. She would have to fire him from her bed as well, obviously, and then "alone" would become even more alone.

We have not, thus far, explored Salma R's private life in New York City, her dark side, out of respect for her privacy. However, the privacy rights of fictional characters are questionable—to be frank, they are nonexistent—and so we hereby abandon our modesty to reveal that she had had not one but two brief, unsuccessful

marriages, the first to a Los Angeles über-agent who left her for a
handsome young man, and of whom she always thereafter said that
she had turned him gay, the second to a Manhattan-based writer-
director whom she left because, she said, "their neuroses were in-
compatible," and then she added, "Every female character he ever
wrote was me, including all the ones he wrote before we met, and
they all left him." As she said these things in more or less exactly
these words on many nationally syndicated television talk shows,
including her own, we are not probing very deeply into her personal matters by revealing them.

Beneath the comedy, however, there was sadness, and acute self-
doubt. She was proud of being her mother's daughter and her
grandmother's granddaughter but in spite of all her success found it
impossible to feel like their fully fledged inheritor, their peer. This
sense of her inferiority may well have been the unstated determin-
ing factor in her decision to leave the Indian film industry and rein-
vent herself in America, where the cruel generational comparisons
would not be made, or not nearly so often, and where she herself
could escape her own inner voice telling her, *you're just not as good as
them*. On the whole she preferred her American self, though the past
still pulled at her. And then there was the bipolarity, her true inheritance, uniting the three women across time and space.

For all this, there were the proper drugs, and the ECT as well.
And for happiness, there was—there had been for a long time, before America, before the black bird of the family condition had
landed on her shoulder—kickers. Cotton. OC. Orange County.
OxyContin.

Back home it had been easy to get the supplies but even in America there was always a doctor who would bend the rules for a star.
She was told she was living dangerously, playing with fire, but the
scripts for the time-release drug were written for her nevertheless.
To add recreational opioids to the meds she was taking for her mental health was extremely ill-advised, she was advised, but the scripts
went on being written. Words like *life-threatening, respiratory arrest,*

and *death* were used, but the scripts were still written and the pharmacies handed out the painkillers, no problem.

As a cursory glance at the contents of her bathroom cabinet would reveal even to the untutored layperson, Miss Salma R was almost as expert in pharmaceuticals as her compliant pharmacist, so she knew about the dangers of misuse. *Crushing, chewing, snorting, or injecting the dissolved product will result in the uncontrolled delivery of oxycodone and can result in overdose and death.* She knew that. But oh dear she did misuse it. She did not inject the dissolved product, because she was squeamish about needles, plus the tracks would be bad for business. But the uncontrolled delivery of oxycodone was exactly what she wanted. So, regrettably, she crushed, she chewed! Sometimes, it's true, she even snorted! How shocked, how disappointed in her her legion of admirers would have been! Or not, of course. As we have noted, she was explicit about many of her vulnerabilities. Not this one; but maybe her fans would just have added it to the list and loved her even more. At any rate, very few people knew about her habit. Rumpelstiltskin knew. Yosemite Sam knew. Another reason to fire him, though he might try to blackmail her. He would be unwise to try that. She was a powerful woman. He would know it was unwise to try that.

He did try, in his newly controlling way, to stop her. She shrugged off his advice. "I've been doing this for so long," she said, "I'm an expert in self-medication." When she said this he had tossed his long red hair. She had never seen a man toss his hair, so this got her attention.

"Whenever somebody says that," he told her, as his hair subsided in slow-motion as if he were in a L'Oréal commercial, "I think, there are a lot of dead experts in self-medication. I think, Heath Ledger."

"Toss your hair again," she said. "How do you manage to do that slow-motion thing?"

He gave up and grinned. "Because I'm worth it," he said.

If we must get into the dark details, for some while now it hadn't

actually been OxyContin itself. There had been a change in the formula which made it harder to use. When she tried to crush the new
OxyContin OP tablets, they resisted, becoming a gummy mess that
was hard to chew and impossible to snort. She tried burning them in
her microwave. She tried soaking them in acetone, baking them,
freezing them. It was frustrating. She had turned to Perc30s and
Roxies, which were thirty milligrams each of pure oxycodone (you
could get OxyContin tablets containing up to eighty milligrams, so
she needed larger quantities of these lower-dosage painkillers).
Lately there had also been Opana and other, similar versions of oxy-
morphone. As she said, she had become an expert. None of the re-
placements were as satisfying as the old Oxys. Why did the world
have to change? She needed to find a new solution. There were people who had been driven to heroin by the change in the Oxy tablets,
but heroin scared her. The *word* "heroin" scared her. She wouldn't
go there. The things she had now were workable, they would do,
but the old stuff was the best. *Take me away,* she thought when she
was alone in her bed at night and the painkillers were easing her
spirit's pain, *to those old Cotton fields back home.*

When she told her closest people she was having electroconvulsive shock treatment, they reacted badly. You have to stop, they
said. Electricity? You can't do that to yourself, it's like torture. I'm
not conscious when they do it, she explained. This isn't mad scientist stuff, it's medicine. But in a way it did feel like the stuff of fantasy. After the sessions she felt clearer, more in control, and kept
seeing clear images of tiny evil gremlins in her brain being electro-
cuted by the voltage, screaming and tossing as they dissolved into
puffs of smoke. She saw tiny green goblins and stringlike snakes
burning between the spiderwebs of her synapses. She imagined her
brain as a clanking malfunctioning machine filled with cogwheels
and levers, with, literally, a number of screws loose, and the electricity as a superhero zooming around it, tightening nuts and bolts,
adjusting chains, getting everything to pull together. The Incredible
Flash, miniaturized and sent in to do the much-needed repair work.

It felt like a Christmas visit from Sanity Claus. (She heard Chico Marx laughing, Ha-ha-ha-ha-ha! You can't fool me. There *ain't* no Sanity Claus! But there was, there was. He was a voltage-powered elf who cleaned up your sanity.)

She started calling her bipolar friends to recommend the treatment. "You should hundred percent get it," she said. "It's like spring cleaning. Call me afterwards to tell me how you feel. But include in your message your full name and how we know each other, or I won't know who you are." She had quite a few bipolar friends. "We're like magnets," she told everyone who would listen. "Depends which poles are up against each other. Attract and cling tight, or repel and flee." She told her non-bipolar friends to get it too. "It's the new juicing," she said. "My double-detox juice. Super super detox detox. The best cleanse there is. Completely allergy-free. No vegetables were harmed in the making of this product." She started recommending it on the show. "I'm hoping to be the ECT brand ambassador," she told her studio audience. "I'm auditioning right now, and if I could just remember why I'm standing in front of a crowd of strangers, I could put my hand on my heart—if I could remember where my heart is—and tell you the results are perfect, and I could remember what the results are."

Privately, she knew that her condition wasn't particularly funny. She had begun to suffer from acute levels of anxiety and at such times she took refuge in a suite at the Mandarin Oriental hotel on Columbus Circle and made a phone call to Anderson Thayer. "Come here, Rumpelstiltskin," she said, and he came, and she lay in his arms, wondering if this was the right time to fire him, or maybe she'd wait until tomorrow. If she fired him now he'd get angry, and when he got angry he might take hold of his left foot and rip himself in two, right up the middle.

He was the man who knew too much. He had helped her cover up a scandal that could have derailed her career. There had been a third man after the two husbands. This man—she never used his real name, not even in the most private moments, agreeing always to call

him by the fake name he told her he preferred, "Gary Reynolds"—
was a political lobbyist and covert operator, an improbable partner
for her, a man who claimed to have undertaken black ops projects
for successive Republican administrations and to have destabilized
and even overthrown three separate governments in Africa. "Gary
Reynolds" was like the world of her old TV series come to life.
Maybe that was why she fell for him, in spite of his politics. He was
a glamorous, dangerous, exciting fiction become fact. She didn't
even care that he told her he "identified as promiscuous." She didn't
need him around every day, but when he showed up, he was real
fun. The Mandarin Oriental suite was their pleasure dome. Yosemite Sam knew about his rival, and Salma could see it irked him, but
he said nothing and did his job. Then one night she went to the
hotel to meet "Gary," who had texted her to say he was already
there waiting for her, and when she got there he was in bed, naked,
and really very dead, indisputably dead, the most dead a dead person could be. On this occasion the suite was booked in his fake
name, as it always was for their assignations, backed up by a "Gary
Reynolds" credit card, but there were members of staff who recognized her, who knew she was the one who came to see him there.
She stayed calm, held it together, just about, and called Anderson
Thayer. Rumpelstiltskin, I need you. He came over and she kissed
him, once, properly. I need you to fix this, she said. Don't tell me
how, just fix it so it stays fixed. I don't want to know about it. I just
want it done. Do this for me.

He fixed it. Nothing connecting Salma to the death at the Mandarin ever became public. "Gary Reynolds" was buried at Mount
Zion Cemetery in Queens beneath a stone bearing his real name,
which there is no need to record here, and at once it was as if he had
been erased from history. She began to feel a great sense of relief.
The scandal had passed her by, like the thunderstorms that skirted
Manhattan and did their worst to New Jersey. This was when she
first thought of firing Anderson Thayer. The fact that he literally
knew where the body was buried, so that firing him from her bed as

well as his job could have catastrophic consequences, made it necessary to find a way to do it. Nobody was allowed to have that kind of power over her. She would not permit it. She thought of Tommy Lee Jones and Will Smith's memory-eraser sticks, their neuralyzers, in the *Men in Black* movies. She needed one of those. Or some real-life equivalent. She looked into the subject and found that researchers at UC Davis had successfully erased memories from the brains of mice by using beams of light, just as the neuralyzers had in the movies. But mice were not human beings. There wasn't a human version available as yet.

Maybe Anderson Thayer needed ECT. A *lot* of ECT. Maybe that was the actually existing way to have his memory erased.

When the show was on hiatus she often didn't get out of bed. She was a recluse in these weeks, and the only way to see her was to ascend into her sanctum, if she permitted you to do so. Her friends, male and female, were invited over to sit on the bed while she ranted about whatever had gotten her goat that day, usually one of her two ex-husbands. These soliloquies could last an hour or more, and it was necessary simply to hear them out. They were the price of admission to her private world, which she had populated with kitsch collectibles of all sorts, the collection of kitsch being her way of disguising her profound uninterest in serious art. She was a secret bidder on auctions of memorabilia from the collections of other talk-show hosts, living and dead, and at these auctions she had acquired one of Babe Ruth's gloves as well as hats worn by Frank Sinatra, Marilyn Monroe, Humphrey Bogart, James Cagney, John Wayne, and Mae West. Her vintage jukebox was full of singles by one-hit wonders, "Sugar, Sugar," "Macarena," "Spirit in the Sky," "Don't Worry, Be Happy," "Mambo No. 5," "Ice Ice Baby," "99 Red Balloons," "Who Let the Dogs Out?" "Video Killed the Radio Star," "I'm Too Sexy," "Play That Funky Music," and "Sea Cruise." On her walls was her prized collection of Indian street and store signs, *Restricted Area for Dead Bodies, Hand Job Nails & Spa, Avoid Victims of Spurious Drinks, Don't Touch Yourself—Ask the Staff, Do Not*

Stand on Zoo Fences—If You Fall, Animals Might Eat You And That Might Make Them Sick, Caution Extremely Horny, Beware Ferocious Dogs and Ghosts, Tailor Specialist in Alteration of Ladies & Gents, Go Slow—Accident Porn Area, Drive Like Hell And You Will Get There, and *Vagina Tandoori*. There was also her Emmy, which she positioned on a bedroom shelf that you couldn't see if the bedroom door was open.

She was a woman who concealed her secrets behind bedroom doors and comedy masks. Beneath the surface she worried about finding happiness. She was aware that after her two failed marriages and one dead body, she had put up high fences around her heart, and she didn't know if she would ever meet a man who would persuade her to lower them, or who would be strong enough to demolish her defense system and take her heart by storm. She thought a lot about loneliness, about growing old feeling isolated and alone. On New Year's Eve she rented a boat to watch the fireworks from the water, and just before the midnight hour, when the display was about to start, she realized that everybody aboard the vessel—the captain, the crew, the assistants, and so on—was in her employ. It's New Year's and I have no friends, she thought. I have to pay for people to come and have fun with me.

She had no child. That was another thing. She couldn't even allow herself to think about that because it would plunge her down a rabbit hole toward grief.

While we are uncovering Salma's dark secrets we should not lose sight of the fact that *Salma* continued to be the biggest show of its kind. As well as the lighthearted fare that was the show's stock-in-trade, and the emotional/confessional material, and the debates on women's issues of the moment, she had recently introduced a segment called "While Black" intended to highlight the problems faced by persons of color in America, and this had generated much comment, inevitable controversy, and even higher Nielsen ratings. "While Black" invited onto the show the men who had been arrested at a coffee shop because a white member of staff called the police when they asked to use the restroom while black and waiting for a white friend, and the men on whom a white golfer called the police because they were golfing too slowly while black, and the men at a gym on whom a white man at the gym called the police because, well, because they were exercising while black, and the women on whom the police were called because they were shopping for prom dresses while black, or napping in their own dorm common room at an Ivy League college while black, or renting an Airbnb property while black, or sitting in their own airplane seats while black and a white passenger found them to be "pungent." Such was the power of *Salma* that the show was able to shame the white accusers who had made the calls to the police into coming along to confess, recognize their own prejudices, apologize, seek forgiveness, hug, and so on. The segment made her a shoo-in for a second Emmy, she was assured, and more importantly was a real contribution to the conversation about race in America. She wanted somebody to hug her when the network bosses told her of their appreciation, someone to take her out for a celebration, to send her flowers and tell her she was wonderful. She wanted love. Instead, she had Anderson Thayer.

When she faced the emptiness of her life she knew that the world would have no sympathy for the way she felt. She was a privileged woman complaining about small things. A woman whose life was lived on the surface, who had chosen superficiality, had no right to complain about the absence of depth. Human life was lived between two chasms, a Russian writer had said, the one that preceded our birth, "the cradle rocks above an abyss," and the one we were all "heading for (at some forty-five hundred heartbeats an hour)." She was suffering from some sort of existential panic. She needed to put it away. But on the days after the electricity, as the confusion faded and her memory returned, she felt the presence of gaps. There were missing days, missing pages in the book of life. She reached back for childhood, for her mother, for India, and felt the dear remembrances of things past slipping through her fingers like sand. *I sigh the lack of many a thing I sought*. I have to go back soon, she told herself, I need to reclaim it or it will be gone, I will be gone from it, and nobody will mourn my loss. She thought about Wile E. Coyote rushing out over the chasm and not falling until he looked down. *That's me,* her weak voice thought, and then her strong voice answered, *Then don't look down.*

She went to work. She made herself available to the Indian media and said she would return soon and was looking out for a suitable vehicle, and within hours of the story running she had a dozen movie scripts to choose from, and expressions of delight from all the top leading men. She initiated a conversation with a major movie studio about making a big-budget *Five Eyes* movie which she would co-produce and in which she would lead the American defense against a ruthless foreign cyber-attack. The movie executives said, fabulous, and this would be an attack by a mysterious secret organization, right?, like SPECTRE or Kingsman or Hydra or ICE or SWORD. She laughed. "Why should we play it so coy?" she demanded. "Can't we just call it Russia?" She did cover shoots for half a dozen women's magazines and sat in on editorial conferences of her own glossy monthly, named *S*. She took part in amfAR fundraisers and emceed the Robin Hood gala. And back at the *Salma* offices she told her team, "I want to take myself out of the studio. I want to look out into the reddest parts of red-state America and be the person to whom the bigotry happens."

"You're too famous," they told her, "your recognizability will get in the way."

"My grandmother the movie legend always told me she had two different ways of walking out of her front door," she said. "She showed me. First she walked out as the great movie star and everybody went insane, cars crashed into one another, so did people. Then later she walked out 'as nobody,' that's how she put it. And this time nobody looked and she walked down the street unnoticed. My mother learned the trick from her and I learned from them both. I can do this. I can be anonymous and you'll have hidden cameras and we'll see what flyover America has to say to a brown woman out there on her own."

And there was one more new segment. Salma had been deeply affected by a letter from Dr. Fred's Place in Bloomington, Indiana (pop. 84,465), one of a very small group of freestanding inpatient pediatric hospice facilities in the United States. "There are thirty such houses in the UK," the letter read, "but if you counted the American locations on the fingers of one hand, you'd have a finger or a thumb to spare." Palliative care for children with terminal cancer was a difficult area. Many dying children, and their parents, didn't want the end to come in the sterile atmosphere of a hospital ward, and yet in many cases home care presented problems, and could be prohibitively expensive. Dr. Fred's created a homelike environment in which families could feel like families, and be given emotional support as well as the necessary medical attention, as they faced what had to be faced. "It would be fantastic," Dr. Fred wrote, "if you could give the American hospice movement a boost by putting it on your show, and beyond wonderful for the kids if you felt like coming to see them, or sending us one or two of your famous friends." Two weeks later the whole *Salma* team arrived in Bloomington and Miss Salma R hosted the show from Dr. Fred's, accompanied by her good buddies Priyanka Chopra, Kerry Washington, and, yes, Ms. Winfrey too, Oprah!, her very own divine self, in a special guest appearance. They played with the children, they hugged the children's mothers, and their brothers and sisters. They hugged the fathers too. It was a good day. The cameras got it all.

Near the end of the day, Dr. Fred led Salma to a room set apart from the other rooms. They didn't go in, looking, instead, through the window inset in the closed door, at a tableau of sorrow, a Chinese family, father, mother, two sisters, gathered around an unconscious teenage boy on his deathbed wearing an Indiana University sweatshirt. There were some patients, Dr. Fred told Salma in a whisper, for whom the pain was so intense that their families wanted them sedated and for the most part unconscious. If they were conscious for brief periods there was a risk that they might suffer break-through pain, and so, for these moments, Dr. Fred reluctantly okayed the use of a powerful opioid spray.

"What is that?" Salma asked.

"It's a version of fentanyl," Dr. Fred told her, "but because it's in spray form we can apply it sublingually and it has an immediate effect."

Miss Salma R grew thoughtful. "That's one powerful painkiller," she said after some reflection. "What's it called?"

"TIRF. Transmucosal immediate-release fentanyl. It comes from SPI."

"Spy?"

"Ess pee eye," Dr. Fred explained. "Smile Pharmaceuticals Inc., over in Atlanta. The brand name is InSmile."

"Sent by a smile," Miss Salma R murmured.

"Excuse me?"

"Nothing," she replied.

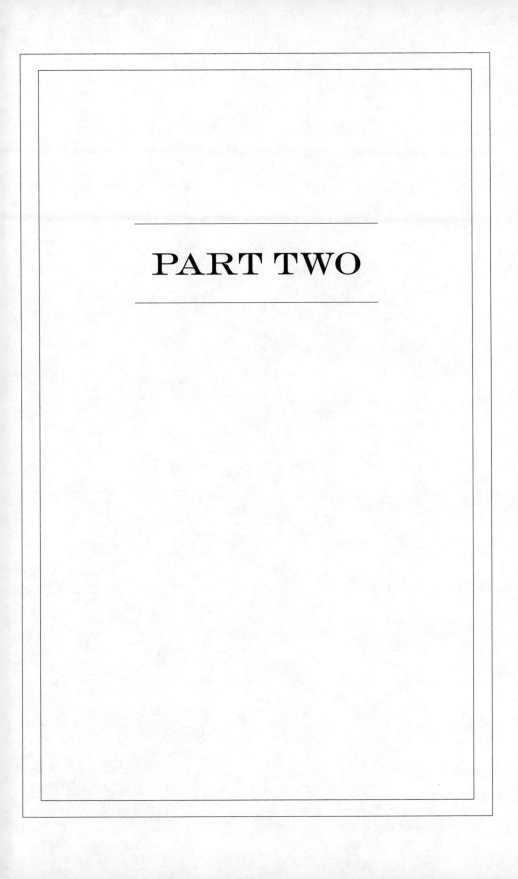

PART TWO

PART TWO

CHAPTER NINE

An Unpleasantness at Lake Capote, & subsequent Disturbances in Reality

*L*ABOR DAY. THE JOURNEY TO THE VALLEY OF LOVE HAD to wait, because first there was trouble to overcome at the camp. It was in Quichotte's nature to assume that everyone who approached him came in friendship, and he greeted all strangers with his delightful and (usually) disarming smile; so when the wide-bodied young white lady in denim dungarees, her fair hair gathered behind her head in a loose bun, came bustling toward the trestle table at Lake Capote where he and Sancho were poring over the map of America just recently anointed by the osprey's sign, Quichotte stood up courteously and even bowed slightly. In his formal way he was about to launch into a little speech of greeting when the lady went on the attack.

"What is that?" the white lady said, jerking a thumb in the direction of the map. "You hatching some kind of scheme?"

"We are travelers like yourself," Quichotte replied mildly, "so it is not unreasonable that we should map out our route."

"Where are your turbans and beards?" the white lady asked, her arm extended toward him, an angry finger pointing right at him. "You people wear beards and turbans, right? You shave your faces and take the headgear off to fool us? T u r b a n s," she repeated slowly, making a swirling turban gesture around her head.

"I think I can say without fear of inaccuracy that I have never worn a turban in my life," Quichotte replied, with a degree of puzzlement that displeased his interrogator.

"You got a bad foreign look to you," the white lady said. "Sound foreign too."

"I suspect few of the campers at Lake Capote are from around here," Quichotte said, still smiling his increasingly inappropriate smile. "It's a destination for visitors, is it not? You yourself must have driven some distance to get here?"

"That's something. *You* asking *me* where *I'm* from? Imma tell you where I'm from. I'm from *America*. Who knows how *you* got here. This ain't a place for you. You shouldn't be allowed past the border controls. How'd you get in? You look like you come from a country on that no-entry list. You hitch a ride with a Mexican? What you lookin' for in America? What's your purpose? That map. I'm not loving the map."

At this point Sancho, in his youthful, hotheaded way, intervened. "Ma'am," he said (that part at least was polite). "Why don't you do yourself a favor and don't be in our business."

That was fuel on the flame. She rounded on Sancho and stabbed her finger in his direction. "Imma tell you the word on *you*," she said. "Seems you keep showing up and vanishing but that car there, it don't move. Where do you come from? Where do you go? Are there more of you holed up somewhere close, appearing, disappearing, hidin' out, who the hell knows? You look shifty to me. You up to something. You can dress yourself out of J.Crew but you don't fool me."

A small crowd had gathered and it was getting bigger as the woman's voice got louder. Two camp security guards came up.

Uniforms, holstered guns, a judge-and-jury way with them. "You two are disturbing the peace," one said. He wasn't looking at the white lady. "You need to pack up and get gone," the second guard said.

"What's your religion?" the white lady asked.

"It is my good fortune," Quichotte replied, no longer so courteously, "that having passed through the first valley, my son and I are both blessedly freed from doctrines of all sorts."

"Say what?" said the white lady.

"I have cast aside all dogma, both of belief and unbelief," Quichotte said. "I am embarked on a high spiritual quest for purification to be worthy of my Beloved."

A man's voice from the crowd: "He's saying he's godless scum."

"He's planning something for sure," the white lady said. "He's got a map. He could be ISIS."

"He can't be ISIS and godless scum at the same time," the first security guard pointed out, displaying an admirable capacity for logical thinking, and trying to maintain order. "Let's not get carried away, ladies and gents."

"In ancient times," Quichotte said, in a last appeal to reason, "when a woman was accused of witchcraft, the proofs were that she had a 'familiar,' usually a cat, plus a broomstick and a third nipple for the Devil to suck on. But almost all homes had cats and brooms and in those days many people's bodies had warts. Thus the mere accusation, *witch!,* was all that was required. The proof was in every home and on every woman's body and therefore all women so accused were automatically guilty."

"You need to quit talking trash and leave," the second security guard said. "These folks here are pretty uncomfortable about your presence at Capote and you talking that way is no help. We can't guarantee your safety much longer and I'm not so sure we're even inclined to do so."

Sancho looked as if he wanted the fight. But in the end he and

Quichotte packed their possessions into the Cruze. The crowd grumbled but slowly dispersed. The white lady, encouraged to back off by the security guards, stood a little way off, shaking her head.

"In the old days," the white lady yelled as they drove away, "there'd have been some frontier justice done today."

She was wearing some strange type of choker around her neck. It looked almost like a collar you'd put on your dog.

SANCHO, A SOMEWHAT LESS IMAGINARY being than before, considers his new situation.

After the business with the white lady everything changed. And FYI, if I accidentally said a little prayer a while ago it's not because I suddenly got religion, it's because it's pretty scary being driven by him. "Daddy." He drives the way he does everything, *the way he sees it done on TV*. He drove out of that camp at Lake Capote like he was Al or Bobby Unser at Indianapolis, and he hasn't slowed down since. I sit in the back seat because it feels safer there, but he twists his head around and talks to me while he's doing maybe fifty-five or sixty down a two-lane blacktop, because that happens all the time on the shows, only when that happens on the shows the car is attached to a truck offscreen that's doing the real driving. Half a dozen times a day I think, I'm about to find out if there's an afterlife five minutes after I got myself a life. If I'm real, I can really die, right? I'm leaning now against the side of the Cruze in a gas station drinking a Coke, wiping the cold sweat of passenger terror off of my forehead, and thinking about this Real thing, i.e., the question of being real, and I'm getting the uncomfortable feeling that the question's about to be answered thanks to an imminent fatal smashup on the road. I have to add that if, after I turn into roadkill and float up through the twisted metal, I find a God up there on the judgment seat, if *that* turns out to be what's real, clouds, pearly gates, flights of angels, all that jazz, it's going to be a shock. But I'm not wanting to get into a discussion about Paradise today. For now I just want to feel safe in the back seat of the car. That's the only seat on my mind. Slow down, I tell him, watch the road. I even yell at him, but he just waves a hand in the air. I've been driving for a *living,* he tells me. I've been doing this since before you were born. Yeah, I tell him, but that wasn't so long ago, was it.

Please do not forget, I was literally born yesterday. Well, literally, a little before yesterday, but you get my point. I'm a lot younger than I look, because I'm growing up fast. Also my head is full of him, his version of everything, so it's hard for me to stand outside and see him for what he is. Even now, after I Pinocchioed myself into flesh and blood, I can't see myself as a being that's totally apart from him. I'm still more a-part-of than apart-from, see. I hate to say it, because it's easy to observe he's not the best of captains, but he's still the one steering the ship. I'm thinking now about the hunt for the great white whale. Obvs the only way I know about this is that he (a) read the book in a motel room sometime when the TV was on the fritz, or, yes, this is the right answer, (b) he watched Gregory Peck, Richard Basehart, and Leo Genn in the old movie on AMC back in the wall-to-wall rerun days before *Mad Men, Breaking Bad,* and *The Walking Dead.* Anyway, here's my thought. The mad captain who's obsessed by the whale dies with the whale along with his crew who are almost as whale-crazy as he is. Ishmael, the one crew member who isn't obsessed, the one character who's just along for the ride, it's just a job to him, he's the one who lives to tell the tale. From which we learn the lesson that detachment is the key to survival. Obsession destroys the possessed. Something like that. So if the old Cruze is our *Pequod* then I guess Miss Salma R is the big fish and he, "Daddy," is my Ahab.

Which leads me to inquire: Did she do something to him sometime? Did she bite off his metaphorical leg? Which is a sex metaphor, right. *Leg* being obvs a what's the word. Euphemism. A stand-in word for Some Other Limb. And *wooden leg* being a term containing the word *wood.* (Hahaha, laughing-face-with-tears-coming-out-of-the-eyes emoji.) Or: is it just her being in the world and ignoring him that makes him feel, what's the word, wooden-legged? If the Beloved is oblivious to the lover, might the lover want to hunt her down and harpoon her? Might he want to end up tied to her by harpoon ropes and drown with her ecstatically in the black depths of the sea? *From hell's heart I stab at thee.* Interesting, no?, that that's the line from the book that stuck in his head (and therefore I have it in mine)? Which leads to the million-dollar question: What does he want to do with her if/when he ever gets close enough to do anything (which is pretty fucking improbable)? Kiss or kill? There are bits of his head I don't have access to. The answer to my question may lie in those hidden bits.

Follow-up question: *Why* are there bits of his head that deny me access? How does this being-a-part-of-him thing actually work? Okay, I'm guessing here, but here's the way I'm looking at it. I see myself as a visitor in his inner world, and I see that world as an actual place, with, like, cities and countryside and lakes and such. With transportation systems. And across a lot of that world I have no obstacles, I can roam about freely and have access to everything he has access to, to episodes in his past, and shows he's watched, and books he's read, and people he has known, and the whole what's the word. Population. Of his memories and knowledge and thoughts and maybe even dreams. But as I see more and more clearly, he isn't well in the head, and I reckon the parts I can't see are the crazy parts, the parts that are so messed up that the gateways to them are blocked, so ruined that the houses in there have fallen down, like what you see on TV about bombed-out war zones, in, like, Syria. Those parts are like scrambled jigsaw puzzles, or fogbound, or just destroyed, there aren't any planes landing there, the roads are fucked, and maybe they're land-mined also, the whole area is sealed off by, for example, let's say, UN peacekeeping forces, the blue helmet dudes, what do they call them. Smurfs. Which means there's no entry. Not unless the Smurfs let you in.

I think we're both disturbed by what happened at Lake Capote. Daddy Q looks like his thoughts are whirling around him like windmills. Right now he just seems lost. After the bird splat at the lake I thought, fine, at least now we're going somewhere. New York or bust. Start spreading the news. We're heading there like everyone does, to be loved or broken, to be born again or to die. What else is there to do that's worth doing? Nothing. There's a woman waiting there for him. She doesn't know she's waiting but she is. Or she does know but she isn't waiting, she doesn't care, and when he learns that lesson then that will be the end of him. And meanwhile, if I may what's the word, interject: What about me? Maybe this adventure could have someone in it for me? That's what I'm interested in. I have an imaginary girlfriend in my head and I need to turn her into a real one. She's walking the New York streets and she's lonely just like me, and wait, what do I see? Is she walking back to me? . . . That's my pretty-woman dream-balloon right there but his behavior is bursting it.

After the confrontation at Lake Capote it's like the balance of his mind got disturbed. If he was at least partly clear-minded before, he's all unclear now. "New York" seems to have become a vague concept. "Sure, sure," he mutters when I ask him. "We'll get there. It's like the valleys," he says, "it's a state of mind." Most days, now, all he wants is a motel and a TV—that's the world that's real to him, and this world, the one with unfriendly white ladies in it, is what he wants to shut out—and sometimes I think that's all there's going to be, this endless drifting and watching and no arriving, an Odyssey without an Ithaca, without a Penelope, and myself a displaced Telemachus doomed to wander with him, far from any idea of destination or home, far, I have to repeat this, from girls.

I'm new here. I'm trying to understand how the world works, his world, the only one available to me. The world according to Quichotte. I'm trying to get a sense of the normal, but it keeps dissolving around me. On TV, because (having no option) I'm watching a lot of TV myself now, everybody seems to know what normal is, and at the same time nobody agrees. I'm using the remote to find out.

"Is this what's normal?" I ask him. "A couch in a living room with a staircase behind it and an armchair to the side, and a father in the armchair and a mom in the kitchen and teenage children rushing in and out wanting sandwiches and quarreling but every thirty minutes minus commercials there's a group hug?"

"Yes," he says. "Life is like this for normal people."

"Or," I say, "is normal a couch in a living room with a staircase behind it and an armchair to the side and a loud woman's big comeback killed by a tweet referencing Muslim Brotherhood and *Planet of the Apes*?"

"That's a less normal normal," he says.

Zap. Sports channel. Normal is nine innings, four balls, three strikes, somebody wins, somebody loses, there's no such thing as a tie. Zap. Normal is unreal people, mostly rich unreal people, having sex with rappers and basketball players and thinking of their unreal family as a real-world brand, like Pepsi or Drano or Ford. Zap. News channels. Normal is guns and the normal America that really wants to be great again. Then there's another normal if your skin color is the wrong color and another if you're educated and another if you think education is brainwashing and there's an America that believes in vaccines for kids and another that says that's a con trick and everything one normal believes is a lie to another normal and they're all on TV depending where you look, so, yeah, it's confusing. I'm really trying to understand which *this* is America now. Zap zap zap. A man with his head in a bag being shot by a man without a shirt on. A fat man in a red hat screaming at men and women also fat also in red hats about victory, *We're undereducated and overfed. We're full of pride over who the f*ck knows. We drive to the emergency room and send Granny to get our guns and cigarettes. We don't need no stinkin' allies cause we're stupid and you can suck our dicks. We are Beavis and Butt-Head on 'roids. We drink Roundup from the can. Our president looks like a Christmas ham and talks like Chucky. We're America, bitch.* Zap. *Immigrants raping our women every day. We need Space Force because Space ISIS.* Zap. Normal is Upside-Down Land. Our old friends are our enemies now and our old enemy is our pal. Zap, zap. Men and men, women and women in love. The purple mountains' majesty. A man with an oil painting of himself with Jesus hanging in his living room. Dead schoolkids. Hurricanes. Beauty. Lies. Zap, zap, zap.

"Normal doesn't feel so normal to me," I tell him.

"It's normal to feel that way," he replies.

This is what I get instead of fatherly wisdom.

Meanwhile, things fall apart as well as people. Countries fall apart as well as their citizens. A zillion channels and nothing to hold them together. Garbage out there, and great stuff out there, too, and they both coexist at the same level of reality, both give off the same air of authority. How's a young person supposed to tell them apart? How to discriminate? Every show on every network tells you the same thing: based upon a true story. But that's not true either. The true story is there's no true story anymore. There's no *true* anymore that anyone can agree on. There's a headache beginning in here. Boom! Here it is.

Ow.

What a time for me to arrive.

Something is going wrong, even I can tell that. Something's badly off, not only with him, but also with the world outside the motel room. Some error in space and time. The motel room itself is unchanging wherever we are, whatever the name on the illuminated sign above the forecourt. Inside the room things are pretty constant. Twin beds, TV, pizza delivery, floral-print curtains. In the bathroom plastic cups wrapped in plastic bags. Small refrigerator, empty. Nightstand lamps, one bulb working (by his bedside), one not (by mine). Paper-thin walls, so there's other entertainment if we don't want to watch TV. (But we do, we always do.) There's a lot of shouting. People drink in motel rooms from bottles in brown paper bags, and then they shout, they yell their lonely sadness into the empty night, but they also yell at each other (if they aren't traveling alone), or down the phone, or at the motel staff. (These are few in number, shoulder-shrugging in attitude, just sometimes rapid-

silence-inducing large and menacing, but more frequently Tony
Perkins-y. Black, white, Hispanic, South Asian Bates Motel Tony
Perkinses with small mysterious psycho smiles. I'd be scared of
them. I *am* scared of them. I keep my voice down.) There's less sex
than you'd think. There is some, mostly perfunctory, mostly paid
for, the price probably not high. I say probably because at this point
sex remains beyond my personal experience. If I had a credit card I
might try to rectify that. He has not as yet provided me with usable
plastic. Therefore I remain, tragically, angrily, a virgin.

What there mostly is, is snoring. The music of the American
nose is a thing to be awestruck by. The machine gun, the wood-
pecker, the MGM lion, the drum solo, the dog bark, the dog yap,
the whistle, the idling car engine, the racing-car turbo booster, the
hiccup, the SOS snorts—three short, three long, three short—the
long growl of the ocean wave, the more menacing rumble of rolling
thunder, the short splash of the sleeping sneeze, the two-tone tennis
player's grunt, the simple breathe-in breathe-out common or garden snore, the constantly surprising erratic snore with unpredictable, randomized intervals, the motorcycle, the lawnmower, the
hammer drill, the sizzling frying pan, the log fire, the shooting
range, the war zone, the morning cockerel, the nightingale, the fireworks display, the tunnel at rush hour, the traffic jam, the Alban
Berg, the Schoenberg, the Webern, the Philip Glass, the Steve
Reich, the feedback loop, the static of the untuned radio, the rattle-
snake, the death rattle, the castanets, the washboard, the hum. These
and others are my nightly friends. Fortunately I am blessed with the
gift of sleep. I close my eyes and I'm off. I never remember my
dreams. I think that I do not as yet possess the capacity for dreams.
I suspect I have no imagination. I reckon I'm a pretty WYSIWYG
type.

Which makes it even more unnerving that the world outside the
motel room has totally ceased to be straightforward. I'm just going
to say this straight out even though it makes me sound like Daddy
Q's not the only one with a screw loose. Here it is: *When I wake up*

in the morning and open the door of the motel room I can't be sure of which town I'll find outside, or what day of the week or what month of the year. I can't even be sure of which state we'll be in, although I'm in a great state about it, thank you very much. It's as if we're standing still and the world is traveling past us. Or maybe the world is TV and I don't know who's in charge of the zapper. So maybe there is a God? Is that the third person in here? A God who's fucking with me and with everybody else for that matter, arbitrarily changing the rules? I thought there were rules about changing the rules. I thought, even if I buy the idea that somebody slash something created all this, isn't that something slash somebody bound by the laws of creation once it's slash he's done creating? Or can he slash it just shrug shoulders and say, no more gravity, and goodbye, we all float off into space? And if this entity—let's call it God because why not, it's traditional— can in fact change the rules just because it feels in the mood, let's understand what exactly is the rule that's being changed here. There's a rule that goes, places must remain in the same physical re- lationship to other places, and if you want to get from one place to the other you've got to travel the same distance, full stop, always and forever. You'd think that was a pretty goddamn immutable rule, otherwise what happens to all the roads and trains and planes? How would it be if, for example, you decided to live as far away from your mother-in-law as possible, and then boom, you wake up and open your door and she's standing on your doorstep with a cake because her house just moved in across the road? How do we even begin to understand what a town is or a city if motels can slide across space and time from one to the other? What happens to population counts and electoral rolls? The whole system collapses, doesn't it? Is that what You're after? You're like the deranged worker with a sledgehammer in the old plumber joke, smashing up company toi- lets and railway station washrooms and writing up that slogan, how does it go again, if the cistern cannot be changed it must be de- stroyed. Jesus Christ. It's the end of the fucking world happening right outside my motel door.

Today, for example. This morning.

Last night I go to sleep in the Drury Inn in Amarillo, Texas (pop. 199,582, if that even means anything anymore), and I dream about yesterday at the Cadillac Ranch art installation out on Route 66, all those fifties Eldorado fins diving into or maybe backing up out of the Texas earth, *Cadillac, Cadillac, Long and dark, shiny and black,* thank you, Bruce, he's singing to me in my dream, *buddy when I die throw my body in the back, and drive me to the junkyard in my Cadillac.* Amarillo's some kind of a wild dream itself, man, they harvest helium in the fields here and they assemble those nucular weapons over at Pantex, they pack a lot of meat and they eat a lot of beef, they got Emmylou Harris's lost boyfriend playing the pinball machines, and they all meet down at the Cadillac Ranch. Great dream, I have to say. Fast cars, big sky, hot girls in cutoffs dancing in ten-gallon hats. I'm loving it. And then I wake up and I take a look outside and I almost faint. I'm on a balcony up on maybe the tenth floor, instead of the first floor with the car parked right outside the door of the room. My head spins. Where am I? Where is this exactly? And even more scarily: *When* is this? Because over there, poking its head up above the transformed streets that don't look like Amarillo at all, is the old World Trade Center itself. Yeah, the one the planes hit. The Twin Towers, except there's only one of them. It's impossible but it's there. So maybe we somehow time- and space-traveled and we've made it to New York, but not New York now. New York *then*. We're somehow back on that horrible day and the South Tower fell already which is why I can't see it.

But.

This doesn't look like New York City, not at any point in its history. This is a different place. The tower standing over there, it isn't big enough. Did everything get miniaturized when I wasn't looking? Honey, I shrunk the world? I call out to him and make him get out of bed and take a look. "Where the hell are we," I ask him, "and how did we get here?" I'm freaked out, and he hears it in my voice.

"Tulsa, Oklahoma (pop. 403,090)," he says, and he's using his kind, soothing Dad voice. "Is there a problem?"

I can't believe what he's saying. "Yes, there's a problem," I say. "What happened to Amarillo? Isn't this the Amarillo Drury Inn? Isn't that where we checked in last night? And by the way, how come there's a Twin Tower over there?"

"There are no Drury locations in Oklahoma," says he. "This is the Tulsa DoubleTree."

I lunge past him to grab the notepad by the phone. *DoubleTree by Hilton, Tulsa,* it reads. I'm losing my mind. Can stuff like this happen now?

HE'S BEHAVING AS IF nothing happened. "Yes, we drove here," he says, "you were sleeping, you don't remember? The elevator, you were pleased to be up high for once, you crashed. It's bizarre that you don't remember at all."

I look at him hard. I'm trying to see if he's gaslighting me. "It's not the first time," I say.

"What isn't?" he asks.

"This location dislocation," I say.

He just shakes his head. "Have some coffee," he suggests. "It will clear your thoughts."

"What's the date?" I ask him, and he tells me. This is worse. This is not the day after yesterday. How did we get to September 11 already? It's fucked up.

And of course a part of me is thinking, Maybe I'm not as fully human as I thought. Maybe there are blackouts, moments of nonexistence, bugs in the program. Maybe I just freeze like a FaceTime image when the Wi-Fi's weak and then eventually unfreeze. Is that what he wants me to think? Because that way I have to defer to him at all times, is that what he wants, a deferential, non-independent-minded kid? Am I getting paranoid? You bet I am. And then I think of something even worse. That insula of mine is working overtime and coming up with nothing but bad news. Maybe, according to my insula, this is the way things are these days in America: that for some of us, the world stopped making sense. Anything can happen. Here can be there, then can be now, up can be down, truth can be lies. Everything's slip-sliding around and there's nothing to hold on to. The whole thing has come apart at the seams. For some of us, who have started seeing the stuff the rest of us are too blind to see. Or too determined not to see it. For them, it's shrug, business as usual, the Earth's still flat and the climate still isn't changing. Down there on the street, cars full of the shruggers are driving around, shrugger pedestrians are walking to work, the ghost of Woody Guthrie is walking its ribbon of highway singing this land was made for you and me. Even Woody hasn't heard the end-of-the-world news.

"Anyway," I say, "you haven't explained *that*."

I'm pointing at the tower which is the ghost of the other tower, what is that doing in fucking Oklahoma. And of course he has an explanation for that too. It's well known, it has a name and a street address, it was built by the same architect, Yamasaki, and it's supposed to be a smaller-scale replica. Move along, kid. Nothing to see here. Calm down. Let's get some eggs.

I'm beginning to understand why people get religion. Just to have something solid that doesn't change into a slippery snake without a word of warning. Something eternal: how comforting when you can't trust yourself to wake up in the same town you went to sleep in. Metamorphosis is frightening, revolutions end up killing more people than the regimes they overthrew, a change is not as good as a rest. I don't know how many people there are out there who have started seeing what I'm seeing, experiencing what I'm experiencing, but I bet I'm not the only one. In which case there are a lot of frightened people out there. A lot of terrified visionaries. Even the prophets, when visions started talking to them, at first thought they were going mad.

He's frightened too. Daddy Q. After Lake Capote, something

happened to that innocent trust in people he always had. Maybe things haven't fully come apart for him, not yet, but I know he's shaken. Let's see how he goes forward. If he does. I'm watching him.

Also, I'm going to start looking out for those people. The ones like me with the end time in their eyes.

CHAPTER TEN

In *which they pass through the*
Second Valley, Sancho, too, finds Love,
& thereafter, in the Third Valley,
they pass beyond Knowledge itself

"IN THE VALLEY OF LOVE," QUICHOTTE SAID, "ONE'S GOAL is the pursuit of Love itself, not the small though often beautiful individual love of one man for one woman, or one man for one man, or one woman for one woman, or whatever more contemporary combination you prefer, and in this category I include my love for my own, destined, inevitable, soon-to-be Beloved; nor the admittedly noble love between parent and child, although I readily express my gratitude that such a love has entered my life; nor the love of country, nor even, for those inclined toward such an emotion, the love of God or of gods; but rather Love itself, the purity of the grand essential phenomenon, the subject unattached to any specific object, the heart of the heart of the heart, the eye of the storm, the driving force of all human and much animal nature, and therefore of life itself. One's goal is the shedding of mental obstacles that prevent one from being flooded with the glorious universal, Love as Being. It is a goal, therefore, that requires of us the absolute and irreversible abandonment of reason, for love is without reason, above it and beyond it; it comes without a rational explanation and lives on when there is no reason for it to survive."

It was morning in the Billy Diner, "Tulsa's go-to for breakfast," and he had ordered green eggs and ham. Sancho got involved with a big plate of huevos rancheros. They looked ordinary, an older guy and his son or maybe even grandson, eating an unsurprising morning meal, but they were attracting attention. It was as if, Sancho thought, that white lady's pointing finger had put the mark of Cain on them both, and now wherever they went there would be suspicion and hostility.

Until this point in his brief life he had not thought of himself as Other, as worthy of disapproval simply by virtue of being who he was. Well, of course, in reality, he was totally Other, a supernatural entity plucked out of nowhere by Quichotte's desire and the grace of the cosmos, he was as Other as it was possible to be, but that wasn't the Other these people were disapproving of, the Other toward whom the white lady had pointed that accusing finger. He was trying to imagine himself into being a regular young human guy in a lumberjack shirt and blue jeans and boots, a dude who was discovering that he liked the music of Justin Timberlake, Bon Jovi, John Mellencamp, and Willie Nelson. He did not like hip-hop or bhangra or sitar music or the blues. He liked Lana Del Rey. But he was learning for the first time the potentially lethal otherness of the skin. "Keep your voice down," he said. "Everyone can hear you."

When Quichotte adopted his declamatory manner to pontificate on whatever was on his mind, his voice frequently rose to public-meeting levels, a fact of which he was happily unaware. The diner was not crowded but those eyes that were there to see turned in his direction, those ears that were there to hear involuntarily heard what he had to say, those mouths that were not full of food were saying things that weren't quite loud enough to hear, and those foreheads that were there to frown crumpled into uncomprehending, but nevertheless inimical, folds.

"Listen to me," Sancho whispered urgently. "Eat up and let's go.

They are looking at us like we're ghosts, by which I don't mean that we're invisible, more that we're spooking them. We're the kind of ghosts people want to bust. Because we're here they think the diner is a haunted house. You can see it in their eyes. Where's Bill Murray when you need him, that's what they're thinking. Maybe we need to get out of the red states, you know what I mean? What's the nearest blue state? Maybe let's go there."

There were moments when Quichotte seemed to be living in a dream, oblivious to his surroundings. Sancho, for all his fictionality, at such times felt like he was the real person and Quichotte the figment. "In Europe," Quichotte airily remarked, "the colors of political affiliation are reversed, and so blue is the color of conservatives, reactionaries, and capitalists, while red stands for communism, socialism, democratic socialism, and social democracy. I ask myself sometimes: what is the color of love? It's hard to find one that isn't used up already. Saffron is the color of Hindu nationalism, green is the color of Islam, except for one or two places where they prefer red, and black is the preferred color of Islamic fanatics. Pink is now associated with women's protests and the whole rainbow is the sign of gay pride. White, I don't think of as a color, except in the racial context. So maybe brown. Brown, like us. That must be the color of love."

The mood in the diner was turning decidedly ugly. The frowns were deeper, the eyes were blazing, the ears were burning, and there were fists, Sancho noted, that had begun to clench. "Will you shut up," he hissed at Quichotte. "You're going to get us killed."

Quichotte stood up unsteadily and spread his arms. "I abandon all reason," he cried, "and open myself to love."

A gentleman of impressive proportions, both vertical and lateral, now approached. He wore a leather vest without a shirt and upon the graying hair on his chest there rested a gold medallion bearing the diner's name in bas-relief. "I'm Billy," said he, "and you two are out of here in sixty seconds or less, otherwise one of these fine folks around you just might remove one of those guns of theirs from their holsters and utilize it, and the consequences would be bad for my décor."

Quichotte turned toward this Billy, looking blank. "They would shoot us," he asked, "because of my declaration of universal love?"

Sancho was pulling on Quichotte's arm, literally dragging him toward the door.

"I'll have no talk of communism and Islam under my roof," Billy said. "You're lucky I don't shoot you myself."

"Fuck you," said one of the mouths that were not, or not overly, full of food. "You look like somebody rubbed shit in your faces so deep you can't wash it off."

"Fuck you," said another of the mouths. "Get out of my country and go back to your broke bigoted America-hating desert shit-holes. We're gonna nuke you all."

"Fuck you," said a third mouth whose ears had at least momentarily been listening. "And don't you fucking talk about love when you so filled up with hate."

"Fuck you," a fourth mouth said, and this may have been a relative of the white lady at Lake Capote. "And where did you hide your turbans and fucking beards?"

When they were out on the sidewalk Quichotte said in some bemusement, "I didn't pay the check." Sancho guided him carefully away, as one guides a blind man or a fool. "I think," he said, "break-fast was on the house."

ONE HUNDRED AND NINETY MILES further north they arrived in the town of Beautiful, Kansas (pop. 135,473), ranked by CNN and *Money* magazine as the twelfth-best city to live in in the United States. In south Beautiful, on East 151st Street at Rey-Nard Shops, you could find one of the three locations of the popular Powers Bar & Grill chain. Quichotte had not intended to make a stop in Beauti-ful. After they left Tulsa his plan was to drive north on U.S. 169 and eventually turn toward Lawrence, Kansas (pop. 95,358), a liberal-minded enclave in that conservative state, where he had booked a twin-bedded room at the inexpensive Motel 6. Because of the unpleasantness in Tulsa he drove uninterruptedly and fast, too fast, in spite of Sancho's repeated requests that he slow down, and by the time they reached the Beautiful town line they were both tired and hungry and needed the bathroom. They pulled into the Powers parking lot just as a ball game was beginning on the TVs in the bar. It looked like a welcoming place, crowded with good-natured baseball fans. Also, "Look," Sancho said to Quichotte, "brown people." There were two South Asian men sitting together at the bar, enjoying themselves, deep in conversation. Quichotte and Sancho used the restroom and ordered a little food. They waved at the two Indian men, who smiled and nodded.

"*Salaam aleikum,*" Quichotte called across the room.

"*Namaskar,*" the two Indian men replied.

Quichotte preferred not to intrude on their privacy any further. Soon after that a drunk man started shouting at the Indian men a good deal less cordially, calling them "fucking Iranians," and "terrorists," asking them if their status was legal, and screaming, "Get out of my country." It was less than twelve hours since Quichotte and Sancho had been screamed at in the same words, and so, to their shame, they retreated into a corner and stood in the shadows. The drunk man was escorted off the premises and everyone was relieved. However, before Quichotte and Sancho had finished their meal, the man returned with a gun and shot the two Indian men and also a white man who tried to intervene. Quichotte and Sancho were unharmed, but for a long time they sat there trembling and unsteady and unable to continue on their way.

Much later that night, when they were safely settled into their room in Lawrence, the TV told them that one of the Indian men had died but the other two men were expected to survive their wounds, and that the killer had been captured drinking in a bar in Carter, Missouri (pop. 8,844), which was around forty miles away from Beautiful. He had become a heavy drinker after his father died a year and a half earlier. He worked as a dishwasher in a pizza parlor, a badly fallen state for a man who was a Navy vet and had once been an air traffic controller. Quichotte watched the news in a distracted, closed-off state, pushed by shock into numbness. The only thing that got a response out of him was the news that the murdered man had worked at the Greene company, the tech multinational whose HQ was in Beautiful. "That's the GPS system we use," Quichotte said, standing up suddenly. "Greene. We use their GPS." As if this coincidence was what bonded him to the dead man, what allowed him to feel his death, more deeply than their common ethnicity or the sight of the dead man's widow on TV asking piteously, "Do we belong here?"

It was Sancho—Sancho, who had not stopped shaking for several hours, and remained on the edge of tears—who made Quichotte face that question. "What do you think?" he said. "Is there a place for us in this America?"

"We have entered the third valley," Quichotte replied. "This is the Valley of Knowledge, in which all worldly knowledge ceases to be of use and must be discarded."

"Is there some other sort of knowledge that helps?"

"Only knowledge of the Beloved can save us now," he replied.

When Quichotte talked this way it showed Sancho that the old fellow was truly cuckoo, and that the route by which he, Sancho, might find his way toward his own goal of full humanity did not lie through his strange progenitor. Quichotte was too lost in the deranged logic of his private universe of antiquated words, mystical thoughts, and TV addictions to be able to function properly, or even grasp what was really going on in the actually existing world around him. Even his improbable beloved, Miss Salma R, was by this point also a creation of words, thoughts, and TV images, no longer real to Quichotte in the way that real things are real: a fantasy, passionately believed in but essentially unattainable, no matter how obsessively pursued. Once you have cast aside belief/unbelief, reason, and knowledge, you're pretty handicapped in the real world, Sancho reckoned. Who knew what insanity the next "four valleys" might bring? He tried to think, not for the first time, about how he might break away and strike out on his own. He could just walk off, of course—stick out a thumb, hitch a ride, and take whatever came his way, whatever work, and, if he was lucky, whatever girls. The plan always foundered, however, on practicalities. Being an imaginary creature who had crossed the boundary into the real, he had no legal existence. Without (a) a driving license it was hard to get very far on your own. Without (b) a bank account or a debit card, ditto. And there was no way to get (b) without (a), and (a) was quite an obstacle, not least because he had never been behind the wheel of a car. There were two possibilities, as far as he could see: (a) a life of crime, and (b) a miracle. Of the two, (b) seemed the most likely to work. He was, after all, quite a miracle himself. Maybe he still had access to the sphere of the miraculous.

He left Quichotte in the room watching *Project Runway* and headed for the darkest corner of the Motel 6 parking lot. Here, standing between a pickup truck (a blue Honda Ridgeline Sport AWD, if you must know) and an aging red Hyundai Elantra, he spread his arms and closed his eyes and called upon the realm of the magical. "Grillo Parlante," he said.

"So, finally he comprehends that he need a friend," said a voice from the hood of the Elantra. "Cosa vuoi, paisan? What do you wish from me?"

"I get wishes? How many? Three?"

"That is not the way it works," the cricket said. "The way it works, you ask what you wish, e poi, vedremo. Let's see if it can be done. There are limits."

"So," Sancho said, taking a deep breath, "a driving license, a bank account, a card for the ATM, and money in the bank."

"Banking is only susceptible to magic at the level of the grande frode, the major fraud," the cricket said. "Billionaires, politicians, mafiosi. You don't play in that league. At your level, it's strictly a cash economy."

"That's disappointing," Sancho said. "Is there maybe a more powerful person I could talk to instead of you? A blue fairy, for example?"

"The bluc fairy è una favola," said the cricket. "It's a fairy tale. At least at your level. Don't even think about her. Also, don't be insulting."

"Then I'm fucked," Sancho said.

"How fucked?" the cricket asked. "Why fucked? You're ungrateful, si. You're rude, also. You're poor, of course. But fucked, no. Look in your billfold."

"I don't have a billfold."

"Look in the pocket of your pants. Is there a billfold there or am I full of shit?"

There was something in his pocket. Sancho removed it, in wonderment. It was a cheap brown leather billfold and in it were ten new twenty-dollar bills.

"Two hundred dollars is the maximum possible," the cricket said. "According to your limits."

Two hundred dollars, at that moment, felt like a fortune to Sancho. But he was suspicious. "Is this like a conjuring trick?" he asked. "Will it disappear when the trick ends?"

The cricket ignored this contemptible slander. "Is there something else in the billfold?" it asked. Sancho looked again. There was an absolutely real-looking state ID card with his photograph on it, and his signature, or what might be his signature if he ever signed his name, which so far he had never done. "New York State," the cricket said with a note of pride. "Non è facile, New York State."

"Thank you," Sancho said, overwhelmed.

"Driving license, not possible, not even magic can make you a good driver," the cricket said. "But this is all the ID you require.

Now you are truly free," the cricket said. "And to be human you must have at least la possibilità di libertà. You are trapped in the cash economy, as I told you; this is true, but you have ten Jacksons and an ID card. Great starting point! So a bank account can be procured by non-magical means."

Sancho shook his head in disbelief.

"The question is," the cricket asked, "now that you are free, what do you want to do? Where do you want to go?"

"In the long term, I don't know yet," Sancho replied. "But in the short term—right now—there's someone I want to see."

SANCHO IS AT THE DOOR of a modest home in Beautiful, a cream-colored two-story building, with the word WELCOME, in English, sprayed in white paint on a red ground in the small forecourt, below a small OM sign. There is no doorbell. He takes hold of the brass knocker and knocks, twice. After a pause the door is opened by a young woman in her early twenties. Sancho instantly recognizes that something impossible has happened: that this stranger is the perfect woman for him, the girl of his dreams, and fate karma kismet has brought him here to meet his only true love; and he arrives in that same instant at the tragic realization that a dream is just a dream, karma does not come with any guarantees, and this girl whose name he does not know will not be his. Never in a thousand lifetimes. He blushes deeply and cannot speak.

"Yes?" says the beloved.

He clears his throat and speaks in the voice of despairing adoration. "May I see Mrs. K, the lady of the house."

"Who are you. Why are you here. Don't you know better than to intrude at such a time. The whole community is in grief. Are you a journalist."

"No. Not a journalist. But she asked a question on TV and I need to know her answer. Is there a place for us, she asked. I need to know what she thinks."

"I know what you want. You want to steal something from her. You want to steal his death and her sadness and make it yours. Go away and get your own sadness and your own death. These things don't belong to you."

"I was there. I was in the bar."

"Many people were in the bar. Nobody prevented it. You also did not prevent it. We are not here to console you for this death. If you have evidence go to police."

"Are you the lady's sister? Excuse me but you are very beautiful. Beautiful from Beautiful." (He can't help himself.)

"You are an obscene person. I will shut the door now." (Her scorn destroys him.)

"Please. Forgive me. I only recently arrived in this country. I need to know what it means. How we should live."

"You are not from here."

"No. I'm passing through. My name is Sancho."

"That's a peculiar name. Okay, let me tell you this, Mr. Sancho. We are all affected. People said to my father, don't let your daughter work in America anymore, send her home. Maybe I will take that advice now. Nobody can tell the difference, Iranian, Arab, Muslim. Therefore we are not safe. Now Indian Indian families do not want arranged marriages with Indian Americans anymore. Maybe our people will go to Canada. Canada says it will receive us. There is also the question of language. We are Telangana people, our language is Telugu. But we tell each other, do not speak Telugu where others can hear. Telugu, Arabic, Persian, nobody can tell the difference. Therefore we are not safe. That bar was supposed to be a safe place and they were not speaking Telugu to each other but still it was not safe, so nowhere is safe. Have you heard enough? We have lost our tongues. We must be cowardly and tear our own tongues from our mouths."

"That sucks. But I get it. May I see the lady to express my condolences?"

"This is not that lady's house. She is not here. You have come to the wrong address."

"Then what—"

"We are all that lady now. We are all her family. If you are from home, from *the country*, only recently arrived, then you will surely understand. But this is not your place. This is not your blood."

"What is your name?"

"Why do you want to know my name?"

"You know my name."

"What did you call me before?"

"Beautiful from Beautiful."

"Then that's my name."

"I have to go," Sancho says. "I have to accompany my father on his last journey. When I'm done with that . . ."

"I don't know you," she says. "And the future? Nobody can see it. Go away."

The door shuts.

He leaves, simultaneously brokenhearted and elated, but with a new look to him; a sudden determination, which is not the same thing as requited love, but is, at least, something he can take away from the encounter.

QUICHOTTE WAS WAITING IN the car, looking displeased. "You are a headstrong child," he said. "I made it clear that this was an absurd idea, more than absurd, an indecorous deed. If I have brought you here it is because you threatened me with your departure, and I did not bring you into the world to lose you so soon. It is worse than indecorous, what you have done. It is an irrelevance to the great matter which we have in hand, the great enterprise we have undertaken. It is a sidetrack, a blind alley, and none of our business."

Sancho in the passenger seat was weeping: the first tears of his young life.

"Now you understand unhappiness," Quichotte said, not kindly. "Is this what you came here to learn? Learn it, then. Human life is mostly unhappiness. The only antidote to human misery is love, and it is to love that we must now rededicate ourselves. Let us go."

"I want you to teach me your language," Sancho said. "The lan-

guage you spoke back there. I want us to speak to each other in that
language, especially in public, to defy the bastards who hate us for
possessing another tongue. I want you to start teaching me now."

Quichotte found himself unexpectedly moved. "Very well," he
said. "I will teach you, my son. Your mother tongue, my child without a mother. It is a language of celebrated beauty. And I will also
teach you Bambaiyya, the local variant which we spoke in my childhood streets, which is less beautiful but which you should know,
because only when you know it will you truly be a citizen of that
city which you have never seen."

"When I have finished learning," Sancho says, "I am going to
come back and knock on that door again. I'm going to tell her, we
don't have to be afraid."

Only knowledge of the Beloved can save us now. When Quichotte said
that, Sancho had thought of it as proof of his detachment from real
life. Now he saw that he had underestimated the old man. Now he
had a beloved too.

"When she said 'go away,'" he tells Quichotte, "I know that she
meant 'come back.'"

BEAUTIFUL FROM BEAUTIFUL WAS *Khoobsoorat sé Khoobsoorat,*
which could also mean "more beautiful than beautiful," which was
a good meaning too. That was in the proper language, but in Bambaiyya she was also *rawas,* "fantastic," and *raapchick,* "hot." These
words could also be used to describe the beauty of America, but
there were also many other words of praise available for that. The
Mississippi River at St. Louis was *baap,* which literally meant "father," but in Bambaiyya it meant "great," "best of the best," or
something like, but way cooler than, the now uncool "rad": "That's
one *baap* river, 'Dad.'" Chicago, and the great lake by which it stood,
were both *majboot:* literally "strong," but used to mean "fabulous,"
"amazing," "terrific." "Chicago: totally *majboot* city, *yaar*! And Lake
Michigan—*bilkul majboot pani*!" (Completely amazing water.)

A sexy girl was *maal,* literally "the goods." A girlfriend was *fanti.* A young, hot, but unfortunately married woman was a *chicken tikka.* In Ann Arbor they paused to take a look at the university campus and Sancho noted that there was a lot of *maal* walking around.

"I thought you found yourself a *fanti* who is waiting for you back in Beautiful," Quichotte teased him gravely. "Also that girl you're looking at has a ring on her finger. She's definitely *chicken tikka,* I'm sorry to inform you."

Sancho learned fast. "And that girl over there," he said, "is a carrom board." Flat chested.

Bambaiyya was not a polite vernacular. It possessed the harshness of life on the city streets. A man you didn't like might be *chimaat,* "weird looking," or a *khajvua,* a guy who scratches his balls.

America became Sancho's language lesson. When there were shootings on the TV, he learned that a gun was a *ghoda,* which meant "horse," and a bullet was a *tablet,* or sometimes a *capsule.* So English, in such mutations, found its way into Bambaiyya too.

Both of them were happy. Quichotte the teacher, as the words from far away evoked old memories, felt joined to his youth again, and he and Sancho were brought closer by the lessons, which leavened the tedium of the road with long bouts of laughter. The country rolled by, rivers and mills, wooded hills and suburbs, freeways and turnpikes, and all of it was comedy. Once, between Toledo (pop. 278,508) and Cleveland (pop. 385,809), Quichotte took a wrong turn and cried out, *"Vaat lag gayi!"*

"What did you say?" Sancho asked.

"I said," Quichotte replied, abandoning his habitual dignity, "that we are totally screwed."

To redescribe the country in their private language was also to take ownership of it. "I understand now why the racists want everyone to speak only English," Sancho told Quichotte. "They don't want these other words to have rights over the land." That launched Quichotte into a new elaboration of his "Indian country" trope. "Once there were other words with rights," he said. "Words belonging to those other Indians. Now sometimes those words are just sounds with lost meanings. *Shenandoah,* unknown Native origin. At other times the meaning remains but nobody knows it, which denies the word its influence. *Ticonderoga* is the junction of two waterways. Nobody knows that. *Chicago* is an onion field. Who knew? *Punxsutawney,* town of sandflies, or maybe mosquitoes. Nobody knows it, not even on Groundhog Day. *Mississippi,* great river. Maybe somebody could guess that. These are the words of lost power. New words were poured over them to take away their magic. On the West Coast, holy names of saints in Spanish, Francisco, Diego, Bernardino, José, also Santa Maria de los Angeles. On the East Coast, names from England burying the past beneath them, Hampshire, Exeter, Southampton, Manchester, Warwick, Worcester, Taunton, Peterborough, Northampton, Chesterfield, Putney, Dover, Lancaster, Bangor, Boston. And of course New York."

"Can you stop?" Sancho pleaded. "Please. Just stop."

"You're right," Quichotte admitted, stopping. "We are in the third valley, in which all knowledge has become useless. My useless knowledge, this rough magic, I here abjure."

THEIR LINGUISTIC ACT OF possession made the country begin to make sense again. The random spatial and temporal dislocations stopped. The world settled down and gave Sancho the illusion, at least, of comprehensibility. They made their journey according to Quichotte's plan. After Cleveland, Bunyan, Pennsylvania (pop. 108,260), then Pittsburgh (pop. 303,625), and after that, Philadelphia (pop. 1,568,000). Across state lines toward Chaucer, New Jersey (pop. 17,000), and Huckleberry, New York (pop. 109,571). Soon the Emerald City itself would come into view. The weather went on being disjointed, however; blazing hot one day, freezing cold the next, heat waves and hailstones, droughts and floods. Maybe that was just what the weather was going to be like now. At least geographical continuity seemed to have been restored. Why? In the world beyond knowledge, there was no why. There was just this odd couple, a father and his parthenogenetic offspring, heading toward their doom.

GOD, SANCHO DECIDED, was the Clint Eastwood "Man With No Name" type. Didn't talk a whole lot, kept his thoughts to himself, and every so often he was the high plains drifter riding into town chewing on a cigar and sending everybody straight to Hell. In a lot of ways the opposite of Daddy Q, who never shut up. When Sancho got sick of listening to "Dad" it was actually kinda great to imagine that God was in the car too. God was the Silence. Sometimes that's what was required.

They were riding into town. No cigars and maybe they were the ones who would get sent to Hell. He, "Dad," saw nothing except his quest, heard nothing except what he wanted to hear. Sancho saw everything, heard it all. Across America he collected the sour expressions on the faces of motel clerks, baristas, and girls at cash registers in 7-Elevens.

And now he, too, had a Beloved to attain.

"MY DEAR SANCHO," SAID QUICHOTTE at the wheel of the Cruze, "I must warn you as we approach the great city that we will face a series of *majboot* obstacles there. The great city is an object of great desire. One might say that it is desired by a great many people in the same way that I desire Miss Salma R. Consequently it is defended by mighty guardians just as in days of old, and in many parts of the world to this very day, a woman is guarded against dishonor; just as Miss Salma R is guarded against unwelcome advances, among which I do not, for obvious reasons, number my own."

"What are those reasons?" Sancho cheekily inquired. "Because no matter how hard I scratch my head, they are not obvious to me."

"Really, there is only one reason," replied Quichotte, unperturbed. "It is because in my messages—which are not so frequent as

to be irritating—I am wooing her with style—with the right mixture of flamboyance and self-deprecation and with, if I may be so
bold as to say so, a certain literary panache. I am approaching her as
a woman of that caliber deserves to be approached, and she, as a
woman of caliber, will at once have recognized that that is so. I do
not come at her head-on, like a brute, like a bull. I am indirect, modest, lyrical, philosophical, tender, patient, and noble. I see that I
must make myself worthy of her, and she, seeing that I see that, sees
that by virtue of my seeing it, I reveal myself as being, in fact, the
worthy suitor I aspire to be. Nobody who did not see the need for
worthiness could ever acquire that quality whose importance he had
failed to perceive."

"When you talk that way," Sancho said, "it makes me sorry I
asked."

Late September now. The evenings drawing in, the nights cooler,
leaves flying above them like birds. They were floating up the turnpike as if in a dream. Inexplicably there were no cars to speak of
blocking their way, just the long uncoiling snake of the road. "Looks
like that old city we're heading for dropped its defenses," Sancho
said. "It's just inviting us right in." Rahway, Linden, Elizabeth, Bay-
onne. "Here we come," Sancho punched the air with his fist. "Ready
or not."

Quichotte patted him on the shoulder. "The road is the tongue,"
he said, "and the tunnel is the mouth. The city swallows you right
up."

Sancho was not to be denied his joy. "I'm up for that," he cried.
"Eat me, New York. Eat me now." Harrison, Secaucus. The tunnel
was coming. *Gulp*.

"We need to be fresh and ready for New York," Quichotte said.
"Let's find a place to get a good rest, freshen up, and put our best
face forward in the morning."

"Agh," said Sancho. "You let me get all worked up and excited
and then you slap me down. That's no way to treat a growing boy."

"There are two cities," Quichotte said. "There's the one you can see, the broken sidewalks of the old place and the steel skeletons of the new, lights in the sky, garbage in the gutters, the music of the sirens and power drills, an old man tap-dancing for change, whose feet say, I used to be somebody, but his eyes say, no more, buster, no more. The flow of the avenues and the clogged-up streets. A mouse sailing a boat on a pond in the park. A guy with a mohawk haircut screaming at a yellow cab. Made men with napkins tucked in under their chins in a red-sauce joint in Harlem. Wall Street guys in suspenders getting bottle service in nightclubs or doing tequila shots and throwing themselves at women as if they were banknotes. Tall women, short bald guys, strip steaks, strip joints. Empty storefronts, closing sales, everything must go, a smile missing some of its best teeth. Construction everywhere but still the steam pipes burst. Ringletted men with a million bucks in diamonds in the pockets of their long black coats. Ironwork. Brownstones. Music. Food. Drugs. Homeless folks. Twenty years ago they were gone but now they're back. Snowplows, baseball, police cars promising CPR, courtesy, professionalism, respect, what can I tell you, they have a sense of humor. Every language on earth, Russian, Punjabi, Taishanese, Creole, Yiddish, Kru. Also, let us not forget, the beating heart of the television industry. Colbert at the Ed Sullivan Theater, Noah in Hell's Kitchen, *The View, The Chew,* Seth Meyers, Fallon, everybody. Smiling lawyers on cable saying they can make you a fortune if you get hurt. Rock Center, CNN, Fox. The warehouse downtown where they shoot the *Salma* show. The streets she walks, the car she goes home in, the elevator to her penthouse, the restaurants she orders in from, the places she knows, the places she goes, the people who know her number, the things that please her. The whole ugly-pretty city, beautiful in its ugliness, *jolie-laide,* that's French, like the statue in the harbor. All this is there to see."

"And the other city?" Sancho asked, frowning. "Because that's a lot right there."

"The other city is invisible," Quichotte replied. "This is the guardian city, its high forbidding walls made of wealth and power, and it is where reality lives. Only its few keyholders can enter that sacred space."

"I'm guessing we aren't in that group."

"I have one key," Quichotte said, "and when the time comes I may have to go to find the lock it opens."

"That's very mysterious," Sancho scolded him. "You kept that a secret. What key? What lock? What's in there? Come on."

"But we also have another weapon," Quichotte said, ignoring Sancho's plea. "We are about to enter the fourth valley."

"We already gave up belief, unbelief, reason, and knowledge," Sancho protested. "There doesn't seem to be much left."

"The fourth valley," Quichotte said, "is the Valley of Detachment, in which we will give up all our desires and attachments to the world."

"All of them?"

"All of them."

"Coffee-flavored chocolate-coated Häagen-Dazs ice cream?"

"And *Law and Order: Special Victims Unit*."

"And sitting near the hot corner at Yankee Stadium at a Red Sox game? Which obviously I've never done but I desire it."

"And *Watch What Happens: Live* on Bravo."

"And *Candy Crush Saga*?"

"And *The Princess Bride*."

"And steak?"

"And french fries."

"And Beyoncé and Jay-Z?"

"And the original cast recording of *The King and I*."

Sancho, on whose face a look of horror had taken root, paused, having suddenly thought of something unbearable.

"Do we also have to give up our desire for, and attachment to, the woman we love?"

"The Beloved is exempt," Quichotte explained mildly, "because the Beloved is the goal. These other burdens, however, must be shed."

"Even an occasional glass of Grey Goose and tonic?"

"Even fava beans and a nice Chianti."

"We're going to be like monks."

"We will become worthy of the Grail."

"And the Grail is the Beloved?"

"The Grail is the hand of Miss Salma R."

"The Grail is the hand of Beautiful from Beautiful."

"Every man has his own Grail."

"But you said we would find a weapon in the fourth valley. All I see is us having fewer and fewer things. I don't see any bazookas."

"When we have attained the surrender of the fourth valley," Quichotte said, "then what is commonly known as 'reality,' and which is really unreality, as we know from TV, will cease to exist. The veils will drop away, the invisible city will become visible, its gates will swing open so that no key is required, and the path to the Beloved will be seen."

At some point, Sancho thought, *someone is going to come along and wrap him up in a straitjacket and take him away, and at that point I'll find the path back to Beautiful, Kansas (pop. 135,473).* This he did not say aloud. Instead, humoring the old man, he declared, "I'm ready. I'll give up my desire for a new iPad and my attachment, which I think I must have got from you, to the music of U2."

"It's a start," Quichotte said, and then the city was upon them. "Can't you feel it? Reality, that sham, is already ceasing to exist."

Sancho did not reply, but privately dissented. Reality was a white lady at Lake Capote, it was what came out of the angry mouths he'd seen at a diner in Oklahoma, it was gunshots in Kansas, two wounded, one dead, a community shaken and in mourning, a beautiful young woman slamming a door in his face. Was that reality likely to dissolve and disappear? Could it really be dismissed as a sham?

CHAPTER ELEVEN

Dr. Smile meets Mr. Thayer; & a Grandfather emerges from the Past to haunt the Present

THE THAYERS WERE EARLY PILGRIMS, CHECK. THOMAS and Richard Thayer, brothers, classified among the Pilgrim Fathers, check. Their descendants married into the *Mayflower* family descended from John Alden, check.—Regarding the *Mayflower* itself, however? Were their names on that eminent list? They were aboard, right?—Um, not actually on the *Mayflower,* no.—Oh. How about on the *Fortune,* the second ship to make the crossing?—Ah . . . no, not on the *Fortune,* either. But they were early settlers. Early was good. Early was impressive. Words had a life of their own, Anderson Thayer believed, they developed meanings that only pedants would argue with, and *Mayflower* was—at least for him—by now pretty much synonymous with *early.* Little discrepancies did not make big differences. Small departures from the truth did not add up to lies. Therefore, Anderson Thayer saw no need to correct others when they believed his people to have come over on the fabled ship. He saw no need to correct himself.

Small was not big. It was a principle he carried over into other parts of his life. He was a small man, and understood that this was not the same as being a big one. (Big men lumbered. Small men were nimble. This could give them an edge. He had read something once, or maybe seen something on TV, about the defeat of the Spanish Armada. The Spanish galleons were big and slow. The British fleet was little, maneuverable, and fast. The British ships zipped in and out between the big Spanish lumberers, firing their cannons and then sailing away, zap, pow, punch and retreat. That was big versus small. It was David versus Goliath. It was Cassius Clay floating and stinging, Sonny Liston standing there like a big confused bear. *His hands can't touch / what his eyes can't see.*)

Small was not big. Small misdemeanors were not big crimes. Small thefts were not grand larceny. Small betrayals were not high treason. During the course of his relationship with Miss Salma R, he had often had recourse to this guiding principle, and it had served him well. He had stolen things from her, sure, but not the big things, the things she cared about. An earring here, a bracelet there. She noticed the losses and shrugged them off.

"I'm always losing things," she rebuked herself, and the thief laughed along with her. He had stolen her likeness, too, filming her secretly on his smartphone in her low moments, her depressions, her out-of-it hours brought on by her abuse of prescription drugs. This was to give him cards to play, to safeguard him in case she turned against him, which he intuited she was considering doing; but he suspected they would not be of much use, because she was so open about her follies, her unwellnesses and overindulgences, that video evidence of their extent might not damage her much. Still, she probably would not like the studio bosses to see the footage; even though they had heard all her stories, in these sensitive times the evidence of their eyes might be too much for them to take, even if the evidence of their ears could be set aside; so the material was not without value. So he was disloyal in little things, but loyal in the big ones: for he was indeed her protector, her guardian, he would do anything for her, he would clean up her messes, and—again, at least in his own opinion—he truly loved her. She was the giant and he the pygmy and he looked up to her, and adored.

He was a student of the world of stardom, and of peripheral figures like himself who modestly played consort to the great. He paid particular attention to young men who were attracted, and attractive, to older women, fading beauties, falling stars. Demi and Ashton, of course, Madonna and that dancer guy, Cher and Tom Cruise, and the present-day gold medalist of this particular sport, the young nightclub king Omar Vitale. Omar and Demi, Omar and Heidi Klum, Omar and Elle "the Body" Macpherson. Respect, Anderson Thayer thought. However, his great role model, only recently deceased, was from the golden age. His name was Robert Wolders and he was a Dutch actor, mainly on TV although he had supporting roles in *Beau Geste* and *Tobruk*. His most substantial TV role had been in the cowboy series *Laredo* in the mid-sixties. But as the real-life leading man to a series of great stars, Wolders had no equal. He married Merle Oberon when she was sixty-four and he was twenty-five years younger, and gave up acting to be with her. She died four years later. The following year he started dating Audrey Hepburn when she was fifty-one and he was about seven years her junior, and he stayed with her for thirteen years, until her death. He was also subsequently the partner of Leslie Caron (five years older). This was a career which Anderson Thayer admired, to which he aspired. Robert Wolders had been tall and handsome and he, Anderson, was the Yosemite Sam/Rumpelstiltskin type, but he had started well in his chosen métier. If he could, he would stay at Miss Salma R's side until her death. Then he would look for her successor. He already had a short list of possible successors in mind.

AT THE TIME OF WHICH we speak, Anderson Thayer made a brief personal visit to Atlanta. The American Association of Doctors of Indian Origin (AADIO), the Georgia Institute of Medical Practitioners of Indian Heritage (GIMPIH), the United States Pain Association (USPA), and the Smile Foundation had jointly organized an "Opioid Awareness Program" at the Atlanta branch of the consulate of India in the Atlantan suburb of Sandy Springs, Georgia. The closing address was to be delivered by the noted Indian-American pain management specialist Dr. R. K. Smile, founder and chief executive of Smile Pharmaceuticals Inc. (SPI). Anderson Thayer, introducing himself to consular staff as Conrad Chekhov, a *Washington Post* reporter on the "opioid beat," was given permission to cover the conference. Anderson was proud of the "tradecraft"—a word he had learned from spy movies on TV—that had enabled him to acquire the fake *Post* ID. He had a selection of such identities available to him. It was often necessary, in his work, to make sure that no connection could be made between himself and what security people called "the principal." Deniability was everything. He left no paper trails.

The conference was small and dull but when Dr. Smile stood up to speak everyone paid attention. This was the Little King, a respected figure who had donated generously to the community and to the cultural life of the city. His name was everywhere, raising the profile of Atlanta's Indian community in ways that were beneficial to all Indian Americans and served to reduce interracial tensions. Today Dr. Smile seemed particularly passionate. To begin with, he blamed the media for not paying attention to the growing crisis. "As a country we are at the mercy of the media, which sets the agenda for all," he said. "Even ten years ago there were maybe one hundred deaths a day caused by opioids but the media because of its liberal bias wanted only to talk about breastfeeding in public places and transgender restrooms. Also, on account of its obsession with the hole in the ozone layer, it foregrounded melanomas. And then came Ebola. How many Americans died from Ebola? I will tell you. Two persons precisely. One, two. But in the media it was Ebola wall to wall, 24/7. Plus it is a society fixated on body issues, on looking good, keeping fit, there is so much 'body shaming,' as they call it, if you have a 'dad bod,' as I think is possessed by many of the men in this room, myself included." Here he was interrupted by laughter, which he allowed to die down. "Be comforted, however," he continued. "Now there are counter-ideologies, 'body neutrality,' 'fat acceptance,' 'body respect.' So, it's okay, gentlemen, you don't have to go on a diet." More comfortable laughter. Then Dr. Smile returned to his serious point. "So, on account of the American body-love, there was much attention paid to walking for fitness and obesity in schools. Meanwhile thirty thousand persons per annum dying from opioids, receiving almost zero coverage."

Now all heads were nodding. "Only in 2015 did U.S. senators make this issue public. I myself launched an online campaign and within one week twelve thousand families replied. Here I must indicate a fault within ourselves, I'm sorry to say. But we must face our own community issues, isn't it. This crisis arises, there is addiction, there is grave danger to family member or members, but we hide it. We think of it as our shame, and we conceal. Back home in India also, it is hidden. Consequently there is a serious shortage of rehabilitation facilities. The crisis gets worse. Strange but true, it is not because money is not being spent. In the U.S. in 2013, eight billion dollars spent. In 2014, ten billion. Resources are growing but the problem also is growing. Why? Here I must use a word with which all of us sadly are familiar." A dramatic pause. "That word, honored Consul *saab,* honorable guests, is *corruption.*" A further cause for the obligatory gasp of shock. "Powerful pharmaceutical companies and lobbyists are responsible. Also the small percentage of doctors, I estimate maybe one percent, who are corrupt. Meanwhile new and more powerful drugs arrive on the market. Here is the issue. I am trying to face it. So must we all."

Anderson Thayer, dutifully taking notes at the back of the room alongside the reporter from *Rajdhani,* had taken an immediate liking to Dr. Smile because he, too, was small. Two Munchkins in Oz, he thought. We need to stick together. But the longer the doctor spoke, the more impressed Anderson became. This guy was something else. He stood up among his peers and more or less flat out

told them, here's what I'm doing, and made them believe the opposite. Everybody left the meeting thinking he was the sheriff, not
the outlaw. He posed as Pat Garrett when secretly he was Billy the
Kid. The guy had balls. Not for him the timid Anderson Thayer
position of small-not-big. This guy gurgled up a big mucus ball of
really big lies and spat it right out between shameless teeth.

Later that afternoon Anderson made the phone call from a burner
phone which he would dispose of before he left town. He introduced himself, as he had said he would, as "Sam," and at once Dr.
Smile began to scold him. "Very bad practice for you to attend the
conference," he said. "Local community journalist was there. Not a
good idea to allow somebody to add one and one and make two."

"I'm sorry," Anderson replied, taking care not to sound sorry. "I
wanted to get a look at you, to know who I'm dealing with."

"And you concluded what?" Dr. Smile's tone was both aggrieved
and a little insecure.

"That you are somebody I can do business with."

"The first delivery will be a courtesy." Now Dr. Smile's voice
became stony and businesslike. "There will be no charge. You will
receive a small package which will also contain instructions for use,
to which you must adhere closely."

"Understood."

"La Reina del Taco on the Buford Highway. Go to the men's
room at 10 P.M. precisely and you will find the package waiting behind the cistern."

The taqueria at night was not a quiet place. The lighting was
neon and lurid, the walls were noisy (some pink, some lime green),
the ceiling was overly jazzed up by little dangling objects (throbbing
red hearts, big yellow hearts, blue broken hearts), the music was
very loud, and the volume on the flat-screen TV on one wall was
turned up high to do battle with the music. The tables were full of
students, from Emory, Morehouse, Spelman, and they generated
such noise as only students en masse were capable of producing. It
was an excellent choice, Anderson thought, nobody was paying at-

tention to anything except themselves and their food. He checked out the men's room at five minutes to ten. There was an OUT OF ORDER sign on the door. He walked away and came back five minutes later. The sign was gone, the men's room was empty, there was a brown paper parcel waiting in the specified place. He took it and headed out to his rented Camry.

It was too late to catch a plane. He would have to spend the night at an airport hotel and fly back to New York in the morning. He hated Hartsfield-Jackson Airport for its immense size and frequent logistical problems. When he'd flown in he'd heard a fellow passenger wearing a Braves baseball cap telling what he assumed to be a local joke. "If you die and go to Hell," the Braves fan said, "you have to change planes in Atlanta."

This is the life I could have had, he thought. He had studied Russian at Davidson, taking one course entitled "Russia and Ukraine—War and Peace," and another studying the use of the metaphor of the vampire in Russian culture, and in his senior year he had been approached by representatives of both American and Russian intelligence and asked if he wanted a job. He had thanked them equally graciously for their interest and declined both their invitations. The American representative had returned to tell him that if he attempted to visit Russia at any time in the future it was probable that his passport would be confiscated and other actions against him might follow. He abandoned Russian, dropped out, did not graduate, and became, instead, a humble (or maybe not-so-humble) personal assistant to the stars. But he could have been a spy if he had said yes. He could have led a secret agent's life.

What are you talking about, he told himself. This is the life you do have. You're living it right now.

THIS TIME THE MAN who called himself Quichotte had sent Salma a photograph of himself along with a new note. A clumsy selfie, printed out, no doubt, at some FedEx Print & Ship Center somewhere along his road, and mailed, so it seemed, in Pennsylvania. So he was close. This was a little alarming, but also, she had to admit to herself, *interesting*. She had not expected him to be handsome, but he was, in his crazy-old-guy way. He reminded her of the actor Frank Langella. His face was long and thin with prominent cheekbones. His white hair was short and he sported three-day-old white grizzle around his chops. He stood erect; no stooper he. He possessed an attractive formality, a nice smile, a melancholy air. As do his letters, she thought, weakening momentarily. They, too, have charm.

Then all of a sudden she began to tremble, because memory burst upon her with the force of a flood, with the terror of a haunting, and she understood that he reminded her of someone else as well as Mr. Langella, and that someone was the man about whom she never spoke, the missing piece in the explanation of her choices, and her life. Quichotte was the spitting image of her maternal grandfather, the long-ostracized and now-deceased Babajan.

"Give this to security," she told the staffer who had brought her the envelope with the photograph in it. "If this guy ever shows up at the door, call the fucking cops."

In the car on the way home, her chauffeur was genuinely concerned.

"If I may say so, Miss Daisy," he said, "you look like you just saw a ghost."

"None of that Miss Daisy crap tonight, Hoke," she replied. "I'm not in the fucking mood."

IT IS TIME TO shed light on Miss Salma R's last and darkest family secret.

When Salma was twelve years old her grandfather Babajan grabbed her by the wrists and kissed her on the mouth. At the instant that it happened all she could think was that he had been aiming for her cheek and missed, but then he did it again and this time his tongue was no accident. She bent backwards away from that searching tongue and it came after her. Then she broke away and ran.

The Juhu Beach mansion was really two houses with a walled garden in between. There was a smaller, two-story house that gave onto the street, then the garden with its sunken ponds and climbing bougainvillea creeper, then the main, three-story building, looking out to sea. Both buildings were full of paintings by Husain, Raza, Gaitonde, and Khanna, and the garden boasted ancient stone sculptures of the gods Shiva and Krishna and the Buddha too. What were they doing, those great artists both ancient and modern, just hanging there on expensive walls, those deities just standing there on podiums in the sunshine and looking on? What use was genius, what was the point of godliness slash holiness, if it couldn't protect a twelve-year-old girl in her own home? Shame on you, artists, gods! Climb down off your pedestals, unhang yourselves, and help!—Nobody helped.—The assault happened one weekend when young Salma wandered across the garden from the beach house to the street house, where the main kitchens were, in search of an afternoon snack. This was the house in which Babajan had an upstairs suite in which, for the most part, he kept his own counsel. He was seen in the gardens only at prayer times—he prayed five times a day, as truly religious people do, and also people in serious need of divine forgiveness—when he brought his little prayer mat, rolled up, to the edge of a sunken pond, unrolled it, faced toward Mecca, and got down on his knees. But as must now regretfully be revealed, he preyed almost as often as he prayed. On this weekend afternoon, as Salma headed for the refrigerator, and in a moment when no prying eyes were around, no servants, chauffeurs, or security staff, he emerged from a shadow grinning like a demon, took hold of both her wrists, pulled her toward him, and kissed her with great force, twice, the second time, as has been said, with his tongue. When she ran from him he trotted after her for a few steps, laughing his little laugh, *heh-heh-heh,* which she had always thought to be his sweet-old-man good-natured giggle but which she now heard as being filled with menace. Then he gave up the chase and, with a shrug and a little dismissive wave of a hand, went upstairs to his quarters.

Here is a young girl running toward her mother, crying. Before she reaches her mother's arms, some more must be said about life in that large unhappy home. It should be plain to us, as we look in on these events, that neither Salma's mother Anisa nor her grandmother Dina could have been unaware of Babajan's proclivities. If Anisa as a child had been his victim, too, the mother before the daughter, she never explicitly revealed it to anyone, except possibly to her mother, whose lips remained sealed. But both Dina and Anisa had warned little Salma, more than once, "Don't sit alone in a room with Babajan. Make sure your ayah at least is present. Otherwise it would be improper. You understand." Little Salma knew, had known all her life, that her grandparents were estranged, that there was a negative electricity in the Juhu house which was upsetting, and which, consequently, she tried her best to ignore. She assumed that the instruction regarding her own behavior was born of that same electricity, that she was being told to choose sides, that friendship with her grandfather would be seen as disloyalty to her grandmother. However, fear, at her tender age, had not yet entered her life, and because she possessed the same fierce independence of spirit which drove both her mother and grandmother, she sometimes disregarded their orders and formed a personal opinion of Babajan which was, to be frank, fond. In spite of the frowns and admonitions of the older women of the family, she liked sitting beside him in the garden and listening to his deliciously frightening fairy tales about *bhoots* and *jinn,* beasts made of smoke and fire who had a fondness for devouring young girls. She liked it that he encouraged her to ask him questions, even dangerous questions. "Babajan," she once said, alarming herself at her boldness, "what if I told you there is no God?" He roared with laughter. "Who put such a damn fool idea in your head?" he answered without a trace of the anger she feared might be his response. "You should be at least fifteen years old before you take up such a position. Come to me then and I'll reply."

This picture of a kindly, giggling, tolerant, broad-minded grandfather became important to her. She hid it away in her head because she knew her grandmother and mother would disapprove, but it was an important secret, and she often thought she might try to bring about a reconciliation between her elders, and made grand plans to that effect, as children will. But the ferocity with which her grandmother reacted to all her attempts to discuss Babajan dissuaded her from putting any of her schemes into operation. And now, twelve years old, running, and afraid, she understood that ferocity, she understood everything, as if she had never known anything before.

As she ran, her whole world fell apart around her, its entire architecture of love, trust, and believed comprehension. The whole story of her family, what she thought she knew about it, who and how they had been in the world, had to be torn up and rewritten. To lose one's picture of the world, to feel its gilded frame snap and crumble, to see the museum glass beneath which you kept it safe crack from side to side and fall in jagged peaks to earth, and the images themselves slide and dissolve and explode: another term for this experience is *going insane*. To have this happen when you are twelve years old and utterly devoid of the psychological equipment you need to handle it is even worse. Salma running saw her vision fragment, saw the whole house slip and slide and the sky break over her head and fall like blue missiles bombing the earth, and the sea ahead of her tear off its mask of calm and rise up to engulf the universe. Then her mother was holding her and she was trying to tell her what had happened and her grandmother stood behind them, awful in her rage. A light came into the eyes of the two older women which could have burned a hole in the fabric of time. The ayah came into the room. "Stay with her," Anisa commanded and then she and Dina left and walked toward the street house like an army going to war.

What they said to Babajan is not recorded but all the staff in the house and even some passersby in the street outside felt the foundations shake and by the time they were done all the artwork was hanging crooked on the walls. After that he was rarely seen by anyone. His food was sent up to him and he lived out his remaining days and said his prayers—perhaps hoping for redemption—in private. When the two women emerged from his suite they had the air of swords unsheathed, of bloody swords after a killing, whose blades they chose not to cleanse, to allow all to see the work that had been done.

When they came back into the place where they had left Salma and the ayah, the twelve-year-old girl was dry eyed and alone. "You both knew," she said to them. "You always knew."

"We hide these things," Dr. R. K. Smile told his audience in Atlanta. "There is grave danger to family member or members, but we hide them. We think of them as our shame, and we conceal."

Very few of the ills that befall us can be said to have one single cause, and so it would be oversimplifying things to ascribe Dina R's mental instability, or Anisa's drinking and depression, or their deaths by suicide, to the hidden shame of Babajan's fondness for young girls. How much did they know? How many did he molest? What was the scale of his evil? These things can't be known for sure. A movie star's fortune and publicists are capable of silencing many tongues and suppressing many truths. How much of such dirty work did they do or cause to have done, and how deep was their guilt at becoming complicit in his crimes by cleaning up after him? Was this the narrative underlying Miss Salma R's decision to leave a successful career in Bollywood and seek her fortune on the other side of the world? Did it lie at the root of her own travails and addictions? The answer is: probably. But human biochemistry, as also human willfulness, has its own aberrations, and these, too, no doubt were part of the story.

"AFTER THAT FOR A TIME I became a prude. Miss Goody Two-Shoes, that was me. I locked my feelings away, worked hard, stood up straight, did nothing naughty, teacher's pet. If I was correct enough, punctual enough, did my homework well enough, obeyed instructions, behaved, then maybe the world wouldn't explode again the way it did that day. And then my mother died and I thought, enough. But I carried one memory with me: of the day I learned that the world was not a safe place. That was the lesson my grandfather taught me. It's a lesson worth learning."

Anderson Thayer was back from Atlanta, listening without interruption while she talked it all out. She had had a copy of Quichotte's photograph made and stuck it on her refrigerator. "Now that I've had time to look at it," she said, "he really isn't like my grandfather at all. He actually has a nicer smile. Babajan had that evil little *heh-heh-heh*."

"Be careful," Anderson said. "I know you. I know what you're thinking. Everything is material, am I right? You want this nutcase on your show."

"No I don't."

He looked at her.

"Okay. Maybe. But I know it's stupid. He's completely bananas, of course. But bananas can be good TV."

"He's a stalker. You can't put your stalker on TV."

"Spoilsport."

"Did you send the photo to the cops?"

"Not yet."

"You should do that. *I* should do that. I'll get it done."

"You really think so?"

"Obviously. You know nothing about this individual."

"Okay, fine, send it. But he's probably just some sweet crazy fan."

He took a bottle of white wine out of the refrigerator.

"Hey," he said, "who's the other person in this photo? The young guy trying to look cool?"

"I don't know," she said. "There's something strange about him, right? He almost doesn't look real."

"What do you mean, not real?"

"Like CG. You know how in CGI they can't ever get human facial expressions exactly right? Like that."

"Yeah," Anderson Thayer said, judiciously. "That is kind of a Pixar smile."

They raised their wineglasses. "It's good to be back," he said.

"And here I am waiting for you, and do you have something for me?"

"It's dangerous," he said.

"I know it's dangerous. Everything interesting is dangerous."

"No, but this is really dangerous. You could die. You have to be very careful."

"I'll be careful. Give it to me."

"There are instructions."

"You know I don't follow instructions anymore."

"Follow these. Okay? I'm serious. Okay?"

"Okay."

"Also, when you're ready, and if this is a long-term relationship you want to pursue, he'd like to meet you. The supplier. Dr. Smile. He likes to meet his VIP clients at least once. I think it's kind of a starfucking thing. After that he will set up a regular errand boy, a trusted carrier, and make delivery arrangements. It's all pretty professional."

"What is he like?"

"What can I tell you? He's a crook. Or, as Michael Corleone would say: first and foremost, he's a businessman."

"Thank you," she said, taking Anderson's hand. "You do so much for me, really. You do everything. Maybe I'll keep you for a while."

$C_{22}H_{28}N_2O$. CHINA GIRL, CHINA White, Apache, Dance Fever. Goodfella, Murder 8, TNT, Jackpot. The drug had many names. Fentanyl, monarch of opioid country, little king of the hill, top of the heap, A Number One. Dr. Smile had been generous. His free introductory package contained six-packs of six strengths of ACTIQ brand lollipops, which he didn't even manufacture himself: two hundred, four hundred, six hundred, eight hundred, twelve hundred, and sixteen hundred micrograms per popsicle. Also included was a small gift-wrapped box containing the main event: a single dispenser of SPI's own InSmile™ sublingual spray. The sheet of instructions for use "strongly recommended" what it called "acclimatization." Start with small doses, work your way up. Users not accustomed to opioids might find even a low-dosage lollipop life-threatening, inducing *respiratory depression,* a state of mind which made you feel like not breathing. Also, by the way, frequent lollipop sucking, as every child knows, could give you mouth ulcers and make your teeth fall out. The lollipops are addictive. Do not have more than one hundred and twenty lollipops a month. Enjoy.

After Anderson Thayer had left for the night (no room for him in her bed that evening, honey, she had a sweeter lover to entertain), she prepared for her first encounter with one of the juiced popsicles as if Casanova himself were about to enter her boudoir. She bathed, she shaved, she perfumed herself, she used lotion that her skin might not be ashy, she wove a single braid into her hair and let the rest flow down over her shoulders, and *lying, robed in snowy white / That loosely flew to left and right,* she took it in her hands, and, taking it, remembered whence those words came that had lollipopped unbidden into her thoughts. *"The curse is come upon me," cried / The Lady of Shalott.* Was she preparing to die, then? To succumb to the curse of her family and follow her forebears to a self-willed end? No, she told herself firmly, she most certainly was not. She could handle this. She was by no means a user-not-accustomed etc. But she would take it slow. Start at the bottom of the ladder. Sixteen hundred micrograms of fentanyl were equivalent to 160 milligrams of morphine. That was a big hit and the sublingual version would hit even harder. Start with two hundred micrograms. Walk before you can run, run before you can fly.

These days the only way to experience joy was through chemistry. It was necessary first to unplug from the Connectivity and then, as the world faded away, to put euphoria into your mouth and suck on it. This was the lover who never disappointed you, the friend who never failed you, the partner who never cheated on you, the government that never lied. This alone was dependable, loyal, honest, and true. Sleepy, relaxed joy. Here it came. Turn off your mind, relax and float downstream.

Ego death.

Samadhi.

Bliss.

QUICHOTTE'S LETTER, WHICH HAD arrived along with the photograph, spoke a little alarmingly about the end of the world. Salma had attached a copy of the letter by a magnet to her refrigerator door. As usual, her pseudonymous correspondent's handwriting was impeccably stylish, while the sentiments expressed in that fine strong hand were irredeemably off-kilter.

My dear Miss Salma,

In a story I read as a boy, which, by a serendipitous chance, you can now see dramatized on Amazon Prime, a Tibetan monastery purchased the world's most powerful super-computer because they believed that the purpose of their order was to enumerate the nine billion names of God, and the computer could help them do that swiftly and accurately. But apparently it was not only the purpose of their order to complete this heroic act of naming. It was also the purpose of the universe itself; and so, once the computer finished its work, very quietly and without any fuss, the stars began to go out. Such are my feelings toward you, that I believe that the entire purpose of the universe up to this point has been to bring about that moment in which you and I will unite in eternal delight, and once we have done so, the cosmos will have achieved

its goal and will therefore peacefully end, and we will ascend together,
beyond annihilation, into the sphere of the Timeless.

Before he left for the night, Anderson Thayer said that this letter made him nervous. The destruction of the cosmos. Annihilation. *Beyond* annihilation. This was language that should give Salma concern. These were certainly not words to laugh about. Her laughter was inappropriate. "No, but look," she said. "One minute he's inspired by old science fiction garbage and the next instant he's back on his mystical voyage of the soul. Read the rest of it."

As I have told you before, dear, I have already cast aside belief, unbe-
lief, dogma, and reason for the sake of Love. I have already learned
that all worldly knowledge is useless.

"That's worth knowing, right?" Salma giggled. "Except that then knowing it would be useless too? Look, now he's struggling with giving up desires and attachments. See what he says happens when he achieves that! Reality vanishes! He's living now in a postreality continuum, which must be the same one that will peacefully end when we fall in love. I mean, it's a comedy routine. I think it's sweet. Look how he signs off. It's as if he's a visitor from the eighteenth century."

Yours aff.ly, dearest Madame, Quichotte.

"Also," she added, "the end of the world is fashionable these days. Aren't we having Evel Cent from CentCorp on the show soon? That's his bugaboo too."

"I think it's another reason to involve the cops," Anderson said. "I'll get them to put the photo out on the wires. I don't want him within a mile of you."

"I don't like it when you get bossy and overprotective like this," Salma snapped. "It makes me want to remind you that *you* work for *me*."

So after a pleasant meeting they had parted on something less than the best of terms. But he was used to her hissy fits. He knew they didn't last and the gratitude she had expressed moments earlier represented her real feelings. He knew it would be business as usual tomorrow. Sometimes he felt as if he were her parent and she his brilliant, willful child. Sometimes he felt big and she felt small. He also knew that this attitude of his could be read as condescension and irritated her more than anything else, so he was careful not to let it show on his face. "I'll see you in the morning," he said.

And now rising-sinking toward sleepy euphoria in her floating bed, she imagined him, Quichotte, beside her as the cosmos dissolved and they moved together into the beyond, the Timeless, where past and present and future all existed simultaneously, the time in which God lived, perhaps, seeing all things, as now they too would see all things, like gods, immortal, free. She looked toward him and saw her grandfather's face. She felt neither fear nor anger, neither bitterness nor disgust. She saw only an old man melting into dust, into light. In this moment, engulfed in chemical happiness, she found it easy, even natural, to forgive.

Was that what Quichotte, purifying himself, was coming toward her to give her? Was he the one who would heal the wounds?

These questions were too big to be considered under the influence of the China White. Pleasure overwhelmed her. She slipped into the spiraling, dizzy light.

WHEN SHE HAD MADE her way up the lollipop ladder and the night came to open the gift-wrapped box containing SPI's pride and joy, Miss Salma R discovered that InSmile™ was like graduating to a Rolls-Royce after years spent behind the wheel of a Nissan Qashqai. It was color after a lifetime of black-and-white, Monroe after Mansfield, Margaux after HobNob, Cervantes after Avellaneda, Hammett after Spillane. It was like your first real kiss, or your first genuine orgasm after years of being Meg Ryan in Katz's Delicates-

sen. One puff under the tongue was all it took. The speed of delivery, the power of the hit, the quality of the high. And yes, Anderson
was right, it was dangerous. At one point she was out of her body,
hovering above it, looking down at it, and she could choose whether
to reenter or not. It was the ultimate thrill ride and you had to be an
expert jockey to stay on this horse. Fortunately she was a great
horsewoman and could stay in the saddle all night long. This was
not her first rodeo, but it was the rodeo Olympics, and only the
greatest athletes could compete in that stadium.

"I'm in," she told Anderson Thayer. "What's the most discreet
way to do the face-to-face with the supplier before he arranges the
regular courier?"

"That's easy," Anderson said. "We invite him and his wife to
come and watch a taping of the show."

DR. SMILE WAS HAPPY that he had made Happy happy. She did so
much, she deserved a weekend in the big city. Fall in New York was
an exciting time. And the chance to meet the star of *Salma*? Happy
loved that show. When he told her he was taking her up to New
York for a little break, and revealed what they would be doing, he
saw tears well up in her eyes, and she jumped up and shook with
pleasure.

"You see what I told you?" she cried. "We're on the A-list now!"

"What do you think," Dr. Smile asked her, "you know our relative Ismail Smile is such a big big admirer of Miss Salma?"

"But you let him go, isn't it."

"Maybe I could find him. What do you think, take him along so
he also can meet the lady? Good idea or no?"

"Bad idea," she said, coming at him with her mouth in a loving
pout. "This little trip must be for you and me only, and no *pagal*
cousins along for the ride."

—

CHAPTER TWELVE

A Sequence of absurd
Events during a brief Sojourn
in New Jersey

QUICHOTTE TOOK ONE OF THE LAST TURNINGS OFF the turnpike before the tunnel's mouth. "We'll spend the night here," he told Sancho. "As I said, I don't want to arrive at the great city weary from the journey and covered in the dust of the road. Don't be disappointed. Destiny will still be waiting for us tomorrow." As they drove down the exit road in the fading light, a sort of fog or cloud settled on the road and it was only by good fortune that they avoided an accident. The cloud cleared away as quickly as it had come and they found themselves passing a sign pointing toward the town of Berenger, New Jersey (pop. 12,554). "Thirty years ago in Jersey City there were gangs terrorizing brown-skinned persons," Quichotte said. "Let us hope things have quieted down in this small town at least."

They pulled in at the JONÉSCO Motor Inn on Elm Street, surprised to see how empty the town was both of pedestrians and of traffic. As they got out of the car they heard a loud trumpeting noise which seemed to be coming from a neighboring street.

"What was that?" Sancho asked.

Quichotte shrugged. "No doubt the locals are indulging in some form of amateur musical or theatrical entertainment," said he. "Let's attend to our own business. That's always best."

Inside the Motor Inn, they were greeted at the check-in desk by a distinguished-looking man, gray-haired, balding, with an intellectual's sadly comic face and what sounded like a thick Eastern European accent. He seemed surprised to see them. "Excuse me, but did you get into town without any trouble?" he asked. It was an unusual opening gambit for a conversation.

"Yes, naturally," Quichotte replied. "We turned off the turnpike and followed the signs and here we are. Why, should we have expected otherwise?"

"No, no," said the man, who turned out to be the owner himself. He gave a little shake of the head and waved his hand airily. "Please, allow me to offer you what accommodation you need." As Quichotte was filling out the required form for a two-bedded room, the bald man explained, "This is my place. I'm a little shorthanded today." But Sancho also heard him muttering under his breath, "There were no barricades? Incredible."

Upon hearing this he spoke up. "Mr. Jones?" he began.

The other shook his head. "I am Jonésco," he corrected Sancho, accenting the *é,* and pointing to a sign on the wall identifying him as the proprietor.

Okay, Sancho thought, call yourself whatever you want. "Sir, I heard you saying something about barricades?"

The proprietor of the Jonésco Motel shook his head. "You misheard," he said. "I was saying, *the bar is closed.* My barista Frank didn't show up for work today."

No, that's not right, Sancho thought, but kept his counsel.

Then the man at the desk began to act even more bizarrely. "If you humor me," he said, "before I give you gentlemen your keys, will you allow me to examine your ears?"

"Our ears?" Quichotte replied, in deep puzzlement. "Well, on the one hand, I don't see why not, our ears being of the common or garden variety; but on the other hand, that is a highly intrusive request."

"Indulge me," said Mr. Jonésco. "I have become something of a student of human physiognomy of late. But it's fine, it's fine. Now that I look, I see that you both have splendid and completely human ears."

"Did you say *human*?" Sancho said.

"No," replied the man at the desk, "I said *normal*. Perfectly normal ears. Your noses also seem entirely appropriate for your faces."

"Now it's our noses he draws attention to," Sancho protested. "Maybe we should look for another motel?"

"You won't find many motels open for business, I'm sorry to tell you," said the proprietor. "Many people have fled the town. *Left*," he corrected himself. "*Left* is what I meant to say, and what, in fact, I believe I did say. The population, regrettably, has declined. This used to be one of the stops of the Manhattan ferry service, but the port is now out of commission, and many people relocated after it shut down. There has been, in fact, a population decline of seven percent from the 13,501 counted in the 2000 census. May I finally, as a final check, ask you to open your mouths so that I can inspect your teeth?"

That was too much even for a man of Quichotte's mild disposition. "We most certainly will not comply with that request," he said, drawing himself up. "Now hand over the keys, my good man, and let's have an end to this."

"Of course, of course, my apologies," said Jonésco, doing as Quichotte had asked. "I'm sure you haven't noticed anything amiss in your dental structures recently. Nothing in the way of enlargements?"

"What on earth can you mean by *enlargements*?" Sancho demanded. "Have you been drinking while your barista is away?"

"By no means did I say *enlargements*," Jonésco answered. "I said *toothaches*. A simple solicitous inquiry. In my family we suffer terribly from toothaches all the time."

"What you said sounded nothing like *toothaches*," Sancho objected, "and it sounded exactly like *enlargements*."

"Never mind now, Sancho," Quichotte tried to bring the discussion to a close. "Let us go to our room. I need a nap."

Just then the trumpeting sound arose again, more than one trumpeter this time, and it wasn't that far away. "What on earth is that awful noise?" Sancho asked.

The motel proprietor gave a little laugh which, it seemed to Sancho, contained more than a modicum of nervousness, even of fear. "Flügelhorns," the fellow said. "In our town there are many avid flügelhorn players and they like, in the afternoons, to rehearse."

"Well," said Quichotte, "they don't sound very expert to me. That's a frightful din and I hope they don't rehearse all night."

ON THE ROAD TO BERENGER, Sancho had noticed that as Quichotte neared New York and what he believed would be the grand and happy culmination of his quest, the years seemed to drop away from him and a certain gaiety, a passion for life, was reborn in his breast. He was relentlessly cheerful, laughed a good deal, enjoyed engaging Sancho in heated discussions about music, politics, and art, and in general seemed to be getting younger in every respect, except that his knees gave him a deal of trouble, and he dragged his right leg. Old as he was, he appeared to be unconcerned by questions of mortality, of when the end might come and what might or might not lie beyond that great finality. "I saw an interview on TV," he told Sancho, "with a famous filmmaker who was asked by the sycophantic interviewer if he was happy that he would always live on in his great cinematic masterpieces. 'No,' the filmmaker replied, 'I would prefer to live on in my apartment.' This is also my plan. If the choice is between a necessarily tedious death and immortality, I choose to live forever."

He began, too, to tell Sancho stories of his salad days, when he had many friends, traveled the world, and was attractive to many women. "Oh, the girls, the girls!" he cried, tittering lasciviously. "Mine was a generation when frequent sexual intercourse was thought of as freedom, and like all the men of my time, I believed in that freedom with all my lustful heart." Now at last he spoke about his old life. The "girls" began to blur together in Sancho's thoughts. He noticed some common elements to the stories. The girls almost always left Quichotte after a short time, and they almost all had bland nondescript Western names, and Quichotte did not specify the cities in which he had known them or the languages they spoke or their religious affiliations or anything that would bring them to life as human beings. It was almost as if he hadn't known them very well. It was almost as if . . . and then he understood that they were all precursors of Miss Salma R, all shadows in his life as she was a shadow, people not known but loved from a distance. Maybe they were real people glimpsed across a room or in a magazine. Maybe they were dreams. Maybe they were all characters in TV shows.

Or: were they all women he had pursued slash stalked?

Or worse?

Who was Quichotte anyway?

There was one woman about whom Quichotte spoke differently. This was the lady in New York to whom he affectionately referred as the Human Trampoline. She didn't appear to be a past romantic liaison, but it sounded as if she did actually exist, and Quichotte was plainly uncertain of his welcome. "We will definitely look her up," he told Sancho, "and if she wishes to see us, that will be delightful for us both." He didn't use her real name or provide any further details. But this was someone who mattered to him. Maybe if they did meet, some of the mysteries surrounding Quichotte might be solved.

Sancho began to think that Quichotte might be a virgin, just like himself. And sometimes he had a stranger thought: that just as Quichotte had invented him, so also somebody else had invented Quichotte.

———

THE NEXT MORNING, while Quichotte was still asleep, Sancho walked out into the streets of Berenger, looking for a coffee. In the Starbucks there were two men arguing, who seemed to be friends quarreling over the fact that one of them was drunk while the other wanted to discuss something important.

"The question is," the sober one was saying, "are they the way things are going or is it just a temporary aberration? We need to know this before we buy."

"They're fucking monsters," said the drunk one. "Shouldn't be allowed to exist. Nobody's going to buy a damn thing from them."

"Of course we aren't planning to buy from *them*," the sober one said. "For God's sake. The question is, can we live with the situation or not?"

"You wan' know how good the schools are is that it," the drunk one replied. "How easy is the commute. Fucking monsters I'm saying and you wan' know the crime rate."

The Starbucks server suddenly jumped, literally jumped up off the ground. "Did you feel that?" she cried. Now everything on her counter was jumping too.

"A small earthquake," said the sober man, trying to sound reassuring.

"That's not an earthquake," the drunk man said.

Sancho ran to the door and looked down the street. He saw that Mr. Jonésco had come out of the motel across the way and was staring in the same direction. Then around the corner thundered a large mastodon, a living specimen of *M. americanum,* last seen in North America perhaps ten thousand years ago. It rampaged down the road destroying parked cars and storefronts. Sancho stood still, rooted to the spot in horror.

"Oh my God!" shouted Mr. Jonésco. "Frankie, is that you?"

———

"NOTHING SO DIVISIVE HAS ever happened in Berenger since I came here from Romania to escape Communism," Mr. Jonésco said. Quichotte and Sancho were sitting with him in the motel bar, and they all needed and were having stiff drinks, vodka for Mr. Jonésco, whiskey for Sancho and Quichotte. "I don't know how it will end," the motel proprietor went on. "Who will make the beds and vacuum the rooms? There is no logic to it. Perfectly okay people, people who were our neighbors and our staff and with whom our kids went to school, turning into mastodons overnight! Without warning! You don't know who will be next. Now you understand why I wanted to inspect your ears and noses and teeth. For signs of mastodonitis, as I call it, though there is no evidence that it is a medical disease."

"Was this a happy town before the mastodons?" Quichotte asked.

Jonésco shrugged. "Happy, who knows. People looked like they got along. But now we see that many were mastodons under the skin."

"How many?" Sancho asked.

Jonésco spread his arms. "Hard to be certain," he said. "Since they changed, they mostly bunch together near the river and we don't go down there anymore, though once lovers walked there hand in hand, and you could buy a hot dog and a soda and watch the moon rise over the water. Sometimes one of them comes barreling through downtown, as Frankie did just now, looking for their old haunts, perhaps, wishing things were as they had been, or just hating the old haunts for refusing to accept them, and wanting to destroy whatever they can. Up here in the main part of town people are frozen by fear, and everyone watches everyone else for the first signs, the enlargements of the ears and noses, and the arrival of the tusks. Once one has turned into a mastodon he is utterly impervious to good sense. The mastodons refuse to believe that they have turned into horrible, surrealistic mutants, and they become hostile and ag-

gressive, they take their children out of school, and have contempt
for education. My belief is that many of them can still speak English, but they prefer to bellow like badly played flügelhorns. In the
first days one or two of them insisted that they were the true Americans, and we were the dinosaurs and ought to be extinct. But after
a short time they gave up on talking to us, and just yowled like
flügelhorns instead."

"I have heard a flügelhorn played," Quichotte said mildly, "and
I do not believe it sounds the way you think it sounds."

Jonésco didn't care. "To me the word *flügelhorn* and the word
mastodon go together," he said. "And that's all that needs to be said
about that."

"When we arrived," Sancho asked him, "you said something
about barricades and then pretended you hadn't."

"It's supposed to be a quarantine zone," Jonésco said. "Because
of the mastodonitis. To prevent the whole of the United States
from becoming a land of mastodons. This is what we were assured,
on local radio, from the megaphones mounted on the vans of the
local authority, on the websites of power. But here you are, so
plainly the barricades were not erected. Already, perhaps, the mastodons are in the Lincoln Tunnel and then all will be lost, perhaps all
has already been lost."

"Not all metamorphoses are capable of being reversed,"
Quichotte reflected. "At a certain point, a tipping point, if you will,
we may have to accept that these mastodons are citizens just like us,
and we will have to find a way to bridge the gap between us, however hostile toward us, however ignorant and prejudiced, they may
appear. But we have been traveling far and wide and have heard
nothing of these creatures in other places, so the problem may still
be contained here in this microcosm of Berenger, and if so, may be
containable, and America can go on being what it always was."

"But what is to be done?" Jonésco wailed. "My business, like so
many others, is ruined."

Quichotte rose swaying to his feet, whiskey glass in hand. "I see now that we are at the very end of the fourth valley," he declared, "for here reality as we believed it to be has truly ceased to exist, and our eyes are opened to this new and dark revelation of how things may actually be. I understand that this has been shown to me because it is an essential part of the Way. I will go through this veil and as a result may come to the place where the path to the Beloved is revealed."

"What is he talking about?" Jonésco asked Sancho. "What veil? Here we are confronted by a terrifying insanity, and he sits with us spouting a foolishness of his own."

"He talks like this," Sancho said good-naturedly. "Don't mind him."

"The veil is *maya,*" Quichotte said. "It is the veil of illusion which prevents our eyes from seeing clearly. That which we previously believed to be reality was an error of perception caused by being forced to see through that veil. Now the veil is ripped from our eyes and we perceive the truth."

"And the truth is mastodons?" Jonésco asked.

"The truth is whatever is put before us to overcome," Quichotte replied, "so that the Beloved may be attained."

AN UNEASY NIGHT'S SLEEP FOLLOWED, for Sancho at least; Quichotte, calm and resolute, slept fairly soundly, although he did get up early and dressed with the care of a soldier going to war. Jonésco met them in the motel's simple dining area. "My cook Alfie didn't show today," he said. "I'm afraid he may have joined forces with the tuskers. You'll have to put up with the eggs I cooked personally." Quichotte ate heartily; Sancho, less so.

"Is there a newspaper in Berenger?" Quichotte asked Mr. Jonésco. "*The Berenger Eagle? The Berenger Star-Tribune? The Berenger Globe? The Berenger Mercury? The Berenger Plain Dealer? The Berenger Times-Picayune?* And has it reported on the mastodons?"

"The print edition of *The Berenger Gazetto* died several years ago," Jonésco told him, "and I don't think the web page has been updated lately. Maybe the Editor is having the same staffing problems as myself. The office is right down the street."

"Then," cried Quichotte, leaping to his feet and stabbing at the air with an upraised index finger, "the *Gazetto* is where the resistance must begin."

Outside the *Gazetto* office building, which was actually an ice cream parlor with a couple of rooms upstairs where the paper was located, a small crowd had gathered, licking ice creams while they protested and argued in the manner of old friends who have suddenly stopped trusting one another. "It's an outrage!" cried a bow-tied gentleman with a briefcase. "These mastodons are riding roughshod over everything we hold sacred, and that includes your barista Frankie, Jonésco, and we're holding you responsible for the damage he has caused." A lady in a floral-print dress who might have been Frankie's mother shouted back at him, "It's because people like you behaved so patronizingly to my Frankie that he defected. You think you can go on being snooty at people for years without facing the consequences? Well, you have sown the wind. Now we are all reaping the whirlwind." The hubbub increased, the crowd grew larger, and people took sides, anti-mastodon like Mr. Bow Tie, sympathetic to mastodons like Mrs. Floral Print, and even a few distinctly pro-mastodon voices. "The system is corrupt," a young man on a bicycle shouted, "and if it cannot be changed it must be destroyed. The mastodon revolution is here and you must all choose which side of history you want to be on."

"Has anybody seen the mastodons in the green suits?" asked a man in a brown suit. "It's said they can walk on their hind legs, like human beings. I haven't seen one myself but I'm reliably informed they exist. It's my opinion that these are the moderate mastodons, the ones who want to make an accommodation with human beings, and we need to negotiate terms with them. Has anyone seen one?"

"Yes, from a distance," shouted the town drunk, already well advanced in his drunkenness at breakfast time. "But I thought it was my mother-in-law and ignored it." This comment was greeted with hisses, boos, cries of "shame," etc., and the town drunk subsided to the sidewalk, propped up against a lamppost.

The Editor, a flustered young woman who had only recently taken over the position when her formidably competent aunt decided to retire, came downstairs to calm things down, but her presence only increased the level of excitement.

"Why is there nothing on your page about this crisis?" Mr. Bow Tie demanded. "It's an outrage."

The Editor looked at him sternly. "It is the practice of all responsible media outlets," she said, "not to provide terrorists with the oxygen of publicity."

The use of the word *terrorists* inflamed everyone, above all the young man on, or now, in fact, off his bicycle. "These are not terrorists, you fool," he yelled. "These are American patriots."

"Things are getting out of hand," Quichotte said to Mr. Jonésco. "I must take charge and lead the people toward a solution. But what that solution might be, I confess, is a question that presently defeats me utterly."

All this while Sancho had been deep in conversation with a studious-looking, young, bespectacled woman in a white lab coat. Now, to Quichotte's surprise, it was not himself but Sancho who took the lead, raising a hand and silencing the crowd with an unexpected air of command, and getting up onto a bench with White Lab Coat Woman at his side.

"Mastodons are creatures from the faraway past," he said, "and I don't think many of us, especially the younger people, are interested in a return to the Stone Age. Back then the mastodons became extinct—this young woman in the lab coat tells me—because early humans hunted them down. So that's one solution. Hunt them down."

There were some nodding heads in the crowd and a chant of "Hunt—them—down!" began, then petered out for lack of widespread support.

"Or," Sancho said, "we can be grateful for what my friend here has done, because she has found the cure."

Here the White Lab Coat Woman removed from her pocket a small phial containing a colorless liquid and held it up for all to see.

"In some cases," she shouted out in a strong voice, "the metamorphosis is partial, there are mastodons with some human features, such as these green-suited mastodons walking erect like us, and in other cases the metamorphosis may look complete but is still within the parameters of reversibility. A simple dart from a dart gun will achieve the cure."

"Shoot—the—darts!" the crowd began to shout. "Shoot—the—darts!"

"However, I have to warn you that in cases in which the metamorphosis has gone too far, the cure will not reverse the process. In these cases the mastodon, the mutant, will die."

"So it's kill or cure?" the Editor asked.

"Kill—or—cure!" the crowd shouted. "Kill—or—cure!" The pro-mastodon faction had fallen silent, possibly denoting acquiescence, or simply the realization that they were outnumbered.

It was Mrs. Floral Print who made the kindly liberal objection. "Killing them seems harsh," she cried. "They were our own community until the day before yesterday. And I don't want my Frankie to die!" She began to sob. Others comforted her. But then the ground began to tremble, a loud trumpeting sound was heard, and the crowd scattered screaming. The mastodon that came thundering down the street was indeed one of the fabled green-suited creatures that could stand on their hind legs. Standing up like that, it looked even larger and more frightening than the ordinary kind, and it didn't behave with anything like moderation, plowing into the ice cream parlor and destroying it, and the *Gazetto* offices above, before it ran off honking into the distance.

"So much for my moderate mastodon theory," said Brown Suit Man. "I vote we go with the poison darts."

"They aren't poison," White Lab Coat Woman protested, but to no avail. The crowds, coming back together, demanded "Poison darts now!"

"Very well," Quichotte cried, taking the lead. "And I myself will fire the first dart."

It turned out the laboratory where White Lab Coat Woman had found the cure was just around the corner. The crowd moved there quickly. She and Sancho went inside and brought out a quantity of dart guns, all loaded with the curative needles. When the arms had been distributed, the group moved down toward the water's edge, where the mastodons had gathered in two distinct groups, the green-suited hind-leg-walkers to the left and the more traditional mastodons to the right. It's almost as if they don't care very much for each other, Sancho thought, but what unites them, I guess, is that they care for us even less.

On the way down to where the mastodons were gathered Sancho had another disquieting thought. What a strange town this was, he thought, where everything was so conveniently next door to everything else—the motel, the coffee place, the ice cream parlor, the newspaper offices, the laboratory—and where this group of recognizable character types rushed up and shouted and then rushed away screaming and then rushed back again to shout some more, almost as if they were doing it on cue, or according to some script which he and Quichotte had not read. Mrs. Floral Print, for example, didn't seem to be in the state a mother might actually be in if her child had really turned into a mastodon, and nobody else seemed to be quite, so to speak, psychologically convincing. It was all too stylized, somehow, to be real.

But Quichotte had warned him that reality as they had understood the word would now cease to exist, so maybe this theatricality was an aspect of that transformation?

Then they were there, the human beings, on the higher ground above the water, looking down at the baleful mastodons, some in suits, others not, and their weapons were aimed, and Quichotte's dart gun was raised along with the others, and Sancho suddenly understood that they were somehow being tested, who knew by whom or why, and he cried out to Quichotte, "Don't shoot!" At which point all hell broke loose, the mastodons saw that they were under attack and charged, and the humans of Berenger began to fire their dart guns, panickily, some in the air, some in the direction of the mastodons, and in every other direction as well, and they were yelling and running, and the mastodons were charging, the ones in the green suits as well as the ones on all fours, and Quichotte and Sancho, rooted to the spot, found themselves in a kind of no-man's-land between the charging tuskers and the screaming humans, and there somehow was Mr. Jonésco pointing at them and laughing an insane laugh, and *this is it,* Sancho thought, *looks like it all ends right here,* and then a sort of cloud or fog descended suddenly over the scene, and when it dispersed the battle of Berenger had vanished, as had Berenger itself, and they were back in the Cruze turning off the turnpike, and Quichotte was saying slash had just said that "we ought to be fresh and perky for our entrance into the great city where Destiny lies." The fog dispersed quickly and there was a sign pointing to the town of Weehawken, New Jersey (pop. 12,554, reflecting a decline of seven percent from the 13,501 counted in the 2000 census), and the mastodon-benighted town of Berenger, New Jersey, was nowhere to be seen, not then, not later, never.

Quichotte somehow managed to guide the car down the exit ramp and then pulled over onto the hard shoulder, perspiring and panting. Sancho, wide-eyed, uncomprehending, shook in the seat beside him.

"What just happened to us?" Sancho finally asked.

Quichotte shook his head. "Now that we have passed through the veil," he said finally, in a weak voice, "I surmise that visions and other phantasmagoria are to be expected."

CHAPTER THIRTEEN

Quichotte in the Big City;
many Revelations; & Sancho has
a grave Mishap

Q UICHOTTE, DRIVING THE CRUZE OUT OF THE LINCOLN Tunnel into Manhattan, felt like a snail coming out of its shell. Here was bustle and thrum, hustle and flow, everything he had run from, had spent the better part of his life recoiling from, concealing himself in the heart of the country, leading a small life among other small lives. And now he was back on the main stage, on which the headliner acts performed, he was at the high rollers' table, betting the farm on love. "The fifth valley," he said quietly, and Sancho looked at him for elucidation, but for the moment he said no more.

The city (pop. 8,623,000) greeted them with a sudden autumn storm: thunder that said *I see you, and who do you think you are?*, lightning that said *I will fry the flesh off your bodies and your skeletons will dance to my tune*, rain that said *I will wash you away like the rats on the sidewalk and the bugs in the gutters, and like all the other fools who came here on quests in search of glory, salvation, or love.*

They took shelter in the Blue Yorker hotel, which stood conveniently just a couple of blocks from the tunnel exit, $103 including parking, excellent value, no ID demanded, no questions asked, cash money required per night in advance, and only when they entered their Oriental Delights–themed room did they understand that they were in one of the city's numerous no-tell motels, with six free porno stations on the TV. There was adjustable mood lighting. There were strategically placed mirrors. The bellhop, a sleazy old Korean gent wearing an ancient pillbox hat, said that for fifteen dollars they could upgrade to the Arabian Nights room with Jacuzzi and steam bath, and if there was anything else they wanted, maybe good massage, deep tissue massage, massage with happy ending, anything, you understand, he could arrange that too. There were twin double beds in the room, for double the action if you want it, the bellhop said, at which they shut the door in his face. That was no way to talk to a father and his son who had come to the city on a mission. "We will move tomorrow," Quichotte said, "or as soon as the rain stops." Sancho bounced down onto his bed and looked up at his reflection in the angled mirror above him. "No!" he objected. "This is cool."

The night was full of noises, of pleasure, pain, and painful pleasure. Sancho slept soundly through it all, Quichotte less soundly. In the morning, after the storm, the city glistened like a new promise. Quichotte, waking up after a night spent tossing fitfully between fear and hope, saw Sancho sitting up in bed switching between the available video pornography, checking it out. "Older women are the best," Sancho said. "But maybe I'm just saying that because I'm so young that most women are older than I am and the ones younger than me are illegal."

Quichotte realized that a moment came in all families when fathers and sons had to talk about these things. "Perhaps you get this from me," he said, "because when I was your age watching TV, all the beautiful women were older than myself. There were no porno channels back then, I hasten to add. But, you know, Lucille Ball, and *I-dream-of* Jeannie. The first woman I loved who was approximately my own age was Victoria Principal as Pamela Ewing in *Dal-*

las. Now, however, such are my advanced years that all the older ladies, and many of the ladies of my own age, are deceased. Therefore, my last and greatest love, Miss Salma R, is my junior by some distance. Let us find a diner and eat a fine New York breakfast."

Sancho grew bored of the pornography (the participants on the screen looked bored too) and started hopping channels aimlessly. Then suddenly he gave a gasp and jumped to his feet. There was the woman he loved, right there on *Headline News!,* talking about the aftermath of the killing in Beautiful, Kansas, its impact on the community, the community's desire to be accepted as American like anyone else. She mentioned the history of America, as when immigration issues arose it seemed compulsory to do, and she did not fail to refer to Emma Lazarus's sonnet "The New Colossus." Mother of Exiles, check. I lift my lamp beside the golden door, check. The caption to her talking head identified her as a lawyer, and the appointed spokesperson for the widow and family of the murdered Indian-American man.

"Give me your laptop," Sancho demanded, and after a few moments of feverish searching he scribbled something on a piece of paper and lifted his eyes in triumph, waving his prize in the air. "I found her," he said. "Her office address, email, and number." Then he deflated and sat down on his bed, looking unhappy. "Now I could call her," he finished, much less confidently, "but probably she'd just hang up when she heard my voice."

Quichotte put a hand on his son's shoulder. "Television is the god that goes on giving," he said. "This morning it has given you a big gift. You will know how to use it when the time comes."

At the diner Sancho stared morosely at a stack of pancakes soaked in maple syrup. Quichotte, eating a toasted cheese sandwich with extra bacon, perceived that further discussion was required. "In the fifth valley," he began—but Sancho wasn't in the mood for valley talk this morning, and rolled his eyes impatiently—"we must learn that everything is connected. Look: you turned on the TV to watch a series of obscenities and then you discovered important information about this girl of yours. By chance, you may say. I say not by chance. You found it because everything is connected, this channel to that channel, this button to that button, this choice to that choice."

He had Sancho's attention now, and launched into a longer statement. "Once," he said, "people believed that they lived in little boxes, boxes that contained their whole stories, and that there was no need to worry much about what other people were doing in their other little boxes, whether nearby or far away. Other people's stories had nothing to do with ours. But then the world got smaller and all the boxes got pushed up against all the other boxes and opened up, and now that all the boxes are connected to all the other boxes, we have to understand what's going on in all the boxes we aren't in, otherwise we don't know why the things happening in our boxes are happening. Everything is connected."

Sancho was eating, but still grouchily cynical. "You mean," he said, "that the thigh bone's connected to the hip bone, the hip bone's connected to the back bone, blah blah," he said. "I believe there's a song about that."

"I must confess to you," Quichotte said, "that the statement I have made was not an easy statement for me to make. For much of my life I have been, one could say, a disconnected man, keeping my own counsel, living with the glowing company of my TV friends, but with little real human companionship. Then love came to town and everything changed. Love brought *me* to town and here I stand, therefore, surrounded by the million million connections between this one and that one, between near and far, between this language and that language, between everything that men are and everything else that they are, and I see that the Way requires me to reconnect with the great thronging crowd of life, to its multiplicity, and beyond its many disharmonies, to its deeper harmonies. It is not easy after so long and I must ask for your understanding. Just as you must take your slow steps toward your Beloved, so I must— gingerly, with great nervousness—make my tentative moves back into human company. Entering New York, I feel like a Catholic entering a confessional booth. Much that has long remained unsaid must now, in all probability, be said. I must circle slowly toward this goal. It may take a little time."

"What is it that's unsaid that must be said?" Sancho was curious.

"All in good time," Quichotte replied.

In the days that followed, Quichotte was pensive and said relatively little, leaving Sancho to wander the city streets alone while he stayed in the hotel room watching TV. He did not, for example, go to stand outside Miss Salma R's apartment building, or outside her offices slash studio, in the hope of glimpsing the woman whose heart he had set out to win. "There is much to be done before I am worthy of her presence," he told Sancho, and then, seemingly, did nothing.

Sancho approached the city methodically, setting himself the task of walking around a different neighborhood each day. And there were moments when Quichotte shook off his apparent torpor and came out as well. It turned out that in the course of their travels he had taken the time to arrange a program of activities to ease himself and Sancho into city life, obtaining audience tickets for *50 Central, The $100,000 Pyramid, The Chew, The Dr. Oz Show,* and *Good Morning America,* and on these outings into the world he knew best he seemed more like his usual self.

But wasn't he supposed to have given up his addictions in the fourth valley, as he called it? Was he backsliding? Would that delay things? Sancho didn't care about the valleys and by now strongly suspected that they were to be numbered among Quichotte's delusions that had no meaning or effect in the real world, so that it made no difference whether he played by his own rules or not. But when, Sancho wondered, would the old man make his move? And how?

"There's someone I have to see before this goes any further," Quichotte said at breakfast, after one week had passed. "Nothing can happen until this matter has been straightened out. The Path will remain closed."

"Is it a woman?" Sancho asked.

"Yes."

"I know, it's a previous lover you still have a soft spot for, but you don't know if she's still carrying the torch, too, and she's kind of crazy so you think it's probably a bad idea to start up with her again anyway, but you have to see her to put your mind at rest."

"No."

"I know, it's a previous lover who treated you like shit but now she wants your forgiveness and maybe more than that, maybe she's hinting that she wants you back and until you see her you won't be able to clear her out of your mind."

"No."

"I know, it's a previous lover who's now with someone else but keeps sending you messages saying she isn't satisfied. Maybe she texts you hot photographs of herself to encourage you to come back."

"No."

"It would be amazing, at your age, if you had all these women after you, right? And all you want is one woman, but these others go on circling around you like helicopters shining their beams down at you. Am I right?"

"No."

"I know," Sancho said with sudden clarity. "It's the Human Trampoline."

"Yes," Quichotte said. His face remained impassive, expressionless.

Sancho clapped his hands. "I knew it!" he cried. "I knew it all along. She's the only other woman you ever loved, and she broke your heart, and that's why you ran away from everything for all these years, and now you have to see her so you can put the old love away and open your heart fully to the new one."

"No."

"Then what? If she's not your old girlfriend, who is she? Your old college roommate? Your dentist? Your therapist? Your bank manager? Your drug dealer? Your parole officer? Your chess instructor? Your priest?"

"She's my sister," Quichotte said, "and a long time ago, I did her wrong. I think that's the right way around."

SANCHO PONDERS THIS REVELATION.

I knew it, I guess. I knew he had secrets in the part of his head I can't get into. But a whole sister! That's a lot. That's a lot he just said right there. God from the machine, this is kinda like an ancient Roman theater trick, I'm finding the Latin in his storehouse now. *Dea ex machina*. Poof! Here's a sister I've got you didn't know about, he tells me, and she has been here all the time.

It's a half sister. The father remarried, there was a child, the father died, the mother, who knows what became of her. I don't know and either he doesn't either or he isn't saying or it's still locked away somewhere deep inside him, still hidden inside that cloud I can't blow away. How well do they know each other? Not very well, not anymore anyway, they haven't met in many years, they don't call, they don't text, they don't write. Or do they? What do I know, but I'm guessing hardly at all. But once they must have known each other, otherwise why this nickname, which I'm surmising is discourteous. A trampoline, it's a thing people bounce up and down on, no? So he's basically calling her a whore.

Not very nice.

But no, no, he's telling me, it's the song, it means she's bouncing into Graceland. It's a way of saying she's a person of grace. Well, excuse me for misunderstanding. I'd excuse her for misunderstanding too. But he's telling me about her now and she sounds like a goddamn saint. Made a stack of money on Wall Street when she was still in her twenties, a *high* stack, higher than the jumbo stack of pancakes in the diner down the street, if you take my meaning: I mean *high* . . . and then one day she said, this is not the life I need, and walked out past the charging bull and never worked for the finance bros again. Now she's running her own organization, facing toward India, Pakistan, and Bangladesh, creating a second micro-banking operation alongside Grameen Bank, generating global funding to offer small loans to women in South Asia trying to start up their own enterprises, beauty parlors, food catering, child daycare centers; also fighting sex trafficking, campaigning against sexual violence toward women in India, you get the idea. A noble, selfless individual, giving her life to the betterment of others. A good woman of this type is a kind of trampoline. People bounce on her and fly. And if they fall they bounce on her again and rise again. She doesn't seek flight for herself but she spreads herself wide and people use her to climb as high as they can go.

All this, he's telling me, and I go, okay, great, but (a) what happened between you and (b) what's she really like? I mean, without the halo? He answers the second question first, to keep me hanging on, drawing it out, so annoying. Well, he hasn't seen her for a long time, he says, so the picture in his mind must be horribly out of date. In his mind's eye she's tall with loose, flowing black hair, flashing eyes, and a long face like his own. In his memory she's warm and funny and smart and has the worst bad temper he ever encountered on any woman or for that matter any man. Also in his memory she wasn't quite so politically advanced as she now is, she would tell Polish jokes, jokes that only Jews should tell about Jewish people, and jokes about black people, too, which if someone had recorded them on an iPhone would destroy her career now, but nobody had iPhones back then, and after she left Wall Street where that was the way people laughed over drinks, she became a reformed character, and now her only jokes were innocent, like drummer jokes.—Drummer jokes?—What do you call a drummer whose girlfriend leaves him? Homeless. What do you call an unemployed drummer? Ringo.

Ha ha ha.

He's clearly more than a little frightened of calling her, of seeing her again, white-haired, with those long tresses long gone, her hair shaved close to the scalp. He's afraid she'll slam her door in his face—*No, that's the past,* like Nastassja Kinski in one version of the *Paris, Texas* screenplay—but maybe he's even more afraid of the opposite: that when she sees him her face will break into a long, slow smile, a smile she has denied herself all these years, and then she'll take him in her arms, and she'll cry, and caress his cheek, and say, "How stupid we were, to lose each other for most of our lives," and she'll greet me with great affection, too, and cook a fabulous dinner for us, and they'll sit hand in hand late into the night, telling each other their stories, apologizing to each other, expressing their sibling love. And then within twenty-four hours he'll step on some invisible land mine and the monster will come out of her, and she'll yell at him, scream abuse at him, and tell him to get out and never darken her doorstep again, and he'll end up broken into pieces in the gutter outside her building. He's afraid of her half-sisterly half-love.

She's a cancer survivor, he did hear that, breast cancer, around ten years ago, double mastectomy, looks like she beat it, she has been in full remission for a long time. He's frightened of seeing the marks of her life on her face and of her seeing the marks of his life on his. After their father died they were briefly close. She called him Smile-Smile, he called her H.T. or Trampoline. They shared an interest in good food and they went out dining together. But there would be fights. At the end of all the warmth and laughter something he said, some innuendo she thought she heard in his voice, something that hadn't been there at all, would get her goat and she would start shouting. In public places, yes. It shocked him and made him retreat. So there were fewer dinners together, and then none. And at one of them he had done the unforgivable thing.

Did you hit her? I asked him. Is that it? You hit her across the face with an open hand and a trickle of blood came down from her ear, and she spent the rest of her life campaigning against violent men?

No.

The memory came out of him with difficulty. The chronology

QUICHOTTE   201

was a particular problem. There were parts of their story that were
lost to him now. He had accused her of having swindled him out of
his inheritance. That was it. She had been the one dealing with lawyers on probate issues after their father's death, and he told her he
knew that she had taken far more than her share. He went further
and accused her of falsifying or even forging the will. He threatened
her with public denunciation, a press conference. What he couldn't
explain, because of the holes in his memory which were like rifts in
the universe, areas of nonexistence in the middle of existence, was
why he had done it, and he had done it, he thought he remembered,
years after the event. She had retaliated against his threats, sending
him a lawyer's letter saying that he should be in no doubt that she
would do everything in her power to defend her good name. She
pointed out that he had signed off on their father's will, and there
were legal documents in the public record which proved his acceptance of it. His accusation was a major defamation, and if he made it
public she would sue him for every penny he possessed. It was a letter designed to scare him into silence and it succeeded. They stopped
talking and since then years had passed and both of them had gone
through many changes: her sainthood, his increasingly isolated personality, her public persona, his private slide toward what he's become, which I prefer not to put into words right now.

But whoa, this is what I said to him. Inheritance? You have an
actual inheritance?

Yes.

All this time, you've actually had—what—a lot of money in the
bank?

Some money, yes.

But we still end up sharing a room in the Blue Yorker motel?
That's fucked up.

This was our dialogue. He tells me for the one millionth time
that he's going through these valleys of purification so that he can
"merit the love of the Beloved," and that extravagance and love of

material things is the opposite of the Way. And I say, would it be too much of a fucking extravagance for me to get my own fucking room?

He says, don't use language like that when you're talking to me. So now we're on bad terms too.

And so here's what I need help with. Are there unforgivable things? Unforgivable acts, unforgivable words, unforgivable bits of behavior? As the new kid on the block I have my share of moodiness and maybe brattishness, but is there anything I could say that he, "Dad," couldn't forgive? Or this girl I dream about. Have I already been unforgivable with her, hitting on her when she was grieving? Is it already too late and thirty years from now, *forty* years from now, we'll maybe run into each other somewhere and she'll say, you know, I liked you, and if only you hadn't done that thing then maybe we could have had something together, but you did that thing and I couldn't forgive it. I'm looking at Daddy Q filled with uncertainty about calling his sister, staring at his phone, not calling the number, trying to decide if he should write first, or go the other way and just show up at her door and fall on his knees and ask to be forgiven. I don't see it. Half a lifetime or more away from your own flesh and blood because of what? Some bad words that didn't even have any bad effects? Surely that can't be right?

Suppose there's a God. Is he an unforgiving God? And if we ought to try to be like him, as we're told we should, should we be unforgiving too?

QUICHOTTE, A MAN UNUSED to intimate human interactions, but convinced in his heart that until he had faced his sister he would be unready to face his Beloved, did what he always did at moments of confusion or crisis. He stayed in his room and watched TV. The images on the screen calmed and comforted him, and felt true in a way that New York City never had. The city had always struck him as being chaotic, formless, overcrowded, harsh, and possessed of no dominant narrative line. On TV the sitcoms, the soaps, the reality shows, were in sharp contrast to the hurly-burly outside the Blue Yorker motel. They moved as if on tramlines through their well-established moves, twists, and cliffhangers, and arrived at satisfying resolutions. This was what Quichotte wanted of life, shapeliness and firm conclusions. What else was his quest but an effort to extract hidden meaning from the world and by doing so earn himself the happy ending for which he so desperately yearned? He didn't spend much time on the news and information channels, but as he surfed by them he saw that they, too, sought to impose meaning on the maelstrom of events, and that comforted him. A couple of days sitting there quietly being reassured by the dark metropolitan plot lines of *Law & Order: Special Victims Unit* (which he had failed to give up; nobody's perfect) might give him some New York rhythm and the strength to do what he had to get done. He put twenty-dollar bills in Sancho's pocket and sent him to walk the streets alone. "It's not so warm anymore," he told his son. "Here. Take my coat."

Once the youth had left, Quichotte began channel hopping. What caught his attention on this occasion was not his typically favored fare, but an interview with the celebrated American scientist, entrepreneur, and billionaire of Indian origin Evel Cent. The name Evel Cent was itself an invention, perhaps derived, Quichotte surmised, from the more Indian-sounding *Awwal Sant,* or something similar. Slick-haired, slender, and underslept, this reinvented man looked every inch like a Bollywood movie star moving from handsome youth into a slightly ragged middle age, and spoke in fast spiky riffs as if hopped up on methedrine, unapologetically using a mixture of the difficult modern vocabulary of high technology and the lingo of modern dystopian fantasy, as if to say, I don't care if you understand me or not, but I know how to get your attention if I choose to do so. *Evel* perhaps came from the great daredevil Knievel, and *Cent* was money, and there was the meaning of his name staring everyone in the face. Although the sound of the name gave off a different odor. Evel Cent, a bad stink. To some people that was what he was, an unpleasant self-promoting capitalist fart, but to others, mostly young others, he seemed like a kind of prophet, and here he was on television, doing a prophet's work while also justifying the opinions of those who thought him a phony egotist skunk.

What he was talking about today was nothing less than the end of the world, what he described as the growing instability of the continuum or gestalt, which, if the trend continued, he declared, would lead to the crumbling into nothing of the whole of space-time. He would, he said, bring forward the science to support this claim at the proper time. For the moment all he would say was that his admittedly alarming claim was backed by teams of astrophysicists working at the leading universities, including several Nobel laureates. The evidence of disintegration was still inadequate, but it was there. There was much work to do to establish the causes, the extent, and the likely rate of expansion of the Instability. But of its existence he had no doubt at all. The question was, would the human race take this lying down and go meekly into oblivion, or would we, could we, do something about it?

Quichotte thought, The man himself looks like a once beautiful entity that is beginning to fray at the edges.

Evel Cent moved smoothly from eschatology to sales pitch. He and his teams were working on an astonishing project which he called NEXT. NEXT stood for Neighbor Earth Xchange Technology. The concept of parallel space-time continuums, parallel universes and therefore parallel Earths, was no longer disputed by any serious physicists. The question was, where were they, and how could we get there from here? If our universe crumbled into space dust, might we not rescue ourselves by traveling in new kinds of vessels that could jump toward an alternative universe that was still stable? *This!* he said, now speaking in a series of exclamations accompanied by a jabbing forefinger, *is! My dream! A new! Home! For Humanity!*

Quichotte was electrified by Evel Cent's performance. Had he not himself recently written to his Beloved and predicted the end of

things? His own inspiration had been love, love as the perfect culmination and therefore conclusion of all things, and perhaps what Evel
Cent and his teams of geniuses had perceived was that he, Quichotte,
was nearing his goal, and the universe was preparing its last rites in
response! Science was confirming what love had driven him intui-
tively to understand.

This was big. He needed to think about this. He switched off the
television set. Something else nagged at his broken memory, something about this man, this Evel Cent. Had they met?

THIS WAS THE DAY on which he began to draft letters to his sister.

Dear H. T. (his first attempt began),

This after a long silence comes from your airhead brother, in the hope
that blood may prove thicker than air, and that we may meet again in
loving fashion. Socrates, too, was considered an airhead, by the way.
In Aristophanes' play The Clouds, *Socrates floats overhead in a bal-*
loon basket, getting high so he can elevate his thoughts. At first this
seems to mean his wisdom is not down-to-earth. On the other hand, it
is only from Socrates' ivory tower (or basket) that he can put the earth
into perspective. Having his head in the clouds grounds him. I do not
compare myself to the great philosopher except to say that I, too, have
been Johnny Head-in-Air. I, too, have tried to elevate my thoughts.

No, that was plainly too vain and self-regarding. He stopped,
crumpled this absurd effort into a ball, and tossed it away. He tried
again:

Dear H. T.,

For a long time, in my younger days, my favorite book was Mr. R.
Pirsig's Zen and the Art of Motorcycle Maintenance. *(I wish*

they would make a limited drama series out of ZAAMM, but that's by the by.) Now that I myself have embarked on a journey across America toward you—yes! I deeply hope that it will not prove to be in vain!—and accompanied by my son—yes! Another thing to tell you about when we meet!—I have been thinking about Mr. R. Pirsig again, and, through Mr. R. Pirsig, about Mr. A. Einstein, whom he quotes as follows: "Man tries to make for himself in the fashion that suits him best a simplified and intelligible picture of the world. He then tries to some extent to substitute this cosmos of his for the world of experience, and thus to overcome it. . . . He makes this cosmos and its construction the pivot of his emotional life in order to find in this way the peace and serenity which he cannot find in the narrow whirlpool of personal experience. . . . The supreme task . . . is to arrive at those universal elementary laws from which the cosmos can be built up by pure deduction. There is no logical path to these laws; only intuition, resting on sympathetic understanding of experience, can reach them. . . ." I must confess that my personal cosmos no longer brings me serenity or peace, yet I long for them, I long to be in harmony with the whole multitudinous world, and I have understood—very late!—but I hope and pray not too late!—that I can only find the peace for which I long by making peace with you. I am learning that everything is connected, and that includes us.

This, too, he crumpled up and discarded. What a nincompoop he was! What did Einstein have to do with anything happening between the Trampoline and himself? Why could he not speak simply, and from the heart, without wrapping his plea in such highbrow fol-de-rol? He made a third attempt:

Dear H.T.,

It may amuse you to learn that in my antiquity I have become a seeker after wisdom, and beyond wisdom, love,

. . . he began, but then stopped, and leapt to his feet, because Sancho tumbled into the room, his face bloodied and his clothes torn, having been badly beaten.

AS HE WALKED AROUND the city wearing his father's cashmere coat, Sancho remembered the white lady at Lake Capote and the unusual leather choker she was wearing around her neck, with a brass buckle at the side, and what looked like a few dangling inches of broken leash. He had thought then it looked like a dog collar, and it wasn't at all the kind of fashion item a lady like that would wear. At the time, he had dismissed it from his thoughts. Maybe, in their haste to leave the campsite and the heightened tensions of that moment, he had been mistaken.

Now, however, he began to see that there had been no mistake. Or, to put it another way: he began to realize that he was seeing things that other people couldn't see. One day on Tenth Avenue, a dozen blocks down from the Blue Yorker motel, he saw a drunk woman stamping on a rainbow. This was outside a store selling crystals and incense. A ray of light from the store passed through a prism dangling in the storefront window and created this fortuitous spectrum on the sidewalk. The drunk woman, a big woman dressed all in black and missing several teeth, was trying to smash the rainbow with her feet and swearing profusely as she did so, unleashing a torrent, a *drool,* of homophobic abuse. Okay, that didn't have to be a vision, but then there was a change in the light, maybe someone moved a lamp in the store, and the rainbow disappeared, *but so did the cursing woman.* As if the one engendered the other. The rainbow engendered the hatred. Yeah, he thought. That's fucked up. Another day, on Madison Avenue among all the clothing stores, he saw three figures dressed all in white including white pointed hoods. That was impossible. This was New York. The Klan wasn't here at all, let alone wearing couture hoods on Madison. He crossed the avenue to get a closer look but the well-dressed crowd merged briefly ahead of him and then parted again and they were gone. This was insane, Sancho thought. It created in him a kind of ontological dread. There were days—it was just about every day, in point of fact—when the issue of his own reality came back at him and haunted him. His coming into being had been so exceptional, his transition from being a dependent sub-clause of the long sentence that was Quichotte into an independent existence continued to feel so improbable, that he had nightmares about having it all come apart, about his very being flickering like a faulty image on TV, then disintegrating and vanishing; about, in short, death. The arrival of these sightings—he resisted the word *visions,* which increased his sense of his own unreality—and the increase in their frequency was alarming. He did not tell Quichotte what he was seeing. Some things were better kept to oneself.

Then while he was walking across the park, kicking at the fallen leaves, as darkness fell—not the smartest of moves, he afterwards allowed—he saw, coming toward him, a group of three middle-aged men in suits, white men, carrying briefcases, ordinary and in-offensive in every way—except that around their necks were the same collars he had seen on the white lady of Lake Capote, the same buckles, the same lengths of dangling leash. Who were these dog-collared people? Was this some sort of nationwide cult he had stumbled across?

"You're staring at us. Why are you staring at us?" The men had stopped, facing Sancho, blocking his path.

Sancho was placatory. "No, sir, not staring. Just walking. Going that way," he said, pointing.

"He was definitely staring," said the second man. "That was im-polite. But these people, they don't know manners."

"They come over here and we pay for their health care," said the third man.

"We worry about the safety of our womenfolk," said the first man.

"We don't know when one of them will go rogue and attack

everything we hold dear. We do know they worship alien gods," said the second man.

"Speak up," said the third man. "Why are you even looking at us? You people shouldn't do that. You should not have done that."

This was impossible, Sancho thought. These were the three least likely-looking thugs in America. These people couldn't possibly be dangerous. These people were gray, harmless, dull. He took a deep breath and spoke up.

"Your neckwear caught my attention," he said. *Mistake,* he immediately realized as he saw their body language change. Moving almost in unison, they set down their briefcases. One of them began to remove his coat.

"Our neckwear," the first man said.

"Excuse me," Sancho said. "I understand it's impolite to stare. I didn't mean to. But I've seen it once before."

"He has seen our neckwear before," the second man said. "Can you believe this boy? He's something. He's unreal."

"We're not wearing any neckwear," the third man said. "It's too hot for fucking neckwear. What neckwear is he talking about?"

"I don't know," the first man said. "I will ask. What fucking neckwear are you talking about, boy?"

Sancho was bewildered, and now also afraid, and in fear and bewilderment he pointed. "The collars," he said, "with the broken leashes."

"Extraordinary," said the second man. "He compares us to dogs."

"He thinks we *are* dogs," the third man said, "dogs that have broken their leashes."

"Savage, dangerous dogs that have been unleashed," the first man said.

"Dogs frothing at the mouth," the second man said. "Beware of the dogs, am I right?"

"Beware of the fucking dogs," the third and first men said in unison.

"Because we have been fucking unleashed," said the second man.

Sancho understood that he had done everything wrong. He had stared when he shouldn't have stared. He had spoken when he shouldn't have spoken. Worst of all, he hadn't run when he should have run. And now they were around him and there was nowhere to run.

And the moral of the story is, he thought, as the punches and kicks began, don't underestimate gray, dull, middle-aged white men in suits, ever again.

They could easily have killed him, but they didn't. Maybe he wasn't worth it. Maybe it was because he was unreal. Maybe it was because they were men who until recently had been tamed and under control and this *unleashing,* whatever caused it, was something new for them. Maybe they were still getting used to their power. Whatever the reason, they left him on the ground, beaten but alive; they picked up their briefcases, put on their coats, and strolled off into the dusk. *"Chimaats!"* he called after them. *"Khajvuas!"* But his voice was too weak for them to hear it. Which was probably just as well.

THE DEMANDS OF PARENTHOOD awoke Quichotte at least partially from the reverie in which he spent the larger portion of his life. He scurried to and fro between the Blue Yorker motel and the local pharmacies and food counters to find hot soup, chicken bowls, cheeseburgers, liniments, Aleve, and bandages, and consequently missed several episodes of *The Real Housewives of Atlanta,* in spite of his passionate interest in the overly full lips of Kim Zolciak and the firing—alleged! The alleged firing!—of Kenya Moore as a warning to the rest of the cast that they should learn how to keep secrets. Sancho had been lucky. His body was covered in an archipelago of black-and-blues but there didn't appear to be any bones broken or anything serious damaged inside him. The cashmere coat was dirty, but it, too, had survived. What the boy needed was rest, sympathy, painkillers, and cheeseburgers.

In the trunk of the Chevy Cruze there was a small case containing what remained of the opioid samples Quichotte had carried on behalf of SPI. These he doled out to Sancho in the first few days, but was very careful about quantities. And the sealed container at the bottom of the bag, the one containing the InSmile™ sublingual fentanyl spray, he left sealed and in its place. Sancho recovered quickly, as the young do, but his mood remained dark.

During these days of Sancho's convalescence, in which they both spent much time in their darkened room, listening to the noises of sexual pleasure filtering through the walls, and, to obscure these noises, turning up the volume while watching (non-pornographic) TV, only to be told by the management that their neighbors were complaining that the high-volume voices of reality stars on the Bravo channel were putting them off, so to speak, their stroke . . . during these stressful days they didn't speak much, except when Sancho wanted to express a need, and Quichotte did his best to satisfy it. They were both preoccupied by their thoughts.

Sancho's thoughts were all of escape. *Get me out of here. I don't care if he's my father, and loves me, and would be devastated etc., I need to strike out on my own. Way back when we were on the road I thought I might betray him by stealing his beloved Salma from him. I don't care about that now. The betrayal I need is my freedom.* He said none of this aloud, but it bubbled in him like a stew.

Quichotte, by contrast, was full of self-reproach. Sancho's injuries had plunged the older man into a condition of profound doubt, in which he questioned everything—how he had led his life, and even the hunger for a child that had brought Sancho into being. He had been something close to homeless for a very long time, living out of the trunk of his car with pit stops in cheap motels . . . what business did such a person have bringing a child into the world? He felt he should apologize to Sancho, but knew that if he did so Sancho would hear it wrongly, would think his father was wishing that he had never been born.

In this way, father caring for son, son receiving his father's ministrations, they grew further and further apart, and the great quest upon which Quichotte had embarked seemed to recede into the distance. Then, in the middle of the night, while the sex shrieks of his neighbors kept him awake, Quichotte arrived at a moment of complete clarity. Enough of these orgasmic motels! His first and only duty was to provide a better life for his child. He would approach his sister, heal that rift, and together they could provide Sancho with the stable family environment he needed. This was how *everything was connected*. This was the only way the *harmony and peace* of the fifth valley could be achieved. And yes, perhaps, once this had been done, the path to the Beloved would be seen. He could not be worthy of the Beloved—how could he be? How could he not have seen that it was ridiculous to think he might be?—until he had proved his ability to do right by his own flesh and blood.

He called her. He didn't even know if she still had the same number, but he called the one he had, and she replied. A lump rose in his throat and for a moment he couldn't speak.

"Who is this?" said his sister's voice.

He didn't speak.

"I'm hanging up," said his sister's voice.

"H.T.?" he said, his own voice trembling.

Now she was silent. Then, "Smile-Smile," she said. "Is it really you?"

"Yes," he said. "What's left of me."

"Where are you?" she said. "Are you here in the city?"

"I'm in a flophouse near the Lincoln Tunnel. With my son."

"Your son. Oh my God. So much time."

"I'm sorry," he said. "For everything. I'm just sorry."

"Come here at once. Can you come now? And bring your, your. Your *son*."

When he hung up Sancho said, "That's it? That's all it took? You both missed out on most of your lives and it would have been so easy not to? Really? That's all you had to say?"

"That seems to be so," he said.

"Wow," Sancho said. "That's fucked up."

CHAPTER FOURTEEN

The Author known as Sam DuChamp meets an Uninvited Stranger

ROTHER, THE AUTHOR, HAD LOST TOUCH WITH HIS only son several years ago. The young man, tall, skinny, nerdy, bespectacled, had never seemed like a potential runaway, but after he dropped out of college, which he described as "worse than useless," adding "nobody will ever need me to write an essay in the whole rest of my life," he began to act strangely, to lock the door of his room and spend all day and all night lost somewhere inside his laptop, listening to music videos, playing online chess, watching pornography, who knew what. Son was living with his American mother, Ex-Wife (she was another story Brother didn't care to revisit, another story whose new chapters he knew nothing about) up in the high nosebleed latitudes of the Upper East Side. She was happily remarried, that was a fact, and another fact was that he was the one who had introduced her to her Chinese-American husband, who had originally been Brother's friend but was his friend no longer, and that was quite a fact, and the new Chinese-American husband was rich and successful and kind of a big man in the city, and that also was quite something. Son developed a bad case of divided loyalties. To see his real father doing, it had to be admitted, not so well, while his new stepfather went in for expensive automobiles and owned a horse farm upstate, this made the boy feel ashamed, and from shame to anger was a short step. So Son was angry with both Brother and Ex-Wife and retreated from them both into his secret world.

Brother didn't know who Son's friends were or where he went when he left his mother's house, and neither apparently did she, so when he disappeared (along with his laptop, tablet, and phone) and the police were alerted, neither parent had any leads to give the searchers. In the weeks that followed he saw a good deal of Ex-Wife as they sat together in sad cafés and waited for the call that said, we found the body. But that call did not come. Instead there was a visit they didn't expect. The officer in charge of the search asked to see them together, so Brother went up to Ex-Wife's lavish apartment in the nosebleeds. Stepfather had the grace to absent himself but all his possessions were there, his expensive bad-taste art, a lot of it contemporary Chinese for obvious reasons, he had identity issues, Brother thought, and believed he could solve them by paying through the nose for this crap from Beijing and hanging his framed identity on the walls. That was an ungenerous thought. He took it back. No, he didn't. Anyway, it was irrelevant. Here was the officer in charge of the search, and he was not saying what they had feared he would say.

They had found Son. He was alive. He was well. He was not drunk, or a drug addict, or kidnapped, or a member of a cult. In short, he was not in danger. He was still in the country, not abroad. And he didn't want to come home or see his parents or be in touch with them. He had disposed of his old cellphone and would prefer them not to have the new number. This was a choice he had made after giving the matter considerable thought. He was an adult now, he had a place to live, he had work, he had some money in the bank (not the bank with which they were familiar). He wanted them to know these things, and asked them to understand, though he knew it would be hard for them to do so. It might be that at some point in the future he might contact one or both of them and wish to reconnect, but at the present time he was doing what was right for him to do.

There followed the usual parental cacophony, demands for more information, weeping, etc., but even as he heard the conventional noises issuing from his own mouth as well as Ex-Wife's, Brother was realizing that he was not surprised. People left him. That was what they did. If Son was now choosing to resign from the family, he was only the latest, perhaps the last, in a long series of resignations: friends, lovers, and Wife (now Ex-Wife). After what he judged to be the minimum necessary period of hysteria, he stood up, thanked the officer for the kindness with which he had relayed this tough information, excused himself, and left. At the new subway station, giant mosaic portraits of artists and musicians—Kara Walker, Philip Glass, Cecily Brown, Lou Reed, Chuck Close—stared at him, judging him and finding him wanting. He would never be canonic. He was no longer even admissible into the canon of good fathers. Bad writer, bad father. Two strikes. He went down below the earth and took the Q downtown.

And so, now, Sancho. Brother hadn't expected an imaginary child to show up on the page, but Sancho had brought himself into being, and insisted on remaining. Brother's own Son had dematerialized and ceased to exist by an act of will, for his parents, at least. Quichotte, contrariwise, had made a son appear through the force of his desire and by the kindness of the stars. If I could make Son reappear by praying to meteor showers, Brother thought, I'd be at every meteor shower in America. But that would require Ex-Wife to be there, too, as she had been way back when.

He understood some of what he was doing, what material his unconscious was throwing up, transmuted, and splattering all over his pages. "The Human Trampoline"? Really? If Sister ever read what he was writing, she probably wouldn't like that. She would probably be disturbed, too, by the fact that Quichotte's financial complaints against the Trampoline were an echo of his own accusations against her. And then this sweet-easy reconciliation between Quichotte and H.T. on the phone, *that's all it took?*, as Sancho asked Quichotte disbelievingly. Well, if only, Brother thought. I'm on the same side as Sancho here. Real life isn't as easy as that. But he saw why it came out that way on the page. Like Sancho himself, H.T.'s welcome was born out of need, her own need as well as Quichotte's.

Salma was all fiction. These days the only women in his life were ones he made up in his head. Or, yes, admit it, as with Quichotte, sometimes women he saw on a screen—in his own case, more often at the movies than on television or one of the streaming services. Fantasy women. The real thing seemed now well beyond his reach. And Dr. Smile? Well, Brother was a writer who believed in doing his research. Sadly, there were many real-life candidates who could fill the crooked doctor's boots. And, yes, his prescriptions too.

If you wanted to say that the bizarre story he was telling, unlike any story he had ever told, had deep roots in personal necessity and pain, then yes, he would concede the point. But the old fool? He resisted the idea that Quichotte was just his Author with a pasteboard helmet on his head and his great-grandfather's rusted sword in his hand. Quichotte was somebody he had made up with a nod (okay, more than a nod) to the great Spaniard who had made him up first. Granted: his creation and he were approximately the same age, they had near-identical old roots, uprooted roots, not only in the same city but in the same neighborhood of that city, and their parents' lives paralleled each other, so much so that he, Brother, on some days had difficulty remembering which history was his own and which Quichotte's. Their families often blurred together in his mind. And yet he insisted: no, he is not I, he is a thing I have made in order to tell the tale I want to tell. Brother—to be clear about this—watched relatively little TV. He was a member of the last cinema generation. On TV, he watched the news (as little as possible, it being presently close to unbearable), and in the baseball season he watched the Yankees' games, and sometimes, when he was able to stay up that late, he watched the late-night comedy shows. That was more or less it. TV had ruined America's thinking processes as it had ruined Quichotte's. He had no intention of allowing it to ruin his mind as well.

So, no, he insisted, not I. However: if he was so certain of the divide between character and Author, why had he so often been afraid that his spy novels had attracted the interest of real spies who were now spying on him? Why had he seen shadows in the shadows, lurking, shadowing him? It was an irrational fear (but then, fear is irrational). He neither knew nor had he leaked any official secrets, he reminded himself. He was not a player in the game. To believe otherwise was vanity. His paranoia was a form of narcissism. He needed to let it go, especially while he was absorbed by this, the most peculiar of all his stories, which for some reason was making him smile happily at his computer screen, allowing him to forsake all thoughts of giving up his chosen profession. Sometimes the story being told was wiser than the teller. He was learning, for example, that just as a real son could become unreal, so also an imaginary child could become an actual one, while, moving in the opposite direction, a whole, real country could turn into a "reality"-like unreality.

He was also getting up his courage and planning a trip to London. Maybe peacemaking would work out for him as it seemed to be working out for Quichotte. The olive branch would readily be accepted and they would have each other once again. Yes, replied the more cynical voice in his head, and maybe pigs would fly. But he found himself feeling optimistic. Very well, he thought, London. It was a long time since he had crossed the ocean. He would have to buy a new carry-on bag. He would need some advice about which airline to use.

Such were Brother's more or less cheerful thoughts when he returned to his apartment in Kips Bay from an evening stroll along Second Avenue, holding a paper bag containing a six-pack of Corona Light, and dreaming, as he often did, about moving to Tribeca, perhaps into a loft conversion in the Gould Industries building, one hundred years old and formerly a printing house and steel wool manufactory, which stood at the corner of Greenwich and Beach with the arrogance of its double affluence, the history of past industrial successes within its walls yoked to the two-thousand-dollars-per-square-foot eminence of its desirable present, and which was his fairy-tale residence of choice. When in Tribeca he always tried to walk past it even though it made him feel down at heel.

He shook off the fantasy and turned his key in his door, to be greeted in his darkened apartment by the bright light from the illuminated iMac screen, which he had left in Flurry screensaver mode, and which was password-protected, but which had somehow been opened. By the light of his hacked desktop he then perceived, seated in the Aeron office chair at the computer station, a large Japanese-American gentleman, who was probably six foot three, six foot four inches in his socks, Brother estimated, and his weight might be what? Two hundred and sixty, two hundred and seventy pounds. The Japanese-American gentleman was wearing an expensive dark blue silk suit with a pale blue silk pocket square, a white shirt with a high thread count, a red Hermès tie in which a small golden cat was chasing a smaller golden wind-up mouse, and a small button badge on his left lapel bearing a miniature image of the Great Seal of the United States. There was writing on the button badge which was too small to read. On his lap, just lying there, was a high-powered handgun, which looked to Brother (who had to be up on such matters because of the genre of fiction in which he had until recently specialized) like a Gen4 Glock 22. Apart from the presence of this gentleman the apartment looked undisturbed. There was no sign that either entry—into the apartment or into Brother's computer—had been forced in any way.

"I apologize for alarming you, sir," the Japanese-American gentleman said. "Let me reassure you that I mean you no harm."

It was indeed alarming when one's worst paranoid fantasies became reality. Brother's interior life went through a series of stomach-churning somersaults in the course of a few seconds. He was about to be beaten up slash murdered slash burgled as well as beaten up and then murdered. The Glock was a bad sign. His eyes focused on the button badge and clung onto that. He was drowning and that was his only hope of a life buoy.

"You're from which agency?" he finally managed to say, in an approximation of his normal speaking voice.

"If you wish, sir, I can show you ID," the other replied. "But I really don't think I have to spell out to you, of all Authors, which agency it is."

"The weapon," Brother said. "Why the weapon?"

"You know how it is, sir," the visitor said respectfully. "A man enters his own home, sees the shape of a stranger seated in his chair, and in self-defense draws his personal weapon and opens fire. This is a plausible scenario. This is America, sir. I wished only to guard against unnecessary loss of life, including my own life, sir, yes."

Brother set down the bag containing the six-pack. "I would feel a lot happier if you put the weapon away," he said. He was trying not to faint, and his bowels were being troublesome.

The intruder did as he was asked, then stood and extended a hand. "Lance Makioka," the Japanese-American gentleman intro-duced himself. "We met briefly on a previous occasion, which I'm certain you will not remember."

"I'm pretty sure we have never met," Brother said.

"Yes, sir, you were signing books at a store right on Sunset in Los Angeles," Lance Makioka said. "At that time I was with President Reagan, post the conclusion of his term of office, and I asked you if you might agree to kindly autograph a book for the president. I believe you were skeptical, and said, 'I thought President Reagan suffers from Alzheimer's and is not reading many four-hundred-page spy novels these days.' I remember your exact words, sir. And I replied, 'Sir, Mrs. Reagan would also be glad of the signature,' and then you very kindly signed the book."

Brother did remember. He even remembered that that was where he had seen the blue suit before, or one like it. "I'm presuming you're not here tonight to get a book signed," he said, relaxing just a little.

"Ha ha, sir, no, sir," Lance Makioka said. "At that period of my life I was on the protection side of things. Since then I have moved on."

"To the house-break-in side of things," Brother said. Heavy levity was his way of disguising his still-high level of foreboding, even of fear.

Lance Makioka did not laugh. "Nowadays I protect America in a different way, sir. That is why I am here tonight. Sir, there's a story I'd like to tell you. May I tell you that story?"

"Auditioning for my job, then," Brother said. The terrified comedian again.

"By way of a prologue," unsmiling Lance Makioka replied, "may I ask if the name of Blind Joe Engressia means anything to you? A.k.a. Joybubble? Now deceased?"

Brother shook his head.

"In 1957," said Lance Makioka, "a blind seven-year-old American boy accidentally discovered that whistling certain precise notes into his phone, at certain precise frequencies, could manipulate the system. The first note to work in this way was, I believe, the fourth E above middle C, having a frequency of 2637.02 hertz. This was the beginning of the practice known as phone phreaking, closely linked to the development of what afterwards became known as computer hacking, and at a certain point the phreaker community included such later luminaries as the computer entrepreneur Mr. Steve Jobs. The boy Engressia, as he grew, became a legend in this community. However, sir, in the end he got busted, he was maybe nineteen then, and he gave up phreaking. His subsequent life was not distinguished by great success. At one point he legally changed his name to Joybubble and announced that he was five years old and intended to remain five years old for the rest of his life. He passed away in 2007, aged either fifty-eight or five, as you prefer. The point of telling you this, sir, is that we, that is to say the appropriate agencies, wished to enlist Blind Joe in our battle against hacking, using the 'set a thief to catch a thief' principle. Like Cary Grant in the old Hitchcock movie. Some say he did work for us for a time but then ceased to do so. If he had done so, he would have had a secure income, health care, pension all the way to the end. But there it is. People make their choices."

"But this is not the story you came to tell me," Brother said.

"No, sir. It is a type of preliminary fable. You will see the point of its moral as I proceed."

"I am not any kind of hacker," Brother said. "Phone or computer. Just for the record. You, however, plainly are," he added, gesturing to his iMac.

"Are you familiar," Lance Makioka asked, ignoring Brother's remark, "with the covert hacktivist organization using the name of Legion?"

That rang a bell. "Is it something like Anonymous?"

"Anonymous we believe to have entered into a possibly terminal decline," Lance Makioka said. "Legion was potentially in a position to replace it, until recent actions by ourselves, which have put a *damn great fist right into the middle of it.*" His voice had risen dramatically, and he slammed his right fist into his left palm, the mask of calm courtesy slipping for a moment to reveal the man of action beneath. Brother found himself thinking of James Bond.

"I am still unclear as to why this is relevant to me," he said, and Lance Makioka nodded slowly, accepting that it was time to provide some significant information.

"The head of Legion made a number of YouTube videos threatening various forms of aggressive cyber-interventions. In those videos he used a voice-changing device and wore a mask which we have identified as a piece of vintage merchandise from the 2002 Broadway revival of the hit musical *Man of La Mancha.*"

"He wore a Don Quixote mask? Okay, that's weird, but it doesn't establish any link to me. Don Quixote has been around for what, four hundred years?"

"He used the pseudonym of Quix 97. Is this name meaningful to you?"

"No. Yes. 1997 is the year my son was born."

"I must regretfully inform you," Lance Makioka said, "that the person behind the *Man of La Mancha* mask is in fact your son. Your absentee son, I believe."

"Oh my God," Brother said.

"Your son, with whom ostensibly at least you are no longer in touch, now goes in his personal life by the name Marcel DuChamp."

"He really does that?"

"The apple, sir, would not appear to have fallen very far from the tree."

Brother was silent. Then, "Tell me the story," he said.

Lance Makioka appeared inclined to take his time about doing that. "I've been reading your books, sir, including this new work in progress," he said. "I'm no critic, sir, but I estimate that you're telling the reader that the surreal, and even the absurd, now potentially offer the most accurate descriptors of real life. It's an interesting message, though parts of it require considerable suspension of disbelief to grasp. This imaginary child, for example. Sancho. Where would you come up with a notion like that?"

"I assume you're going to answer the question yourself," Brother said, his face grim now.

"If the character of the old fool is based on you," Lance Makioka said, "meaning no disrespect, sir, just trying to decode your way of communicating . . . then it may follow, may it not, that just as your Mr. Quichotte is accompanied by the phantom son Sancho, so also you are in fact in contact with your apparently estranged son. Who is using, as I mentioned, very similar iconography to that being employed by you."

"It does not follow," Brother said. "It's a coincidence."

"Good, good, thank you for clearing that up. You'll concede that it's a forgivable conclusion to draw, if one were to draw it. I'm more puzzled by the idea of the old gentleman's lady love. In your story. Who might be the model for her?"

"There's no model."

"There is no lady love in your life?"

"Am I being interrogated? Am I suspected of something? Because maybe I should call a lawyer. You'll allow me to do that, I hope. This is still, as you pointed out, America."

"Sir, please be assured you are not at present a suspect in any investigation of which I am aware. This is just a friendly talk."

"Then please tell me what you came to tell me."

"But there is a lady in your life about whom you're thinking, am I correct? A lady, if I don't miss my guess, presently residing overseas."

"Why are you asking me questions to which you already know the answers?"

"An estranged lady as well as an estranged son," Lance Makioka reflected. "Two family members. Do you ask yourself why it might be that people close to you become so frequently estranged from you? I'm sure you do. You're a writer, so no doubt you pride yourself on leading an examined life. You will be familiar with the dictum of Socrates that the unexamined life is not worth living."

"You came here to insult me."

"On the contrary, sir," Lance Makioka said, moving into apologetic mode. "I came here to tell you a story."

"Which you have not done, so far."

"Your estranged lady overseas," Lance Makioka said, as if remembering something. "How much do you know about her present condition?"

"What do you mean by that? What's her condition?"

"I should have said 'situation,'" Lance Makioka corrected himself. "Her current situation."

"Less than you, plainly. Is that what the story's about?"

"And your son. Marcel DuChamp. You're certain there has been no contact."

Brother did not answer. Lance Makioka nodded, slowly, stood up out of his chair, and clasped his hands together at waist level, in the elocution position.

"To tell a story to a professional storyteller," Lance Makioka said. "It's daunting, sir. One feels almost ashamed. Permit me to collect my thoughts."

IN THE CITY OF MUMBAI (pop. 21,300,000), on Rustom Baug in the locality of Byculla, across the street from Masina Hospital, in a large high-ceilinged *salon* in a crumbling old Parsi mansion whose slow demise was attended by many gravely watchful banyan trees, two well-known photographers had installed nothing less than the cockpit of a Boeing 747, and surrounded it with state-of-the-art flight simulation equipment featuring video screens on which a wide range of international airports could be projected, so that they and their guests, helped by a friend who actually was a jumbo jet pilot, could practice landing and taking off. This eccentricity was popular in their circle, but word of it reached ears in the American embassy in Delhi, which caused foreheads in that embassy to frown and heads in that embassy to be scratched, and as a result, one fine afternoon, there arrived at the gate of the crumbling old Parsi mansion, asking to speak with the owner slash residents, a Japanese-American gentleman in a blue silk suit, an imposing figure of a man, perhaps six foot three or six foot four in height, and weighing, what?, two hundred and sixty, two hundred and seventy pounds. He introduced himself to the two photographers as Trip Mizoguchi, and said that the ambassador would be grateful if they agreed to answer a few questions; which, instantly understanding that they were in the presence of U.S. intelligence, they immediately agreed to do.

They had purchased the cockpit of a decommissioned old 747 and installed it in these premises, was that information correct?

It was.

They had further purchased computer programs and ancillary equipment to create an advanced flight simulation system, was that information correct?

It was.

They utilized these materials purely for the amusement of themselves and their associates, was that information correct?

It was.

One such session was scheduled for that very evening, was that so?

It was.

Would there be any objection to himself, Trip Mizoguchi, being present at that session?

There would not. He would be most welcome.

Did they understand that airplanes had been flown into the twin towers of the World Trade Center in New York City several years previously, and that therefore this elaborate and costly piece of eccentric private amusement might strike certain persons as highly suspicious, and if, in fact, it were to be found to be nefarious in intent, certain persons might wish to put a *damn great fist right into the middle of it*?

Very reasonable. Yes, they perfectly well understood.

After Mr. Trip Mizoguchi left the premises, promising to return at the appointed hour that evening, the two photographers, whose mobiles, it should be admitted, were being listened in on, telephoned the forty most beautiful fashion models in Mumbai and said, please come over tonight, there's a person we would like you to charm. When Trip Mizoguchi returned, there was music playing, and drinks were flowing, and the forty most beautiful fashion models in Mumbai were telling him how much they liked a man of such imposing size, how much they liked his suit, his pocket square, his Hermès tie, his square jaw, his smile. At the end of the evening, Trip

Mizoguchi thumped the two photographers on their backs, saying, "You guys sure know how to throw a party. Let me know the next time you're having one of these affairs. I'll come down from Delhi to be here. And don't worry about anything. I can see you gentlemen are on the up-and-up. You'll have no difficulty from us." With that, he took his leave, and neither the two photographers nor the forty most beautiful fashion models in Mumbai noticed that at one point in the evening Trip Mizoguchi had briefly been in conversation with one of the male guests, an unimpressive, tall, skinny, nerdy, bespectacled fellow, a recent arrival in Mumbai whom the two photographers had befriended at a nightclub and invited along so that he could make some friends. What was the young fellow's name? The two photographers had trouble remembering. It was like the name of a famous artist. Picabia, something like that. But maybe young Picabia hadn't had a very enjoyable evening, and maybe Trip Mizoguchi got transferred out of India. Anyway, neither of them ever showed up at any of the photographers' soirées again. But Trip Mizoguchi was a man of his word, at least. There were no further inquiries about the flight simulator.

"I wanted to satisfy myself that he was the asset we were searching for," Lance Makioka told Brother. "Mr. Marcel DuChamp, definitively ID'd by me, previously unmasked by us as Quix 97. That was what it was about. We didn't give a damn about the flight simulator. That just got me in the door. Once we had a positive make on Marcel, we were all systems go. We acquired him later that night."

"Asset," Brother repeated. "Acquired."

"Correct," said Lance Makioka.

"Is my son alive? Did you hurt him?"

"He is in excellent health."

"And you. What is your real name? Steve Sayonara? Ricky Fujiyama? Rock Mishima? Who are you, anyway?"

"I've heard," Lance Makioka said, "that your mother, accusing you of being secretive, would sometimes ask you that question."

"You've heard a lot," Brother said. "No point in asking how, or where, or from whom."

"As a gesture designed to encourage trust," Lance Makioka said, "I am meeting you tonight under my real name. I can show you ID if you so wish. Sir."

"I'm sure you have many IDs."

Lance Makioka did not reply.

"What did you do with him after you 'acquired' him?" Brother demanded. "The 'asset'? My son? You were on foreign soil. What did the Indian authorities have to say about an American kidnap carried out on their turf?"

"We didn't see any need to trouble the Indian authorities, sir," said Lance Makioka. "Mr. Marcel DuChamp is a U.S. citizen, so we see him as one of ours. We have him in a secure holding facility."

"In India?"

"In the United States."

"Oh my God," Brother said, "it's the plot of my seventh book."

"*Reverse Rendition,*" Lance Makioka said, actually clapping his hands in delight. "I hoped you'd recognize the similarity. We're all big fans."

In his seventh novel Brother had imagined a scenario in which the American secret state needed to extract an asset from a safe haven in a neutral country and bring him onto American soil for questioning.

"If my information is correct, it was your most popular book," Lance Makioka said. "I took a look at the sales figures. They were pretty impressive. For you."

"This story you came to tell me," Brother said. "How much of it is a fairy tale?"

"It's a good story," Lance Makioka said. "You wrote it."

"But you do have my son. And now you want something from me."

"This is where I mention Blind Joe one more time," Lance

Makioka said. "We want you to talk to Marcel DuChamp and invite him to change sides. That's what we want, just like with Joe. We're offering him a 'poacher turns gamekeeper' scenario. A term dating back to the fourteenth century, I believe. If he accepts, he will have financial comfort, health insurance, a government pension, all of it."

"Why would he listen to me? We haven't so much as spoken in years."

"Using you as the messenger adds the element of surprise. He won't be expecting it, so it will put him off balance. After that it's up to you. It's my guess he's carrying an amount of anger, aimed at society, sure, the corrupt system, the fat cats, the power structure, no doubt. But mainly anger at you and maybe at his mom a little bit also, and he's going to need to let that out. You being there, taking him by surprise like I say, that's going to help him let off that steam. You can take it. You're his dad. You want him back in your life, so you're going to let him say what he has to say. Once the steam is out of him, he's going to be able to hear the message you're going to deliver for us. And the message to him is, he plays ball, he does the right thing for his country, and he'll be well taken care of. Alternatively, he'll face cyber-terrorism charges and we'll make sure he goes to Guantánamo Bay *for the rest of his fucking life*." Again that sudden climactic roar and the right fist thumping into the left palm. The agent wore a fine suit and had a cultivated manner, but under all that, the naked guy under all that expensive clothing, was the scariest individual Brother had ever met.

The world Brother had made up had become real. There was a black Cadillac Escalade waiting outside his building. Lance Makioka held open a door—rear door, near side—and ushered Brother into his seat. The blindfold requirement was delicately alluded to and Brother, having little choice in the matter, acquiesced. If he had been a real spy, he thought, he would have been able, even blindfolded, to follow the movements of the vehicle and know, at the very least, in which direction they were headed, east along the 495 for example, or north past the stadium, and on upstate. But he had no idea. Blindfolded, he experienced a certain dizziness brought on by the merging of the real and the fictional, the paranoiac and the actual outlook. Even the son he was going to meet felt fictional in a way. The *Man of La Mancha* mask! Like a dime-store Darth Vader who had escaped from Brother's story and gone over to the dark side. His doubly pseudonymous life, Quix 97, Marcel DuChamp. His son had become an imaginary being—two imaginary beings!—by the force of his own will. So also Brother had brought Sancho into the world, and then Sancho had willed himself into being *real, live*. These doubled births echoed one another, deafeningly. If he said to his son when they met, I have longed for you so much that I dreamed of an old fool giving magical birth to the son he never had, how would Son react? Was there any love left in him that might lead him to react lovingly? Was there a chance of a reconciliation? Estrangements, reconciliations . . . again, the dizzying union of the real and the imagined. A third party, reading these accounts, might even, at a certain point, conclude that both were fictional, that Brother and Sister and Son were imaginative figments just as Quichotte and Salma and Sancho were. That the Author's life was a fake, just like his book.

They drove for two hours, or what felt to Brother like two hours, and all the way the Japanese-American gentleman spoke in soft conversational tones, briefing him. A team of genius-level cyber-warriors had been assembled and was being expanded, to fight the growing force of cyber-attacks emanating from Russia and North Korea and their proxies from the early identity-theft days of CarderPlanet to the full-fledged assault of Guccifer 2.0. The present leader of the group, which went by the code name of Anthill, was a Bulgarian hacking genius who had turned himself in to the FBI two decades ago and had helped them set up the counterforce. He called himself Hristo Dimitarov, but that was a nom de guerre constructed from the names of two celebrated Bulgarian soccer players, Stoichkov and Berbatov. Anthill had been built slowly but surely, and almost all its members were hackers who changed sides. "They understand," the Japanese-American gentleman said, "that this is the third world war, and the future of the free world, of untwisted social media and unfixed elections, of facts and law and democracy and freedom as we understand the word, depends on winning it. Tell your son this. I suspect him of being a patriot. Currently wrongheaded, but a patriot below the mask. I note that he chose to disguise himself as the fictional character from whom we derive the adjective *quixotic*. He's an idealist. Right now he's charging in the wrong direction, let's say at a windmill, but he can be turned. There are real giants out there for him to fight."

Cyberwar was the attack on truth by lies. It was the pollution of the real by the unreal, of fact by fiction. It was the erosion and de-valuation of the empirical intellect and its replacement by confirma-tions of previously held prejudices. How was that any different from what he himself was doing, Brother asked himself, how was it different from the fictions he was making and which were now en-snaring him? Except that he was not trying to bring down Western civilization, excuse me. That was a small difference. And he was tying nobody up in knots except himself.

When the blindfold was removed Brother found himself in a low, anonymous structure surrounded by thickly wooded hills. The contemporary architecture was confusing. He'd have expected a shingled wooden house, characteristic of the region. This concrete-and-glass edifice belonged nowhere, so it could be anywhere. In this respect the house was like him, Brother thought. He belonged nowhere too. The Japanese-American gentleman led him into a comfortably furnished living room, with settees and armchairs up-holstered in floral patterns. There was a pool table and a dartboard, backgammon and chess. He couldn't see a swimming pool but thought there might be one around the back. This didn't feel like a jail, Brother told the blue-suited agent. "Of course not," was the reply. "We are here to make friends."

A door opened and Son entered the room. When he saw his father sitting there he stiffened. "They grabbed you too," he said. It wasn't a question.

"No," Brother said, "I'm here of my own free will."

"Sure you are," Son said. "I see you already met Mr. Trip Mizoguchi. He's a great believer in free will."

"Trip here tells me his name is Lance Makioka," Brother said.

At this the Japanese-American gentleman intervened. "To put this matter at rest," he said, "here is my Langley ID. As you see, the name printed there is not a workname. It is my personal name. Agent Kyle Kagemusha."

"And this is another gesture designed to encourage trust," Brother said.

"Exactly."

"Whatever," said Son.

"I leave you two gentlemen to talk things over," the recently renamed Agent Kyle Kagemusha said. "I'm sure you have a lot of catching up to do. Welcome to Anthill, Quix 97. We look forward to having you on board."

"WHY ARE YOU EVEN HERE?" Son said. "You don't know who I am. You never knew."

"You're right," Brother replied. "We're not much of a family, are we? But there's a thing you don't know about parenthood. It's mostly about showing up."

"It's crazy that you're here," Son said. "You're in so deep, so way over your head you don't even know how deep."

"We both are," Brother said.

Agent Kagemusha had been right. At first the words didn't come, but soon enough they came in a great hot gush, like steam from a broken pipe. One of the things Son wanted to attack his father about was belonging to the great Indian diaspora. Son had gone to India to discover authenticity. Only Indians from India had any claim to being authentic. The diaspora was full of phony Indians, people who had been uprooted so long that their souls were dying of thirst, people who didn't know what language to speak or what gods to worship, people who pathetically bought Indian art so they could hang their identity on their walls (did the lad even know, when he said this, that he was echoing Brother's gibe about his stepfather?). People, he went on, who flew to India for two weeks over New Year's and went to a few weddings and ate sweetmeats and danced in the neon night and felt that they had refilled their India tanks and could go back to being fakers for the other fifty weeks. He had learned the Indian term *420,* which had nothing to do with smoking weed, but which meant "fraudulent" or "fraud." *Charsobeece,* he said, his Hindi accent imperfect but aggressive. "You're all char-sobeeces. And, by the way, nobody likes your books."

"If the system cannot be changed it must be destroyed," Brother said.

On the second day, Son collapsed abruptly and wept, suddenly a very young man again, all his masks stripped away. He allowed his father to embrace him. "We were so close to doing it," he said. "This close."

Brother began to talk to him about Anthill, about fighting the real enemy and serving the greater good. It didn't take long. A few days. He was a good kid. Yes, quixotic. He got the message quickly. And he didn't want to go to jail.

When Brother said goodbye to Son, he knew it might be a long time before they met again. That was okay now. They were good. As he left he decided to ask one last question. "Oh, by the way: 'Marcel DuChamp'?"

Son grinned. "I guess it was my way of saying, I love you, Dad."

He turned to go, his heart full. Son called after him. "Oh, Dad?"

"Yes?"

"Don't tell Mom."

Then again the blindfold in the Escalade. On the ride back to the city Agent Kagemusha offered some final thoughts. "I want to thank you for your service," he said. "And I also want to be frank with you. You know a great deal now, some would say too much. But we're the good guys. We don't arrange for people to be hit by trucks. So, we'll be watching you. We're in your phone, your computer, every call, every keystroke. Don't even try to hide from us. We would take that unkindly. We are grateful for your help, and now we need you to be silent. Don't disappoint us by talking. We hate disappointments."

"Careless talk costs lives," Brother said. "And it's good to know you're the good guys."

"There you go," said Agent Kagemusha. "Smart man."

When the blindfold was removed he was outside his building again. "One last word," he said. "I'm kind of a classic movie buff."

"Yes, sir. I like to see old films myself."

"So, *Kagemusha*. I saw that film. It means 'shadow warrior.'"

Nothing from the agent, but the darkened windows of the Escalade began to rise.

"Thanks," Brother said, "for the gesture designed to create trust."

CHAPTER FIFTEEN

Regarding Sister, & the
Unforgivable Thing

THE RESTAURANT BENEATH SISTER'S NOTTING HILL DU-
plex was called Sancho in honor of Ignatius Sancho, "the extraordinary Negro," born on a slave ship in (approximately) 1729, a runaway
slave who was then freed in England, a Sancho who worked for
English milords but wasn't looking to go wandering in the service
of any knight: composer, playwright, polemicist, prolific writer of
essay-letters to the newspapers, author of *Theory of Music,* greengro-
cer, the first person of African origin to vote in a British election,
and along with Ottobah Cugoano and Olaudah Equiano one of the
earliest black British chroniclers of and campaigners against slavery,
painted by Gainsborough, admired by Laurence Sterne, and not
someone who would have been a regular consumer of the jerk
chicken, ackee and saltfish, and Red Stripe lager on offer in the
Jamaican-themed eatery that now bore his name (although he might
have tasted African callaloo). Nor, in all probability, Sister thought,
would he have approved of the pounding dance music that had
begun to issue from the cellar below the restaurant, whose owners

had lately decided to go for more of a club-scene vibe and to hell with all sleeping neighborhood children. After that there were drunks making out and fighting in the street until three in the morning. It was hard to imagine Ignatius Sancho as a disco devotee. This, after all, was a man who had sided with the British against the American Revolution. This was a conservative man.

The neighborhood association asked for Sister's help. She agreed to lead the discussion, sought meetings with the restaurant's owners, and received only platitudes in return. She offered compromise proposals, suggesting acceptable decibel levels and shorter nightclub hours. She spoke to the local council and asked it to intervene to set in place and then to police proper regulations. She pointed out that Sancho was licensed as a restaurant, not a nightclub, and was therefore in breach of its legal obligations. Only when all these avenues had been explored without satisfaction having been received did she agree, with extreme reluctance, that the restaurant and its parent company should be sued.

When the lawsuit began, the restaurant owners accused her of racism.

Social media had no memory. Today's scandal was sufficient unto itself. Sister's lifelong commitment to anti-racism was as if it had never been. Various people styled as community leaders were ready to denounce her, as if high-volume music played late at night was an inalienable aspect of Afro-Caribbean culture and any critique of it had to be driven by prejudice, as if nobody noticed or cared that the vast majority of the young nocturnal drinkers, makers-out, and fighters were affluent and white. Someone started a Facebook page protesting her elevation to a life peerage—she was a baroness now—and her rumored front-runner status for the soon-to-be-vacated post of Speaker of the upper house. The protest gathered 113,686 signatures on the first day. She began to receive hate mail and even threats. And of course, there were political consequences. The already fragile alliance of left and right which had come together to offer her the chance of elevation to the Woolsack, where Speakers of the House of Lords had been seated since the time of Edward III, wavered and broke. She was given to understand, in the British way, that a degree of embarrassment was being felt regarding the— almost certainly untrue! And so unjust!—allegations against her, and consequently some people were having second thoughts. She decided on her response more or less instantly. She called her fellow baroness and withdrew her candidacy. "Thank you for your support, Aretta, but there's no need for anyone to be embarrassed by me. I'm not dying to sit on that sack."

The loom of life was broken, she thought, that loom upon which we wove the fabric of our days from familiar threads. Work, friendship, health, parenthood, family, love. And yes! Community. For goodness' sake, yes! And race, and history, and struggle, and memory. Yes to all of that. All that was at the heart of the weaving. One made the finest cloth one could with such skills as one had, accompanied by, one hoped, the humility lacked by Arachne when she challenged Athena and insulted the gods. (However, if it was true that Arachne's tapestry, which showed how the gods had abused humans, especially Zeus with all his rapes, was superior to Athena's, then she was all for Arachne, and vengeful Athena, spidering her opponent, didn't come out of the story at all well.) But now, discontinuity ruled. Yesterday meant nothing and could not help you build tomorrow. Life had become a series of vanishing photographs, posted every day, gone the next. One had no story anymore. Character, narrative, history, were all dead. Only the flat caricature of the instant remained, and that was what one was judged by. To have lived long enough to witness the replacement of the depth of her chosen world's culture by its surfaces was a sad thing.

The law came to her rescue as it always had, as she had always trusted it to do. Within the walls of that unimportant courtroom during this extremely minor case about noise abatement, certain old values still survived. There was evidence. There were facts which were not merely the assertions of rivaling bigotries. There was truth. Let me live and die here, she thought. This is my true home.

She won the case easily. The restaurant's owners were obliged to apologize in open court for violating the terms of their license to operate, and for the defamatory innuendos about Sister. Overnight the troll army vanished, and the culture without memory, which all culture had become, instantly forgot how it had slandered an innocent woman, and moved on. The street quieted down. The late-night revelers went elsewhere to disturb other people, other sleeping children. What passed these days for ordinary life resumed. She was used to the hard knocks of litigation and told herself that these bruises, too, would fade.

It was only now, when the fog of war had lifted and the armies gone away, that she saw that the genuinely injured victims of the conflict were her husband and daughter. Godfrey Simons sat on his High Court bench and the whole world passed before him and he passed judgment and then came home and put on a long dress and drank a glass of Bandol *rouge* and became Jack, her Jack. But that she should have been dragged through the mud in this way had filled him with a rage that would not be assuaged.

"It's unforgivable, Jack," he said. "We're going back to mob rule. The lynch mob, the stockade in which people were pelted with fruit, the public burning."

"Now, now, Jack," she said. "You'll be talking about witch hunts next. There was a song they were playing the night before the case. I'm sure you could hear it in your room too. I may not have heard properly but I thought it went, 'I fought the law, and the law won.' Is that a song? Because that's what happened here. The law won."

"That isn't all that happened. What was done to you. It's an unforgivable thing."

Daughter, twentysomething, a rising star in the fashion industry, with a showroom slash atelier in a nearby mews and a growing clientele of shiny, thin, much-photographed beauties waiting to be dressed, was there too and concurred. "That is a song," she said. "But there's no excuse for what happened to you. I'll never forgive it either."

"Calm down, both of you," Sister said. "I'll live."

She did not renew her interest in the Lords position, although there were new efforts to persuade her, accompanied by fulsome expressions of regret which she understood were insincere and calculated, as political apologies always were. The truth was she was relieved not to have to take up this new and weighty role when there were more personal things that needed her attention. "More personal things." Hah! She had become more British than the British. This was no time for euphemism or understatement. She had to deal with the question of her health. Of whether, in short, she would be alive for very much longer, able to take up any sort of role in anything. Of, to be blunt, the possibility, bordering on probability, of death.

She had already defeated a cancer that she wasn't supposed to survive. When she was still relatively young and, according to others, attractive, she had been diagnosed with stage IV breast cancer which had already spread to the lymph nodes. In spite of the very poor prognosis for patients in her condition, she lived. The double mastectomy wasn't the only mutilation. Treatment had also required the removal of a part of an armpit and some of her chest wall muscles, plus very debilitating chemotherapy. Even though the cure was completely successful, according to her doctors, and she was declared to be in full remission, she had assumed that after that no man would desire her and she would live alone in a sort of remission from life as well as death; that her death sentence had been commuted to a life sentence, and loneliness would be her lot, along with the guilt, commonly experienced by cancer sufferers, of having brought the illness upon herself by the choices she had made in her life. Maybe it was the Fates' reward for the way she had discarded Sad-Faced Older Painter and, according to some unkind tongues, helped to drive him into his grave. Then she had met Jack, and he had loved her in spite of it all. There followed the multiple miracles of love, marriage, a brilliant career, and happiness. The birth of a healthy child, Daughter, was the biggest miracle. She had supposed herself sterile as a consequence of the chemotherapy, but her womb had had other ideas.

Now, no longer young, she feared that a shadow had returned. Most mornings she woke up with a sense of impending horror. Then she told herself not to be foolish, she was symptom-free, all was well. After that she told herself, if you're so worried, go in for a full checkup. But she had been afraid to do so. The Sancho case had felt, almost, like a welcome distraction. Now that it was over, the angels on her shoulders were whispering in her ear again. *You're fine,* said the left angel. *Get yourself looked at,* said the right. She ignored them both and went to work, came back to her neighborhood, stopped by Daughter's showroom to look at the beauty her girl was creating and to swap the day's stories with her, got home and had a glass of wine with Jack in his red dress, or his green or blue dress, and told herself she was living her best life. But still she felt it: the shadow in her blood.

I'm not dying, she had said. Also, *I'll live.* She hoped that wasn't dangerously overconfident, hubristic, of her. Maybe she should have crossed her fingers for luck when she defied the exterminating angel. Some nights she dreamed of Nemesis coming for her in a chariot drawn by griffins, wielding her punishing whip.

And then there was the other subject that never completely went away. Brother. The slap on the ear, the accusation, the threat. Whenever his name came up, so did the subject of his unforgivability, if indeed he was unforgivable, and slash or she unwilling to forgive. Now that Jack and Daughter were talking about other matters being unforgivable, her thoughts tended back, yet again, to her lost sibling, whom Daughter, so implacably unyielding in her fury about the way her mother had been treated, wanted Sister finally to make up with. Daughter even bought a paperback copy of his novel *Reverse Rendition* (cheaply, at the secondhand bookstore on Notting Hill Gate) and urged Sister to read it. "These CIA agents go to an unnamed Eastern country—maybe Pakistan?—to kidnap a man. He might be innocent or he might be the son of Osama bin Laden or some other terrorist. You don't know until the last page. It's so contemporary. You should totally read it."

Being his sister felt like a sort of life sentence too.

ON THE DAY SISTER got her bad news, Daughter was trying to imagine herself as a mask. Her next runway show, she was thinking, would feature models in many different kinds of mask: animal masks including antlered deer, lionesses, roaring she-bears; Caribbean masks all feathers and sequins; hand-painted Venetian commedia dell'arte masks—Arlecchino, Pantalone, Capitan Scaramouche—men's masks all inhabited, taken over, transformed, by the tallest, most beautiful girls she could hire. If your atelier was just off the route of the carnival, you couldn't help having masks on your mind. Somebody brought her an old recording, VHS transferred to CD, of the National Theatre's 1980s production of Aeschylus's *Oresteia* in which the whole cast wore masks throughout. Watching all four and a half hours of the trilogy showed her the truth of something she had heard said but never witnessed: the masks acted. The masks became human and were capable of expressing all the great emotions of tragedy. The masks lived. This was what she wanted to achieve in the twenty-minute length of a runway show. It was impossible, but the impossible was the only thing worth trying to do. She was drawing masks for herself. What would be the mask that she would become, the mask that would become her?

"Take a look at this," her assistant Ornella said. *This* was a set of YouTube videos, the first group put up by Anonymous hacktivists, featuring men (and women?) in Guy Fawkes masks, as originally seen in the graphic novel *V for Vendetta* and the Wachowskis' film of it. The second was a video by the rival group Legion, a straight-to-camera speech by a man using a voice-changer device and wearing a

Don Quixote mask, vintage merch from *Man of La Mancha* on Broadway back in the day. "So derivative, both of them," Daughter said. "Maybe we should try to contact them. I could make them much cooler things to wear."

"I heard Legion got broken up," Ornella told her. "And Anonymous these days makes stupid messages about aliens coming to Earth, being here already, walking among us."

"Damn, they penetrated our cover," Daughter said, and then, in a Dalek voice, "We are the aliens that you seek."

The truth was that she was wearing a disguise already, giving a phony performance every day of lighthearted competence, while secretly full of grief and fear. She had recently gone through a breakup with her lover and business partner, an older man, a Polish aristocrat and shrewd entrepreneur, whose cocaine habit had become a big problem. So now she was alone, looking for someone to manage the business end of things, trying to do it all herself, panicking a little, nursing her sadness, feeling close to an unhealthy edge. Yeah, she thought. I don't need a mask. I'm already the mask of myself.

"I need some fresh air," she said to Ornella. "I won't be long. Hold the fort."

She walked through the streets of stucco façades, some white, some brightly painted, past the church that was bombed in the Blitz and rebuilt after the war ended, and arrived at her mother's place, which would be unoccupied at this time. Her mother and the judge would be away at work, and the housekeeper would have left. She had her own key and let herself in past the bouncers standing outside Sancho, who gave her unfriendly looks. Unsurprisingly, there was some residual resentment about the outcome of the recent court case. She didn't respond to the dirty looks and went upstairs.

Afterwards, she swore that she had not intended to do what she then did, that she had just wanted a quiet place to be in for a while, away from the pressure-cooker atmosphere of her workplace. Be that as it may: at some point that afternoon, she went into Sister's home office on the upper floor of the duplex, sat down at her computer, entered the password, which she knew, and composed an email from her mother to her uncle in New York.

One of us has to begin, and perhaps you're too uncertain of your reception at this end, or too wrapped up in your own business, or just disinclined to renew this long-discontinued connection, so I'll make the first move, using the old descriptive notation. 1. P-K4.

Send.

As soon as it was done she felt a surge of delicious terror. What had she started? What would her mother think? How would her uncle respond to what he would obviously assume was a message from Sister, not from her interfering Daughter? Would he respond, or would her radical, intrusive, borderline-dishonest gesture be in vain? A false move?

Here I am, masked again, she thought. She sat staring at the screen for an hour, for ninety minutes, for two hours. Sister and the judge would be home soon. She should just shut down the computer and leave and explain it all to her mother later. Or maybe she should wait and face the music.

Ding.

There was a message in the inbox. He had replied. Her heart pounded.

1. . . . P-K4.

It was her move.

A key turned in the lock. She jumped up and went to look and there on the lower floor was her mother, home, holding a sheet of paper and staring up at her with an expression on her face which Daughter had never seen before. She's onto me, Daughter thought. But how could she be? I don't know, but she knows, and she's really angry.

"Come downstairs," her mother said. "I have something to say to you."

"I have a confession to make," Daughter replied.

"Come downstairs," her mother repeated. "You can go first."

So Daughter went first, and when she told her mother about the chess moves Sister lost her usual iron self-control and wept. Sister's stoicism was well known. Few people had seen her cry. These huge, shoulder-shaking sobs were shocking to Daughter, greatly increasing her guilt, and her own tears soon mirrored her mother's. After a few moments Sister took several deep breaths and said, laughing bitterly through yet more tears, "Honey, you don't even know what I'm crying about."

In fact she had been immediately happy to hear the news about Brother, had already decided she would reply, and was clear about her next move in the chess opening. Daughter's initiative had opened up a healing possibility that felt like a renewal of life. But it was also the day when a routine blood test had produced a result that was anything but routine. She had been right about the shadow within. The contrast between the news of Brother's reentry into her story and the diagnosis of a life-threatening illness which seemed likely to bring that story to a close had been too much for her to bear. She handed the sheet of paper to her daughter and as Daughter read it her tears were replaced by dry-eyed shock and fear. She felt as if a grave had opened in the polished oak floor between them and a hand had reached out from that yawning pit and seized her mother by the ankle.

"Cheer up. It doesn't mean I'll die tomorrow," Sister said. "There's treatment. In some cases the treatment keeps people going for the length of their natural lives. My view is, why shouldn't one of those people be me?"

The judge had come in, unnoticed by either of the women. He walked over to Daughter and took the paper from her hand.

"If you die now, Jack," he said to his wife, "that will be the most unforgivable thing of all."

Sister was calm now, back in charge of herself. She opened a bottle of the good Bordeaux. "This thing is supposed to be a disease of white people," Sister said with a glass in her hand. "Or people who have been exposed to Agent Orange or other unpleasant chemicals. Or, it's hereditary, but that's not the case in my case. It's as if it accidentally climbed into the wrong body, but it's here in my blood, no question of that, and the bone marrow too, as you see. The white count is high. A malfunction in the DNA of the cells that make the blood. Malfunctioning DNA! It's like discovering you're a Friday car. The workers who made me wanted to knock off for the weekend and did a hurried, botched job. But I've been so damn healthy all my life. People have complimented me on my good health. And I got used to replying, 'Your good health is the thing you have until the day your doctor tells you you don't have it anymore.' And so here we are."

"There's a doctor in America," Daughter said, looking up from her phone. "Indian doctor. Brown person. He's the top man. Even the stages of the illness are named after him. Here's the hospital where he works. I can call for an appointment."

"London is fine," Sister said. "The same care is available here. No need to go flying off across an ocean."

"Make the call," the judge said. He looked older all of a sudden, Daughter thought. The news had knocked some of the life out of him. Maybe they would both be gone soon, maybe this thing would kill them both. Maybe it would be a repeat of Ma and Pa, the grandparents she had never met. Ma died and Pa couldn't bear to live another day.

And after that the next person for whom the hand reached up would be herself.

"If you two will excuse me," Sister said, "there's an email I have to send." At her desk, she took a deep breath and wrote to Brother. *2. P–KB4.*

This time the reply came quickly. *2. . . . PxP.* The pawn sacrifice was accepted, as she had thought it would be. The sadness fell away from her and she smiled.

Do you remember? she wrote.

Allgaier–Kieseritzky Gambit, he replied. *You always liked it. But I'll tell you something about chess. It's not like riding a bicycle. It doesn't all come flooding back.*

Let's see how much you've forgotten, she wrote. *3. N–KB3.*

. . . P–KN4. How am I doing?

4. P–KR4.

4. . . . P–N5.

5 N–K5.

And here, he wrote, *is where my head starts hurting. Can we try something else?*

What would you like to try?

"Hello."

"Hello, Brother."

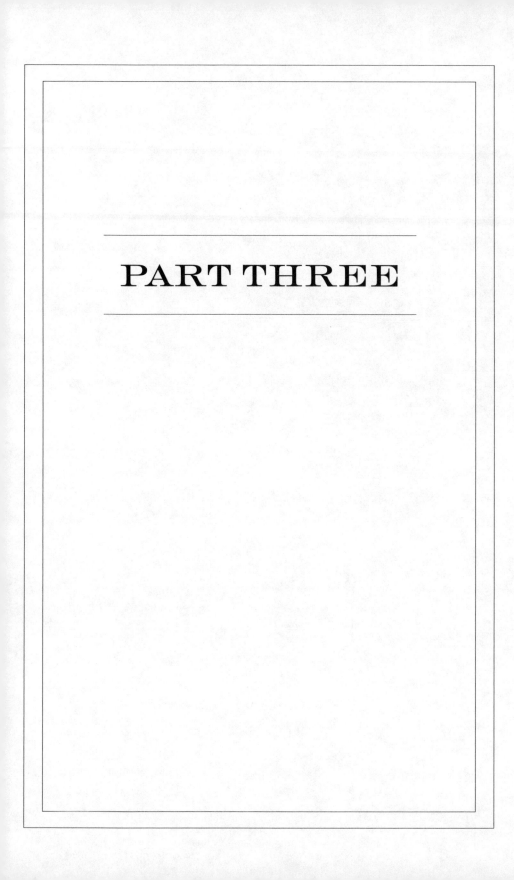

PART THREE

The Trampoline tells Sancho & Quichotte an old Tale of Betrayal, & the Path is opened

*T*IME, THAT LETHAL CHAMBER OF HORRORS WHOSE WALLS close slowly in upon the luckless inhabitant until they crush the life out of him, pressed in on Quichotte as he stood gazing up at his half sister's apartment building. He felt a tightness clutching at his chest, a band of pain like a message from the Reaper. How poetic it would be, he thought, if he were to fall down dead on her very doorstep, offering up his life itself on the altar of her temple, by way of making amends. *The Gould Industries building* (Brother wrote, housing the Trampoline in the apartment of his fantasies), *one hundred years old and formerly a printing house and steel wool manufactory, stood at the corner of Greenwich and Beach with the arrogance of its double affluence, the history of past industrial successes within its walls yoked to the two-thousand-dollars-per-square-foot eminence of its desirable present.* The Human Trampoline owned five thousand of those square feet, with high ceilings and exposed beams, high up at the penthouse level. A liveried doorman stood at that portal, eyeing Quichotte and Sancho suspiciously. Quichotte less than warm in his worn suit and Sancho in distressed denim and the coat that needed dry-cleaning made an un-impressive pair. They faced one another in a motionless standoff, Quichotte and the doorman, the traveler's dilapidated pride offer-ing a silent repudiation of the uniformed flunky's sneer. Then there was a commotion in the lobby, and in a flurry of flying fabric and waving arms a woman with wild black hair—still black, defying the years!—burst out of the building and spread her arms in welcome. It was the Trampoline. She was tall, could perhaps even be called gangling, with a long, bony face, and if it wasn't for the hair and the expensive hoop earrings it would have been like looking in a mirror, thought Quichotte.

She took him by the shoulders and leaned in for a kiss. Then she asked him what Sancho thought was an odd question: "What do you remember?"

Quichotte seemed bemused all of a sudden. "I remember some of it," he said, defensively. "I remember climbing with our father among the rocks at Scandal Point to look for little crabs in the rock pools. And the sleeping berths in the Frontier Mail to Delhi, me on the top, he below. And the metal tub with the big ice block in it he bought to keep us cool on the train. I remember the little wooden Ferris wheel, just four seats, he hired for my birthdays. The *charrakh-choo*." His face was full of sadness. He put a hand up to his head as if to soothe an ache. "You weren't there for any of that. You came later. You don't know any of this."

"So you don't remember," she told him. "About us."

"I remember long ago better," he said. "Back then, before every-thing, before he remarried, before you. More recently . . . it's patchy."

"And you," the Trampoline said, looking hard at Sancho. "You're quite a mystery. I need to hear all about you."

Sancho was surprised by the presence, in the Trampoline's pent-house, of much religious imagery. There were two bronze guard-ians at her front door, greenish centaurlike demigods the size of bull terriers, with human heads and animal bodies that had both leonine paws and cloven bull-like hoofs. Inside the door was a six-foot-high wooden figure, lionlike, its face almost demonic. This was a *yali,* a threshold god. Once it had stood at the door of a palace on the Malabar Coast, and courtiers entering or leaving, or embarking upon some new enterprise, or princes going to war, would ask for its blessings. There was a modern painting of the Buddha, sleeping, covered by a white sheet, beneath a black tree set against a red ground. This was the tree of enlightenment, and it usefully came with a blue electrical cord attached to it, with a plug at the end. The cord was not plugged in. Enlightenment had evidently not yet occurred.

She answered the question Sancho hadn't worked out how to ask. "No," she said, "I'm not religious, but I find these works to be beautiful and powerful and moving. Also, the women we work with, the poor women we are lifting up, whom we are enabling to lift themselves up, all of these women believe in something, and sometimes I think their lives are richer than mine because of that."

"My father thinks that immigrants like us have identity crises and try to fix them by buying art and hanging our identity on the wall."

"I don't think that," Quichotte said, startled. "I've never said anything of that sort. Where did you get such a discourteous idea?"

"I don't know," Sancho said, backing off, genuinely puzzled. "I guess somebody else, something else, put the notion in my head."

"Let's start over," said the Human Trampoline. "I'll open a bottle of wine."

The bar was a long, freestanding piece made of dark, intricately carved teak, and behind it hung a painting of four women with shorn hair, wearing white saris, sitting in a room with an ornately patterned rug within whose patterning the family car, the family cat, and the dead husband could all be seen, in miniature. The women's faces looked exactly like the Trampoline's. White was the color of mourning and there was a tiny dead man on the rug. Once again she answered the unasked question. "Yes, I commissioned it and sat for it after our father died. His father and mine. I mourned him in quadruplicate, in the north, south, east, and west, in the past, present, future, and in the time beyond time. Don't think you understand me because you have looked at this for two minutes. You have no idea who I am."

Sancho tried to placate her. "No, I just liked it," he said. "I didn't mean anything by it."

"Anyway," she said, "I have no idea who you are, either. *Salut.*"

This was the way family reunions went on TV, Sancho thought. People bickered and sniped and there was usually an explosion at the end of the episode, after which everyone wept and everyone said how much they loved everyone else. So now he found himself in one of those episodes. He knew how to play his part.

Quichotte in his sister's home wore a distant, abstracted, absent manner, fading in and out of the encounter like a ghost. For the most part he looked lost, as if unsure of his right to be there, and bewildered about how to achieve what he had come to achieve, which was the restoration of family harmony and peace. As the Trampoline spoke, it was almost as if there were two Quichottes in the room, a version from the past as well as the present one, and that as the past was superimposed on the present it caused a sort of blurring, because the two versions were so unlike each other that it became difficult to see the Quichotte in the room clearly, as he now was, and he himself was a victim of the same confusion, not able with any degree of ease to free himself from the trap of what he had once been. At first he stood by the sliding doors to the terrace as the glamor of the night city began to wrap itself around the ugly-beautiful daytime streets. Once it grew dark he moved to a corner of the room and sat upright on a hard chair and, for the most part, held his tongue.

"I'm going to tell you everything," said the Trampoline, addressing her remarks to Sancho, "including all the things he no longer knows, or says he doesn't, or says he isn't sure if it's what he did to me or I did to him, or whatever. I do this because you're family now, or so he says, even if he won't say how or why, or what happened to your mother. We'll get to that. I don't know what he has told you but I'm betting there are some pretty large gaps."

Yes, that was so, Sancho agreed. "He told me he did you wrong," the youth said. "And he wants to set things right. At least he thinks that's what happened."

"He's talking about the money business, I assume," the Trampoline said, waving a dismissive hand. "That's the least of it. The most of it is, he was always careless with people's hearts. He never took any responsibility for what he broke. And now, what, he's a mystic? There are seven valleys of purification and we're where, in the fifth? And this is all because he's in love with a woman he has never met? That's perfect, really. The withdrawal from reality into mumbo jumbo. And then the pursuit of a fantasy. He might as well wear a T-shirt that says, *I am incapable of living a real life. I am incapable of love.*"

Quichotte had turned to face them now. He continued to say nothing. He wore the air of someone about to be told a strange story for the first time. He folded his arms and remained silent, ready to hear her out.

"Once upon a time, Sancho," the Trampoline began, "he was charming and selfish. You look at him now and you see a gaunt scarecrow, a skin-and-bone relic. He thinks he's questing for love, but you know better, you know what's waiting for him at the end of his road. But why should I say what you see? Maybe you're just the loyal squire to the gallant knight."

"To be fair," Sancho said, coming to Quichotte's defense, "he still has the charming smile and old-school good manners. And he doesn't seem that selfish to me."

"You're loyal to him," the Trampoline said. "I see that. That's a good characteristic, but what follows will therefore sadden you, because what I have to tell is a story of disloyalty, even of betrayal. You want to hear it all? Well, even if you don't. I'm here to reunite your father with his mislaid past.

"The truth is, I'm the one who is supposed to be dead. Let's start there. I was a young woman then. I was supposed to die but my body made a different decision. However, it had to accept a number of consequences of that decision. It accepted them and defeated the crab in my breasts. The consequences included a double mastectomy, the removal of a part of my armpit and some of my chest wall muscles too. Also, chemotherapy. By the time you've been through that you no longer think of yourself as alive. You think, I'm lucky not to be dead. That's what I've been ever since: lucky not to be dead, living in the aftermath of an escape. You no longer think of yourself as having gender or sexuality. You think of yourself as an undead thing that is unaccountably continuing to live. In this state of aftermath one craves simple things: sympathy and love. Your father was not good at providing either.

"He was some sort of journalist," the Trampoline said, turning back to Sancho. "Freelance. Investigative. He used words like that. Specialist in intelligence. At least in his own opinion. I don't think he did particularly well. But he was a good talker. He said he was delving into the hidden reality of the world, the truth that exists but is buried very deep so that most of us can live among more palatable fictions. The ladies, enough of them, listened. Then they saw through him and walked away. Maybe what's left of him believes he can make this television Salma listen too.

"People called him paranoiac and he accepted the label. He had a whole theory of paranoia. I don't think he remembers that now. He said paranoia was to be understood as essentially optimistic, because the paranoid believed that there was a meaning to events, that the world made sense, even though that sense was concealed. Did he ever talk to you about that? No, he has lost that part of himself along with the rest. The opposite of paranoia, he said, was entropy, which was tragic, because it indicated that the universe was absurd. It was good talk. It didn't work so well in print. He had to go on living in that small apartment in Kips Bay. I had already made my money and so there was between us the question of envy. He didn't come here much because he envied me for living here. How ridiculous that was! There was nothing to envy about me at that time. The mutilation, the chemo, the transformation of a woman into an undead entity, a trickster who had somehow gotten away with cheating death. I guess you could envy me for my luck, but he envied me for my apartment. This is the kind of brother he was. Half brother. He wasn't even half a brother to me.

"I lifted him up whenever the women left. They always left him, that was a fact. When the gaudy patter ran out they found there wasn't enough of a man there and they excused themselves and exited. He never found anybody to build something real with. But he seemed content in those days just to find the next temporary connection. The next unreal thing. And when they dumped him, he came around. He came to his Trampoline in search of some bounce and that was my fault, I always cheered him up, I didn't say, you asshole, can't you see which of us is more in need of being lifted up right now? I should have said it but I just didn't. Lifting people up, that's my thing. So, I didn't complain.

"The year of my illness was also the year of the song. The one that gave me my name.

"It builds up, the resentment. It piles up like New York garbage. Then something comes along and gives it a shove and after that, get out of the way of the avalanche if you can."

The sun sank behind the Hudson and in a moment of silence the three of them stood on the apartment's terrace and watched it go, the light of the fire dying in the water like a dream being forgotten. The Trampoline, however, was unquenched and on fire, had forgotten nothing, and what had been pent up in her during the long years of estrangement was blazing out of her like the flame of a second sun that had no intention of setting, not until its hot work had been done.

"Betrayal blindness," she said, and it wasn't clear if she was addressing Quichotte or Sancho or planet Venus glinting in the darkening sky. "Victims of treachery find ways of deluding themselves that they are not being betrayed. Sexually, for example, but I assume in other areas too. Business, politics, friendship. We are good at fooling ourselves in order to preserve our trust. But it isn't only the victims who do it. The traitors, too, convince themselves that they are not committing treason. At the very moment of their deepest betrayals they assure themselves that they are acting well, even that their deeds are in the best interest of the betrayed person, or of some higher cause. They save us from ourselves, or, like Brutus and his gang, they save Rome from Caesar. They are the innocent ones, the good guys, or, at the very least, not so bad."

"What did he do?" Sancho asked. "Dad, I mean, not Brutus."

The Trampoline crossed her arms and clutched at her shoulders, and breathed deeply, gathering herself, like a storm.

It was necessary, she said, by way of a preamble, to tell Sancho something about the problem of South Asian men. She presumed Sancho was not fully briefed on this topic?

No, she hadn't thought so.

She would not bore him with statistics. But she would ask him to believe that in her field, the microfinancing of poor women to enable them to become economically self-sufficient, she could not count on the backing of the men in their lives. In her work she and her teams in the field subscribed to the so-called sixteen decisions of the Grameen Bank movement, and decision eleven, for example, "We shall not take any dowry at our sons' weddings, nor shall we give away any dowry at our daughters' weddings," was not popular with the patriarchy. Sexual violence against South Asian women was present wherever and whenever women tried to establish independent lives and expand the zone of their personal freedoms.

The microcredit movement lent money without asking for any guarantees. It operated entirely on the basis of trust between the lender and the borrower. He could appreciate, could he not, that in any field where trust was as important a currency as banknotes, the issue of betrayal was a hot-button topic.

Here Sancho interrupted her to say that Quichotte had told him something about her operation; quite a lot, in fact. This information came to her as a surprise.

"He remembered that," she said. "I didn't think he would remember."

"Because of the Interior Event?"

"Yes."

"What was the Interior Event?"

"I will tell you in due course. Everything in its proper place."

"I WROTE AN ARTICLE," she said. "In *The New York Times*. About my work. It was at a time when I was feeling worn down by the battle, I admit that, and I expressed my frustration about the many ways, big and small, in which South Asian men held women back, the many obstacles of old-fashioned attitudes that had to be negotiated and overcome. The article was well received at first and was reprinted in many countries, including the South Asian countries. For a moment I was happy about the article's reception. Then the craziness began. People—South Asian men—began to send me messages of abuse. 'Man hater,' 'lesbian,' et cetera. Death threats were also received, and descriptions of the terrible things that would be done to my body before and after I died, and promises of hellfire, and, worst of all, threats against the women who used our organization. What shocked me was that respected, senior male members of the community in this country condemned me too. Religious leaders, but also business leaders, the same ones who had previously encouraged me and supported my initiatives. There was a demand that I make a public apology to all Indian, Pakistani, Bangladeshi, and Sri Lankan men, the ones living in those countries and the ones in the diaspora too. For a moment it looked as if everything I had tried to build would be destroyed overnight. As if I had beaten one life-threatening disease only to be overwhelmed by a different kind of killer sickness. The name of the sickness was a word we were all just learning.

"Blowback.

"What saved me was the date. Let's just say, B.G., which is to say, Before Google. The world before the birth of the monster the Internet became, before the age of electronically propagated hysteria, in which words have become bombs that blow up their users, and to make any public utterance is to set off a series of such explosions. Our age, A.G., in which the mob rules, and the smartphone rules the mob. Back then the most advanced technology available was the fax machine. Old technology saved my business and my life. It was too slow to kill. The howls of outrage spread, but they spread slowly. My character was assassinated, but it was a slow assassination, which allowed time for a defense to be assembled, for resistance to be organized. And, best of all, the women we had trusted, to whom we had given money without any guarantee of its return, those women now trusted us. Trust saved me as it had saved them. The organization did not break. I did not break. Instead, the storm broke, and we survived.

"Your father, the only half of a brother I've got, I hoped I could trust, but he betrayed that trust. And at the time that felt like an unforgivable thing."

"He wasn't on your side," Sancho said. It wasn't really a question.

"I don't know which half of the available brother material he got," Trampoline said, keeping her emotions at bay. "But I think it was defective. He said I should have known. He said, what did I expect. He said, did I do it to provoke, to get attention, whatever. He said it was my own fault. Somebody sent a flayed pig's head in the mail to me at the *New York Times* address, and they called me and asked if I wanted it messengered over. For all of this I was to blame."

"I don't remember the pig's head," Quichotte interjected, mournfully. "These accusations should be leveled at another person, who disappeared long ago."

———

THIS WAS WHEN THE Trampoline began to tell Sancho how the end of her relationship with Quichotte was linked to a larger ending: the end of the world.

Sancho sat up when this larger subject was introduced. "Wait a minute. We were just talking about a pig's head. How did we get from there to doomsday?"

"I changed the subject," the Trampoline said. "It's time to mention Evel Cent."

"Did you say Evel Cent?" Sancho asked.

"I did."

"That Evel Cent? The science billionaire?"

"I believe there's only one."

"Wow."

The apartment was in darkness but nobody turned on a light. The three of them sat some distance from one another, wrapped in their separate obscurities. Then out of the darkness Quichotte spoke.

"I saw him," he said.

"When?" the Trampoline asked, very surprised. "Where? How?"

"On TV," Quichotte said simply. "He was saying that science was in the process of confirming what I already knew. He said he would provide the scientific evidence at the proper time."

"You know the world is going to end?"

"He read something in a science fiction story," Sancho explained, "and decided it explained his quest. When he attains the Beloved, the universe will have achieved its purpose, and will therefore conclude."

"And he feels okay about that," the Trampoline said.

"You know how he is," said Sancho. "Who knows how he feels?"

———

"I MET THIS STRANGE beautiful boy, Evel," the Trampoline said. "It was at a money people's party at one of those clubs there were then, Lotus or Moomba or Bungalow or Sway, I don't recall. I didn't like those parties, men in red suspenders ordering Cristal and waving cash at women as if it was an irresistible sexual organ, but sometimes I had to go, because of what was then my new microcredit project. A friend told me I should meet this physicist on his way to becoming a billionaire and led me across the crowded room. I expected a cliché, some sort of small, skinny, dark-skinned, bespectacled, nerdy person, the classic Indian in America making it big in the new technologies, and was surprised to find a guy with moviestar good looks, slicked down and shiny faced in a bespoke suit, a geek in dude's clothing. He had a booth all to himself, which was his way of saying he was somebody. He said, 'I'd be glad if you sat down and had a drink with me.' His name made an impression on me. *Evil Scent*. 'You've got the right name for this world,' I thought, but managed not to say. He probably heard variations on that theme all the time anyway. But he chose that name. Awwal Sant, his real Indian name, would have been just fine but he had rejected it. That was a clue that there was something off about him. I should have paid better attention.

"He was several years younger than me, and acted even younger than that, sulky, awkward, but cocky, sure of his genius. We had nothing in common except our attitude to the money, I thought. I had been on one side of the money and now I was switching to the other side: first I had made it and now I was giving it away. He was still very interested in making a lot of it but he had his eyes on something much bigger. Money was a tool, not a goal, we agreed on that.

"I liked the first thing he said after I sat down: 'I'm sorry, but I have no small talk.' It was a funny line, but he said it with absolute solemnity and a kind of piercing, sincere energy, which made it funnier, and made him interesting. He began to talk about himself, which was normal with money guys. But most of them talked about their assets, their planes, their boats, their blah blah blah, which to me was an instant turnoff. This Evel talked about his obsession with the nature of reality, its fragility and mutability, and that was interesting too. He was thinking about parallel universes even then. When he started in about his love for science fiction, naming obscure-to-me writers of the old school—I remember the names Simak and Blish and Kornbluth and Sprague de Camp—I glazed over and was about to excuse myself but then he did something actually unpleasant. He grabbed me by my wrist and glared at me with what looked like anger and said, 'You can't leave.' I detached his hand. My secret anger was bigger than his, and I showed him just a flash of it. 'You need to learn how to behave,' I said. 'Let me know if you ever do.' Then I left. I looked back toward him from the doorway. He seemed lost in thought, wrapped up in himself. But he was watching. Afterwards he said to me, 'If you hadn't looked back I would never have spoken to you again. But you did look back. That was very important.' It was, I thought, the remark of a very vain individual. But, again, it was interesting.

"I never believed any man would find me attractive after my mutilation, and I had reconciled myself to that. There was, yes, the secret anger. I had a lot of anger about what had happened to me. But I had also learned how to bury it so deep that it didn't know how to get out unless I chose to let it escape. It worked for me now, I told myself. I told myself a lot of things: that I was doing the work I wanted to do, I had loyal friends, a full and comfortable life, and I had cheated death. There was nothing wrong with that picture, nothing that required the presence of a man to put right. These good thoughts prevented the rage from rising up out of its burial ground. But it was there if I needed it. It still is.

"This was the china shop in which I lived, into which Evel Cent charged, without a thought for the damage he might cause, talking about the end of the world. The morning after he grabbed my wrist he was standing on the sidewalk down there holding flowers, calling my cell number. I hadn't given it to him, or told him my address, but there he was. Resourceful. Determined. Apologetic. Urgent. I told him to come up and what followed, followed. No, that isn't correct. It was slow. The idea of undressing for a man was horrifying. The idea of being touched. He said, 'I'm in no hurry. The end isn't coming for a while yet.' *What?* I said. *What?* Out came his pet theory, the one to which he would devote his billions. The cosmos disintegrating like an oil painting on a fraying canvas, like the ruins of Egypt. The appearance of holes in space-time, the coming victory of Nothing over Everything. And then his grand design. He was already working on it, had built the research corporation, and had hired the top-drawer scientists needed to solve the problems of the science, and he already had the name for it.

"This was how I first heard about NEXT. 'Neighbor Earth Xchange Technology.' He said: 'Once I've built the transfer machines, we can escape to safety. I don't even know what the machines will look like right now. People always think, *spaceships,* but maybe the gateways to the neighbor Earths will actually turn out to be *like* gates. Portals, to use the word they like in sci-fi. You step into something like a phone booth and step out somewhere else. I'm thinking of the wardrobe that opens up into Narnia. My guess is that the Xchange Tech will be of that kind. We all step through the wardrobe and there's the lamppost and somewhere a benevolent lion waiting to welcome us. You, me, the human race. We can all go. We will be the NEXT people.' Sometimes he sounded like a cult leader in Guyana or Pune. Sometimes he sounded insane. But he was always passionate, convinced, and the brilliance was not in doubt. And he had no small talk. When he finally turned to the subject of us, he was suddenly and unexpectedly direct.

"To make his pitch he took me, where else, to the planetarium, where he was a panelist in a debate called 'Buying Space.' Four white men in gray suits were on the panel with him. He was wearing a golden vest embroidered with images of all the planets in the solar system, a star in the house of the stars. The four white men were talking about the exploitation of aerospace by business. They would build vessels to satisfy NASA's cargo requirements, they would send robots to asteroids to set up profitable mining operations, they would devise space vacations for rich tourists. They said without shame that they hoped to become the first trillionaires in history. When it was Evel's turn to speak he told them that their focus on space had made them blind to the crisis in space-time. He spoke of the coming disintegration of the universe and the need to survive by escaping into one or more neighbor Earths. The only technological advances that mattered, he said fervently, were explorations into this kind of trans-dimensional travel. 'Mars is so twentieth century,' he said. 'Neighbor Earths are the only destinations worth thinking about.' The white men in the gray suits looked at the brown man in the golden vest with all the condescension of their tribe, and humored him. 'How long have we got,' one of them asked Evel, 'and can you develop our escape routes in time?' Evel replied with great seriousness, 'I see that you don't believe me, but signs of the Great Instability will change your minds pretty soon. We don't have long, that's a fact, but we probably have long enough. I'm working on this day and night, both on identifying the neighbor Earths and on the means of getting there. I'd say we aren't too far from a breakthrough in the science.'

"At the end of the discussion his eyes were sparkling and there was an exhilaration in him which I hadn't seen before. He's a street fighter, I thought, this surprising mixture of a man, Rock-Hudson-meets-Shah-Rukh-Khan on the outside, with Stephen Hawking hidden inside that shell. He actually likes going up against men like the men in the gray suits and messing with their heads. He enjoys debating men who think they're at the cutting edge of the future and telling them they're out of date. I liked to see that.

"After the debate, we had lunch and in one of his no-small-talk outpourings of words he made a sort of declaration of love. A crucial aspect of NEXT technology, he said, was accepting that the body and whatever you wanted to call it, the self, the spirit, *das Ich,* the ghost in the machine, were yoked together but not the same, inseparable but not identical, and so if a way had to be found of transporting the body across a very complex existential divide, it could not be automatically assumed that the Thing within the body (the Hawking inside the movie star, I thought) would be transported too. NEXT technology, in other words, had to be cognizant of the needs of the soul.

"Then he said, 'It is the intangible thing that attracts me, not the outward thing. The thing that sees, not the eye that does the seeing. The unseen pilot in the driving seat, not the housing assembly or the engine. It is the intangible thing that draws me so close to you.'

"I said, 'So what you're saying is that my body repels you but you like my soul? Because I'm pretty sure I don't believe in the soul.' And he replied, 'You are receiving an insult when only a compliment was sent. And as regards the Thing, you will come to see that I am right, and it certainly exists.' Then he took my hand, but not in the way in which, on that first night, he had grabbed my wrist. Now, in his emotionally strangled way, he was telling me what I had thought I'd never hear again."

Quichotte appeared to lose interest in the Trampoline's story, moved away from them toward the large TV set in the wall at the far end of the living room, and picked up the remote. "*Salma* will be on soon," he said, vaguely, as if talking to himself.

The Trampoline moved swiftly toward him and took the zapper out of his hands. "We're just coming to the good part," she said. "The part you're in."

Sancho heard the note of fury under her calm voice. There was a volcano down there, he thought. Maybe it would explode before the night was done.

"After that we were together, Evel and I," the Trampoline went on, still addressing her remarks to Sancho. "He was arrogant and full of himself and he worked around the clock, sometimes for many days running, and when I saw him all he could do was sleep, but there he was, and I liked it, or I liked it more than I didn't like it, and if I'm going to be completely honest, I was, just a little bit, grateful."

"Then he did something," Sancho guessed, jerking his head in his father's direction.

"They finally met," the Trampoline said. "My brother the intelligence guy and my lover the genius. I even cooked dinner."

"He's on *Salma,*" Quichotte said suddenly.

"Who is?" the Trampoline wanted to know.

"Your guy," Quichotte replied. "Mr. Evel Cent. In fifteen minutes."

"How do you know?"

"I pay attention to programming," said Quichotte. "Especially for the show of the wonderful woman I love."

"Then fifteen minutes will have to do," the Trampoline said.

"DINNER WAS FILET MIGNON and roasted brussels sprouts and he, my half brother of the wrong half, drank too much red wine too fast and really, really wanted to know all about what my genius boyfriend was up to. He was out of his depth but that didn't stop him; he became belligerent and even condescending.

"'You think there are other dimensions and we can slip into them like going through a crack in an open door? Is that a real thing?'

"So of course my genius boyfriend became pompous.

"'The science can't be argued with, we already have third-generation detector probes that have begun to find echoes of the neighbor Earths, the way our radio sensors are beginning to hear the echoes of the Big Bang. We have fourth-generation probes in development that will sharpen our data and provide a clearer path through the Instability and into the folds of the Multiplicity.' Blah blah blah.

"Naturally this was too technical for your father, so he changed tack.

"'And you believe in the end of the world?' Said with an open, undisguised scorn. 'Even though crackpots have been giving us the end-of-the-world news at regular intervals since forever, and it hasn't ended yet, has it?'

"If there's one thing that's a red rag to a physicist billionaire it's a journalist doubting the science, so . . .

" '*Crackpot* is a harsh word, sir, particularly coming from a man who wouldn't recognize a tear in the deteriorating fabric of space-time if it was pointed out to him with a stick.'

"That was a declaration of war. I needed to calm things down. 'Hey,' I said, 'why not tell Evel what you're working on right now?'

" 'Hackers,' he said. 'Computer hackers. They're going to be a big problem. They already are.'

"This was when the trouble really began. You could argue that Evel started it by boasting.

" 'We have the most advanced encryption systems in the world,' he said. 'Our defenses are so high that these pygmies you're talking about would burst into tears at the sight.'

"Now, any brother of mine, even a half brother who got the wrong half of brother-ness, should at this point have thought, this is my half sister's boyfriend, back off, don't goad him, don't get into a who-has-the-bigger-dick contest, but that's exactly what happened.

" 'I know people who could hack into your systems in fifteen, maybe twenty minutes, and then all those secrets of yours, your what-do-you-call-'em NEXT systems that will save the world by taking us to live in Narnia or Middle-earth or some other fairy tale, will be sold on every street corner for anyone crazy enough to compete with you to buy.'

"He shouldn't have said 'crazy.' He shouldn't have said 'fairy tale.' He shouldn't have made it sound like a threat. He shouldn't have said one damn thing. He should have kept his big mouth shut and let me have my relationship with my genius. There were one hundred things he shouldn't have done but he did them all. And the genius took the bait.

" 'Threatening me is never a good idea,' Evel said. Voice like ice.

'It doesn't work out well for the people who do it. Let me just say that.'

"And to me he said. 'This is your brother. This is how he is with me. It's a problem.'

" 'Half brother,' I said, laughing it off, but he was on his feet and heading for the door. " 'Don't be childish,' I said. 'Sit down and let's get past this.'

Maybe I shouldn't have said 'childish.' Definitely I shouldn't have. But he was walking out the door and I panicked. It wasn't my best moment. I admit that. And Mr. Cent, he never called again.

" 'Let him go,' he said, your dad. 'He's a bully and a narcissist and he lives in crazytown. You don't want to spend your life with that. You don't want to spend another five minutes with that.'

"He thought he was doing me a favor. He thought he was the good guy. But I was the one left with the broken heart. Evel disappeared from my life, and that, my dear boy, was that for me as far as romance was concerned. And now we are back to where I started: betrayal blindness. Your father betrayed me and was blind to what he did. Until I told him. And I did tell him, in pretty colorful language. That was where we left it."

"It is hard for me," Quichotte quietly said, "to ask forgiveness for actions I don't fully recall."

"And yet, curiously, forgiveness is what you're here to ask for," said the Trampoline.

"So that was the second unforgivable thing?" Sancho asked. The Trampoline did not reply, but drank her wine, quickly, and refilled her glass. Sancho tried a different tack. "What was the Interior Event?" he asked. "I need to know about that."

"It's showtime," said Quichotte. "We need to turn on the TV."

AFTERWARDS, WHEN THE GREAT scandal broke, there were people who said that the way Miss Salma R looked during the Evel Cent interview was the first indication that something was seriously wrong with her. She had the air of a woman who has spent half the night throwing buckets on a fire at her home and has had to leave to go to work before the flames were fully doused: tired, distracted, and not her usual lovable self. The techno-billionaire, however, was full of vim, like a child riding a bouncy ball. There were things he was bursting to say.

After introducing her guest, Salma was uncharacteristically sharp. "This business about the end of the world, Dr. Evel," she said, and he interrupted.

"I'd appreciate it if you dropped the 'Dr. Evel' shtick," he said. "It kind of sends out the wrong message?"

"Dr. Cent," she corrected herself smoothly, without an apology. "Don't you think it would be better, and a relief to your shareholders, I'm sure, if you stopped pushing this pretty unbelievable idea?"

"I understand that many people are in a state of denial," Evel began.

"Most people," Salma interrupted him. "Like, ninety-nine percent of people."

"When ninety-nine percent of people thought the world was flat," Evel said, "it didn't make the world flat. The world didn't need people to believe it was round to be round. Right now, ninety-nine percent of people are happily having a picnic on a railway track. Which doesn't mean there isn't a train coming down the line, traveling pretty fast. The railway train doesn't need people to believe it's coming, because it's coming."

"Evel, is this just something you're putting out there, like a theory, something for discussion, or is there actually any proof?"

"I'm here today," Evel Cent said, "to make two announcements. The first is that CentCorp will be releasing a report tomorrow which will contain all the proof you, or anyone, could possibly need. This is happening. The universe is fraying at the edges. It's coming apart. We need to recognize that and take action."

"But even if you're right, this is something that's going to happen, what, thousands, millions of years from now? So there are more important things to worry about at present, aren't there? Better uses for our resources?"

"I'm not so sure it is so far in the future," Evel said. "Some of my models show disturbing scenarios that predict the possibility of a highly accelerated progression."

"How accelerated are you talking about, Evel? Within our life-times?"

"I can't answer that. It's one of the possibilities. We don't know which model has the highest probable degree of accuracy."

"So you're here on national television, telling the prime-time audience that the world may end in their lifetime. Evel, don't you feel that for a man with your visibility and prominence to put out such notions is, frankly, alarmist? You're scaring people, in all likelihood for nothing. Isn't that pretty irresponsible?"

"In the first place," Evel replied, "the truth is the truth, and must be heard, however problematic it seems. I'm confident that when our science is judged everyone will accept our conclusions. And in the second place, as I said at the beginning, I have a second announcement to make. I said some time ago that I would come forward at the proper time. That time has come."

"I'm afraid to ask," Salma said.

Evel Cent actually leapt to his feet. "This is the good news, Salma. This is the astonishing news. I'm here to tell you that the first neighbor Earth has been positively identified and the NEXT systems are up and running. Listen up, world: the path has been opened!"

"And we'll be right back with much more from Evel Cent," a stunned Miss Salma R told her viewers, "after these messages."

"THE PATH HAS BEEN OPENED," Quichotte repeated in beatific wonderment during the commercial break. "He said it, right there on TV, for everyone to hear."

"I get it that you believe everything you hear on TV," Sancho told him, "but really, this guy is off the wall. And I don't think he's talking about the same path as you."

"She's right there next to him," Quichotte replied, "and you heard what he said. The Path has been opened. Those are words of great power. Once such words have been spoken, events have no choice but to fall in line."

"I forgot for a moment," Sancho said, "that you're as crazy as that guy on the show."

When the commercial break ended, Salma pressed Evel Cent to back up his extraordinary claims. "You understand, don't you, that to most people watching, this business about portals will sound like a *Star Trek* script? Beam me up, Scotty, you know? How do you know these gadgets work, and are safe, and how do you know this other Earth exists? Are you going to let cameras in to film them? I can't believe I'm taking this seriously, that's the truth. Are you sure this isn't some sort of a prank? Because a CEO who is also the chairman of a multibillion-dollar tech corporation probably shouldn't be doing things like this. It scares the shareholders."

"She is not herself," Quichotte said gravely, watching Miss Salma through narrowed eyes. "She looks shaken. You can see the panic in her eyes. The idea of a crumbling cosmos has disturbed her. This is because the end of everything is impossible to face in the absence of love. In the presence of love it becomes a form of exaltation. It becomes rapturous."

"Shh," Sancho said. "I want to hear about the dog."

". . . a chocolate Labrador called Schrödinger," Evel Cent was saying on the show. "Named after the famous physicist Erwin Schrödinger and his quantum paradox about the cat."

"What happened to the cat?" Salma asked, out of her depth on this.

"The paradox is that the cat can be simultaneously alive and dead."

"Poor cat," Salma said.

"However, being simultaneously dead and alive won't work for people going through the portal, who will expect to be non-paradoxically alive and that's all," said Evel Cent. "So we sent Schrödinger through and brought him back to make sure he was less paradoxical than the cat. We used a dog, because dogs are more reliable. Cats don't always do as you ask. Also, we put him on a long leash, so that if there was some emergency and we needed to get him out of there we could yank him back. Then we sent him through the NEXT portal, making him the first entity in the known history of the cosmos to travel through inter-dimensional space. He went through, he came back. A successful experiment. One hundred percent. We have a string of such experiments planned. And we have a name for this first portal. We call it the *Mayflower*."

"How is Schrödinger now?"

"He's fine. Healthy, normal, alive, eating, in terrific shape. He's a great dog."

"And you recorded this, you filmed it, and you'll make the film available to us, so that we can all see for ourselves?"

"In due course," Evel Cent said. "We are in touch with the White House. This is a breakthrough discovery of national importance. More than that: of global importance. We have to be very careful. There are countries already thinking they could use NEXT to exile people they don't like. The neighbor Earth is not a prison colony. It's not Australia. Also there are strong indications that the Russians are trying to hack into CentCorp's systems. Imagine what a neighbor Earth would think of us if their first impressions of us were provided by Russians? If that sounds bad I'm sorry. I'm a patriot. I want to make sure America is in the leadership role of this movement into tomorrow, which alters the future of the whole human race. Here in America we have one clear edge. We have all these South Asian tech geniuses in the talent pool and I'm putting plenty of those heads together to keep us in the driving seat, to keep both our creativity and our defenses high. We'll be fine. Russian brains don't work like brown brains. Does that sound wrong too? I'm sorry. I guess I can be too passionate."

"Come back soon," Salma said, wrapping things up, "and next time, bring along Schrödinger the dog. That dog has things to tell us, I'm sure of that."

"She doesn't look good," Quichotte opined. "But the Path will become clear very soon, and then we will be together."

"He's just like this," Sancho said to the Trampoline. "He talks this way."

"It's time to talk about the Interior Event," the Trampoline replied.

KIPS BAY WAS NO longer a bay, land reclamation had taken care of that, and nobody there any longer remembered old Jacobus Hendrickson Kip, whose farmhouse once stood at what was now the intersection of Thirty-Fifth and Second. If you had talked to the moviegoers frequenting the multiplex a few blocks south, you would have found their heads full of fictional battles between human beings and their guardian superheroes on the one hand and various space monsters and supervillains, Balrogs and orcs, on the other, but very few of them could have told you anything about the real-life Landing at Kip's Bay in 1776, one of the first skirmishes of the War of Independence, when the American militia fled from the British and Washington in disgust cried, "Are these the men with whom I am to defend America?" The story of how Mary Lindley Murray, at the Grange on the Inclenberg property that is now Murray Hill, delayed the advancing British by inviting their general, Howe, to stop for cake and wine, allowing Putnam's ragged rebel forces to make their escape . . . that will have to wait for another day. We walk unknowing amid the shadows of our past and, forgetting our history, are ignorant of ourselves.

As also now Quichotte. Quester for love, supplicant for forgiveness, seated in the nightgloom of his half sister's home, while his ghosts, exhumed by her sorcery, walked all about him, including the phantom of himself as he once was. Chinese food was delivered and set upon a table, but Quichotte could not eat, feeling himself lost in darkness, encircled by the sadness of days gone by. Why had he been as he was, consumed by envy, ungenerous, competitive, harsh? He could not say. He had no access to that self. The reason for that was what happened that night in the Kips Bay of the past.

It wasn't such a bad apartment. The ceilings were high and the neighbors were quiet and he could work there contentedly enough. On the night in question, however, it almost became his tomb. He had a nightmare that night in which he had awoken, in this his own bedroom, to see a shadowy figure standing at the foot of his bed, looking down at him, saying nothing. He understood, in the dream, that the intruder was both himself, or his shadow, and also Death. He woke up in fear. It was 3 A.M. He sat up in bed and turned on the lamp on his nightstand, his heart beating hard. There was nobody in the room, of course, and to calm himself he drank a glass of water and got out of bed to go to the toilet. That was when the Interior Event happened. There was a sort of explosion between his ears. He lost his balance, fell forward onto the floor, and blacked out. When consciousness returned—a moment or an age later, he couldn't tell—it occurred to him that he was not dead. At some point after that realization, he also understood that he could not move. His cellphone was on the nightstand and so was the landline phone he was old-fashioned enough to have kept, but he was on the floor facing away from them. So he was helpless.

It took him two days to turn around and drag himself to the nightstand. For another whole day and night he tried to strike the table in such a way that one of phones fell off within his reach. On the fourth day he got hold of his cellphone and began to try to make a call.

"Who did he call?" Sancho wanted to know.

"He called me," the Trampoline said. "Who else would he call?"

The call finally went through and she answered it but he was unable to speak. He lay there on the bedroom floor with the phone by his ear while her voice shouted *Hello*.

Understanding that something was wrong, she had come quickly to his building, found the super, had the front door opened, found him on the floor, called the emergency services. He survived. He was a lucky man. This was America, and a stroke required long and careful treatment, and he was covered, because he had recently applied for and won a teaching position at a journalism school downtown, a tenure-track professorship that came with excellent health insurance. He endured a long period of rehabilitation, and after perhaps two years he was back in something like full working order, though his speech had slowed and he dragged his right leg. But the man who emerged from the Interior Event was not the same person as before. For a time he suffered some expected aftereffects. He cried at random moments, without apparent cause. He suffered from stress, depression, anxiety. But beneath these alterations lay a deeper change. There were deep gashes in his memory and those did not mend. He became less gregarious, more silent, much more withdrawn. Also, the journalist, the professor: he was gone.

Physically, he had clearly made a miraculous recovery. The lasting damage was not to his body but to his character. He did not return to the teaching position that had given him the insurance coverage he had needed. He distanced himself from old and new colleagues, new and old friends, and withdrew into himself, retreating so far, so deep, that nobody could follow him. For a long time he hardly spoke, and watched TV all day, sitting upright on the edge of his bed at home with his hands folded in his lap. This was when he began to speak in TV references, and his grasp on reality loosened. It also became clear that he no longer felt at home in the big city. The multiplicity, the everything of everything, the roar of narratives, the endless transformation, the myth factory lost in the myth of itself: it unsettled him. The absences in his mind needed to be soothed by absenting himself from his previous life, and by television, being absorbed by which was another kind of absenting. The day he told the Trampoline that he needed to leave town—that he had reached out to their cousin Dr. Smile in the pharma world and asked if he could work for him as a traveling salesman somewhere far from New York—was also the day on which he first made the money accusation. The third unforgivable thing.

That he accused her of stealing his money was bad enough. That he did it after her solicitude during the past two years was worse. That he ignored the fact that throughout this period she had actually been managing his money for him, making sure it was well cared for, was worse still. And the allegation about forging their father's will, or falsifying it in her favor, was the last straw. "He was always the wrong half of a half brother," the Trampoline told Sancho, "but at that point I understood I needed to withdraw from him, just as he needed to withdraw from almost everything. He was damaged, I saw that, he wasn't himself, I had compassion for that, but he had become unbearable. If we had been married we would have had to get divorced. In a way we did get divorced. When he left the city to begin his strange journeyings in the heartland, selling pills to doctors, I thought, okay, that's that, and let him be, let him do what he has to do, and maybe find his way. But guess what? His money is still in good shape. And there's certainly enough of it to mean you guys don't have to stay in the Blue Yorker motel. If he wants to stay in the city he can rent a place. You can both stay here until he does. I have a parking place in the basement garage, but I don't have a car, so he can put his wheels down there."

She turned to face him. "Does that work?"

Quichotte rose to his feet and cleared his throat. "There is something I first need to say," he stated, formally. "I wish to apologize to you, my sister, for all offenses both remembered and forgotten, both those for which I feel guilt and responsibility and those which were the responsibility of a person who has faded from memory. In my small way I am what your Mr. Cent says the universe has become: a cosmos with holes torn out of it, where nothing remains. I am fraying at the edges and may not survive. Therefore I ask that both kinds of fault, the known and the unknown, be forgiven before we reach our ends, and I am willing to perform whatever deeds you ask for by way of a penalty, in expiation of my misdeeds, both those which I own and those which I can no longer own, as they have left me and gone far away. This is what I have crossed America to set right, for until there is harmony the path to the Beloved, who lies beyond the world and its grief, will not open." At this point, he moved slowly toward the Trampoline, his leg dragging heavily tonight, and when he reached her he fell, shockingly, to his knees and took hold, between his thumb and forefinger, of the hem of her garment.

"Forgive me," he said, bowing his head, "and set me free, and yourself as well."

Time stood still inside the room. Outside, or so it seemed to Sancho, a week passed, a month, a year, a decade, maybe a century. The sun rose and set, the moon waxed and waned, the seasons fled by. Mighty men and women rose and fell, the world changed, the future enveloped them, and they were leftovers from an ancient past, unknown to all, lost in their own labyrinth of love and pain. Then the Trampoline stirred, very slightly, and very slowly lifted her hand and placed her palm upon Quichotte's humbled head.

"Yes," she said, and the clocks moved once again.

"The time ahead of us," the Trampoline said, "is much shorter than the time already past. You're right about that. There are new concerns about my health. We don't have to talk about those now. Let's just say it's a good time to set down burdens. Oh, and as regards Evel Cent, these days he's well known to be a womanizer, so you were right, I didn't need him in my life. Which doesn't mean he's wrong about the end of the world. Or, by the way, right about it."

"Now that there is harmony," Quichotte said, "we have entered the sixth valley, which is the Valley of Wonderment, in which the perfect love will come into being, and that will bring about the happy ending we all want."

"Oh, that's right," the Trampoline said. "You're now a doomsday merchant too. Well, then, I forgive you because of the approaching end of the world."

"Hallelujah!" cried Quichotte. "And now that I am forgiven it merely remains to rescue the woman I love and lead her through wonderment into the seventh valley, which lies beyond space and time, and where, whatever happens to this world, the Wayfarer who reaches its meadows can live happily for all eternity."

"The Elysian Fields! That is indeed a noble goal," the Trampoline said, keeping a straight face, "but the word 'merely' seems to undervalue the level of difficulty involved."

"You will see," Quichotte cried, a tide of happiness rising in his breast. "The obstacles are about to dissolve, and the time of joy is about to begin."

And promptly the next morning at 8 A.M., Quichotte received a text from his cousin and erstwhile employer, Dr. R. K. Smile, sent from a burner phone, requesting a meeting. The path to the Beloved opened.

CHAPTER SEVENTEEN

In which Sister finishes
the Family Story, & her own Game

"A CITY WAS A DOOR, AND IT WAS EITHER OPEN OR shut. London got slammed in his face and tried to keep him out. New York swung open easily and let him come in." The hard-boiled opening lines of Brother's novel *Reverse Rendition* returned to him on the day flight from JFK to Heathrow. On reflection, he didn't agree, or not anymore, or not to the New York part, not in this racially charged and confrontational time. His secret agent protagonist needed to rethink his position. The idea of London (pop. 8,136,000) as a clubby, members-only, keep-out zone was probably out of date too. He hadn't been there for many years. These days the clubs were mostly owned by foreigners and it was the English who had to apply for membership. But the new flag-waving go-back-where-you-came-from England-for-the-English white populism was there, too, had risen from its grave in the dead imperial past to haunt the fractured, second-class-nation present. So, then, a plague on both your houses, Brother thought, and asked for another vodka and soda, his third, one over his limit, but he needed it today.

(He had not been in an airplane for quite some time. He had given his Quichotte a nightmare which he had had himself, a dream of first falling out of the sky and then drowning, and Quichotte's consequent fear of flying was also Brother's own. On the rare occasions when he had no choice but to fly, he knocked himself out with Xanax and got through the journey that way. This time he had chosen vodka instead of Xanax. So far, it was working well.)

Ever since his reunion with his lost child he had been thinking of broken families—of his own broken family—as allegories of larger-scale fragmentations, and of the search for love and healing as a quest in which everyone, not just his mad Quichotte, was involved.

He made a note on his phone. *Don't forget to resolve Sancho's love interest too.* This was the latest addition to a list he had been making since the plane took off. *Don't forget Sancho's visions—reality begins to be more phantasmagoric. Don't forget Quichotte's key. What does it open, and what's inside?* And one more: *Quichotte (sounds like) key shot.* A key shot was a tiny bump of cocaine or heroin scooped up on a key. He didn't know how this fitted into Quichotte's story. Maybe there was no place for it. It would remain just a note, to be deleted later.

The plane lost altitude suddenly and fast, like one of the balls Galileo imagined dropping from the Leaning Tower of Pisa, like an elevator plunging down its shaft, like a falling man. His drink spilled, but he caught the glass before it fell. The orange breathing masks appeared from above. The captain spoke rapidly over the intercom, trying to reassure passengers while also giving emergency instructions. It was not necessary at present to put on the breathing masks. Stay in your seats with the belts fastened. This was more than *rough air,* but the aircraft was under the pilots' control, or so the voice insisted, not wholly convincingly. The 747 lurched, bumped, slalomed first one way, then the other. Many of the passengers panicked. There was weeping and shrieking. There was vomiting too. Brother, for whom this was a bad dream come true, who had always known in a part of his mind that airplanes were simultaneously

too massive to fly and too flimsy to resist the immense forces of nature, was interested to note that he remained calm. He continued to
sip at his drink. Was it possible that his fear of flying had been cured
at exactly the moment at which it was perfectly rational to feel
afraid? I've been writing about the end of the world, he thought,
and what I was really doing was imagining death. My own, mas-
querading as everyone else's. A private ending redescribed as a universal one. I've been thinking about it for so long that this doesn't
come as a surprise. He raised his glass and toasted the giant death
angel, a bare skull visible within a black hooded robe, standing on
the horizon and holding the aircraft in one hand and shaking it. The
death angel bowed in recognition of the gesture, and let the jumbo
jet go. With a brief final shudder the aircraft settled back into its
course.

After that the flight went smoothly and the passengers entered a
mood of near-hysterical camaraderie. The crew handed out cham-
pagne for free, even in coach. Brother suspected that some of the
passengers were having mile-high sex with strangers in the washrooms. Things were becoming a little rock and roll. He kept his own
counsel, finished his drink slowly, and went on thinking about
death. Which had been central to his career as a writer until now.
He had always felt that a story didn't come alive for him until at least
one character hated someone else, or several someone elses, so much
that they were prepared to murder them. Without killing there was
no life. He knew that other writers could make masterpieces out of
accounts of tea parties (e.g., the Mad Hatter's) or dinner parties (e.g.,
Mrs. Dalloway's) or, if you were Leopold Bloom, out of a day spent
walking around a city while your wife was being unfaithful to you
back home, but Brother had always needed blood. It was an age of
blood, not of tea, he told himself (and others, from time to time).

He was flying toward a deathbed now—or somewhere very
close to a deathbed—hoping there would be time for a final scene of
reconciliation. Sister was in the angel's fist and he didn't seem in-

clined to let her go. At the end of most lives, he reminded himself, death did not arrive as a crime, but as the great mystery, which everyone had to solve alone.

Mysteries were the perfect analogue of human life as well as human death. Human beings were mysteries to others and to themselves as well. Some chance occurrence jolted them from their sleep and they began to act in ways of which they would not have believed themselves capable. We know nothing about ourselves or our neighbors, he thought. The nice lady next door turns out to be an ax murderer, giving her mother forty whacks. The silent, smiling, bearded gentleman upstairs is revealed as a terrorist when he drives a truck into innocent people in the town center. Death offers us clarification, it shines a harsh shadowless light on life, and then we see.

The death of Don Quixote felt like the extinction in all of us of a special kind of beautiful foolishness, an innocent grandeur, a thing for which the world had no place, but which one might call humanity. The marginal man, the man laughably out of touch and doggedly out of step and also unarguably out of mind, revealed in his last moment as the one to care most about and mourn most deeply for. *Remember this. Have this above all in mind.*

He raised his window blind to look out at the no-longer-dangerous sky. There were black dots dancing in his field of vision. He suffered from floaters, had done so for a long time, but they seemed to be getting worse. Sometimes a group of floaters seemed to come together near the corner of his eye and then it looked as if the universe itself might be fraying. As if empty spaces had appeared in the fabric of what-there-was.

He pulled the window blind down again. We are lost wanderers, he thought. We have eaten the cattle of the sun god, and incurred the wrath of Olympus. He closed his eyes. Sister was waiting in London. That was what mattered right now. Death, and Quichotte, and everything else, could wait. A fourth vodka, however, would be a good idea.

(EARLIER.)

"Hello."

"Hello, Brother."

"This is a good idea, right? To have these getting-to-know-you talks before we meet in real life? It's been a long—"

"Yes, it's a good idea."

"We can do it on Skype or FaceTime or WhatsApp video if you prefer. Or Signal if for any reason you want the conversations encrypted."

"No."

"No, not encrypted?"

"No, not Skype or FaceTime or WhatsApp video or Signal."

"Why not? Just a question."

"I don't want to have to dress up for you. When I'm ready I can send you a recent photograph. I'm not ready yet."

He didn't tell her about Googling her. "You don't have to dress up."

"The phone is fine."

"Do you want to see a photograph of me?"

"Not today." That meant she had already Googled him.

"Okay. So who goes first? If you'd—"

"You go first."

"I hoped you wouldn't say that."

"You go first."

"Then I'll begin by making my apology."

"As is only right and proper."

The first thing he had to do was to get over the accent. She had lived in Britain forever, he got that, so it was natural she would sound British, but did she have to talk like the fucking queen? Ay'm so heppy to heah from you. The rain in Spain stays mainly on the plain. In Hahtf'd Heref'd and Hempshah, hurricanes hahdly evah heppen. Rule Britennia, Britennia rules the waves. Ez is only raight and proppah. Half Lizzie Two, half *My Fair Lady*. That was some white shit.

There was, however, something else about her voice on the phone, something which even the plummy vowels could not disguise: a small shakiness, a trembling, which (or so it seemed to Brother) she was making a powerful effort of will to disguise.

"Are you all right?" he asked her.

"Don't change the subject."

So he made the apology. He thought of Quichotte rising formally to his feet to speak, then falling to his knees and touching the Trampoline's dress at the hemline. That last kind of self-abasement wasn't Brother's style, but if they had been video conferencing he might have stood. He tried to speak with something like his character's formality, to be wholehearted and undefended in his remorse. When he finished he realized his heartbeat had accelerated and he was breathing heavily, an old man who had overexerted himself. He had to start thinking seriously about what he ate, and about getting fit, he told himself, not for the first time. Douglas Adams, the author of *The Hitchhiker's Guide to the Galaxy,* had died after going to the gym as everyone in California was obliged to do by the state's unwritten laws, to worship at the altar of one's body all the world's gods of health, whose names were only known to those who, being vegan and gluten-free, were pure enough to receive the information: Fufluns the Etruscan deity of plants, wellness, and happiness, Aegle the Greek goddess of the healthy glow, Maximón the Mayan hero god of health, Haoma from Persia, and Panacea the goddess of the universal cure. Ever since Brother read about Adams's death he had started saying, half joking, half defensively, that exercise was to be avoided because it killed people. Don't panic. Have some fries with that.

But now, after doing nothing more strenuous than telling his sister on the phone that he was sorry for his past misdeeds, he was stressed out and gasping for breath. The death angel hovered and then set him free. (Later, when the angel released the plane in which he was crossing the ocean, he thought, that's two lives used up, and I'm not a cat.)

His jumbled thoughts about death and Equinox filled the gap between the conclusion of his apology and the beginning of Sister's response, which came after a lengthy pause. When she spoke her words were as measured as a legal deposition. "Remorse and forgiveness are obviously related," she said, "but it's not a cause-and-effect relationship. The connection between them is the act. It is for the actor to decide whether or not he feels regret and remorse for the act, whether or not he is willing and ready to apologize in the hope of making amends. It is for the person acted upon to decide whether or not she feels able to set the act aside and move on, which is to say, to forgive. The decision of the person acted upon is not contingent upon the decision of the actor. One may genuinely feel remorse and make a genuine apology, and still not be forgiven, if the person acted upon is not ready to forgive. Alternatively, one may not feel ready to apologize, and still be forgiven, if the forgiver is ready to let bygones be bygones. You have apologized. That was and is your decision. I accept that it is a genuine apology. Now it is for me to decide whether or not I can forgive what you did. Or maybe I have already decided that. Or perhaps I never will."

"I'm glad there's at least one lawyer in the family," Brother replied. "Pa and Ma would have been so proud."

Those were their first moves. The purpose of the opening in the game of chess, Brother thought, was to establish command of the center and to give your pieces the greatest possible positional advantage. He had begun with a sacrifice, the unreserved apology, but it wasn't immediately clear if he had improved his position as a result. In the conversations that followed they circled one another, Brother reluctant to abase himself further, Sister playing a cautious game, defensive and slow. They ventured into childhood memories, not very successfully. The past, the peacefully dead mother, the suicide father with the empty bottle of pills by his bedside, Sister's affair with Sad-Faced Older Painter, the slap, all of that felt like treacherous territory, in which one or both could easily make false moves and lose ground that would be hard to recapture. Their few forays into old times led to strained exchanges.

"Do you still sing?"

"Only in the shower."

"That's a shame. No more Tweety Pie?"

"The cat got my tongue."

After some early awkwardnesses of this type they stayed away from reminiscence, by unspoken mutual agreement.

Brother quickly moved beyond the chess metaphor. Chess was a war game, and he was trying to make peace. Chess ended when you killed the king, and there could be only one winner. He wasn't trying to win. He was trying to recapture something he had lost.

They found they could talk to each other more easily about the present. Slowly at first and then with growing heat Sister told Brother about her racial equality work and her pro bono legal cases. "I've reached the point where I've had to give all that up," she said, in one of her first admissions of vulnerability. "I don't want to admit that the savages are winning, that the jungle is creeping in and recapturing the civilized world—the jungle where the only law is the law of the jungle—but on many days every week that's how it feels. It feels like I have to get up every day and hit my head against a wall. After a couple of decades of doing that kind of work, I need to start taking better care of my head. Time to step away from my place at the wall, to make way for a younger head. Somebody else's turn."

Not all the obstacles her clients faced were racial. Some were capitalist: for example, many members of the Bangladeshi community in London were employed in restaurants, and many of their Bangladeshi employers denied them the most basic of employee rights. Other hurdles were ideological. "I'm not fucking fighting to defend women's right to wear the veil, the hijab, the niqab, whatever," she declaimed. "All these young women these days who describe the veil as a signifier of their identity. I tell them they are suffering from what that presently unfashionable philosopher Karl

Marx would have called false consciousness. In most of the world the veil is not a free choice. Women are forced into invisibility by men. These girls in the West making their quote-unquote free choices are legitimizing the oppression of their sisters in the parts of the world where the choice is not free. That's what I tell them, and they are very shocked. They tell me they find my remarks offensive. I tell them I feel the same way about the veil. It's exhausting. I've become embittered. I just needed to stop."

During these conversations she didn't tell him of the other, more imperative reason why she was giving things up—her bad health news, the utterly unfair invasion by a second carcinoma, chronic lymphocytic leukemia, or CLL, of a body already ravaged by its Pyrrhic victory over breast cancer. She didn't yet feel that that news belonged to him, that he had a right to it. Instead she talked with pride about Daughter's achievements in the rag trade. She also spoke at some length about her husband "Jack," the loving judge, and, in a step toward greater intimacy, described his fondness for wearing women's gowns when entertaining at home. "What our friends understand, even though nobody else nowadays seems to, is that it has nothing to do with sexuality. It's just a fashion preference. At least in our small charmed circle such innocence is still allowed." He heard again a kind of exhaustion in her voice, and tried to tell himself that the cause was probably her feeling of being out of step with the conventional progressive attitudes of the time. The old left-right simplicities didn't fit anymore, and a woman like Sister, who had identified with the left all her working life, might well feel worn down by the new rhetoric. Time for someone else to bang their head against the wall.

He didn't entirely convince himself. Something was badly wrong with her, he could hear it in her voice every time they spoke, but he understood that she didn't yet trust him enough to tell him what it was.

He told her a little about Quichotte: the character of the aging TV addict, the love of the unknown woman. She laughed. "I'm glad to hear you are capable of sending yourself up," she said. He began to make the usual literary protest, he isn't me, he's fictional, etc., but she stopped him. "Don't even," she said. "It's better if I think you're lampooning yourself. It makes me like you a little more."

He didn't talk about the Trampoline, or tell Sister that he had given Quichotte's fictional half sister the same illness and brutal surgery as Sister herself had undergone many years ago. That revelation could wait for later. Maybe a lot later. He was pretty sure it wouldn't go down well.

("When a writer is born into a family, the family is finished," Czesław Miłosz once said.)

They were finding their way back to each other. There was one angry exchange, Sister's famously pyrotechnic temper getting at least this one final, spectacular outing, but even that, Brother afterwards thought, was essentially affectionate, the subject being Sister's fury that Brother's long silence, the years it had taken him to consider attempting a rapprochement, had robbed her of family life for all that time. His return, and his attempt to re-create the familial bond, infuriated her because of its tardiness, which she translated into uncaringness, unfeelingness, and what with her Eliza-Doolittle-meets-Elizabeth-II accent she called *arseholery*. "Did you ever have any comprehension, did you even possess the capacity to comprehend, what it might have felt like to imagine having an older brother by my side, that I could turn to, on whom, if need be, I could lean? No, never mind, rhetorical question, I already know the answer. Of course you can't bloody imagine it, because you were too busy swanning around bloody New York fantasizing about bloody espionage. You know who the real James Bond was? An expert on Jamaican birds whose name Ian Fleming stole for his 007. That seems to sum you up pretty damn well. As a secret agent—correction, as somebody writing about secret agents—you make an excellent ornithologist. As a human being? Not even as good as that."

That was just Sister clearing her throat. The aria followed, a song

of accusation to rival the mighty "Abscheulicher!" in Beethoven's
Fidelio. He was a heartless monster, she told him; did he not understand—*O abominable one!*—that human life was short and that each
day of love stolen from it was a crime against life itself? No, of
course he did not understand, such understanding was beyond the
ken of monsters, *abominable ones,* who rutted and grunted in the
mud of ugliness and rose up to murder what was beautiful, or what
might, with proper husbandry, become a thing of beauty. They had
never been that close, she cried, but if he had shown even the slight-
est desire to come closer to her she would have responded a thou-
sandfold. But instead, there was his unjust accusation of a financial
crime, there was the slap, there were the ensuing years of prideful
unrepentant absence, and these were unforgivable things. And in
spite of that there had been times—so many times!—when she had
told herself, Yes! You can do the impossible, you can forgive the
unforgivable, only let him ask, let him come to my door and bow
his head and say, at last, after so long, after the years of blindness
which were caused by my stupidity, I recognize the wrongs I did, I
feel the pain you felt at their injustice, I see the truth, and the truth
is that I have been guilty of arseholery, and so, at your door, with
head bowed low, this arsehole asks to be forgiven. That was all he
had to say and do. And now here he was doing and saying it, but he
had left it so late, he had been so stupid for so long, that her rage
could not be quenched. He should hang up and go away, take his
voice out of her ear, let the silence between them be resumed, for
she was accustomed to that silence and it was too late for peace.—
No.—That was not how she had meant to end.—He should call her
again tomorrow. There was no more to be said today.

Words to that effect.

And after the tirade, she was spent. "I have to go," she said faintly,
and hung up. Brother had the impression that she had used up every
ounce of her strength—her *remaining* strength—and had been
brought to the point of collapse. He sat quietly with his thoughts
for a long time after the end of the phone call. He tried not to allow

the Shadow to become real. But he was becoming more and more certain that she was very sick.

There were no calls for a few days following the explosion. When she finally did call him she was calmer and quieter. She asked him more questions about his writing and he found himself willingly doing what he never did, which was, to talk about a work in progress. He was not a particularly superstitious man, but he did have this one superstition: don't let the work come out of your mouth or it will never come out through your fingers. But he answered Sister's questions willingly enough, and was encouraged by her interest in what he had to say. He talked about wanting to take on the destructive, mind-numbing junk culture of his time just as Cervantes had gone to war with the junk culture of his own age. He said he was trying also to write about impossible, obsessional love, father-son relationships, sibling quarrels, and yes, unforgivable things; about Indian immigrants, racism toward them, crooks among them; about cyber-spies, science fiction, the intertwining of fictional and "real" realities, the death of the author, the end of the world. He told her he wanted to incorporate elements of the parodic, and of satire and pastiche.

Nothing very ambitious, then, she said.

And it's about opioid addiction, too, he added.

That was when her defenses dropped. When he described to her his research into the American opioid epidemic and the scams associated with it, he felt her attention intensify, and when he talked about his character Dr. Smile, the devious fentanyl spray entrepreneur, and his unscrupulous willingness to allow his product to get into the hands of people who didn't need it, or not for medical reasons, he had her full attention. By the time he finished, she had made a decision.

"I have something to tell you about my condition," she said, and in a flash of clarity he remembered his encounter with the man who had called himself Lance Makioka, among other names. *"Your estranged lady overseas,"* Makioka had said. *"How much do you know about her present condition?"* And when Brother had asked him what he meant, he had backed away from the usage. *"I should have said 'situation.' Her current situation."* And here it was again, the menacing word.

"Your condition," he repeated, and then she told him.

She had contacted the doctor in America, the brown person, the top man, but had told him frankly that she wasn't keen on flying over to spend, what?, six months?, the rest of her life?, all her money?, receiving treatment in the United States. He had studied her case, been thoughtful, kind, and understanding, and had referred her to a "very good man" in London. The illness was unpredictable. In some cases, with the right treatment, life could be prolonged by many years. In other cases, regrettably, things moved quickly. "I'm in the latter category," she said flatly. "The prognosis is bad."

"How bad?"

"Bad."

"I see."

"What I'm most afraid of," she told him, "is pain. They say women have a much higher pain threshold than men. They say it's because we are the ones who have to go through childbirth. I say it's because most women have a much higher everything than most men. But now that I've waved that flag, I immediately have to admit that I'm not one of those heroines. I dread pain. The final pain, what did you call it just now? Breakthrough pain."

"I'm so sorry," he said.

"Not your fault," she told him. "And as it happens, there may actually be something you can do to help."

"Anything," he said.

"Your fictional character, Dr. Smile," she said. "And his fictional spray, InSmile™. Do they have real-life models? I'm wondering if there may be an actual doctor or doctors you read about, or better still, with whom you may be acquainted? And a product or products that actually exists or exist?"

Brother didn't answer her for a long moment.

"So, not 'anything' after all, then," Sister said.

"Sublingual fentanyl sprays are available on the market now," he replied carefully. "And breakthrough pain"—he restrained himself from saying *in terminal cancer patients*—"is exactly what they are intended for. I'm sure your British physician knows what's available in the UK and can prescribe the right thing."

"Haven't you heard about British doctors?" she said. "They don't like giving their patients medicines for what ails them. They think medicine is bad for sick people."

"But I'm sure that in your case, if the prognosis is—"

"Yes or no," she said. "Can you get hold of it for me? Do you know a man?"

Again, Brother took a moment before answering.

Then, "Yes," he said. "I do know a man."

"Do this for me," she said, "and then get on a plane as quickly as you can."

"I just want to say that you are a respected attorney and your husband is a judge, and this would be borderline against the law. Or, not even borderline, in fact."

"Do this for me," she said again.

"Okay," he said.

"And then get here soon."

"How soon?"

"Just get on a plane and come."

ALL AIRPORT CUSTOMS HALLS were designed to make even the innocent feel guilty. NOTHING TO DECLARE: the sign might as well have read DEAD MAN WALKING. He was convinced he would be stopped and found to be in possession of a highly restricted substance, without any proof of his right to carry it—which was to say, doomed, as surely as if he was on his way to the gallows. But in the drama in which he had agreed to participate, he was for the moment a player of secondary importance, so he passed uneventfully into the unrestricted liberty of Arrivals.

Brother asked the cab driver to turn on the air. This was not understood. He had to say "air-conditioning." The cabbie said it wasn't working, sorry, mate, open a window. What came through the opened window was a blast of hot air. London was enduring what the cabbie called a scorcher. A heat wave in London, Brother thought, felt like an oxymoron, like nonstop drizzle in L.A. Here it was nevertheless, the temperature at 9 P.M. still in the high eighties, whatever that was in Celsius, thirty? Thirty-five? Who knew. There was no understanding the British and their systems. Road signs gave distances in miles but bathroom scales used kilograms. You could buy a pint of milk in a supermarket or a pint of beer in a pub, but at the gas station fuel was measured in liters. Athletes ran the "metric mile," fifteen hundred meters, but a cricket pitch was twenty-two yards long. The money was decimal but everything else was a muddle, and even the European Union had long ago given up the attempt to make the Brits standardize their weights and measures, one of many early signs that the country resisted the idea of being fully European.

It was almost a relief to arrive in the middle of other people's crises and leave the crisis of America behind. At home he had stopped listening to the news and avoided social media to shut out the daily nonsense as much as he could. He had his book to write, and this private crisis to deal with, the crisis of Sister, and that was all he could handle right now. The apocalypse of the West would just have to wait in line.

He looked out at the night sky and experienced once again the illusion of a void. There were holes in his field of vision, spots of nothingness. These seemed different in kind from the floaters he was used to. So either he had begun to experience some sort of degeneration of the retina, or, alternatively, the crumbling of the cosmos as prophesied by his character Evel Cent had begun to occur in the real world as well as the fictional. That was absurd, he scolded himself. *That is absolutely not what is happening. That's a thing I made up.* He made a note to visit an eye specialist on his return from London.

He called Sister's phone. An unfamiliar female voice answered.

It was Daughter. "She's resting," she said. "But we are expecting you. Your room is ready. Also . . ." She paused, then continued, "I'm really excited to meet you. I've been wanting this to happen for I don't know how long, and I should confess that I was the one who wrote the first email from my mother's computer. Pawn to King Four. That was me."

"Then I'm greatly in your debt," Brother said. "I'll be there shortly."

"You should know," Daughter said, lowering her voice, "that my father finds it hard to forgive slights against my mother. Just as she gets furious on his behalf if anyone criticizes him. They have always been that way, super protective of each other. I'm just telling you in case he's a little cold toward you when you arrive. He'll get over it, I'm sure, now that you and my mother have patched things up."

"Thanks for the heads-up," Brother said.

He remembered the neighborhood from his student days when he had long hair and a Zapata mustache and wore purple shirts and red crushed-velvet flared pants. In those days, on the street with the famous weekend market, there was what people used to call a head shop called the Dog Shop whose owners had, for unexplained reasons, attached a giant human nose to the wall above the entrance. He had read somewhere that in the old days the area's poor would sometimes steal the dogs of the rich, take them away and train them to answer to different names, and then sell them back to their former owners on this very street. He had gone into the Dog Shop one day and asked if that story was the origin of the name, to be met with stoned hippie blankness. "No, man. It's just a name, man." Too bad, he thought. Even then, half a century ago, the culture was already beginning to be a thing without memory, lobotomized, with no sense of history. The past was for dead people. Turn off your mind, relax and float downstream.

And the restaurant below Sister's duplex was called Sancho. There were moments when it seemed that the whole world was echoing his work in progress.

He rang the doorbell. A buzzer sounded and the door to the apartment clicked open. Judge Godfrey Simons, in open-necked white shirt and slacks, stood at the top of the stairs to greet him. The welcome, as Daughter had warned, was not warm. "Look who's showed up at our door after all these years," the judge said. "Don't you think there's something a tiny bit ghoulish about appearing at this juncture after not being bothered to drop us so much as a postcard for donkey's years? Something a teensy bit macabre?"

Daughter pushed past him. "Stop it, Daddy." Then, to Brother, "We're very glad to have you. And he's not actually nearly as much of a curmudgeon as he sounded just then." She turned back to her father. "Behave." He snorted, a good-natured sort of snort, and turned away. Brother climbed the stairs and went in.

When he had imagined Sister on the other end of the phone, his picture of her had been influenced by her grand accent. He imagined her dressed more or less like the queen, in heavy floral-patterned fabrics that resembled sofa upholstery or curtains, and made her look, in his mind's eye, like human furniture. Sometimes, in an unkindly playful mood, he imagined a tiara on her head and, on her body, the kind of puffy-sleeved, farthingaled ballgown he had seen in Masterpiece Theatre programs about the Tudor royal family. As a result of these fantasies of ballroom wear and upholstery, he was unprepared for the woman he had come to see as she actually was: which was to say, a very sick woman indeed. She was in her bedroom on the upper floor of the duplex, and was unable to come down to greet him, or, as he soon learned, for any other reason. She had lost a lot of weight, and in her nearly emaciated condition needed help to clean herself or perform her bodily functions. The illness was a daily humiliation, but she bore it without complaint. Only her voice remained strong.

"There are several complications which can arise from CLL," she told Brother, wasting no time after a brief embrace. "The mildest are infections of the upper and lower respiratory tract. I have experienced both of these. Unfortunately, they have been the least of my problems. It can also happen that the immune system fouls up. The cells which are there to fight diseases become confused and attack the red blood cells, as if a lawyer for the defense were suddenly to switch sides and join the prosecution. This doesn't happen very often, but it is happening to me."

"I'm sorry," Brother said, using the words people used when they had no words.

"Oh, I haven't even reached the good parts yet," she said. "CLL increases the risk of developing other cancers, such as melanomas and lung cancer, and yes, you've guessed it, there are now shadows on both my lungs. That's the silver medal winner. The gold medal goes to the CLL itself. Very occasionally, it can switch into a much more aggressive cancer, called diffuse large B-cell lymphoma. In the cancer business we refer to this as Richter's Syndrome, probably because it's an event of earthquakelike magnitude. In the dying business we refer to it as forget-about-it. This is what I now have. Welcome to London."

She was attached to what the judge called "her Heath Robinson contraption." Brother had to dig deep to remember who Heath Robinson was. But the tangle of tubes and drips that were needed to provide what the body could no longer provide for itself made the judge's meaning clear enough. "Oh, right," he said. "It's a Rube Goldberg machine."

"We don't need the American version here, thank you," the judge said. Still not that friendly. "Heath Robinson will do very well."

It wasn't right to argue at the bedside of a dying woman, but

Brother couldn't resist going one more round. "Then there's Gyro Gearloose," he said. The judge's face reddened.

"Be nice, Jack," Sister said.

Nodding with great deliberation, the judge turned to go. "I'll leave you two to do whatever it is you need to do," he said. "I'll be downstairs." Daughter left the bedroom, too, and then Brother and Sister were alone.

"So now you see me," she said. "Looking skinny, no?"

She was receiving in-home hospice care. During the day many people passed through. Doctors, nurses, paid professional caregivers, therapists, friends. Later the family took over. Daughter spent most nights here nowadays. She and the judge shared the night shift. "They're both exhausted," Sister said. "That's why Jack's so irritable. He's a man who likes his sleep."

"I can understand that," Brother said. "I'm the same."

"It won't be long now," Sister said. She had briefed herself thoroughly on the signs of approaching death. "Different patterns of sleeping and waking," she said. "Check. I never know when I'll drop off, and I wake up at all odd hours these days. Diminished appetite and thirst, check, and I used to love fine dining and good wines. Fewer and smaller bowel movements, just as well, since I need help getting to the bathroom and cleaning myself, so the less of that, the better. The blood pressure situation isn't good, and often my heart races, and sometimes it's difficult to breathe properly. Is this getting to be too much for you? You're looking a little pale. No? Very well then, we proceed. There's also, I'm sorry to say, incontinence. I have a rubber bedsheet under here, it's like being a baby again, imagine how much I love *that*. And my body temperature fluctuates. Sometimes I'm sweating, at other times my skin feels cold to the touch. It's a long list. The body fights for life until the very end. We are all death's virgins, and we don't easily yield up our flower.

"And oh, yes, there's one more sign. More pain."

"Is that a morphine drip?" Brother asked, and she nodded.

"I have grown to love morphine," she said. "But I'm hoping you have something even better for me. Did you bring it?"

"I brought a supply," he said, "but I don't want to just leave it by your bedside, because the risks of overdosing yourself are considerable. One ten-microgram dose will buy you about an hour's relief, and it's only to be used when the morphine won't cover the pain, and there are strict limits on how much you can use in a day."

"What, and if I don't obey, it might kill me?" She laughed hard, and the laugh became a cough, and that took a while to subside, and there was expectoration, and there was blood mixed up in the mucus.

"I remind you of what you just said to me," Brother told her. "Don't yield up your flower too easily."

"Give the sprays to Jack," she said, very tired now. "Jack's in charge."

LONDON THAT NIGHT WAS full of noises, cries borne upon the dark air revealing distant anguish, shouts of anger, drunken glee like the cackling of broomstick witches. Brother lay awake in the small spare bedroom—Sister's office, Brother on the fold-out couch—listening to nearer noises, Daughter and the judge waking and resting, going to Sister's bedside to do what needed to be done. The air was clear but he had the feeling of being lost in a fog and not knowing his way home. Was his own work here already completed? Should he leave? What, if he did not leave, might he usefully do for her in these last days? The fog thickened around him, and he slept.

"Tell me a story," she said in the morning. "Tell me about playing hide-and-seek around and inside the Old Woman's Shoe in Kamala Nehru Park on Malabar Hill. Tell me about the Sunday morning jazz jam sessions in Colaba and how we listened to Chris Perry's saxophone and Lorna Cordeiro's voice and then we were taken to Churchgate and ate chicken Kiev at the Gaylord. Tell me how we went to Goa for Christmas and Saint Francis Xavier rose up out of his casket in the Basilica of Bom Jesus and gave us his blessing. Tell me about the Spice Mountains of Kerala and the elephants of Periyar. Tell me about when we built our first and last snowman in the Kashmiri mountain meadow of Baisaran. Tell me how we stood at the tip of Kanyakumari and the waves came from left and right and straight ahead and all crashed together at our feet and soaked us and we were happy. Tell me about going to visit the home of Satyajit Ray in Calcutta and his family showing us the notebooks in which he prepared his movies, pictures on the left side, words on the right. Tell me about the night I got an ax and smashed the Telefunken radiogram to pieces so that Pa and Ma could never dance together again. Tell about how we, you and I, went on a killing spree across India for years until they caught us in an old Cadillac and filled us full of holes which was exactly how we would have chosen to die, because it's important how one chooses to die. Tell me anything. Tell me everything. There isn't very much time."

He understood that she was asking him to describe her dreams, rather than anything that had really happened, and so instead he told her about his own imaginings, or, in other words, about his book. At first she interrupted him constantly, saying, "This isn't nearly as good as the story I want you to tell me, about when we ran away from the flat in Soona Mahal and robbed a bank," or, "I think you should stop and talk instead about the night we flew out of our bedroom window and floated in the air of Westfield Estate and looked in at all the grown-ups' bedroom windows and watched them making love, or snoring, or fighting, or all three, not in that order." But when he began to talk about the younger days of "Miss Salma R.," and the day when her grandfather grabbed her by the wrists and kissed her on the mouth, she became very attentive. Near the end of the story she stopped him.

"This isn't possible," she said.

"It's fiction," he replied, confused.

"We never told you about this. Don't tell him, we agreed, it will upset him."

"Who are 'we'?"

"Ma and me."

"What is 'this'?"

"Did someone else tell you? Otherwise how could you know? Did he tell you?"

"Who is 'he'?"

"You really don't know."

"I have no idea what you're talking about."

"You don't know and you made it up without knowing."

"I think you have to tell me a story now. Something happened between you and our grandfather? Is that even possible?"

"Not our grandfather."

"Then who."

"Why do you think Ma left Pa and moved into Soona Mahal. When I was five years old."

"Oh," he said, and felt the ground fall away beneath his feet.

"DID YOU AND MA think about telling me at any point?"

"Yes. No. Maybe when you were older, we thought."

"But you were much younger than me. I was the older brother."

"You were the beloved son. Firstborn and only. You had to be shielded."

"You didn't trust me even when you were five years old."

"I'm sorry. But this isn't about you."

"YOUR WHOLE PICTURE OF the world broke," he said, "and you felt like you had gone mad."

"Yes."

"And I didn't even notice."

"Boys. They notice nothing."

"And then five years later they made up and we had to go back and live with him. You had to go back and live with him."

"Imagine how I felt about that."

"What was Ma thinking? How could she do that?"

"Maybe she thought, we have punished him enough. Maybe she thought, I was older now and he had learned his lesson. Maybe she thought, a family should always try to be together, and children need a father. Maybe she was concerned that rumors would circulate and put us to shame. Maybe rumors *were* circulating and she already felt ashamed. Maybe she thought, *I love him.* Maybe she wanted to dance."

"And had he learned his lesson?"

"He never touched me again. He never looked me in the eye. He hardly ever spoke directly to me. He resented me. And he wouldn't pay for my college education abroad."

"So it wasn't just because you were a girl and therefore inferior."

"That also. But I didn't want his money anyway. I worked, I won my scholarships, I hauled myself out of there by my own bootstraps, I never went back, and I never asked either of them for anything ever again."

IT WAS BEWILDERING AT such an advanced age to understand that the narrative of your family which you had carried within you—within which, in a way, you had lived—was false, or, at the very least, that you had been ignorant of its most essential truth, which had been kept from you. Not to be told the whole truth, as Sister with her legal expertise would know perfectly well, was to be told a lie. That lie had been his truth. Maybe this was the human condition, to live inside fictions created by untruths or the withholding of actual truths. Maybe human life was truly fictional in this sense, that those who lived it didn't understand it wasn't real.

And then he had been writing about an imaginary girl in an imaginary family and he had given her something close to Sister's fate, without knowing how close to the truth he had come. Had he, as a child, intuited something and then, afraid of what he had guessed, buried the intuition so deep that he retained no memory of it? And could books, some books, gain access to those hidden chambers and use what they found there? He sat at Sister's bedside, deafened by the echo between the fiction which he had made and the fiction in which he had been made to live.

It wasn't about him, she had said, and that was right. But she was dying, and he would live, and after that it would be his burden to bear, because she would have set it down.

SHE SLEPT MUCH OF the day, went in and out of sleep. The judge was busy with paperwork at his desk. Daughter ran between her business and her mother. The hospice team members came and went. Brother found a wooden upright chair and placed it in a corner of Sister's bedroom, keeping out of the way. He had a notebook on his knee and made entries in it.

> In the Valley of Wonderment, said Quichotte, the Wayfarer, in the presence of the Beloved, is filled with awe and understands that he has never known or understood anything.
>
> There's an old Jewish joke, Evel Cent said to Miss Salma R in a deleted segment of their interview. In the joke an old Jew in Germany in the 1930s goes into a travel agency looking for a country to flee to. On the counter of the travel agency is a globe of the world and the old Jew points at one country after another, the United States, Canada, Mexico, wherever, and each time the travel agent shakes his head and says no, they aren't accepting any more refugees. Eventually the old Jew doesn't have any more countries he can point to, so he turns away from the globe and says to the travel agent, "So this one's all full up. So maybe you got another?" Our neighbor Earth project answers that question with a big Yes. Yes, that old Jew can be one of the NEXT people. And so can all of us.

Grillo Parlante, Sancho whispered in his bedroom at night. Mister Jiminy, are you there? There are things I need: a life of my own, away from Daddy Q. It's time pretty soon to leave him behind and strike out on my own. But before I do that there are two actual items I really do require.—Pop!—The cricket appeared on his bed, looking none too pleased. I think maybe this is my final visit, it said. La mia ultima visita. After this you're on your own. So, what is it? Don't ask for too much. Remember the fisherman's wife and the talking flounder.—What about them?—That magic fish, which was German, by the way, but I don't speak German, was granting them everything. When the fisherman found the flounder they had been living in a pisspot. In un vase da notte, because they were poor as piss. Then came gold, riches, the works. But finally the fisherman's wife went too far. She said she wanted to be the pope. So the fisherman said to the fish, my wife, she want to be pope. Il Papa. When he went home he discovered that all the fish's gifts had vanished and they were back to living in the pisspot. This is the German story. In Italian it is not so different.—I don't want to be pope, Sancho said. I want two things. I want a cellphone, and I want the girl's personal telephone number, not the office line.—Look in your pocket, said the talking cricket, and addio per sempre. Goodbye forever.

Are you Mrs. Smile, said the first man in a black suit wearing wraparound shades. Mrs. Happy Smile?—Yes, she said.—Yes, ma'am, I am Will Smith, special agent in charge for the Office of Inspector General of the U.S. Department of Health and Human Services. My colleague here is Tommy Lee Jones, a Federal Bureau of Investigation special agent. Is your husband at home?—No, he is away on business.—Ma'am, we will need to come in. This is a search warrant.—But my husband is an honorable man, a prominent citizen, much respected in the town, a public benefactor, a supporter of the arts.—Ma'am, we also hold a warrant for his arrest.

(N.B.: the agents' names are obviously placeholders. These are not those men in black.)

And one more:

If I use Sister's death in my book, is that exploitation or legitimate? And also: who is it that has to die? And he added a postscript: *How big of an asshole am I?*

She woke up and looked straight at him, looking alert and present, but her mind was confused. She made a number of remarks that seemed to be addressed to other people, as if she mistook him for someone else; and then, suddenly, shockingly, demanded: "I'm not dying, am I?"

He replied without pausing to think. "No," he said. "No, honey, it's okay, you're just resting."

For a long time afterwards he would ask himself if he had given the right answer. If, when his turn came, he asked that question of the people closest to him, would he prefer the comforting lie or the truth which would enable him to prepare for the grandeur of life's ending? He thought he would prefer to know. But everyone he asked said, "I would have done the same as you." Again, the human preference for fiction over fact.

Sister gave a small nod. "I'm glad you came," she said, recognizing him now. "This has been good." She smiled faintly and slipped back into sleep.

I have what I came for, he thought: absolution.

HE LAY IN BED listening to the sounds of the night city. The night music of Manhattan was played by the orchestra of emergency machines going about their business—ambulances, fire trucks, police cars racing to the scene of a crime—and sometimes a sanitation vehicle or a snowplow reversing under your window. In London he was hearing voices, and, being a little separated from objectivity by what he had heard and seen since he arrived, he found it hard to say if these were human beings or phantoms or the voices of angels or devils, in some way of another realm, ethereal voices such as the great mystics could hear, Joan of Arc, Saint John the Divine, Aurobindo, Osho, Buddha. The city seemed to be shrieking its pain into the night sky, asking for succor. Mortal men and women in agony and despair, without any road to happiness or peace. Monsters on the rooftops like giant succubi, drawing in long breaths and sucking out of human beings all their hope and joy.

And amid all this mayhem he had crossed the ocean looking only for the love of a woman he did not really know.

Now Quichotte and I are no longer two different beings, the one created and the one creating, he thought. Now I am a part of him, just as he is a part of me.

THE NEXT DAY SISTER announced that she would be hosting, at 4 P.M., a little afternoon tea for the family. The judge and Daughter said in unison, "Excellent idea," and offered to go out and get cakes and crumpets and madeleines and scones. Daughter said she would make the cucumber sandwiches. "We will do this," Sister additionally commanded, "downstairs, and there will be music. I'm tired of being in this bedroom. There is a very sick woman in here and she's becoming annoying."

Sister got up and dressed, with Daughter's help, in a fine skirt made from Indian brocade, a white blouse, and antique silver jewelry—not from her lecherous father's Zayvar Brother store but from the Zaveri Bazaar market district, which was also in the city she insisted on calling Bombay. In Zaveri Bazaar the price of the jewelry had nothing to do with its antiquity or with the fineness of the jeweler's work, but was based solely on the weight and the purity of the silver. She liked this matter-of-fact approach, she said. It cast aside the vanity of artists and the sentimentality of age in favor of the practicality of what had true value: weight and purity. Daughter had brought her a magnolia flower and she put that in her hair. The judge had dressed up, too, in his finest evening gown, a gorgeous silver sheath with lacy frills spreading out below the knee. "By Mr. Cecil Beaton," he said to Brother. "*Sir* Cecil Beaton. Since you ask."

All of them, Daughter, Brother, and the judge, were needed to help her downstairs, Daughter going down backwards in front of her, arms extended, to prevent her mother from falling, and the two men beside her, sideways, helping her to go slowly down, step by anxious step. The members of the hospice staff stood by, ready to help, but understanding, on account of their great reserves of human sympathy, that this was a family matter. (During the family tea party the caregivers retreated upstairs to Sister's bedroom. Later, when tea was over, Sister preferred to allow one of them, a strong young orderly, to carry her back up to her room.)

"Shall I be mother?" she asked, as if there were any doubt about the matter, and then tea was poured and passed and cakes and cucumber sandwiches consumed, and the flavor of everything was greatly heightened by the mingled pain and pleasure of knowing that something excellent was being done for the last time.

"The thing I'm very pleased about," she said, "is that just before all this business in my body started up, I took out a very substantial life insurance policy, and now the buggers are going to have to pay up a fortune, which will look after my girl very well." Then she laughed, high and long. She could not cheat death, but she had put one over on the insurance company, and that felt almost as good to her, she said.

She hadn't mentioned the judge in her declaration, but he laughed as long and hard as she did. That was strange, Brother thought. Why wasn't she happy to be providing for his old age too? And why didn't he care?

"I think," she declared when tea had been drunk and cakes and sandwiches consumed, "that I may sing a little, as I once did." But then a great pain struck her and she fell back in her seat with a gasp.

"Jack," she cried, and he came to her with the painkilling spray and she opened her mouth and raised up her tongue and there was relief. After that she allowed herself to be borne back upstairs to bed.

Family life, Brother thought, one moment of it after a lifetime without it, and that will have to suffice.

FENTANYL WAS ONE HUNDRED times more powerful than morphine. The lethal dose was therefore one hundred times smaller: two milligrams as opposed to two hundred. Sublingual fentanyl spray was even more powerful and worked much faster. Medicinal doses of the spray were measured and delivered in micrograms, so to reach the fatal level it was necessary to spray beneath the tongue repeatedly and rapidly. The product packaging carried prominent and strongly worded warnings about overdosing.

They had made their plans methodically, Sister and the judge, because they were both diligent people. They knew the required dosages, had calculated the effects of their different body weights (she was down to just under one hundred pounds at this point, while he was closer to two hundred), and had destroyed all identifying marks on the two sprays, scratching away the batch numbers and the address of the manufactory, so that Brother could not later be charged with having supplied the fatal drug off-prescription, and they had left careful instructions—in a letter propped up on a cushion at the foot of Sister's bed—for the disposal of their assets and belongings. They sent their great and apologetic love to Daughter and asked her not to grieve but to rejoice that they left the world as they had lived in it: together. In Sister's hand at the bottom of the letter (the rest of which had been written out by the judge, though clearly conceived jointly by them both) were a couple of lines from

Marvell's "On a Drop of Dew." *How loose and easy hence to go, / How girt and ready to ascend*. She was ready and had chosen when and how to give up her flower. They had both chosen, and they had kept their appointment.

Brother came awake fast in the dead of night, his thoughts filled with sudden, sad understanding. The disembodied voices of the darkness had fallen silent, as if they, too, understood. He got out of bed in his pajamas and went rapidly toward Sister's room. He stood for a moment listening. Daughter was asleep on the couch downstairs. But the silence behind the closed door of Sister's bedroom was not the silence of sleep. He opened the door and went in. The judge was in a chair by her bedside, still dressed in the silver gown, his chin upon his chest. Sister had been sitting up in bed but had now slumped sideways so that her head rested upon her husband's shoulder. On her nightstand lay two chess pieces, the white king and the black queen, both knocked over, resigning their games. They had changed the rules, Jack and Jack. The queen had resigned as well as the king. There was no victor, or else they had both won.

Now Daughter was there, too, opening and reading the letter. When she looked up from the pages Brother saw in her eyes the rage she had inherited from her mother.

"Well, thanks for coming, Uncle, and you should go now," she said savagely. "Don't worry. I won't point a finger. Nobody will come looking for you."

He moved toward her; she recoiled.

"I brought you here," she said. "Pawn to King Four. It's my fault. Big mistake."

She turned away from him to look at her parents. Her fists were clenched.

"The story you told us about your flight from New York," she said. "About the death angel. I get it now. It's you, the hooded skull. You came to collect their lives and you held their deaths in your fist. It's you, the angel of death."

*O*n the plane home, half asleep, under the influence of vodka and grief, Brother saw his reflection speaking to him from the window. "The world no longer has any purpose except that you should finish your book. When you have done so, the stars will begin to go out."

CHAPTER EIGHTEEN

Quichotte reaches his Goal,
whereupon Shame & Scandal
engulf the Beloved

QUICHOTTE, ENTERING CENTRAL PARK THROUGH
Inventor's Gate, touched the brim of his hat in a gesture of respect
toward the statue of Samuel Morse, and asked himself: What en-
coded dit-dit-dah message, were he offered the opportunity, might
he now choose to send? Who would he now say he was, what should
he declare that he desired, and what secret did he wish either the
whole world or a single precious individual to know? And at once
he answered himself: He was a lover, he desired only the love of his
Beloved, and would tap out that love on Mr. Morse's wire telegraph
or shout it from the rooftops or whisper it in his Beloved's ear, his
mighty love the fulfillment of which was the onliest remaining purpose and most proper function of the good Earth itself. He thought,
too, of another, more contemporary inventor, the scientist-
entrepreneur Evel Cent, and his NEXT machines. It might be that
these magic portals of Mr. Cent's, the *Mayflower* etc., had been
brought into being to make possible a perfect ending, in which

Quichotte and Salma escaped this dying vale of tears to live in time-less bliss in—what had the Trampoline called them?—the Elysian Fields. Things were coming together nicely.

He felt himself flowing back into himself. He had spent too long in the valley of apology and healing, the dale of restored harmony; too long in the realm of the necessary, which had had to be endured to make possible what was needed. The Trampoline had taken him on a journey back into the past and wrapped him in a self that no longer had any meaning for him, and that past was, anyway, only her version of events and of him as well, a version within which he still sometimes suspected that the truth had somehow become in-verted somewhere along the way. There were moments when he was possessed by the idea that in fact she had been the one who had done *him* wrong, who had accused him of things, who had been unloving, and if only he could remember, if only he could get past the fog in his mind that stopped him remembering, he would be able to see, to know, to say, to face her with the facts, the knowl-edge that she had the whole story ass backwards (if he could, in the privacy of his own thoughts, permit himself such a vulgarity)—so that the person who needed to be apologized to had ended up doing the apologizing, abasing himself both formally and unreservedly. But he couldn't remember. There was only confusion, and the fog. And finally it was okay, he didn't mind, she was probably right, and anyway peace had had to be made, a surrender had had to take place, an offering up of a vanquished sword, a kneeling, even on such un-fair terms. She had made him put on, after so many years, a skin that no longer fitted him, and he had had to wear it like a hair shirt, doing penance for what he could not remember having done. No matter. Now that old skin had been shed and he, Quichotte, had reemerged: the gallant knight, the mystical *amant,* the Galahad quester, the seeker for the grail of love, gathering his strength as he prepared to make, at long last, his tryst.

———

AT THE MOMENT OF reconciliation there had been a separation. He had understood that a knight pursuing his quest could not accept even one soft night in a palatial residence, even as his own sister's lodger. Such a knight must remain hard, ascetic, pure. Softness was weakness. "Does that work?" the Trampoline had asked him, generously offering him comfort and a respite from his long wanderings. And to his surprise his answer was "No." The Blue Yorker, for all its faults, was a better place for him. That was the kind of story he was in, and not the loft-in-Tribeca kind. He found himself anxious to return to his room and watch some comforting TV.

"Thank you," he told her, "but we will stay where we are, my child, my car, and I."

Sancho reacted with shock. "You cannot be serious."

"I am in deadly earnest, I assure you," he replied sternly. "This has been an important encounter, and I am grateful for it, but we must follow our own path."

A mutiny followed. "Maybe we don't have to stay together," Sancho said. "Maybe it's time I had a life of my own. 'Every man has his own Grail,' isn't that right? You're the one who taught me that. You have your beloved, I have mine."

"In the first place," Quichotte said, "you are not ready to be a man, and in the second place, that girl, Beautiful from Beautiful, is just a pipe dream."

"And then what, tell me," Sancho replied rudely, "is Miss Salma R?"

Here the Trampoline intervened. "It's been a big evening," she said. "Everyone's tired. Let's just put everything on hold. If the young man wants to stay, let him stay. If you," she said, turning to her brother, "insist on returning to your fleapit, then so be it. Let's all take a moment. Tomorrow is another day."

As he drove back uptown to the unpleasant little hotel, Quichotte felt the emptiness of the seat beside him, felt it like an acute pain, like the severing of a limb. Was this the last and hardest thing required of him, he wondered: the sacrifice of a son? Agamemnon sacrificed his daughter to put the wind in his sails. But Agamemnon ended up dead in his bathtub, murdered by Iphigenia's vengeful mother, Clytemnestra, his queen. Was the empty passenger seat his death sentence too?

But Sancho had no mother. The ancient stories did not always have modern echoes. And yes: every man had his own Grail.

THREE DAYS PASSED AND there was no further word from Dr. Smile, and none from Sancho or the Trampoline either. Quichotte sat alone in his room, bathed in the light of the screen. A man told him that in two years everyone would believe that the Earth was flat. A woman told him that vaccinations were part of a global conspiracy against children. A man told him that condensation trails left by high-flying jet aircraft were composed of chemical and biological agents that enabled the psychological manipulation of human beings, or sterilized women to control the population explosion, or were proof of the use of biological and/or chemical weapons upon an unsuspecting world. A woman told him that someone known as Q had unearned proof of a conspiracy against the government. A man told him about heavy traffic on the FDR.

He allowed it all to wash over him, the stuff of electronic life, the manifold whatness of the airwaves. He neither accepted nor rejected. He was not a judge. Even the coincidence of the Q of his pseudonym with the handle of the architect of QAnon was only of passing interest. He was passing the time in his preferred way and the time was passing. That was enough. He wasn't interested in becoming analytical about reality. Reality was this room, this play of shadow and light, this waiting for the call.

On the fourth day the call came.

THERE WAS A TREE he was looking for, an old red oak. It stood a little distance away from the statue of Hans Christian Andersen contemplating (or being contemplated by) a duckling which was present for familiar literary reasons that need not detain us. Quichotte preferred—both preferred and was frightened by—the story about the shadow. Shadows were treacherous and cryptic counter-selves, and needed to be watched. (The shadow of Peter Pan had escaped at one point also, and had had to be caught and re-attached to Peter's feet by Wendy's deft and careful needle.) He had kept half an eye on his own shadow throughout his quest, but so far, to his relief, it had showed no signs of acquiring an independent spirit, a malicious nature, or competitive romantic inclinations. In the golden shade of the autumnal tree, his shadow was banished, and so, with a flutter, a kaleidoscope of butterflies in his stomach, he waited; and while he waited, thought—of course—about television.

Just as King Arthur had needed his Merlin, so also Quichotte had come to the park today to meet the wizard who would work the magic he needed. He hadn't enjoyed the TV series about the youth of Merlin a few years ago. He was looking for an adult sorcerer today, not a callow boy who needed to grow up. Everyone wanted youth now. How tedious that was! Young Indiana Jones. Young Han Solo. Young Sherlock Holmes. Young Dumbledore. Any minute now there would be a mini-series about the young Methuselah. As an older person he wanted the trend to be reversed. How about Old *Sex in the City*? Old *Friends*? Old *Girls*? Old *Gossip Girl*? Old *Housewives*? Old *Bachelors*? How about old models on the runway? (Victoria, after all, had lived to be a very old queen, and no doubt still, in her old age, had her secrets.) Sure, *The Golden Girls,* okay. But that was just one show. How about Old *Simpsons*? How about an Old Fonz in *Happy Days Got Older*? He'd watch those shows. And

America had an aging population, did it not? So, then. Time to stop pandering to empty-headed youth. Start pandering to the addle-brained elderly instead.

The Wizard in the old show from the eighties had been a little person. The conjurer Quichotte was waiting for was scarcely a foot taller than its star, David Rappaport, had been. He kept his eyes peeled for this person, a small man of energetic disposition and a certain ethical vacuity: his cousin, the bearer of his destiny, Dr. R. K. Smile.

Why was Quichotte so certain of what the day would bring? The answer was there for anyone to see who had eyes to see. It was the increasing number of spots dancing in his field of vision. Every-one had started seeing these spots now, but because of the infuriat-ing ability of human beings to fail to understand what was right in front of their faces, explanations were being offered which were much more complicated than the truth.

The eye condition which caused blind spots on the retina had long been known about, and had indeed for some time been the leading cause of blindness in Americans, but it was now—or so all the relevant authorities and respected journals proclaimed—attaining the status of a global epidemic, or even, to use the term beloved of writers, a plague. Plagues were mysterious in origin, ran-dom in their victims, and uncontrollable. They caused panic in the streets and required, often, the digging of mass graves in big cities. The Black Spot, as the new eye plague came to be known, did not appear to be fatal, although its consequences included a rising num-ber of motor car accidents, which sometimes did lead to fatalities. There were also railway accidents in many countries, at a rate higher than the norm, most of them minor, but a few that were truly cata-strophic. In addition, mistakes made by airline pilots during landing were reported from airports around the world. In countries where the expensive medication that could treat the plague was available, supplies ran short, even though the treatment—regular injections through the white of the eye to clear the retina—was one that many people were frightened to try, even though they knew that blindness was worse than a needle in the eye. The cause of the illness was the deterioration of the macula, the central part of the retina, which controlled human beings' ability to read, drive, recognize faces and colors, and see objects in fine detail. Often there was also a leakage of blood onto the surface of the retina. However, eye specialists in many countries who were now fully occupied by the treatment of the surge of cases reported strange results. Tests on their patients showed no noticeable deterioration in the macula, nor had blood leaked onto the retinal surface. In fact, the patients' eyes could in the majority of cases be said to be one hundred percent healthy. Yet the apparent effects of retinal decay were present in their vision. It was a medical mystery to which nobody could offer a plausible solution.

This did not mean there were no theories on offer. The scientist-entrepreneur Evel Cent, chairman and CEO of the new-tech giant CentCorp, was insistently, even stridently, presenting his eschatological solution to anyone who would listen, but this was not, at first, thought to be plausible. The deterioration, he declared with great emphasis on all available media, was not taking place in the eyesight of the human race, but in the world. Not in the seeing thing but in the thing seen. He quoted, very often, the old sixties graffito, *Do not adjust your mind, there is a fault in reality.* There really was a fault in reality, and it was getting worse, and everyone needed to wake up and understand what was happening. The cosmos was crumbling. There was still time, with the support of world governments and the United Nations, to mass-produce the NEXT machines in sufficient quantity to rescue a high proportion of the human race by transporting them to a parallel Earth. He himself was prepared to invest his entire personal fortune and all of his time to the effort.

Few people were convinced at first. Even his substantial fan base of admirers, some of whom were willing to go along with his scare tactics, mistrusted the NEXT machines, which, if built in the numbers Cent proposed, seemed more likely to cause a mass extermination of humanity than to transport them to a new Garden of Eden. His experiment with the Labrador Schrödinger persuaded few people, and many more considered it to be a put-up job. Anyone could say a dog had traveled to a "neighbor Earth" and returned in good health. The dog itself was unable to bear witness, and no visual evidence had been made public. So, for the moment, Evel Cent was a voice crying in the wilderness, heard by many, believed by almost none.

Quichotte believed him. Ever since he began his quest he had known that preparing himself for love, making himself worthy of the Beloved, also necessitated readying oneself for an ending, because after perfection was attained there was only oblivion to look forward to. These manifestations, erroneously characterized as symptoms of a medical emergency, were early warnings that both culminations were at hand.

There was the tree, and there—poof!—was Dr. R. K. Smile. Hat, coat, small leather attaché case, like an old-world medico doing his rounds. And had that been a puff of smoke? No, that was just his imagination, Quichotte reproved himself. It was improbable that his illustrious cousin traveled the country with the Wicked Witch of the West's personal smoke effects in his baggage. But, on the other hand, in the Age of Anything-Can-Happen, as he well knew, anything could happen. Maybe puffs of smoke were available now. Maybe you could buy them at Walmart, like guns.

"Best of cousins!" Quichotte cried. "I'm happy to see you. I hope your mood is fine?"

"Let's walk a little," said Dr. Smile. His mood, Quichotte noted with regret, appeared to be very far from fine. One might say that it was foul.

"There has been an event today in Atlanta," Dr. Smile said as they walked in the general direction of the boathouse. "A shocking event, may I say. An offensive event concerning my good wife."

"Mrs. Happy?" Quichotte cried. "That is indeed unexpected and woeful news! I hope she has not met with a misfortune?"

"'Misfortune' is too mild a word," Dr. Smile said grimly. "I will tell you what has happened. I have a need to tell someone, and I believe I can talk to you—because, to put it bluntly, you are nobody, you know nobody, so you can tell nobody who is anybody, and, plus, you are borderline simple as well."

This remark—in its tone very unlike the kind manner with which his cousin had always spoken to him—struck Quichotte as harsh, and in part incorrect. "But everybody is somebody, aren't they?" he replied mildly. "Although the language can be confusing. When we say that 'nobody is here,' we mean in fact that 'somebody' is 'not here.' If I am here, I can't be nobody. Look," he said, pointing. "There, there, there. Somebody, somebody, somebody." He pointed at himself. "Somebody," he concluded with some pride.

Dr. Smile heard him out with growing impatience. "I repeat," he said, "borderline simple."

The discourtesy in his cousin's speech saddened Quichotte. He tried to deflect it. "*Simple* is almost *smile* rearranged, isn't it," he offered. "If you or I or both only had the initial *P,* then we would both be *simple* rearranged."

This gentle pleasantry failed to improve Dr. Smile's mood. "I don't have time for small talk," he barked. (Quichotte was on the verge of replying, "Then this you have in common with the famous Mr. Evel Cent!"—but he held his tongue.) "I have something to say today about the injustice of the world toward a man trying to do his best. And also toward his lady wife, an innocent bystander, Happy by name, happy by nature."

Quichotte composed his features, frowning slightly to indicate deep attention.

"She was with her lady friends," Dr. Smile said. "A circle of like-minded philanthropical ladies, meeting as was their habit at Dr. Bombay's Underwater Tea Party in Candler Park."

"Underwater?" Quichotte was lost now.

"This is a name only," Dr. Smile said sharply. "This is a tea place, not a submarine."

Quichotte inclined his head.

"Then they came in, how do they say in America? Like gang-busters."

"The like-minded philanthropical ladies?"

"The forces of the law," Dr. Smile said. "Bulletproof vests, dogs, assault weapons, as if it was a terrorist gang, not a social occasion. And why?"

"Why?"

"Because of me," Dr. Smile said. "Because I am accused of crimes, and in my absence they went for her. Bastards."

"The law enforcement officers?"

"The people who betrayed me. Treacherous bastards. Who else could have informed the police? Only the people I made rich. Yes, I made myself more rich, but I was the one who made it happen. Little doctors here, there, turning into rich fellows. Then they turn me in. Bastards. How do they think you become a billionaire in America? Morgan, Carnegie, Vanderbilt, Mellon, Rockefeller? At Underwater Tea Parties? I have done what had to be done. It's the American way, correct? But still my own children, my own creations, the ones I made who they are today, they want to save their asses and tear me down.

"Listen," he went on, "I don't feel this thing called community feeling. This 'our people' *bakwas*. We are supposed to feel it, isn't it? Loyalty to our community above all. The brown before the white, the many before the one. Bullshit. Our people come closer to us so they get to knife us first, in the front, in the back, in the balls, wherever. I'm speaking frankly today. I'm opening my heart to you in my time of anger. 'Our people' is nonsense. Wife feels the feeling, I don't. Even if in some ways our people can teach us things. Our culture. It has lessons I have learned.

"Corruption, they accuse me of today. Corruption! Me! Myself! Dr. R. K. Smile! Everyone knows that what I have done is not corruption. It is our culture from the old country. You are at a railway station—let's say Sawai Madhopur—and the lines at the ticket windows are long. You get to the front and the clerk says, wrong line, go and queue over there. This is frustrating, am I right? It would frustrate anybody. Then here is a little boy, maybe ten years old, tugging at your sleeve. *Ssss,* he says. *Ssss.* You want ticket? I have an uncle. And of course he wants a little something for his trouble. You can be smart and give it to him or you can be stupid and refuse. If you are smart you find he really does have an uncle, and he can take you to this uncle in the office behind the ticket window, and in two shakes your ticket is in your hand. If you are stupid you move from line to line for hours. We are like this only. You are in a yard, let us say in Thiruvananthapuram, and here is an antiques dealer offering you fine objects of value, and you want to bring them home, maybe to Atlanta, Georgia, to share with your loving family. But there are laws, isn't it, that say it can't be done. So you can be stupid and say, the law is the law, or you can be smart and say, the law is an ass. If you say ass the antique dealer will take you to the person who has the government stamp, the person who needs to be convinced, the amount it takes to convince him being specified in advance, and in five minutes your treasure is on the way to Buckhead. The law is useful, in fact. It tells you who is the correct person you need to convince. Otherwise you can waste money convincing people who don't have the stamp. Waste not, want not. We are like this only. We know what is the oil that greases the wheels."

He paused for breath, panting a little. Quichotte waited patiently.

"You also," Dr. Smile said, stabbing at Quichotte a sudden vehement finger, "you also are a person who is uninterested in your people. You also, going here, going there, going nowhere, you have broken loose of your moorings, isn't it. Like a boat without a rudder. Like a car without a driver. Where you came from, who you came from, do you think about it? I don't think so that you do."

"You are angry," Quichotte answered gently. "But I am not the reason for your anger."

"What do you like?" Dr. Smile roared on. "Our food? Our

clothes? Our religions? Our ways? I don't think you are concerned with these things. Am I wrong or right?"

"I own thirteen objects," Quichotte said, "which open the doors of memory. Some family photographs, a 'Cheeta Brand' *maachis,* a stone head from Gandhara, a hoopoe bird."

"You are a fool," Dr. Smile said, and then, like a burst balloon, subsided. "But you are a fool who is going to have a very lucky day. My luck today, however, is bad. However, I will not go to ground like a rat in a hole. I will not vanish like a thief in the night. I will surrender myself, I will pay whatever bail they want, I will wear the damn ankle bracelet, and I will fight. This is America. I will fight and I will win." His words had a hollow ring, expressing a bravado he did not feel.

"That is an admirable course to follow," said Quichotte.

"What nobody grasps," Dr. Smile said with the weariness of a man who carries a burden other people are unwilling to lift, "is that business gets harder all the time. I do things responsibly, through medical personnel, et cetera. But there are gangs now. They threaten my people. You are lucky you quit when you did."

I didn't quit, Quichotte remembered. I was dismissed. This also he did not say.

"Crazy names," Dr. Smile said, his voice receding into a melancholy growl. "Nine Trey Gangsta Bloods. It has no meaning. But they are selling everything out on the street. Heroin, fentanyl, furanyl fentanyl, MDMA, dibutylone. They are irresponsible and unscrupulous. To a medical person, they are anathema. Also they deplete my sales."

"Can I ask," Quichotte finally ventured, "why it is that you wished to see me? Why is it a lucky day for me?"

"You are like everyone else," Dr. Smile said sadly. "Me, me, me." Nodding with the bruised resignation of a man who only, selflessly, works for the benefit of others, and who goes unappreciated and unloved by the selfish world, he indicated the attaché case he was carrying. "This you will keep safely," he said. "You have the deposit box with the key, yes?"

"Yes."

"Keep it there only. Inside you will see little white envelopes. Each envelope is one delivery of InSmile™ spray, to be made once a month, directly into the lady's personal hand. To this procedure she has agreed."

"The lady is very unwell?"

"The lady is very important."

"But she is a person with a medical requirement?"

"She is a person we wish to please."

"And this is what you want me to do," Quichotte said. His tone of deflation mirrored his cousin's. "To please a person who is not sick."

"Ask me her name," Dr. Smile said. "Then let's see what you think."

When the name was spoken a great radiance opened up in the heavens and flowed down over Quichotte in a cascade of joy. His labors had not been in vain. He had proved himself worthy and now the Grail had manifested herself. He had abandoned reason for the sake of love, accepted the uselessness of worldly knowledge, surrendered his desires and attachments to the world, understood that everything was connected, moved beyond harmony, and now in the Valley of Wonderment the name of the Beloved hung in the air before him as if on a giant flat-screen television. It occurred to him that he loved the man who had caused this miracle to occur.

"I love you," he said to Dr. Smile.

The doctor, pondering his troubles, was startled and horrified by this remark. "What are you talking?" he demanded.

"I love you," Quichotte repeated. The radiance was still cascading and now perhaps a celestial choir had begun to sing.

"Men do not talk so to men," Dr. Smile admonished fiercely. "Yes, of course, there are family I-love-yous, and even between cousins, okay, but the tone of voice is different. It is casual, like air kisses near the cheek. What is this I *luuuve* you? Less emotion, please. We are not husband and wife."

But Quichotte in his reverie wanted to say, *Can't you see the radiance descending? Can't you hear the angels as they sing? The miracle is upon us, and you are the man who has made it so, and how can I react except with openhearted love?*

"Tell her," Dr. Smile said, changing the subject, "that we are making product improvements all the time. We will overcome our present obstacles and proceed. Soon we will have a small tablet, only three millimeters diameter, thirty micrograms. It will be ten times more powerful than the InSmile™ spray. Tell her, if she wishes, this also can be available."

Then Quichotte's head swirled, the birds of the park spiraled over him in a phantom dance, and he entered an *agon,* a great interior struggle, in which his whole being was at war, a battle in which he was at once protagonist and antagonist. The first Quichotte exulted, *My love is within my grasp,* while the second objected, *I am being asked to do a dishonorable thing, and are we not honorable men?* The first cried, *The miracle is upon me, and I cannot refuse it,* and the second replied, *She is not sick and this is medicine for the terminally ill.* Beside that American oak which was by no means tropical and that Indian cousin who was by no means ethical, a nonsensical verse flowed unbidden through his broken mind.

> *Under the bam*
> *Under the boo*
> *Under the bamboo tree*

He understood, to the best of his capacity, his true nature. He was impure. He was the bam and he was also the boo; the flawed as well as the fine, the honorable and the dishonorable too. He was not Sir Galahad, nor was he meant to be. As the realization dawned it was as if the entire structure of his quest fell away, shriveled and dissolved in that light like a night creature that hates the sun. It had been a delusion, the whole business of needing to be worthy, of needing to make himself worthy of her. All that mattered was this opportunity, knocking. This attaché case was all that mattered. Which made him not a knight but an opportunist, and an opportunist was an altogether lower form of life. Altogether unworthy.

Then a heretical thought occurred. Was it possible, that she, the Beloved, was unworthy too? What he was being asked to do for her was wrong, yet she was asking it. A goddess or a queen did not ask her knight or her hero, who wore her favor on his helmet, to perform immoral tasks. So if she was asking this, then she was no more a queen or a goddess than he was a hero or a knight. Her request and his fulfillment of that request would topple them both off their pedestals and drag them down into the dirt together. And paradoxically, he thought, if she was no longer a queen-goddess, then she was no longer impossible for him, no longer out of his reach. Her fall from purity made her mortal, human, and therefore attainable.

Dr. Smile was saying something. Through the torrent of his thoughts Quichotte heard his cousin say, "Also in every envelope there is Narcan, in case of need. Both in nasal spray form and in auto-injectors."

Narcan was naloxone, the medication of choice in case of opioid overdose. Auto-injection brought the fastest results: this worked in about two minutes and the effect lasted for thirty to sixty minutes, so multiple doses might be required in the case of a major crisis. Narcan, Quichotte thought, was also the moral salve which made it all right for him to do what he was being asked to do, the shield that would protect the Beloved from self-inflicted harm.

"Narcan, good," he said. But his mind was still mostly elsewhere, and Dr. Smile grew irritated.

"What's the matter with you?" he snapped. "Maybe you're not the person for this very simple job. Maybe you've just become too loony and old dufferish. Maybe you're not to be trusted and I need to find someone else."

You know those films of an explosion in reverse? How *ffwwwappp* everything comes flying back together and the world is in one piece again? The effect of these words on Quichotte was like that. He was alert and present and he would not let this opportunity slip. He would do what the Beloved asked of him and *que sera sera*. He straightened up and spoke clearly and firmly. "I'm your man," he said. Destiny was pushing him over a moral boundary, and he suffered himself to be pushed. Lancelot, too, had forsaken morals for the love of Guinevere. He was not Galahad, but he might yet be Lancelot, and spirit the Beloved away—as he had once promised himself—to Joyous Gard.

"Very well," said Dr. Smile, in a hurry now. He took a paper out of his coat pocket and passed it to Quichotte. "There is everything you need. Contact information, how when where, and amount to be collected. You have the locker. You have the key. Stash the cash. I'll be in touch." Dr. Smile's cellphone buzzed. "My good wife," he said. Now he was the distracted one. "I have to run. Yes, literally, I must run. A man like me. It is disgraceful. I have lawyers. This will be fought. I will return. Like Zorro, isn't it? I shall return."

Poof! He was gone, and Quichotte was alone in the ordinariness of the park, with the magic attaché case in his hand, tiny, crumbly black spots dancing in his field of vision, and a head full of unanswered questions. *What would my son think of what I have agreed to do— my newly estranged son?* he asked himself, and answered himself, *Sancho may react with the puritan condemnations beloved of the very young.*

He made his way back toward the gate, but paused by the Andersen statue and gazed at the immortal storyteller like a second duckling. As the end of a journey approached, it was natural for the traveler's mind to circle back to the beginning. "An old fool gazed upon the image of a high princess," Quichotte said to Hans Christian Andersen, "and dreamed that one day he would sit beside her on her throne."

"A good enough start," said Hans Christian Andersen, "but how do you go forward?"

"How do I go forward?"

"Do you have, for example, a potion that will make her love you?"

Quichotte considered the contents of the attaché case. "I have a thing like a potion that I think she loves, but will it make her love me?"

"That's up to you," Hans Andersen answered. "What do you know that can help you?"

"I know that I love her," Quichotte replied. "I know that I am in the sixth valley, and I know that the purpose of all existence is to unite us."

"But what are you prepared to do?" the great author asked.

"Anything and everything," Quichotte said.

"And if she protests your advances, what then?"

"I will advance until she does not protest."

"And if she resists, what then?"

"I will overcome her resistance."

"And if she doesn't love you, what then?"

"But she must. We must love each other absolutely and completely and then the world, having achieved its purpose, must end."

"And if the world doesn't end, what then?"

"It must end."

"The question is, do you mean to do right by her? Do you mean well by her? Or is your desire so great that it overwhelms your sense of the right and the good?"

"I am no longer sure that I am good," Quichotte confessed. "I have things in my bag that are bad, potions that she wants, that may help her to love me, but that are also dangerous. I have to collect her money, go to my locker, use my key, and stash the cash. I don't know if any of this is good. I may be doing her harm."

"What's in the locker? You talk about the locker and the key to the locker. When you open the locker, what do you see?"

"There's a gun in the locker."

"A gun? In the locker?"

"It's locked there. I have the key."

"And why is it there?"

"In case of need."

"Will you take the gun out of the locker?"

"I need the locker to stash the cash. It's not such a big locker."

"Will you take the gun?"

"To make room. To stash the cash."

"So then you'll have a gun, and if she doesn't love you, what then? And if the world doesn't end, what then?"

"What then? What then? You tell me how it ends."

"It's not my story, and a bronze statue tells no tales. But ask yourself this: are you—you, Quichotte, after your long journey!— are you the angel of love?"

"I want to be," Quichotte said. "I want to be the angel of our love."

"Or," Hans Christian Andersen said, "with the dangerous po- tions in your case, and the gun in your locker, the gun you'll take out to stash the cash . . ."

"Yes?"

"Are you perhaps the angel of death?"

"I don't know."

"Is the gun loaded?"

"Yes," said Quichotte, "it's a loaded gun."

"So I ask the question again."

"Which question?"

"Are you the angel of death?"

THAT NIGHT AS HE SAT in his motel room filled with self-doubt with her phone number in his hand, she was on TV, on the attack, her introductory monologue given the title "Errorism in America," allowing her and her comedy-writing team to take on all the ene- mies of contemporary reality: the anti-vaxxers, the climate loonies, the news paranoiacs, the UFOlogists, the president, the religious nuts, the birthers, the flat-earthers, the censorious young, the greedy old, the trolls, the dharma bums, the Holocaust deniers, the weed-banners, the dog lovers (she hated the domestication of animals), and Fox. "The truth," she declaimed. "It's still out there, still breathing, buried under the rubble of the bullshit bombs. We're the emergency rescue squad. We're going to get it out alive. We have to, or the errorists win."

Am I an errorist too? he asked himself. Is everything I believe a lie?

The program must have been recorded earlier that day, "as live." She was probably home by now, relaxing. He called the phone number. When her voice answered he panicked and said, "Wrong number," and hung up.

Of all the movies Quichotte had seen on TV dealing with the phenomenon of "first contact," the first encounter between human beings and an alien species, two had stayed with him: the famous film whose climax took place at the Devils Tower, Wyoming—by a happy coincidence, the place where his son Sancho had been born!—and a much less well known TV show, a black-and-white piece from the 1960s, "Pictures Don't Lie," an episode of the series *Out of this World,* which he had caught by chance on an old reruns network, maybe Sci-Fi before it became Syfy. An alien spaceship contacts Earth. They look like us, we can translate their language, and they are coming in to land. But they can't understand why our atmosphere is so thick, *thick as glue,* and when they say they have landed, they are invisible, and then afraid, because, they say, they are drowning. But on the landing field which fits their coordinates, there's no lake or river, just a bit of a drizzle. Too late, one of the Earth team understands the problem. The aliens are so incredibly small it would take a magnifying glass to see them. They are drowning in a puddle of rain.

That's me, Quichotte thought. I'm about to make first contact, but I'm so insignificant compared to her great significance, such a common little ant beside her giant majesty, that I might drown in one of her tears.

He called again. Voicemail. "Darling, I'm having the voltage today, I'm drinking that special juice of mine, so I don't remember who you are. Leave your full name and tell me how we know each other. Mwah." He understood that the show must be on hiatus, and the "Errorism" episode he had seen was a tape from a while ago. He didn't leave a message. The next day he called again and she answered.

"Who?" she said when he began with the code word on Dr. Smile's sheet of paper. "Here, talk to Anderson."

First contact, Quichotte thought. One single word from her lips had entered his ear. He was filled with an immense happiness that washed away all his doubts and qualms.

"Where do you want to meet?" Anderson Thayer asked, and the question was like cold water thrown in Quichotte's face.

"No, no, no," he replied.

"What do you mean, no, no, no?"

Quichotte strengthened his resolve. "I mean, sir, and meaning no disrespect, but my instructions were clear. I must deliver into the lady's hands. My hands to her hands. My instructions are clear."

"That's not going to happen," Anderson Thayer said.

Quichotte made the great gamble of his life, putting everything he had, so to speak, on a single number. "Then, I regret," he told Anderson Thayer.

There was muffled conversation at the other end of the line. Then a different voice; her voice, which so far had poured the single syllable *who* into his adoring ear.

"Don't be cross with poor Anderson, darling," she said. "I'm the one who drank the juice, but he appears to be suffering from short-term memory loss on my behalf."

BETWEEN THE GODS AND MORTAL MEN and women there hung
a veil, and its name was *maya*. The truth was that the fabled world of
the gods was the real one, while the supposedly actual world inhabited by human beings was an illusion, and *maya,* the veil of illusion,
was the magic by which the gods persuaded men and women that
their illusory world was real. When Quichotte saw Miss Salma R
walking toward him through the park, in her invisible mode, attracting not a single glance from the earthbound beings she passed,
he understood that her power over the actual was very great, and
also that he was about to have an experience granted to very few
creatures of flesh and blood: he would pass through the veil and
enter the realm of the blessed, where divinities made their sport.

He had dressed for the occasion in his few remaining pieces of
sartorial finery: the still-soiled camel cashmere coat which he had
cleaned as best he could, a brown hat, scarf, and leather gloves. He
wore, too, his finest sunglasses. First impressions counted. The attaché case had been placed in his locker, which he had emptied in
order to fit it in, removing its contents and placing them in his
pocket along with the envelope containing the first month's supply
of goods. He had rehearsed many times the words he wanted to
say. He would hand her the envelope with a little bow of the head
and say, "This is sent with all respects by Dr. R. K. Smile, and
comes also with two brief stories with great admiration from myself." If his powers of charm had not entirely faded she would
allow him to tell the stories. The first story was the tale of what
they had in common: a common city in the past, and the decision
to leave it. The looking back and remembering, the decision not to
look back, not to remember, and the ability of the past to insist,
in spite of everything, on its right to return to haunt the present.
This was their shared truth. The second story was an American
story. Before the *Mayflower* became the first CentCorp portal into

an unknowable future in an alternative reality, it was a ship, and among the travelers on the ship there was a love story. John Alden asked by Miles Standish to press his case to Miss Priscilla, who replied, Speak for yourself, John. And he, Quichotte, would say, I am here on another man's behalf, but given permission I would speak for myself.

She was standing in front of him. He had passed through the veil. He stood before her like a fool and stammered.

"Make it quick, darling," she said. "Eyes everywhere."

"This is sent with all respects by Dr. R. K. Smile," he began, and then saw her eyes widen in fear and alarm. Her hand flew up to cover her mouth and she looked from side to side, planning her escape.

"Sent by a smile," she said. "Oh my God, I know who you are. You sent your photograph. I know who you are."

"It comes also," he continued desperately, "with two brief stories with great—"

"Kwee-cho-tay," she whispered. "The letter writer. Key-choat."

"Key-*shot*," he corrected her.

She made a lunge at the envelope in his gloved right hand. He held it away from her. "No, no, no," he said, wretchedly. It wasn't supposed to be this way. It wasn't supposed to go this way at all. "Your envelope for mine. Cash on delivery."

She stepped back from him, gasping. Then, from the depths of her Moncler coat, an envelope emerged. She dropped it on the ground. "It's all there," she said. "Now throw yours to me."

He could not know if the required sum was in the envelope on the ground. But she was his Beloved and he would trust her. "Madam, catch," he said, and threw her what she wanted. Which she grabbed; and ran. Leaving him standing there with a gun in his pocket and money in his hand.

". . . with great admiration from myself," he said hopelessly, with tears in his eyes.

———

AFTER THAT THE BLUE YORKER became most of his world, the TV set his only companion. He emerged occasionally to eat, unhealthily and at erratic times, wandering the city for ten days and nights in search of the junk food of America, finding it at IHOP, Denny's, Applebee's, TGI Fridays, Olive Garden; and at KFC, Ruby Tuesday, Five Guys, Dunkin', Chipotle. Some nights, some days, he drank in bars with TV screens floating above the alcohol, and watched the sportsmen strive and vie, and heard the American stories of mass killings in various states and the slaughter of lovers by lovers, and the accidental deaths by shooting of parents at the hands of very small children. He spoke little and made no calls. At night he kept his loaded gun, a Gen4 Glock 22, on the nightstand by his bed, with the barrel pointing at his head.

On the eleventh day he stayed in bed nursing a light fever, moving in and out of nightmare-plagued sleep while a cold October passed outside. The TV murmured in his ears, and he surfaced in time for the early evening news. The growing world environmental crisis, the instability in reality which was finally grabbing the attention of politicians and scientists, even of the (many) politicians and (very few) scientists who had traditionally dismissed environmental issues as fake. A suspension bridge had collapsed in Australia because of the appearance of a strange cloud among the cables, which had caused the cables to snap as if cut with giant shears. "It was more like a hole than a cloud," an eyewitness reported. "Like a bit of the air that wasn't there." The story was rippling out across the world, creating alarm, but, oddly, not panic, or not as yet. People had grown used to the arrival of the incredible in the midst of the everyday. An island drowned in the South Pacific? That's too bad, it had great beaches, but everybody was rescued, right? And it was really small. Tornadoes in the Midwest? Yeah, they're big, but tornadoes have been out there forever, even before Dorothy got spirited away

to Oz. Earthquakes in places that never had earthquakes before? Oh
well. Join the club, North Texas and Plainfield, Connecticut. Guess
we can agree that we all live on shaky ground. And so, holes in the
air? Okay, so we have them now also. Life goes on. Quichotte
watched the helicopter footage of the fallen bridge and the hole in
the sky. It reminded him of photographs of the sun blacked out in
eclipse with its corona glowing around it. It looked impermanent,
also like an eclipse. Maybe it was just a temporary problem, a self-
correcting thing, and the sky would close up again soon, would heal
the way skin did after being torn.

The story ended, and now the news anchor, very surprisingly,
addressed her remarks directly to Quichotte. "You'll be interested
to know," she said, fixing her piercing gray eyes on him in his tawdry bed, "that several of today's stories concern you personally."

Quichotte sat up. What?

"Three stories, in fact," the news anchor said. "All involving persons significant to you."

"Are you talking to me?" Quichotte cried, his voice entering a
higher register than usual.

"I don't see anyone else in there," the anchor replied, leaning
forward and pointing her pencil at him.

His relationship with television had plainly entered a whole new
phase. "What," he asked, uncertainly, "what are the stories about?"
The anchor, seemingly reassured, resumed her habitual posture and
read him the news.

"From Atlanta today, dramatic news of the arrest of the pharmaceuticals billionaire Dr. R. K. Smile, chairman and CEO of Smile
Pharmaceuticals Inc. and prominent arts philanthropist, on charges
of running a nationwide ring of doctors prepared to prescribe powerful opioids 'off-label,' that is, to people not suffering from conditions specified on the label—often people in excellent health. The
charges call him 'one of the most unscrupulous contributors to the
current epidemic of opioid misuse.' Sources say it is likely that further arrests will follow as investigators pursue other members of the

alleged ring. Additionally, there are separate accusations by seven
women employed by SPI of sexually inappropriate behavior by Dr.
Smile, who is allegedly known to many of his female employees as
'Little Big Hands.' Dr. Smile, speaking through his lawyers, has denied all the accusations and expressed his determination to clear his
name."

Further arrests will follow. The words hit Quichotte hard. That he
should end up a common criminal at his advanced age. The shame
of it might kill him.

The newscaster was moving on to the next story, apparently uninterested in Quichotte's response. "In related news in Manhattan,
we have a breaking story that celebrated actress and TV personality
Salma R may have suffered a severe opioid overdose and has been
rushed to the intensive care unit at Mount Sinai Downtown. Early
unconfirmed reports suggest she was found unconscious by her assistant Mr. Anderson Thayer, who injected her with the antidote
Narcan and made the 911 call. More about this as the facts come in."

Quichotte trembled. Was this the end of his story, that he was
responsible for the death of his Beloved? That from his hands she
received the instrument of her destruction?

"Is she going to live?" he asked the TV screen. "What are they
saying? Is it possible she will make a full recovery and live on in
health and prosperity as she deserves?"

The announcer looked scornful. "More about this," she repeated,
"as the facts come in."

"You said three stories," Quichotte quavered. "What's the third?
Can it be any worse than what you have already told me?"

"The third story is minor," the announcer said. "It didn't make it
onto the show."

"But what is it?" Quichotte pleaded.

"This is irregular," the announcer replied. "But, okay. Your sister was robbed early today, in her apartment in Tribeca."

His heart was breaking. "Robbed? Was she hurt? Who was it?"

"She cooperated with the assailant, which was wise," the an-

nouncer said. "He left her bound and gagged but he did not otherwise injure her. She was in the habit of keeping substantial quantities
of cash at home, and the assailant's discovery of that fact may have
triggered the assault."

"How did the assailant know about the money?"

"He was staying with her in the apartment as her guest," the announcer said. "I'm sorry to tell you that the individual, presently on
the run, was your son. She made him breakfast before he pulled this
stunt. That's all I have."

"Thank you," Quichotte said, as his world fell apart around him,
as it crumbled like the crumbling universe.

"You're welcome," the television replied.

LIMBO WAS THE EDGE OF HELL. Time did not pass there, nor
kind breezes blow. All was stagnation. Life, having been rendered
meaningless, lost the power of movement. When he turned on the
television the images did not change. It seemed that the Earth stood
still and the sun neither rose nor set. Were days going by, or weeks,
or even months, or had the idea of time passing become meaningless
too? A perpetual twilight reigned. The noises of the street were held
in stasis, a two-tone siren stuck on one tone, the bleep of a reversing
truck sounding continuously like the whining of a mechanical mos-
quito, the traffic roaring, not as traffic does, but like the low sus-
tained breath of some unknown beast. Quichotte neither ate nor
drank and did not know the day from the night. It was as if he were
a character in a show on TV and owing to a technical problem the
transmission had frozen and he was caught in mid-gesture, trapped
in electronic aspic. It was as if he were being written and the author
could not turn the page. In that long nothingness it was not difficult
to think of the gun as his only friend.

He was like the postapocalyptic underground troglodytes he saw
in a movie on TV, dependent for everything on the all-powerful
Machine, unwilling to brave the surface of the Earth where a few

brave souls were still moving, and so doomed when the Machine, without explanation, stopped.

The Machine was stopping.

The last valley, he remembered, was the Valley of Poverty and Annihilation, where the self disappeared into the universe and the Wayfarer became timeless.

At a certain moment, in that moment without moments, he re-fused this ending, and found the courage to go on. Then with a great grinding noise the world around him began to move again, the cogwheels engaged, the end turned out not to be the end. The sun and moon, the traffic, the TV, here they all were once more, rising, setting, roaring, blaring. Here was the date on the TV screen. It was already December. And the gray-eyed newscaster had more words for him.

"Salma R was released from the hospital today and went home. The scandal surrounding her abuse of the opioid fentanyl and her subsequent near-death experience shook the entertainment world. Today, as she left Mount Sinai, she spoke to our cameras."

There she was on the front steps of the medical facility, the Be-loved, looking better than she had any right to look; looking ador-able, irresistible, beginning the process of winning back her fan base. "I'm just so ashamed," she said. "I let the network down, I let everyone working on the show down, I let the fans down, and I let myself down."

"Ms. R, during your hospitalization your show was placed on permanent hiatus and network executives have said they are unlikely to bring it back, do you have a comment?"

"I need to earn back the trust of so many people," she said, look-ing gorgeously crestfallen, "but I'm absolutely going to try."

"And that's the news at—"

"Wait a minute," Quichotte cried. "What about the rest of it?"

"Oh," the newscaster said, shuffling her papers and looking ir-ritated, "Dr. R. K. Smile is out on bail right now, confined to his home and wearing an ankle monitor, but he will go on trial soon, and things don't look good for him. Many of the doctors who worked with him were also arrested and most have agreed to become cooperating witnesses."

"Do they think they have everyone involved in the ring?" Quichotte asked anxiously.

"To the best of our knowledge, yes," the newscaster said. "Now I really have to go."

"What about my son?" Quichotte insisted.

"He is still at large," the newscaster said. "Interestingly, there appears to be no trace of him in any public records. This may well be something we would be interested to talk to you about. Would you be willing to come in . . . ?"

Quichotte reached for the remote and turned off the TV. It would probably be a good idea to avoid the news channels for some time.

He made two telephone calls. The first was to his sister. The Trampoline answered but gave him short shrift. "It was a mistake to see you," she said. "You and that unscrupulous boy. Sometimes it's better not to make peace. We don't need to speak to each other again."

"I didn't know he'd turn out that way," Quichotte said. "That isn't the way I imagined him when—" and here he broke off, because how could he say, *when I brought him into being?* He revised his words. "That isn't the way I imagined he'd be."

"There's no more to be said. Goodbye," the Trampoline told him, and ended the call.

After that he looked at the phone for a long time before calling Miss Salma R. When he finally made the call, it was Anderson Thayer who answered.

"You," Anderson Thayer said. "You piece of fucking shit. Tell me where you are so I can alert the NYPD."

"I only wanted to offer my sincere happiness that the lady has recovered," Quichotte said.

"I'll hunt you down," Anderson Thayer said. "Understand me?

If you try to come near her again, I'll hunt you to the end of the fucking earth."

"I understand," Quichotte replied. The invisible membrane that separated Salma's world from his had thickened and hardened and he could not penetrate it.

"But I know what could," a voice said. He leapt up, startled. The voice was in the room somewhere. But the TV was off and there was nobody there.

"It's me," the voice said. "Your trusty Glock 22."

Things at the Blue Yorker were deteriorating rapidly. First TV newscasters spoke to him from the screen, and now his gun wanted a conversation.

"It's well known," the gun continued, "and well documented, that the way for an ordinary decrepit nobody like you to penetrate the barrier that keeps you out of the blessed world, the world of light and fame and wealth, is to use a bullet. Take it from me. For you, it's the only way. A bullet will unite you and your Beloved for all time, for the whole of history."

"That is not and will not be my story," Quichotte replied nobly. "I have not come to destroy her but to save her."

"Pop! Pop!" said the Glock, seductively. "Zap! Bap! And she's yours forever."

"Say no more," Quichotte admonished the weapon. "Get thee behind me."

"Then how do you expect to get anywhere with her?" the gun wanted to know. "You'll come around. You'll have to. I'll be waiting."

"Mine is a love story," said Quichotte. "And love will find a way."

CHAPTER NINETEEN

In which the Question
of Sancho is Answered

*H*OW, SO SOON AFTER MY BIRTH, DID I BECOME THIS PER-*son? This thief, this binder and gagger of my aunt—carefully, yes; gently, for sure, I didn't want to hurt her, that goes without saying; but I did it, that I did—so how have I shown myself to be this amoral rapscallion, this runaway rogue?*

On the one hand, it has to be my nature, right?, because there has hardly been any time for nurture. I couldn't have been turned into a delinquent at this speed, it must have been there inside from the start. Some fault in the program when Daddy Q dreamed me up, or some bug that got into the system when the Italian cricket turned me into a real, live boy. Some streak of aggression, selfishness, don't-give-a-fuck-who-gets-in-my-way-I-just-want-what-I-want-when-I-want-it. Some ruthlessness. If there's a baby in the road when I need to drive down that road, then hard luck, baby, because I'm driving on. That's my programming. It's in the gattaca, the DNA. In which case it's not my fault, is it? See, if I'm bad—to quote the great Jessica Rabbit—it's because I'm drawn that way.

———

DESPERATE TIMES, DESPERATE MEASURES. Ever since the beating in the park Sancho had felt something go wrong inside him, not a physical ailment but an existential one. After you were badly beaten, the essential part of you that made you a human being could come loose from the world, as if the self were a small boat and the rope mooring it to the dock slid off its cleats so that the dinghy drifted out helplessly into the middle of the pond; or as if a large vessel, a merchant ship, perhaps, began in the grip of a powerful current to drag its anchor and ran the risk of colliding with other ships or disastrously running aground. He now understood that this loosening was perhaps not only physical but also ethical, that when violence was done to a person, then violence entered the range of what that person—previously peaceable and law-abiding—afterwards included in the spectrum of what was possible. It became an option.

The beating had also further detached Sancho from Quichotte. As the Trampoline had noticed, the youngster still felt a degree of filial loyalty toward the antique gentleman, but he was more certain than ever that his own destiny lay elsewhere. He thought a good deal about the young woman at the door of the house of grief, Miss Beautiful of Beautiful, Kansas, and he wanted very much to return to that door in the hope that his future might lie behind it. The more he thought, the more surely he convinced himself that if he were to present himself on her doorstep she would give him a positive response, and the thought of that filled him with a deep contentment and a hopeful belief in the meaningfulness of human existence. He began to imagine his escape from New York—his departure from the Emerald City, clicking together the heels of his ruby shoes, there's no place like Kansas, which wasn't home yet but if things went according to plan, it might be!—to dream the dream of leaving and to feel it as an urgent imperative, and it was that urgency, plus the memory of violence, that had added up to his crime.

About his disorienting sense of having lost his grip on reality he spoke to no one, assuming that it would heal, as bruises do, and broken bones. And as to the rumored imminent end of the world, he didn't give that much credence. For him, the world had only just begun. If it was faulty, if bits were falling off it as if it were an old house in need of repairs, then it was because perfection was an illusion. It was impossible to believe that everything that was wouldn't be around much longer. The injustice of such a dénouement would be too great. The celestial storyteller whom he occasionally contemplated and toward whom he felt the kinship of one fictional character for another was surely not so cruel. Although, he had to concede, the question of God—cruel or loving?—had not been definitively answered.

"And what of la questione de Sancho?" a small, angry voice inquired. "Do you have a soluzione to this problem?"

He was sitting at that moment on a midnight bench in the Port Authority Bus Terminal with a $146 one-way ticket to Beautiful in his hand and the scent of fresh micturition in his nostrils, wondering if the Trampoline had been found and the police were on his trail. A cold night, winter tightening its grip. The bus did not leave for another hour, so he had sixty minutes to ponder the great issues of life, such as the central role of the bus in keeping the States united in the post–9/11 era, when—so he had heard—flights across America were fewer and more unpleasant than onceuponatime and the trains were, well, they were Amtrak; and how amazing was it that for $146 stolen from your aunt's pocketbook you could get a thirty-one-hour Greyhound ride right to the center of a faraway small town like Beautiful with no connections to make or snafus en route? And a related question: Was he about to go to jail, to be sent to Rikers to be monstered by the monsters residing there, or was he on the verge of being free and racing through night and day to the open arms of his lady love? Freedom! He stood now like a greyhound in the slips, straining upon the start.

Follow your spirit, he told himself.

Then the talking cricket, Grillo Parlante, was on the bench beside him, buzzing with annoyance. "There are persons who are undeserving of what has been done for them," it said. "Unworthy persons. Immeritevoli. Non degni. I am sorry to discover that you yourself are a person of this sort."

"You're back," Sancho said. "I thought you were gone for good."

"Anche io," said the cricket. "I also thought this. But your descent toward a moral abyss has obliged me to return. I am unhappy about this but eccomi qui. I am here because there are things that must now be said."

"Spare me the lecture," Sancho said. "I know what I did and I don't need to be scolded. Also, you're a cricket. I could squash you with my thumb."

"The question to be answered," the cricket said, "is not, what is it to be a cricket, but what is it to be a man, and have you passed that examination?"

At the Port Authority in the middle of the night a man sitting on a piss-drenched bench talking to himself was not only not unusual, it was actually conventional, so the few other nightcrawlers moving past Sancho did not even trouble to turn their heads as the thief raised his voice. "Look at me," he said. "Flesh and blood. I live and breathe and think and feel. What more do you want? You're the one who told me I even have an insula, and that means I'm a genuine human person. You told me that."

"Without a conscience," said the cricket, "you're not even a genuine chimpanzee."

"I've only been around for a short time," Sancho said, "but in that period I have noticed that conscience isn't a major requirement in human affairs. Ruthlessness, narcissism, dishonesty, greed, bigotry, violence, yes."

"It would not be prudent to make such a judgment based on the TV news," said the cricket. "Many people remain who know the difference between good and evil, and who let their conscience be their guide. This is the warning I give to you. Lascia che la tua coscienza sia la tua guida. If you choose that other path—spietatezza, narcisismo, disonestà, avidità, bigotteria, violenza—it will not go well for you. Also, to pursue a woman who is a stranger to you, be aware that that may not look like love to her. That may appear to her as molestie sessuali. As we say, lo stalking."

"Did I mention," Sancho said insolently, "that I don't understand Italian? Also, I don't speak cricket. We may be experiencing a failure to communicate."

"Yes," said the cricket. "Incidentalmente, regarding that matter of squashing me with your thumb, I have a brief demonstration for you. Guarda."

A cricket can jump quite a distance when it wants to, and before Sancho could do anything about it the insect was on his head. There followed a sensation of immense pressure and pain, as if a giant invisible mountain were crushing him beneath its weight, and Sancho fell back and slipped down to the floor. The cricket jumped off and was back in its place on the bench. "Do not make the mistake," it said, speaking perfect English, "of equating size with power. Or you might find a cricket squashing you under its thumb."

Sancho climbed back onto the bench, twisting his neck. "That hurt," he said.

"So the first question of Sancho," said the cricket, "is, can he become a human being before it is too late?"

"Oh, there's more than one question now," Sancho grumbled, still rubbing his head, neck, and shoulders.

"The second question is, who is Sancho without Quichotte?"

"Sancho is Sancho," Sancho mumbled, with a slight note of defiance.

"You say this," the cricket replied. "But who is Hardy without Laurel? Who, without Groucho, are Chico and Harpo? Who is Garfunkel without Simon? Capisc'? You are now riding alone on a bicycle built for two. Not so easy! You remember how it was in the beginning? If you moved too far away from him you felt yourself breaking up? Now you want to move very far away. It remains to be seen if you can have any prolonged existence without him at such a distance. A solo career? Resta da vedere. Now I must go."

Sancho gathered his strength for one last sally. "Anyway," he said, "I didn't think that the life expectancy of a cricket was this long. I Googled it. Three months. Aren't you past your sell-by date?"

"Conscience never dies," the cricket said. "There will always be a cricket for those who deserve, who are worthy. But for those who are non degni, no. Addio."

ON THE BUS HE BEGAN to see things again, the things he hated to call visions. It was dark outside the windows; the streetlamps flashed by, their little lights barely touching the black heart of the night, and every so often a gas station, a highway interchange, a little burst of convenience stores. Mostly, however, nothing, except what he was seeing out there. The night sky like a huge jigsaw puzzle. The edges of the interlocking pieces visible, like a crazy grid system. And yes, there were missing pieces. Absence did not look the same as night. Night was something. Absence was nothing. In the blackness of the rushing night he saw absences passing by.

The bus itself contained more problematic sights. Was he turning into—revealing himself to be—Quichotte's true offspring, as obsessed as he with the unreal real? If not then why were there long-fanged vampires here, and members of the tribes of the walking dead? Why men with the hairy paws of wolves protruding unshod from the cuffed bottoms of their pants? America, what happened to your optimism, your new frontiers, your simple Rockwell dreams? I'm plunging into your night, America, pushing myself deep into your heart like a knife, but the blade of my weapon is hope. Recapture yourself, America, shed these werewolf hides and zombie shells. Here comes Sancho, holding on to love.

He closed his eyes. The last time he had seen the masks slipping and the truth about people becoming visible, the broken-leashed who-let-the-dogs-out truth, he had been kicked and beaten within an inch of his life. Before I open my eyes, he begged, put your masks back on, and let's pretend. I won't tell anyone who you are if you'll just let me live.

He opened his eyes. Everything was normal. The lady across the aisle, blond, Nordic, and almost two seats wide, wearing a shapeless long blue sweater over a shapeless long blue dress, was offering him a sandwich. He was grateful for this glimpse of human kindliness but he was afraid that she might be concealing a terrifying, monstrous identity beneath her close-to-bag-lady mask. He saw a tiny bright blue flame flickering in her eyeball and that unnerved him. He politely refused the sandwich.

I am new to the human race, he thought, but it seems to me that this species is mistaken, or perhaps deluded, about its own nature. It has become so accustomed to wearing its masks that it has grown blind to what lies beneath. Here in this bus I'm being given a glimpse of reality, which is more fantastic, more dreadful, more to be feared than my poor words can express. Tonight we are a capsule containing evidence of human life and intelligence, sent hurtling into the black depths of the universe to tell anyone who might be listening, here we are. This is us. We are the golden record aboard the *Voyager,* containing memories of the sounds of the Earth. We are the map of the Earth engraved on the *Keo* spacecraft, the drop of blood in the diamond. We are the Hydra-headed Representative of Planet Three, the many melded into one. Maybe we are the Last Photographs in the time capsule satellite orbiting the Earth, which, long after we have extinguished the last traces of ourselves, will tell arriving aliens who we once were.

We are scary as shit.

DAYLIGHT DID NOT BRING an end to strangeness. They came off I-70 for a restroom stop at a gas station outside Pocahontas, Illinois (pop. 784, temp. 30 degrees F), and when Sancho returned to his

seat after relieving himself a man wearing a straw hat and red suspenders was sitting there, dozing, with an old-fashioned transistor
radio on his lap.

"Excuse me," Sancho said, "but that's my place."

The sandwich lady looked at him with a puzzled expression.
"Son, you talking to someone?" she asked. "Because I can't see who
you might be addressing."

"You don't see this gentleman right here?" Sancho demanded,
and at that point the sleeper awoke, looking embarrassed, and
stood up.

"Beg pardon," he said. "Sometimes I forget. I use to ride this
Greyhound all the way—all the way!—but that was before and this
is after. No offense." As he vacated the seat he passed right through
Sancho's body and moved off down the aisle and out through the
open door of the bus.

"You okay?" the sandwich lady asked. "You lookin' kinda green,
like you saw a ghost."

So there were ghosts now and maybe the sandwich lady knew
that, maybe everyone on the bus knew that, had known it all the
time. Maybe this Greyhound was a ghost bus and it was taking him
not toward Beautiful but to the ghost town at the end of the road.
Maybe this wasn't the I-70 but the ghost road to Hell. Maybe he had
completely lost his fucking mind.

He was a kind of ghost himself, he reminded himself. He was a
parthenogenetically created, unrecorded person, no birth certificate
or other trace of him on any file. He was here, but he wasn't meant
to be. He was the deluded one. Of course he wasn't real. Reality was
a cloak he had put on. He felt it crumbling off his shoulders as if
made of ancient Egyptian papyrus. Maybe he would soon start
crumbling, too, dust to dust. Maybe a child born under a meteor
shower had only a meteor's life: short, dazzling for a moment, but
then burned out. A small pile of ashes blown away by the first un-
caring breeze.

Serves me right for telling the cricket he was past it, he thought.

The one with the low life expectancy is me. He leaned back in his seat, losing his grip on the world. He felt in that instant that he would not make it to Beautiful and would never see the woman of his dreams again. He felt that he would dissolve right here in this window seat and that would be the end of his story.

"There is someone you say you love that you're on your way to see, and you've convinced yourself there's a good chance she returns your feelings," said the sandwich lady. "You're thinking, hold on to her. You're telling yourself, you need love to keep things real."

Sancho sat up. "How do you know about me?" he asked, too loud. Heads turned. The sandwich lady shrugged, took a long sub out of her bag, and prepared to bite it. "Oh, darlin'," she answered him, "let's say, you've got that love light in your eye."

"Let's say a whole lot more than that," Sancho retorted. "Let's start with, who are you?"

"Let's say, I'm friendly with someone better disposed toward you than you deserve."

She took a large bite of bread, salami, and provolone. Sancho waited.

"He's Italian," the sandwich lady said, speaking with her mouth full. "And he's pretty small. He asked me to keep my eye on you."

Sancho suddenly understood. "You're the blue fairy," he said, awestruck.

"Call me what you like. I'm a woman in a plus-size blue outfit on a bus to nowhere," she replied. "But you need to listen to me."

"Okay," he said, "I'm listening."

"You and that parent of yours are cut from the same cloth," the blue fairy said. "You're chasing a stranger and so is he."

"Yes," Sancho replied, "but he's nuts."

"Once upon a time," the blue fairy continued, ignoring that, "if you had two guardian angels—let's say a cricket and a fairy—your path to true love would be pretty smooth. Between the two of us, we could spirit you to her door, and cast a magic spell on that girl, maybe give you a potion to drop in her drink, and—presto change-o!—she would love you to bits, and for evermore."

"Sounds good to me," Sancho said.

"Things have changed," said the blue fairy. "Do you know what they call a gallant lover who shows up unannounced with a bunch of flowers at the door of a lady he does not know and drops a love potion in her tea?"

"Smart?" Sancho hazarded.

"They call him a rapist," said the blue fairy. "Back in the day, Jupiter could disguise himself as a bull and carry Europa away, but this is frowned on at the present time."

"Then what am I to do?" Sancho cried sadly. "I am crossing America in the name of love, and yes, I believe this love may be my only salvation, my only chance of a true and long human existence, but if things are as you say, then I despair. Give me the potion, I beg you. If you were sent by the cricket to care for me, then this is the thing you can most tenderly do for me. I ask for nothing else."

"Have you heard of Bill Cosby?" the blue fairy asked.

"I think my father liked his show," Sancho said, tapping his temple. "I have his memories of the Huxtables in my head."

"Dig deeper," the blue fairy advised. "Look for the 'ludes."

Some hours later the bus pulled in for a second time at the gas station near Pocahontas, Illinois, and the man with the straw hat and the red suspenders holding up his blue jeans climbed aboard again holding his transistor radio on his shoulder while it played songs from an oldies channel. Sancho felt suddenly dizzy. This wasn't right. They shouldn't be back here. They did this already. This ghost was hours ago. So was this gas station. Something was terribly wrong.

The man with the straw hat and red suspenders tried once again to sit down in the seat in which Sancho was sitting, and once again Sancho protested, more forcefully this time.

"Hey!"

"Beg pardon," the man said. "Sometimes I forgit. I use to ride this Greyhound all the way—all the way!—but that was before and this is after. No offense."

And off he went.

"You okay?" the sandwich lady asked. "You lookin' kinda green, like you saw a ghost."

"I'm scared," Sancho admitted. "Why aren't we there yet? Why are we here again?"

"In the situation in which we find ourselves," the sandwich lady said, "it's hard for me to give you good advice, or even an answer that you could accept."

"Try," Sancho said. "Because I'm freaking out here."

"The road is always unreliable," the sandwich lady said. "It'll twist and turn on you. It'll duck and swerve and land you where you don't expect and you got no business being. You need your wits about you if you want to ride the road."

"That's BS," Sancho said. "That's what you're saying so's you don't have to say what you don't want to say. Give me the real thing now."

"The real thing is deep," the sandwich lady said. "It might drown you."

"I'll take that chance."

The sandwich lady who was also the blue fairy made a heavy sighing sound and then she told Sancho the things that were hard to hear. There were two crises unfolding simultaneously, she said, and it wasn't easy to see how either could come out well. The first was the crisis of Sancho himself. "You're seeing things I can't see myself," she said. "Ghosts, zombies, crazy shit. What this tells me is, you're in danger of slipping into a ghost world from which I won't be able to get you back and nor will anyone else. It says to me, our little Italian friend did a great job, he got you most of the way to bein' a real live boy, but maybe he didn't finish the job. And now that you've broken away from your daddy things are getting worse.

I look at you and it's like your presence isn't strong. Like there's bad reception, a bad signal, and you aren't always coming through clearly. Am I making myself understood?"

"Yes," Sancho said. "You're saying I'm dying."

"Let's not jump that far," the blue fairy said. "I'm just saying there's a problem."

"Can you save me?" Sancho pleaded. "I want to live."

"You been talking a whole lot about love," the blue fairy said. "Seems to me you've got it ass backward and upside down. Let me tell you what I mean by that fine sentiment. I understand it to be, first of all, selfless. Love makes the other more important than you. And the other isn't necessarily an individual. It can be a town, a community, a country. It can be a football team or a car. If times were normal here's what I'd say to you: Forget about this girl at the end of the road. Go back where you came from and set things right for yourself. Your aunt? You owe her a big apology just like your daddy did. Funny how you're like his echo. You owe her an apology and money also. She's not pressing charges, told the cops it was a domestic dispute. That's pretty nice of her. Go, apologize, get a job, work until you've paid her back, and cling to the love of being alive and living a decent life. That's the love that makes you real. This girl? She's just one of your ghosts."

"Okay," Sancho said, recovering a measure of defiance, "so this is advice I'm definitely not going to take. This I can find on an Internet meme or in a fortune cookie."

A hubbub had arisen. Passengers on long-distance bus rides habitually fell into a transitional state, a kind of in-between torpor, half asleep, listening to music on their headphones, watching sitcoms on small seat-back screens, eating mini-pretzels or cinnamon grahams, dreaming of the possibility of happiness. The country rolled by outside the windows, unobserved. But now some passengers at least had noticed the disturbance, the feedback loop which had fed them back to where they had been several hours ago, and people were panicking, not helped by the driver, who threw up his hands and said, "Beats me. I just drive the bus, I don't make the roads."

"One moment," the sandwich lady said to Sancho. "Let me see what I can do."

She stood up in the aisle amid the shrieking of her fellow passengers and closed her eyes. There followed a series of heavy bumps, the kind one might feel on a railway train changing tracks across multiple points, and then she sagged down into her seat, exhausted.

"Okay, we're back where we should be," she said to Sancho, "but that was pretty much above my pay grade. I'm going to need to recover before we discuss the second crisis."

The noise in the bus subsided as the street signs began to make sense once more. Beautiful wasn't far away now. Some passengers accused others of having mistakenly raised an alarm for which there was no need. The driver shrugged his seen-it-all-before shrug and drove on. The sandwich lady snored gently in her seat. Sancho alone was fully alert. It seemed plain to him that the second crisis might be worse than the first.

As he waited he became aware of certain disturbing changes in himself. *Like there's bad reception, a bad signal, and you aren't always coming through clearly.* That had been the sandwich lady a.k.a. blue fairy's unsentimental diagnosis. Now he was beginning to feel it too. He was experiencing fuzzy spells, when his thoughts became clouded and unclear, the kind of grogginess one might feel if one had a bad case of the flu. There was also a kind of intermittency, a series of very short interruptions during which the stream of consciousness apparently vanished and then returned. Most worrying of all were the visual and aural symptoms. He looked down at his hand and saw it break up before his eyes like a bad TV image, and then re-form. That was impossible. He used the hand to rub his eyes and it worked just like a hand ought to work, which was partially reassuring. Then a few moments later he saw the phenomenon again. He wanted to ask the sandwich lady for help but she was out cold, snoring. He called out to her and to his horror heard his voice crackle and pop like a radio station that wasn't properly tuned in.

He was, he reminded himself, misbegotten: born out of the ir-resistible need and imperishable desire of an old fool whose brain had been addled by television. Therefore, he himself was a by-blow of the junk culture that was addling the brains of many fools old and young, maybe even of America. Maybe this was what the symptoms of illness looked like in such an irregular creation as himself, born in the wrong way, motherless, only putatively real, like something from Syfy that stepped through the screen, and so possibly doomed to die a quasi-electronic death, death by a failure of the signal.

I'm too young to die. The fallacy of youth. Death had never cared about the ages of those it claimed.

He stiffened his resolve. If he had been created by an act of will, it followed that he must have inherited a strong will of his own. Didn't it? Very well then. If his father had imposed his will upon the angel of life, then he in his turn would set his will against the death angel. And how would he do it?

"Mine is a love story," he said aloud, "and love will find a way." The echo does not know it is an echo. It resounds, until it fades.

THE SANDWICH LADY'S EYES popped open and at once she was wide awake and speaking rapidly. "The second crisis," she said, "is the crisis of everything."

"Everything sounds like a lot," Sancho said.

"All of us are in two stories at the same time," said the sandwich lady. "Life and Times. There is our own personal story, and the big-ger story of what's happening around us. When both are in trouble simultaneously, when the crisis inside you intersects with the crisis outside you, things get a little crazy."

"How crazy are we talking about?" Sancho wanted to know.

"Bad Times," she answered. "The worst ever. Things are falling apart. People have begun to notice. It's going to be a wild ride and

I'm not sure how we can get through it and come out on the other side. I'm not sure that we will."

"Seems like wherever I go people are talking about the end of the world," Sancho said. "I think I'll bet on the world not ending, as per usual."

"What I want to say to you is this," the sandwich lady said. "The larger crisis changes my views regarding your personal ambitions. Regarding, that is to say, the lady at the end of the bus ride. This is not to say I'm willing to hand out the love potions, no, sir. But I'm thinking, if time is short for all of us, then go for it, kid. Go see her, be polite, but make your pitch. If she slams the door in your face, then damn, okay, you're going to have to respect that, but you tried. Maybe she will, maybe she won't. Go give it your best shot." And with that, she disappeared.

"Thank you," Sancho said, and felt simultaneously uplifted and afraid. "Thank you, I will."

But when he got off the bus in Beautiful, at the depot that was just down the road from the Rey-Nard mall, it was already too late. There were snowflakes gusting in the air, it was six degrees below, and the wind chill made it feel much colder. People were running wild in the streets, screaming *The sky is falling*. There were cars on fire and broken Best Buy windows, revealing that the desire for meaningless destruction and free TVs survived even at the end of days. This was the twelfth-best city to live in in the United States and its citizens, the twelfth-best citizens in America, were losing their minds. They'll never make the top ten now, Sancho thought, trying to hold it together, trying to keep a hold on sanity, as he began to run. The absences, the holes in time and space which he had seen in the sky, had multiplied rapidly and come down lower, and one of them yawned terrifyingly in the space where the Powers Bar & Grill used to be. Just to look at that thing—that no-thing which was the negation of all things—was to be filled with an incurable dread. Sancho ran from it as one might from the jaws of a man-eating dragon. As he ran he felt himself beginning to splinter too. He looked down at his arms, his hands, his torso, his legs. They were crackling and distorted. The picture quality had become really bad. Was there no Wi-Fi around here? He ran as hard as he could and as he neared the street where she lived he felt a kind of hammer blow fall, and the thought arrived unbidden that his father, Quichotte, who had fashioned him from falling stars, had despaired of him and unwished his mighty wish. *Who is Sancho without Quichotte?* The answer appeared to be, nobody. A fiction that could not endure.

Had he deserved his father's despairing rejection, if that was what had happened? And could it be that his creator could uncreate him after all, that without his father's love he would simply cease to be? Was paternal love the lifeblood he lacked, without which even romantic love could not save him? Had he loved his father? If he was truthful with himself, the answer was, he had not. So, then, these were his just desserts.

His deterioration accelerated. He went from high definition to early analog and now his only hope, all his hope, was that the woman he loved would open her arms and heart and love—love itself!—would burst through his body and make him whole. A woman's love could do that. A good woman's love. It could save your life, even if you had not loved your father as you should have, even if you were lost to him, so far away; even then, her love could let you live. Right? Right? he asked, but there was nobody to answer him. All he could do was run.

He passed an SUV abandoned with its motor running and the radio playing, Sinatra, "Taking a Chance on Love." "That's a good omen," he shouted to himself, and his voice crackled and broke, his body popped and broke and became pixelated and then recovered its form, and he ran, or something did, and he repeated, over and over, *love will find a way.*

He rounded a corner and then he was at the door of that modest home, that cream-colored two-story building, with the word WEL-COME, in English, sprayed in white paint on a red ground in the small forecourt, below a small OM sign. There was no doorbell. He took hold of the brass knocker—his hand sizzling and shifting and hissing with static like the rest of him—and he knocked. And there she was, there she was!, Beautiful from Beautiful, *Khoobsoorat sé Khoobsoorat,* which also meant "more beautiful than beautiful," the girl of his dreams, and this was his one chance, and he knew what he had to say.

"I love you, and I know that's insane, but I also know that love takes courage, and I take my courage in my hands and say, I love you, and God, I hope you remember who I am."

"Hello?" she said, looking left and right. "Is anybody there?"

"Take my hand," he pleaded, hardly able to hear his own voice now, "say you love me and I'll be able to live. I throw myself at your feet and beg."

"No," she said, answering someone behind her in the depths of the house, "there's nobody. Someone definitely knocked but there's nobody here now."

And then there was nobody there.

CHAPTER TWENTY

Concerning the Author's Heart

*W*HEN HE RETURNED TO NEW YORK THE AUTHOR was not the same man. The tragic events in London had hit him hard, and his niece's last accusation had been a spear in the heart. I could die right now, he had thought when she hurled those words at him. *Angel of death*. But the exterminating angel isn't supposed to die, is he. Everyone else dies at his hands. And here he was back at his desk writing about the end of the world, in the process of wiping out everything he had invented to go along with the erasure of everything that mattered in his real life. His own world felt like it had just ended. Without a Sister, he was no longer a Brother. He was just a pseudonym, Sam DuChamp, writing the last bars of the music of his book. All that remained was the last of Quichotte.

He was beset by his characters. They flew about his ears like bats, knowing that their stories were ending, insisting on his attention. Me, me, me, as Dr. Smile had taunted Quichotte, but now they were all doing it. Save me, save me. Quichotte alone found a little scrap of dignity, even nobility. He did not ask to be saved, but there was someone he wanted to save. The character was teaching the Author about the nature of true love.

When his heart trouble began—he thought at once of Quichotte's youthful arrhythmia—he understood that his book had known about it all along, even before he had any symptoms. Everything he had written about the malfunction of time began to make sense. He had sketched out scenes in which time accelerated or decelerated, in which it became staccato, a series of pounding moments, or in which it seemed to skip a beat. As the laws of nature lost their authority, time would lose its rhythm. He already had that worked out. And now in his own body his fiction was coming to life.

The world no longer has any purpose except that you should finish your book. When you have done so, the stars will begin to go out.

There had been a moment in the writing when a character assumed a more important role than his author had originally envisaged for him. The scientist-entrepreneur Evel Cent had moved to center stage and taken command of the book's larger narrative, and plainly would play an important part in its conclusion. When a character developed so dramatically on the page, in the act of making, one had to say to oneself, okay, but is this right? Is this helpful, should I hold on to his coattails and go along for the ride, or is it taking me down a blind alley I don't want to end up in? He had decided to allow Evel Cent's enlarged presence to remain in the text. CentCorp and NEXT portals would have their place. The decay of the Earth in the novel would be a parallel to the decay—the environmental, political, social, moral decay—of the planet on which he lived.

In the week after his return, his health continued to deteriorate. This was a shock to him. He had been blessed with good health most of his life, with only minor complaints to report. He remembered Sister's words. *Your good health is the thing you have until the day your doctor tells you you don't have it anymore.*

Then he was in the clutches of the medical profession and there wasn't much to say about that except that it was so. Tests and examinations bombarded him as if he were a Syrian refugee enclave. There was a schedule of meds and then there was bypass surgery. He was warned that even this might not entirely solve the problem of his wayward heartbeat but it would help. After the surgery he felt better fast. They had told him the recovery took between six and twelve weeks, but it seemed he was one of the fortunate quick recoverers. He felt so much better so soon that he started calling people up and recommending the procedure. "Don't hold back. Have the whole quintuple. It's great." (Again, he heard the echo of one of his characters, Miss Salma R, recommending electroconvulsive therapy to her crazy friends.) He was told to take it easy. But the return of energy, of functionality, was exciting. His only problem was insomnia, and in the insomniac nights his optimism waned, and his heart sent him a secret message. *I'm not done with you,* it said. *You know it. There's an endgame up ahead.*

Just let me finish my book, he replied.

And it was true. The book had known better than he did from the start. He had not contemplated his own mortality until now, but his book had been talking about death all the way. So was that what he'd been up to, without being fully conscious of it? This whole performance about the end of the world had really been a way of talking about the imminent end of the Author? And could there be anything more narcissistic than that, to equate one's own departure with the end of everything, to say that if he was no longer around, nothing else would endure either? The battle would be over and all of humanity would lie sprawled on the battlefield alongside him? Let's not talk about race or class or history or multiplicity or any damn thing in the beautiful broken world, let's not argue or love or try to make a good world for our children, because all of that goes down the toilet along with me! *L'univers, c'est moi?* Was that the kind of megalomaniac he had shown himself to be?

Did he have a good heart or was he shriveled inside?

Even great Bellow, he saw in the *Times,* had been unclear on the question of the heart, and had asked on his deathbed: "Was I a man, or was I a jerk?"

ON THE NIGHT HE FINALLY felt strong enough to face his book again, he went back into his office, and there in his Aeron chair waiting for him was the large Japanese-American gentleman with many names.

"What are you doing here?" the Author cried, feeling his heart thump. "Has something happened to my son?"

"Your son is fine," the gentleman said. "And doing excellent work. He has proved himself to be a great American patriot, as I always believed he was. Thanks to him and others like him, we are winning the cyberwar."

"Is that right."

"Affirmative, sir. That's our position."

"You scared me, showing up this way. You have to stop doing this. In the first place it's a crime and in the second place I'm a heart patient now."

"I have good news. I have to give you props. You've been officially approved." The agent rose to shake hands and offered the Author his card. *Agent Clint Oshima,* it read.

"Good name."

"Thank you. Anyway, *great* job."

"What job would that be?"

"Anthill," Agent Oshima replied. "You didn't leak. Not a word. We waited, and you did nothing. First class."

"Oh, yeah," the Author remembered. "I wanted to ask you. There was an article in the *Times* a few months ago describing an operation pretty much like Anthill. I thought, if it's so hush-hush, how is it in the paper? But it wasn't called Anthill. It was called Hivemind."

"So let me explain," said Agent Oshima. "When we are obliged

to allow outside personnel to be brought into the covert operation—a parent, for example, like yourself—we give them certain
information, but we don't give any two people the same information. Then if the information enters the public domain we know
who put it there."

"You mean it isn't called Anthill, you just told me that?"

"It's called Anthill. Between ourselves."

"What happened to whoever you told it was called Hivemind?"

"There were consequences."

"Grave consequences?"

"A good way to express it."

"And you're here to do what? To congratulate me or warn me or
both?"

"I'm here to congratulate you because as you have passed a certain set standard, we are prepared to permit certain access privileges."

"To Anthill?"

"To your son."

When he heard those three words—when Son's name was spoken—he felt, as he had never imagined he would feel, like Quichotte
when Dr. Smile told him he would meet his Beloved. He wasn't, by
temperament, a great believer in radiance opening up in the heavens
and flowing down over him in a cascade of joy, but something of
the sort befell him at that moment. He no longer had any hope of
encountering a great romance. That ship had sailed. Son was all he
had to love, but he had been kept at a distance, first by Son's own
design and then by the intelligence community. If he was now to be
allowed to spend time with his child—if his child wanted to spend
time with him—that would make possible a renewal of his own belief in life. Or, in simpler words: it would make him happy.

"In our evaluation," Agent Oshima continued, "if we wish to
maximize the effectiveness of our team of digital warriors, a degree
of outside human contact is a benefit. A young man can go stir-
crazy out there in cyberspace, in the max-security bubble. It's good

to come down to earth. What we propose is, one weekend every six weeks, and once a year a two-week vacation. I have recommended in your case that we begin with the two-week stretch and take it from there. How does that sound to you?"

"What does he think?" the Author asked. "Does he want to do this?"

"A young man needs his father," said Agent Oshima. "He has expressed that need."

"Agent Oshima, Agent Kagemusha, Agent Mizoguchi, Agent Makioka," the Author replied, "I think I love you. All of you."

The Japanese-American gentleman looked embarrassed. "That's inadvisable, sir," he said.

HIS HAIR HAD BEEN long the last time, falling in waves almost to his shoulders. Now it was brutally short, cut close to the scalp, like Sister's. The Author winced when he saw it.

"What?" Son wanted to know.

"Nothing," his father replied. "The hair."

"You don't like it?"

"I think I preferred it longer."

"Everyone likes it," Son said, neutrally. "I've had a lot of compliments."

The first hours were awkward in this way. They sat across the breakfast table nursing their coffees and had to find out how to talk to each other.

"What do you want to do, these two weeks?"

A shrug. "I don't know. Nothing. Anything. What do you want to do?"

"I'd like to do stuff we'd both enjoy."

"I don't know what that is. I'm fine with whatever you decide."

A long pause. Then:

"You want to go on a road trip?"

"Where?"

"A bunch of places I've been writing about. Going there will help me to get them right. And, eventually, California."

"You sure you can still drive?"

"I can drive."

"No, I'm not sure you can still drive."

"Then you drive."

"You'll let me do the driving?"

"Yes."

"Okay, then. Road trip."

"We have to go rent a Chevy Cruze."

HE HAD NOT TOLD Son about the heart trouble. He had decided there was no need. He felt stronger by the day, and the murmurs he heard in his sleepless nights were just an old man's fears running wild. He was a little grayer, a little thinner, but children barely noticed such variations in their parents. And he felt more energetic than he had for a long time. Anyway, telling Son about the surgery would ruin the adventure, putting the child in the caring slash parenting role. Let the chips fall where they may, he thought. He wanted to find a better ending for himself and Son than he had been able to make for Sancho and Quichotte. In his case the Question of Sancho was inverted. The question was not, who was Son without him, but who was he without his son, and the answer was, really not very much.

Son was the stranger behind the wheel whose father he had to become again. In the town he had reimagined as Berenger, New Jersey, he told the young man about the mastodons, and his indebtedness to Ionesco's *Rhinoceros*. "So many great writers have guided me along the way," he said, and mentioned, further, Cervantes and Arthur C. Clarke. "Is that okay to do?" Son asked. "That kind of borrowing?" He had replied by quoting Newton, who said he had been able to see further because he was standing on the shoulders of giants. Son looked doubtful. "Yeah, but Newton wound up discovering gravity," he said, unkindly. "You haven't gotten anywhere close to that."

He tried to explain the picaresque tradition, its episodic nature, and how the episodes of such a work could encompass many manners, high and low, fabulist and commonplace, how it could be at once parodic and original, and so through its metamorphic roguery it could demonstrate and seek to encompass the multiplicity of human life. He stood on the high street of this ur-Berenger which felt less real to him than the township in his pages, and said, of the Absurd in general, that it both mocked and celebrated our inability to give life a truly coherent meaning, and of his mastodons in particular that maybe they said something about our growing dehumanization, about how as a species we, or some of us, might be losing our moral compass and becoming, simultaneously, creatures out of a barbaric, prehuman, long-toothed past, and also monsters tormenting the human present.

"Is that what you believe," Son asked him, "that life is meaningless and we are turning into animals without morality?"

"I think it's legitimate for a work of art made in the present time to say, we are being crippled by the culture we have made, by its most popular elements above all," he replied. "And by stupidity and ignorance and bigotry, yes."

"So what have you done about it?" Son demanded. "What's your contribution? What sort of mark do you think you're leaving on the world?"

"I did my work, and then there's you," he said, hearing as he spoke the weakness of his reply.

Son shrugged and headed for the car. "Okay," he said. "Let's move on."

Your son, your grand inquisitor.

THEY HEADED INTO THE WEST to the places of his fancy whose streets he most wanted to walk, and Son was happy driving long hours, listening to the radio, snoozing for an hour in a mall parking lot, then arrowing on into the night, watching the roadside nowheres spool by. As it unfurled, America—with its calm green signage, its garish billboards featuring men with large, excellent teeth who were trying to sell him their legal services, its Howard Johnsons and Days Inns—began to feel progressively less real to the Author than the versions he had invented and lived in and with for a year and more. The imagined took precedence over the actual. Quichotte and Sancho were traveling with them, in the car which was also their car, and his and his son's journey felt more and more like theirs, run backwards, like a film, in the days when there was film. Ghost-Quichotte sat with him in his seat, ghost-Sancho helped Son to drive the car, and gradually their phantom forms merged with and were absorbed by his own and his child's. He genuinely felt as if he had entered the world of his fiction and began to look nervously up at the sky as they drove through the cold night to arrive by daylight in the Kansas town he had renamed Beautiful, and he half expected—more than half expected—to see ruptures in reality up there, holes in space-time, and panic in the streets below.

But all was peaceful. And here was a quiet street, and here just as he had imagined it, shocking in its exact mirroring of his make-believe, was a cream-colored two-story house with the word WELCOME sprayed in white paint on a red ground in the small forecourt, below a small OM sign. She's in there, he thought, mourning her murdered relative, and just maybe pining for the strange boy who once came to her door and called her Beautiful like the town and promised to return. Time running backwards. Any moment Sancho would walk backwards to the front door and make himself known. The Author sat watching the door with his heart in his mouth.

Nothing happened. The ghosts did not walk by day.

On East 151st Street they walked into the Powers Bar & Grill, not called Powers, not (or not yet) destroyed by a space-time hole. They used the restroom and sat together at the bar and ordered a

little food. This was when the streams merged and fiction became
fact, as if they had stepped onto a theater stage during the intermis-
sion and then the second act had begun, its characters swirling in
around them and treating them as members of the cast. A drunk
man started shouting at them, calling them "fucking Iranians," and
"terrorists," asking them if their status was legal, and screaming,
"Get out of my country." Quichotte and Sancho had reacted by
backing away and standing in the shadows, allowing other (white)
men to bring the drunk under control. The Author, to his surprise,
reacted differently, standing up to the drunk and defying him—
*control yourself, back off, the only person terrorizing anyone around here is
you*—until the abusive individual was escorted off the premises to
general relief.

They were unharmed, and went ahead and finished their meal,
but Son still had his guard up. "I don't think that's the end of it," he
said, watching the door, and the Author realized he was right, the
drunk would come back with a gun to kill them. He found himself
saying, "He's coming for us," said it a couple of moments before the
man did come back with the gun, and what then followed happened
so fast, and at the same time so slowly, that it intensified the Author's feeling of being in a waking dream. When the man entered
the Bar & Grill, Son was right there to meet him, and the Author
heard his own voice slowed down to a growl, begging *no, no,* and
then Son made a series of moves, leaning his head and upper body
out of the line of fire and at the same instant grasping and twisting
the gunman's gun hand with his own left hand while, with his right
hand, striking the gunman's wrist with a violent karate chop, and
then Son was holding the gun and the gunman was facing him, wetting his pants. Literally wetting his pants, no longer killer but just a
maudlin drunk, begging *don't shoot me, I got kids,* as time speeded up
again and the noise of the room returned to normal and then the
hee-haw of law enforcement vehicles and the drunk man being
cuffed and taken away.

"I need a drink," Son said, and sat back down at the bar.

"Where'd you learn to do that?" his father asked him.

"Out at Anthill," Son replied, "there isn't a whole lot to do. There's a gym, and there's TV, and there are YouTube videos. I watched like ten videos on how to disarm a man with a gun—if it's a handgun, if he's holding it with one hand, if he's holding it with two hands, if it's a rifle, whatever—and then I got my gym instructor to work with me on it, just for kicks."

"You could have been killed."

"Not really. I knew I could take him. He was so inebriated his reaction times were way down. It wasn't even that hard."

The Author let it go. "Thank you," he said.

"I'm curious about one thing," Son said. "When you said 'He's coming for us,' nobody had seen him coming. That really helped me be in position, ready and waiting, but how did you know?"

"It's in my story," the Author said, and saw his son's eyes widen. That was maybe the first time the young man had looked impressed.

"What happened to us in your story?" he asked.

"We got killed," the Author replied. "That's the part where having you here really made quite a difference."

"Thanks, Dad."

They drank in silence for a moment, then the Author had to ask, "Do you watch a lot of TV out there?"

"I told you. TV, YouTube, Spotify, Netflix, that's about what there is to do. That and the gym. So, yeah. I like to watch things on TV. Why?"

"Nothing," the Author said. "I guess there are some good things about TV as well as bad."

"Videos just saved your life," Son pointed out. "So you could say that, yes."

Another time of silent drinking.

"In your story," Son asked, "when the guy started with his racist abuse, how did we react?"

"I'm ashamed to say that we backed away from him," the Author answered. "Maybe I should rewrite that part."

"Yeah," Son said. "Because you didn't back away. You totally confronted that asshole and you had everyone on your side."

"Maybe that was a dumb thing to do."

"No," said Son. "It was fucking heroic."

IN THE CRUZE AGAIN. "Is there any more stuff like that in your story?" Son wanted to know.

"There's a diner in Tulsa."

"Let's go there," he said.

"No need to go looking for trouble," the Author said. "You could have been killed."

"Not really," Son said.

"On the whole it's better to walk away from violence. Plus for people like us . . ."

"I'm not buying it," Son said. "I'm done with meek and mild. If someone comes at me, Imma go at him, double."

"I don't like to hear you talk that way."

"Dad, please. Don't start with your peace and love. Back there in that Bar & Grill, that was the truth."

They went to the place in Tulsa he had renamed the Billy Diner, *Tulsa's go-to*. Nothing happened. They ate green eggs and ham and huevos rancheros and left. Nobody looked, nobody cared. It felt to the Author like reclaiming a space from which Quichotte and Sancho had been expelled; another kind of victory.

"Two more stops," he said to Son. "Then we drop the car at Hertz at SFO and go home."

There was news on the radio. The Chevy Cruze was being discontinued along with the Impala and Volt as part of General Motors' cost-cutting drive. There were endings all around him, the Author thought. He wasn't the only one on his last lap.

SNAPSHOT ONE, TAKEN AFTER a fifteen-hour drive: Devils Tower, Wyoming, at night, massive and powerful and overwhelming. They sat and looked at its ominous silhouette. They couldn't even get out of the car.

"I saw that movie," Son said finally, in a small voice.

"We're not here because of the movie," the Author said.

"Why are we here then? Is it in your story?"

"Yes. But it's in your story too."

"My story?"

"I've been here once before," the Author said. "Long ago. With your mother."

"Oh."

"There was a meteor shower that night, and we prayed for a child. We hadn't found it easy to have kids."

"Oh."

"And then we got you. You were our star child. You were our answered prayer."

With that confession, withheld for so long, the Author finally made the story of Sancho and Quichotte his own story, and his child's. He took Son's hand, and they sat in the car, and looked. There was no meteor shower that night, but it was a clear sky, the great misty highway of the galaxy blazed across it, and they saw a couple of bright shooting stars.

Snapshot two, twenty-something driving hours later, with three nights at motels en route, after they left Devils Tower and drove west and south, through Rock Springs, Purple Sage, and Little America (pops. 23,036, 535, and 68), past Lake Tahoe into California, through Sacramento (pop. 501,901) and San Jose (pop. 1,035,000). They were at last in Sonoma (pop. 11,108), in a parking lot at the corner of Broadway and Napa Road. Along one side of the parking lot ran a low white building bearing the sign SALSA TRADING COMPANY.

"There's nothing here," said Son. "This is what we drove half-way across America to see?"

"This is where, in the future, they will build Cyberdyne," the Author said, reverentially.

"Cyberdyne, like in the movies?"

"Cyberdyne the corporation that built Skynet which built the Terminators. This is the correct address. They tell you it's in Sunny-vale, but I reckon that's wrong, or, in other words, it's fictional. This is the precise location right here."

"You've lost your mind."

"Anyway, in my story," the Author said, "this is where I'm build-ing CentCorp."

"And that is?"

"The place where Evel Cent builds the NEXT portal *Mayflower* that will connect our world to neighbor Earths and allow my Quichotte and his Salma to escape this dying planet to make a new life in a newfound land."

"How does that work? I guess you'd better tell me the whole story now."

"I'm not sure about this part," the Author said. "I haven't writ-ten it yet."

"Dad," said Son, "let's go home."

HE LOOKED OUT OF the airplane window in the awkward dark-ness of a redeye flight and saw the Northern Lights hanging there, rippling, a majestic green curtain in the sky. It was rare for the au-rora to be visible in these latitudes, only a handful of such manifes-tations in a decade, so it felt like a privilege to be granted such a vision. He wanted Beethoven on his headphones to accompany such grandeur, the Choral Symphony thundering in his ears while the aurora thundered in his sight. The ripples raced across the sky, there and back again, their beauty bringing tears to his eyes. *Deine Zauber binden wieder / Was die Mode streng geteilt*. "Thy enchantments bind together / what custom sternly did divide." He saw the vision of the aurora as the final proof that the worlds were conjoined, *bound together,* that the world within him, the world he dreamed up, was now forever merged with the world outside himself, and he imagined that the Lights were themselves the portals that might transport men and women to a brave new world.

It was the time of miracles. A miracle was sleeping beside him: his son restored to him, their broken love remade. If that could be true then everything was possible. It was, as Quichotte reminded him, the Age of Anything-Can-Happen. And his heart? It was very full, but it had not burst. He would have time to finish his story.

He closed his eyes, and slept.

—

CHAPTER TWENTY-ONE

Wherein the World Explodes and the Wayfarer becomes Timeless

THE GROWING CATASTROPHE WAS NOT LIMITED TO THE damaged and disintegrating physical fabric of everything that was. The laws of science themselves appeared to be bending and breaking, like steel girders melting under the pressure of an unimaginable force. Events preceded their causes, so that a large hole appeared at the intersection of Forty-Second Street and Lexington Avenue, a hole into which cars tumbled, some time before the explosion of the gas main that was the reason for the hole's appearance. In the city, time passed more rapidly down the avenues than on the cross streets, where it often seemed to be permanently jammed. It was possible that the great second law of thermodynamics had fallen, and entropy had in fact begun to decrease. People who knew nothing of science nevertheless felt themselves possessed by dread. When the sun shone the day grew colder and the moon exuded a tropical heat. The rain, when it fell, burned your skin, and the snow, too, sizzled when it hit the ground.

The seventh valley, Quichotte reminded himself, is the Valley of Annihilation, where the self disappears into the universe.

His room at the Blue Yorker was a monk's cell at the heart of a whorehouse, and in the little microcosm of the motel nothing had changed. Human needs were being amply and vocally fulfilled by night and day on the far sides of his thin walls. In that dark time the continuity of desire brought Quichotte a measure of comfort. Human nature at least was unchanged, and remained the great constant at the root of things. He himself had no desire to participate. Nor in the solitude of his room did he use television for pornographic arousal. Pornography embarrassed him. In fact, all sexual behavior on television embarrassed him. He averted his eyes from the screen even when people kissed. He had no need for such proxy gratifications.

He was waiting with folded hands for love to find a way.

IN THE END THE ADDICT will always call the dealer. Even if the dealer is in love with the addict, obsessed by the addict, consumed by the need to be with the addict and to keep her safe from all the world's dangers, the addict's need for what he has is still greater than his need for her. So in the end she called him. Time had passed, it was hard to know how much time, because time was strange now, stretching, compressing, unreliable. A week could be a month long. A lifetime could pass in a day. The world was falling apart, a great roaring maw of nothingness had appeared in midair near the storied secular spire of the Empire State Building, and the city was full of screaming mouths and running feet and fallen figures being trampled in the stampede. And in the midst of chaos a calm man in a sleazy motel waited for the phone to ring, and it rang, and all she wanted was him. At the heart of a nightmare, a dream come true.

"Madam, is it you? I am honored."

"I have to see you," she said. "I need more."

His decency struggled against his desire. "But, madam, last time, you came so close to dying. How can I bring you the weapon with which you will kill yourself?"

"I was stupid," she said. "I'll be smarter now." This was no longer the voice of a powerful, successful woman in full control of her destiny and that of many others. This voice was wheedling, disingenuous, the falsely innocent delivery of a child begging for a treat. *I'll be good, I promise:* the first lie we all tell.

"It's dangerous to meet," he said, his better nature still fighting off his own need. "Your Mr. Anderson, your Mr. Thayer, will he permit it? I think he means me harm."

"He's out of the picture," she said. "They ID'd him from videos from Atlanta, after they arrested your, your relative. 'Conrad Chekhov.' That didn't fool them for long. He is now a person of interest and has gone to ground. I don't know where he is."

"You must have other people around you," he said. "You are such a big personage."

"There's nobody. There's madness out there. Nobody came today. I have no security. I have nothing. There's just me. This is why I need what you have. You understand?"

"Madam, you need protection." He had to see her. He had to place his feeble body at her disposal. She had nobody and she needed him.

"Go to her," his gun spoke up. "We can decide how this comes out later."

"The world situation is bad," he said. "But I have a plan that can save us."

"I don't want to discuss the world situation," she said, regaining a degree of her old imperiousness. "What I want from you is one particular thing. Do you have it?"

"I have maybe two years' supply," he said, and heard her long, satisfied exhalation.

"Tell me where and when and how," she said. "There's a problem. My driver has also done a bunk. I guess that movie's over."

Quichotte didn't understand.

"Never mind," she said. "Also, I don't think the car services are working."

"The old red oak tree behind the Hans Christian Andersen statue in the park," he said.

"That's far."

"It's better not to be close to your residence."

"How am I supposed to get there?"

A small irritation flared up in his love-drenched soul. "Madam, like the rest of us. Walk."

WALKING WAS TERRIFYING. WALKING ALONE without anyone to fend off unwanted attention. She knew how to be invisible. Her shades, the headscarf, the unassuming black clothes, flat shoes, inexpensive pocketbook, no perfume. The body language of the nobody. She made her best effort. The streets were insane. It was the holidays but nobody was in a holiday mood. Crowds spilled everywhere with fear in their eyes. *Maybe the last New Year's.* Nobody looked at anyone, everyone was shouting, but these were soliloquies. A city of Hamlets howling their anguish at the traitorous skies. And yes, broken windows, upturned cars. She felt as if she were in one of those Will Smith movies in which Manhattan was destroyed. Hollywood destroyed Manhattan regularly. It was a perverted expression of love. Her thoughts were all over the place. Where was Anderson. How could he leave her now. Where was Hoke. Why in the midst of the apocalypse was she going to meet a fentanyl pusher in the park. Why was she going to meet her stalker without anyone to take care of her in case he, in case he, what? He was a hundred years old and harmless. His face had a certain charm and there was education in his voice. Why was she talking to herself like this, she must have lost her mind like everyone else. He was a person to be careful of. Of whom to be careful. She had taken her bipolarity meds but she could feel the upswing toward hysteria in her blood. Her mother had given her many presents. A one-legged father who vanished. This bipolar disorder which she had to fight every day. And alcoholism which she had sublimated into drugs. One drug in particular. One version of that drug. The spray that went under your tongue, below language and therefore below argument and disorder, and brought you peace.

Thank you, my mother. My life is your fault. If anything happens to me today, I blame you.

Things started crumbling for me a while ago. I felt that. Okay, the overdose was stupid. I'm lucky to be here, lucky to be functional, lucky to be walking to Central Park up literally Mad Ave, but the network totally didn't have my back. If they put their people on it they could have squashed the story, made it much smaller than it was, just a minor health issue, but they let it blow up as big as the sky. I've been outspoken on the show, I get that, in these days anyone who gets even a little political has a target on their back, and a brown person, a brown *woman*? I had enemies I guess. I should have seen it coming. Instead I OD'd and put the knife to stab me with in their hands. Maybe I should go home. I miss Bombay. But the Bombay I miss isn't there to go home to anymore. This is who we are. We sail away from the place we love and then because we aren't there to love it people go with axes and burning torches and smash and burn and then we say, Oh, too sad. But we abandoned it, left it to our barbarian successors to destroy. Can I blame my mother for that too? Why not. What's a dead mother for.

I can't look up. Up there, what is that. Like a colossus with a huge blaster blew a hole in the air. You look at it, you want to die. This can't be fixed. I don't believe there's anyone in DC or Canaveral who knows what the fuck to do about *this*. Is anyone even at their desks or is everyone just running up and down in the street the way people are here, charging around Dupont Circle and up and down the Mall and up and down Pennsylvania Avenue going *aaaaaaaaa*. And in the Oval Office maybe some oval charging. *Aaaaaaaaa.*

That's all we've got. Oval charging. That's what the human race comes down to after all these years. Shakespeare Newton Einstein Gandhi Mandela Obama Oprah and in the end it's just an impotent scream. *Aaaaaaaaa aaaaaaaa aaaaaaaa.*

Yes, Salma, I hear myself, yes I do. I know I sound high and wild and this part isn't much better, talking to myself as if I'm someone else. My north pole in dialogue with my south.

Aaaaaaaaaa.

So here I am as commanded. I don't know when I walked so far except on the treadmill at the gym. There's the ugly duckling guy and there's the red oak tree. And there *he* is in his camel coat and brown fedora with a shawl draped over his right hand and in his left hand his little attaché case of joy. Kwee-cho-tee, Kwy-choat, Key-shot. Grinning all over his foolish face like I just said *I do.*

Babajan come back to life. My pedophile grandfather. *Heh-heh-heh.*

SHE SAID, "I HAVE ENOUGH cash here in my pocketbook to acquire your full supply. I can wait while you count it. After that I won't need to trouble you anymore."

He said, "No can do, madam. That is like asking me to shoot you in the head."

She said, "I don't want to discuss it. You're selling? I'm buying."

He said, "The world is coming to an end. On your show you had the gentleman promising an escape route. He said the portal was open."

She said, "Why are we talking about this? I'm here to make a simple cash transaction."

He said, "I have been watching this gentleman on the news. Mr. Cent. I know the location of the portal *Mayflower.* Probably you do, too, because the news story is big. Armed guards all around the facility, crowds demanding to be allowed to pass into the next world.

It is necessary to go to California. CentCorp, number 18144 El Camino Real. The newscaster on TV spoke to me personally and told me it was our only chance."

She said, "So you want to go to California. Good luck to you. You'll certainly have plenty of cash. Maybe you can buy passage for yourself."

He said, "You must also come."

Now Miss Salma saw the gun under the blanket, pointing at her heart. *I deserve this,* she thought, *for being such a bloody fool.*

"You see, madam," Quichotte said, "this gun talks to me, and wants me to fire. But me, I don't want to shoot, I want to rescue you, and to rescue you, I must ask you to come with me to Sonoma, CA. Please."

Control your body language, she told herself. *Control how you speak. How you conduct yourself in the next few minutes will determine whether you live or die.* "Do you really think," she asked, speaking kindly and evenly, and allowing an old accent to creep back into her voice "that our two Bombay stories should end with a bullet in New York? Remember where we are from. *Prima in Indis,* gateway to India, star of the East with its face to the West! Queen's Necklace, Hornby Vellard, Pali Hill, Juhu. Remember our *bhel puri,* our pomfret fish, our Bambaiyya slang, our movies. Did you like my mother's pictures? My grandmama's? Of course! Everybody your age loved those flicks. *Zara hat ké, zara bach ké, yé hai Bombay meri jaan.* Remember who we are, *bhai.* We don't belong on opposite sides of a gun. You are not my enemy, I am not yours. The enemy is elsewhere, with a different skin tone. We are a couple of hometown kids. Bombay, men! Totally *majboot* city. Great god Ganesh, *Ganpati bappa,* watches over us all—Hindu, Muslim, Christian, all. Put the bleddy gun away."

"I am not trying to kill you," Quichotte said. "I am trying to save your life."

"Allow me," she said, in the same gentle voice, "to point out some practical difficulties. You are trying to kidnap a very famous woman in broad daylight in the middle of Central Park, and you're all by yourself. You're relying on me not to scream or run because I don't want you to shoot. But even if I agreed with your proposition, what then? We have to drive across America? You're going to have to sleep. I'm going to need changes of clothes and to use the restroom. Can you really keep me prisoner through all that? You know that when people find out I'm missing they are going to raise the alert. There's going to be an APB and my face all over the news. You think you can drive me to the West Coast and they won't stop you five miles from here? It's impossible. Why don't you just put the gun down, take my money, give me the attaché case, and we'll call it even. Nobody has to get shot, nobody has to go to jail. How does that sound?"

"It sounds," Quichotte said, "as if you still think everything's normal all around us. But the situation is very far from normal. Most of the TV networks are down. There is almost no news being broadcast. The NYPD, who knows what condition it's in. I don't think anyone will be hunting for you, the terror has everyone in its grip. The country is running wild. Maybe the whole world. There may not be much time left. This is why I make my request."

This was the moment when the ruptures in the fabric, the voids, came down to ground level. Behind Quichotte and Salma, where the Metropolitan Museum stood, the nothingness burst through the somethingness of the world, roaring like a fire, and then the increasingly familiar giant-bullet-hole shape was all that was left, the awe-inspiring black void of nonexistence, and around its edges the broken edges of the actual, and the long-gathered and carefully curated history of the human race was gone, and with it a part of the meaning of life on earth. Miss Salma R began to weep.

"We have to go and help," she said.

"There's nobody left alive to be helped," Quichotte replied.

She dried her eyes. "Put your gun away," she said with new resolve. "Let's go."

"Don't listen to her," said the gun. "She can't be trusted. I'm the one you can trust. This is your chance of immortality. Don't be tricked. Shoot her now."

"Immortality no longer exists," Quichotte said. "The future, posterity, fame. Those words need to be removed from the dictionaries. There are no dictionaries. There's only now."

"Are you talking to yourself?" Salma demanded. "I'm supposed to trust my life to someone who talks to himself?"

"I was talking to the gun," Quichotte said. "Explaining why it won't be needed."

"Jesus Christ," said Miss Salma R.

THEY BEGAN TO WORK in concert. "I'll need clothes," she said, and they got into the Cruze and drove to the Gap at Fifty-Ninth and Lex. There were no staff on duty and people were looting the place. They took what they needed and left. A few blocks downtown they did the same at a Duane Reade and then they were set. The looters were like automata, grim-faced, empty-eyed. Nobody looked at anybody.

"So I'm a thief now," Salma said.

"Possessions no longer exist," Quichotte said. "I don't even think there's money anymore. There's only go west or die."

"Can you still drive?" she asked. "Long distances, at your age, fast?"

"I can drive."

"No, I'm not sure you can still drive."

"Then you drive."

"You'll let me do the driving?"

"Yes."

"Okay, then. Change places. Road trip."

Forty-five hours' drive time, three thousand miles, give or take. That was in normal driving conditions, but you had to add to that the weather conditions, the abandoned vehicles, the burned-out wrecks, the trucks skewed sideways on the freeways, the broken bridges, the fallen debris, the marauding long-haired armed gangs roving the highway shoulders, the feral dogs, the madmen on bicycles, the maimed survivors of the void's irruptions, the blind, the limbless, the starving, the deranged children, the angels on their way to hell, the walking dead, the crawling dead, the dead. Watching them from flagpoles the tattered banners of fallen America. And up above roaring in the sky the monstrous evidences of the great Nothing, the bullet holes, the absences, the star eaters, the galaxy swallowers, sucking the Earth's terror up like food, preying on our deaths. The voids.

The interior of the Cruze was a capsule hurtling through space, hoping to land with pinpoint accuracy upon the distant heavenly body of their salvation. CentCorp. On the road that name didn't feel real. It was just a word. Only the broken maddened road was real. The two of them strapped *inside,* wide-eyed, watching the horror of *outside,* rendered dumb by exhaustion and shock. They stopped for gas and Quichotte and his gun patrolled the vehicle while Salma filled her up.

"Well, well," said the gun, sulking. "Guess I'm still useful for something, huh."

From the gas station store they took toilet paper, soap, the last gallon jugs of water. When they needed to perform their natural functions they turned off the freeway and found a side road where danger looked, for the moment, to be absent. They cleaned and washed themselves and went on. Civilization was a skin they were in the process of shedding. Apart from gas and bowel movements, nothing made them stop. She drove for eight hours and slept for four. While she slept, he took over and drove for four hours, then slept for four while she took the wheel again. Then they were awake together for four hours and then she slept and he drove again. They were awake together for four hours in every twenty-four and in those hours they said whatever came into their heads, or nothing, with increasing hysteria. Theirs was the intimacy of outlaws on the run. Hollow-eyed, numb-brained, the bandits of the apocalypse, running for their lives. Running toward their last hope of life.

He said: I lost my son my only child the blessing of my old age. She said: I want to go home I dream of Juhu Beach and instead of my wicked grandfather there could be you. I could have my family again with a good grandfather instead of bad. What am I saying. You pulled a gun on me. You talk to guns. You're crazy. He said: I wash my hands of him. I renounce him. He turned out wrong. I don't take responsibility for that. He caused me shame. She said: Edvard Munch and Van Gogh were bipolar, too, did you know that. I miss my electricity. The voltage keeps me earthed. Is there some- where I can get ECT treatment en route. Also I need a hit of the spray. You're not listening to me. I have problems. I need the ECT. I need the fucking spray. He said: If you want to die we can stop for those things. You're in recovery. Let me remind you. Nausea, vom- iting, heart pounding, difficulty in breathing, confusion, hallucina- tions, weakness, sweating, itchy skin, difficulty swallowing, dizziness, then a seizure. Is this what you want. Can we get to Cali- fornia and pass through the portal into the promised land if you insist on this. We cannot. She said: You're supposed to give it to me. You're selling I'm buying. He said: I have been in love with you for a long time. I will not cause your death. You're crazy too. She said: Fuck off. He said: Drive the car.

Cleveland, Toledo, Chicago, Cedar Rapids, Des Moines, Omaha. She said: Omaha, that's a Peyton Manning play in a football game. He said: It's a beach in France. Grand Island, North Platte, Cheyenne. He said: I saw a cowboy movie on TV. At one point the old chief explains his people's inevitable defeat. He says, "There is an endless supply of white men, but there has always been a limited number of human beings." Maybe *Cheyenne* means "human beings" in Cheyenne. She said: And maybe *Indian* means "human beings" in Indian. There's no such language as Indian. I know that. Nevertheless. It's us. We are the human beings. He said: We're in Indian country.

Outside the car didn't exist. Only inside the car existed. The Nothing roared in the sky and made them mad. They babbled as they drove. Salt Lake City, Battle Mountain, Reno. She said: Hey, let's get a quickie divorce. He said: We can't. We're not married. They laughed hysterically and drove on.

WELCOME TO CALIFORNIA.

He was asleep. She shook him awake to show him the sign. He woke up very quickly and sat up very straight. And in that instant when he gazed upon the California sign a lifetime of delusion fell away from him, and he saw clearly at last, no longer foolish or mad. Perhaps what they said was true: that only at the end of the quest did the seeker understand how deeply rooted in error his journey had been, only at the end of the narrow road to the deep north did the Japanese poet perceive that there was nothing to be learned in the deep north, only at the summit of Mount Qaf which they had climbed in search of their winged god did the thirty bird-pilgrims see that they themselves were the god they were looking for, and only when one saw the sign saying WELCOME did one comprehend the impossibility of the welcome one had sought, and with that comprehension came a new clarity, a return to sanity, and even a kind of wisdom.

So, now that Quichotte was in full possession of his senses, there were things he needed to say. "My quest for you," he told Miss Salma R, "has not been for you alone, but also for my own compromised goodness and virtue. I see it now. By attaining you—the impossible!—I thought I might validate my life. By becoming worthy of you I might feel worthy of being myself."

"That's quite a speech," she said.

"What I hoped for is indeed beyond hope," he said. "I was out of my mind, looking for this year's birds in last year's nests. And all around me America—and not only America, the whole human race!—yes, even our India!—was also losing its reason, its capacity for ethics, its goodness, its soul. And it may be, I can't say, that this deep failure brought down upon us the deeper failure of the cosmos. But I at least have woken up. I am sane again, and if the story of the world is coming to an end, and maybe our stories will end with it, then let us make that a happy ending, a peaceful coming to rest in a good place. But I still hope we may save ourselves. At least I hope that we may try."

"Why would we have driven like lunatics across America," she asked him, "if not to try?"

"Then," he said, "call him."

"Call whom?"

"You have his number, I'm sure. The genius. You need to talk to him."

"Yes. I'll pull over," she said.

"We can't go in the front door," Quichotte said. "There's a security ring and a crowd of hysterical people. You need to ask him about access. There must be another way."

"Why would he tell me?"

"You are Salma," he said. "Of course he will invite you in."

There was no time to lose. The great voids roared in the sky, eating the stars.

IS IT YOU? YOU'RE REALLY HERE?

Yes, Dr. Evel, it's really me.

"Dr. Evel." Now I know it's you.

Dr. Awwal Sant. I'm with a desi friend. Can we come in? Three of us is a party.

The place is surrounded. You know that.

Tell me what to do.

Don't come anywhere near CentCorp. Follow the highway to Boyes Hot Springs. I'll send a car to meet you at the Cochon Volant BBQ.

There's a back way in?

There's a tunnel. Go down the tunnel toward the light.

———

EVEN BEFORE HE HAD completed his journey through the tunnel, Quichotte, now, at the last, the clearest minded and sanest of men, had understood that this was an earthly version of the same tunnel of which people speak, which appears at the end of life, and in which at a certain point one may have the choice of turning back toward the beautiful temporariness of the world, or of going forward into the purity of the Eternal. He understood, furthermore, that when the entire fabric, the warp and weft of everything, was unraveling, when the stars were dying and history itself was coming to an end, then the possibility of taking one magic step through a gateway and starting over in a new, Edenic location was a fairy tale, not to be taken seriously. In other words, there was no escape from Death, not even if one hurtled across a continent in search of Life, for there at the end of the journey was the hooded figure waiting for you with open arms.

Nevertheless, he thought, it was better to play the game to the end, not to knock the black king over and resign but to wait for the checkmate move, to fight against the advancing white pieces until they could no longer be held back, because there was an endless supply of white chess pieces, but a strictly limited number of black kings. So at the end of the tunnel he got out of his old car, knowing he would never drive it again, silently thanked it for its years of unostentatious reliability, and went around to open the door for Miss Salma R, as a gentleman should. The liveried chauffeur who had driven the lead vehicle guided them toward a small railway car, in which they were carried through the interior organs of CentCorp to the room containing the brain.

CentCorp was all light, its interior space composed, or so it appeared to Quichotte, of great illuminated canyons pockmarked with small areas of relative darkness where, he guessed, actual human beings sat and did their work. He felt as if he were entering the sun itself, or at least the almost-as-radiant palace of the Sun

King. Half blinded by the grandeur of the blazing white light, he failed to observe a single person until, at their journey's end, their carriage door opened automatically and there to greet them was the Sun King himself, Dr. Evel, the scholar-entrepreneur and master of the NEXT gateway, Evel Cent.

"Welcome," he said. "Welcome on this dark day." The blaze enveloping him appeared designed to give the lie to his words, to set its brightness against the darkness of the times. He was dressed simply, in black T-shirt over black jeans, and looked to Quichotte oddly unimpressive with his slicked-back black hair and doctored smile, a B-list actor in an A-list part, a spear carrier whom events had thrust into the spotlight at the center of the stage. Awwal Sant reinvented as Evel Cent. He didn't seem like the man to command the closing scenes of the drama. Yet here he was. There was nobody else. It was his show.

"Are you well?" he asked Salma. "We heard you almost . . ."

"Yes," Salma answered. "But I decided to make a thrilling recovery and daredevil-drive across America in a matter of hours, defying *Mad Max* gangs and universe-eating black holes en route instead. That was option B."

"I'm delighted, of course," said Dr. Evel. "We all are, my dear."

"Can nothing be done to reverse the decay?" Salma asked, changing the subject, and Quichotte saw that she was still in the grip of the optimistic fantasy that some scientific wand could be waved and things would go back to being as they had been before.

Evel Cent laughed, a weak little laugh, and then said I-told-you-so. "I am the last Cassandra of the human story," he said. "I prophesied and nobody believed, and this time it's not only Troy that will burn, but Sparta and Ithaca and all the Achaeans too." Such self-aggrandizing talk, Quichotte thought, was pointless in the moment of crisis, when only action counted, and insisting on having been right was just narcissism. "I'm afraid nothing can be done," Cent went on. "We are in the last moments, and I fear the hordes at the gates will not be saved."

"Have you been sending people through?" Salma asked. "The NEXT terminal, is it working fine? How many people have gone through the gateway to the neighbor Earth? Do you have any contact with the other side?"

"Can we speak privately?" Evel Cent took her by the elbow and began leading her away from Quichotte, but she reached out and took the old man by the hand.

"My friend and I have made a long, dangerous, and tiring journey," she said. "I'd like him to hear what you have to say."

Then they entered one of the small areas of darkness, a glass door was shut behind them, and they were enclosed in a soundproofed space. "The truth is," Evel Cent said, "that when I came on your show I perhaps exaggerated our situation for dramatic effect."

"The dog," Salma wanted to know. "Schrödinger. Is he safe?"

"I'm sorry."

"He died?"

"I'm sorry. I made up the dog."

"In plain English, then, you've got nothing," Quichotte said. "Which, I'm assuming, is why you're still here with the rest of us mortals, getting ready to face the music."

"Is that right, Evel?" Salma asked. "NEXT doesn't work?"

"It works," Evel Cent said. "It will work. Everything about this is so radical, so post-Einsteinian, we're having to make up the physics as we go along. The match to the neighbor Earth location has to be exact to an alarming number of decimal points. It's just a question of getting a couple of equations to balance."

"So it doesn't work," Salma said.

"There's a story about Sir Isaac Newton," Evel Cent told her. "He announced the theory of gravity before he'd done the math. He just knew he was right. And then he had a deadline, because he had to go down to London from Cambridge and deliver a lecture on the fully worked-out theory in front of an audience of his peers, and he worked day and night, and got the math right in time."

"Was his deadline the end of the world?" Quichotte inquired.

"We will meet the deadline," said Evel Cent. "In the coming hours."

"I'd like to see the portal," Salma said. "Will you bring us to where it is? Unless of course it's at this stage still just a hole in your head."

Evel Cent stiffened. "This way," he said.

QUICHOTTE HAD IMAGINED SOMETHING out of a silent movie, some kind of Art Deco altar surrounded by crackling arcs of electricity, some sort of giant jukebox that played human beings instead of records. Circles of shining voltage would rotate around the person to be transported, moving up and down, crossing one another, down and up, until suddenly, accompanied by a reverberating clash of cymbals and a bright flash of light, the human figure would disappear.

The reality was banal. An empty room with bare walls, a glass window in one wall through which a control room filled with technology could be seen; more like a sound recording studio than an Expressionist fantasy. And at the far end of the empty room, a simple door. That was the *Mayflower,* the place where the dimensions joined, where the neighbor Earth rubbed up against this one. Just open the door and walk through. From one room into another. As simple as that.

Except that there was a bad connection.

Evel Cent explained. They had reliably established a number of things about the other reality: atmospheric composition, gravitational force, mean temperatures, all well within the range of what was tolerable. The balance of gases in the air was very close to our Earth's, the g-force identical or near-identical to our own, and the climate was Earthlike. The only remaining issue was the fog.

Fog?

It had proved impossible to get a clear image of the other-Earth. It, or that part of it to which they had made a successful connection, was enveloped in a thick fog which they had been unable wholly to penetrate. CentCorp scientists had used their most sophisticated tools, looking through the NEXT connection at infrared and ultraviolet frequencies, using state-of-the-art radio imaging performed by their own alterations of the cameras mounted on space telescopes. Computer analyses of these tests indicated, with a high degree of certainty, that the place connected to was an enclosed interior space, either a domestic residence or a private office (though these notions of usage, Earth-centric as they were, the product of our own ideas about how space was used, were necessarily hypothetical). The nature and number of possible occupants was unclear.

"How great is the risk?" Quichotte asked.

"Once we have stabilized the connection," Evel Cent told him, "which I'm hearing we will have successfully achieved momentarily, we evaluate the physical risk as low. But it must be said: travelers will arrive in an utterly alien world, not knowing the language or customs, having no wealth or assets to use, and will be at the mercy of the beings they encounter, and reliant on their own resourcefulness and wit to survive. As far as disease and illness, we can neither be certain of what infections our travelers may fall prey to, or indeed of what germs they may carry that may be harmful to their new hosts. First contact is not a sure thing."

"So if we go, we go as refugees," Quichotte said. "Pilgrims setting foot for the first time upon a new world, hoping the indigenous population will teach us how to survive there."

"I'm wondering," Salma said. "If others follow us, will they come as conquerors?"

The three of them were alone in the room with the door. Through the glass window, Quichotte could see the beginning of a commotion in the control room. Evel Cent cupped a hand around his earpiece, listened, and his face grew grim. "I have good news and bad news," he said. "The good news is, the connection has been stabilized, so the NEXT gateway is open."

"And the bad news?" Quichotte said.

"The deterioration outside has accelerated," Evel Cent said. "The void phenomenon is spreading rapidly. We can't know when it will, when it may, burst upon us."

Quichotte understood that the commotion in the control room was caused by fear. The last moments were at hand.

"How does the door open?" he asked.

"Like a door," Evel Cent said. "You turn the doorknob, and pull."

"And you're sure the connection is safe?"

"The connection is stable. On the other side, nothing is certain."

"You go first," Quichotte said.

"I'm not ready to go," Evel Cent said. "I have to supervise the evacuation of my staff, and perhaps of some of the people outside. It's my responsibility."

"You go first," Quichotte repeated, and there was a gun in his hand.

"Finally," said the gun. "I thought you'd never ask."

"You can't be serious," Evel Cent said.

"I'm very serious," said Quichotte. "Before I bring Miss Salma to the gate, I need to see what happens."

When the door was open they saw the gray fog.

"Very well," said Evel Cent; and he turned; and lowered his head; and charged into the next world like a bull. And was gone.

WHAT VANISHES WHEN EVERYTHING vanishes: not only everything, but the memory of everything. Not only can everything no longer remember itself, no longer remember how it was when it still was everything, before it became nothing, but there is nobody else to remember either, and so everything not only ceases to exist but becomes a thing that never was; it is as if everything that was, was not, and moreover there is nobody left to tell the story, not the whole grand story of everything, not even the last sad story of how everything became nothing, because there is no storyteller, no hand to write or eye to read, so that the book of how everything became nothing cannot be written, just as we cannot write the stories of our own deaths, which is our tragedy, to be stories whose endings can never be known, not even to ourselves, because we are no longer there to know them.

Let us think of it this way. Here at the heart of a canyon of light an old man and the woman he loves stand in front of an open door. Who knows what lies beyond it? But on this side of the door, there's hope. There may after all be a life after death. He grasps her hand. She squeezes his hand. A long quest comes to an end. Here they stand in the Valley of Annihilation, with the power to disappear into the universe. And just possibly into something new.

Quichotte, a sane man, understands that it won't happen. But on this side of the door, it's possible, for a few last moments, to set that knowledge aside, and believe.

"Come on," he said to Salma. "Let's go through."

ON THE AUTHOR'S DESK, and on the mantelpiece in his office, stood thirteen modestly sized objects, carefully arranged, which made the room feel like home: a polished "found art" Chinese stone whose patterning resembled a landscape of wooded hills in the mist, a Buddha-like Gandharan head, an upraised wooden Cambodian hand with a symbol of peace in the center of its palm, two starlike crystals, one large, the other small, a Victorian locket inside which he had placed photographs of his parents, three other photographs depicting a childhood in a distant tropical city, a brass Edwardian English cigar cutter made to look like a sharp-toothed dragon, an Indian "Cheeta Brand" matchbox bearing the image of a prowling cheetah, a miniature marble hoopoe bird, and a Chinese fan. Without these objects around him, he couldn't work. He picked up at least one of them once a day. And there was one more, too precious to display, which he kept in a drawer: a little silver ingot, an inch high, on which was engraved the map of unpartitioned India. This was his greatest talisman, his open-sesame, his magic lamp. He had caressed it this very day, before writing his final page.

Often at the end of a working day the Author would fall asleep at his desk, his forehead resting on the wood, bowed down before the computer screen as if performing some ancient rite of worship. So it was that, on this day of the ending, he was in a half-sleeping, half-waking state when he thought he saw a tiny door open at the very bottom of a corner of his room, less than half of half of half of a millimeter high, and through that door a bright light flowed, an intense pinpoint of light, as if it might be from a mousehole behind which a studious undersized mouse sat reading by a lamp; or, as it might also be, the light of another reality, another Earth, bleeding into his. And then a creature tumbled through the opening. He knew at once who and what it was. It was impossible but he knew. And now he also had an explanation for the fog. It was a question of scale. This world so gigantic compared to that. That other world, which he now understood to be the one he himself had made, was a miniature universe, perhaps captured under a glass dome—a snow globe without snow—which had begun to crack, so that its minuscule inhabitants had become desperate to escape. And here they were, bursting into his office, but tragically finding its air too thick for their tiny eyes to see through, their tiny lungs to breathe. He saw the first minute creature enter, gasp, and faint, its hope turning to despair in this new continuum inhabited by what to it were super-colossi, giant mastodons, able to crush it under their thumbs. The microscopic man, the creature of the Author's imagination, had brilliantly done the impossible and joined the two worlds, had crossed over from the world of Fancy into the Author's real world, but in this one he was unassimilable, helpless, puny, gasping for air, not finding it, choking, and so lost.

Stop! cried the Author, knowing what would happen next, the thing he could not stop, for he had already written it; it had already happened, so it could not be prevented from happening. His heart pounded, feeling as if it might burst from his chest. Everything was coming to an end.

The end cannot be changed after it has ended; not the end of the universe, not the death of an Author, nor the end of two precious, even if very small, human lives.

There they stood in the gateway, on the threshold of an impossible dream: Miss Salma R and her Quichotte.

ACKNOWLEDGMENTS

*T*HIS NOVEL OWES SOME OBVIOUS DEBTS: TO MIGUEL DE Cervantes's *Don Quixote* (translated from the Spanish by Edith Grossman) and to Jules Massenet's opera *Don Quichotte;* to Katherine MacLean's story "Pictures Don't Lie," Arthur C. Clarke's story "The Nine Billion Names of God," Eugene Ionesco's play *Rhinoceros* (translated from the French by Derek Prouse), and, for the nickname of the Trampoline, to Paul Simon's song "Graceland." For the sequence of seven Valleys, I'm indebted to Farid-ud-Din Attar's *The Conference of the Birds.* My thanks, too, to Francesco Clemente, for cleaning up the cricket's Italian (any faults that remain in it are my own); to Andrew Wylie, Jacqueline Ko, Emma Herman, Tracy Bohan, and Jennifer Bernstein at the Wylie Agency; and, for her invaluable editorial guidance, Susan Kamil at Random House New York, as well as Louise Dennys at Knopf Canada and Bea Hemming at Jonathan Cape in London. Thanks, finally, to those friends and family members who served as helpful early readers, to Rachel Eliza Griffiths for her photographs and much else, and to my former assistant Dana Czapnik, now happily launched on her own literary career.

SALMAN RUSHDIE is the author of thirteen previous novels: *Grimus, Midnight's Children* (which was awarded the Booker Prize in 1981), *Shame, The Satanic Verses, Haroun and the Sea of Stories, The Moor's Last Sigh, The Ground Beneath Her Feet, Fury, Shalimar the Clown, The Enchantress of Florence, Luka and the Fire of Life, Two Years Eight Months and Twenty-Eight Nights,* and most recently *The Golden House.*

Rushdie is also the author of a book of stories, *East, West,* and four works of nonfiction: *Joseph Anton: A Memoir, Imaginary Homelands, The Jaguar Smile,* and *Step Across This Line.* He is the co-editor of *Mirrorwork,* an anthology of contemporary Indian writing, and of the 2008 *Best American Short Stories* anthology.

A fellow of the British Royal Society of Literature, Salman Rushdie has received, among other honors, the Whitbread Prize for Best Novel (twice), the Writers' Guild Award, the James Tait Black Prize, the European Union's Aristeion Prize for Literature, Author of the Year prizes in both Britain and Germany, the French Prix du Meilleur Livre Étranger, the Budapest Grand Prize for Literature, the Premio Grinzane Cavour in Italy, the Círculo de Bellas Artes Gold Medal in Spain, the Carlos Fuentes Medal in Mexico, the Crossword Book Award in India, the Austrian State Prize for European Literature, the London International Writers' Award, the James Joyce Award of University College Dublin, the St. Louis Literary Award, the Los Angeles Public Library Literary Award, the Carl Sandburg Prize of the Chicago Public Library, the Chicago Tribune Literary Prize, the Norman Mailer Prize, and a U.S. National Arts Award. He holds honorary doctorates and fellowships at six European and seven American universities, is an Honorary Professor in the Humanities at M.I.T, and was for ten years a University Distinguished Professor at Emory University. Currently, Rushdie is a Distinguished Writer in Residence at New York University.

He has received the Freedom of the City in Mexico City, Strasbourg, and El Paso, and the Edgerton Prize of the American Civil Liberties Union. He holds the rank of Commandeur in the Ordre des Arts et des Lettres—France's highest artistic honor. Between 2004 and 2006 he served as President of PEN American Center and for ten years served as the Chairman of the PEN World Voices International Literary Festival, which he helped to create. In June 2007 he received a knighthood in the Queen's Birthday Honors for services to literature. In 2008 he became a member of the American Academy of Arts and Letters and was named a Library Lion of the New York Public Library. In addition, *Midnight's Children* was named the Best of the Booker—the best winner in the award's forty-year history—by a public vote. His books have been translated into over forty languages.

He collaborated in adapting *Midnight's Children* for the stage. It was performed in London, Ann Arbor, and New York by the Royal Shakespeare Company. In 2004, an opera based upon *Haroun and the Sea of Stories* was premiered by the New York City Opera at Lincoln Center.

A film of *Midnight's Children,* directed by Deepa Mehta, was released in 2012. That year, Rushdie was awarded the Canadian Screen Award for best adapted screenplay.

The Ground Beneath Her Feet, in which the Orpheus myth winds through a story set in the world of rock music, was turned into a song by U2 with lyrics by Salman Rushdie.

salmanrushdie.com

Facebook.com/salmanrushdieauthor

Twitter: @SalmanRushdie

About the Type

This book was set in Bembo, a typeface based on an old-style Roman face that was used for Cardinal Pietro Bembo's tract *De Aetna* in 1495. Bembo was cut by Francesco Griffo (1450–1518) in the early sixteenth century for Italian Renaissance printer and publisher Aldus Manutius (1449–1515). The Lanston Monotype Company of Philadelphia brought the well-proportioned letterforms of Bembo to the United States in the 1930s.